# SECOND
# TIME AROUND

*Recent Titles by Julie Ellis from Severn House*

AVENGED

DEADLY OBSESSION

GENEVA RENDEZVOUS

NINE DAYS TO KILL

NO GREATER LOVE

VANISHED

# SECOND
# TIME AROUND

## Julie Ellis

SEVERN
SH
HOUSE

This first world edition published in Great Britain 1997 by
SEVERN HOUSE PUBLISHERS LTD of
9–15 High Street, Sutton, Surrey SM1 1DF.
This title first published in the U.S.A.1998 by
SEVERN HOUSE PUBLISHERS INC of
595 Madison Avenue, New York, N.Y. 10022.

British Library Cataloguing in Publication Data

Ellis,  Julie,  1933 -

   Second time around
   1.   Women authors – New York  (State) - New York  -  Fiction
   2.   Romantic suspense novels
   I.   Title
   813.9'14  [F]

   ISBN 0 7278 5270 1

Typeset by Hewer Text Composition Services Limited,
Edinburgh, Scotland.
Printed and bound in Great Britain by
MPG Books Ltd, Bodmin, Cornwall

# Chapter One

The sparsely occupied Metro North to Katonah pulled into the station on schedule. Janet Ransome hurried to the parking area, unlocked the driver's side door of her nine-year-old Chevie wagon and slid her slim five-foot-three frame behind the wheel – the plastic seat hot from the June sun. She pushed the ignition key into place, lifted her free hand to brush tendrils of perspiration-wet honey coloured hair from her forehead.

Why had she rushed back to the house the minute she had finished her business–pleasure luncheon with Ronnie? Tim didn't expect her home before six. At twelve and fourteen Lisa and Brian were old enough to survive her absence for the afternoon. A tender smile brightened her face. This was her thirty-eighth birthday, and she knew the kids were plotting a secret birthday cake to accompany dinner. She'd serve dinner early so they would not have to fret too long before presenting the Big Surprise.

She had deliberately chosen today to go in for the conference with Ronnie to allow the kids time to set things up. She'd wanted to be with Ronnie today, she acknowledged sentimentally. At forty-three Ronnie had not succumbed to panic facing that age. Still, at thirty-eight – one birthday removed from staring at forty – she was intimidated.

Divorced six years ago, Ronnie delivered endless stories about the rat race run by unattached women in the city. *"Look. Jan, it's a shitty position to be on the loose without a man after forty. But it's suicidal not to face it with a sense of humour. When you're single, every day of the year is the mating season."*

1

Jan relished these escapes into New York. Nobody in Ridgefield knew she wrote for the 'dying confession' magazine market and the raunchy men's market. She'd been writing for those markets since Brian was eight months old – because they always seemed to need more money than Tim brought home. Thank God, Ronnie edited half a dozen schlocky magazines. Though the confessions were down to one, there were still the 'tit' books, the beauty books, and whatever short-run ideas her boss dreamt up. The cheques that came from Ronnie's firm were keeping them afloat.

Tim had not worked in eleven months. At intervals she bluntly admitted to herself that he wasn't looking for a job. He had not sent out résumés since the first weeks. So he wasn't a kid fresh out of college; at forty-three and with his background he was still corporate executive material. Every two or three years since their marriage he had faced a job crisis – but those other times he hadn't retired from the business world.

Jan drove with a subconscious awareness of the summer beauty of the area. Approaching their hilltop colonial cape she inspected the charming, weathered shingle structure set high above a pair of terraces. She felt none of Tim's pride of ownership. She was ever conscious that they had bought beyond their means – as half their neighbours had done.

She left the car in the driveway and walked into the silent house, grateful for their central air-conditioning. She knew Tim was home. His almost new Olds was in the garage. She'd start dinner right away. Tim would drive down to the community swimming pool to pick up Lisa and Brian.

She frowned at the sight of the vacuum cleaner sitting in the middle of the living room. Damn! She had meant to vacuum the lower floor this morning. What had stopped her? Oh, somebody had called about helping with a fund-raising drive and she'd got derailed.

The house was silent. Usually Tim had the radio or TV blasting. He must have wandered over to visit with Jack Adams, she decided. Jack was home on vacation this week.

But Tim shouldn't leave the house open – too many daytime burglaries in the area.

Jan started up the carpeted stairs. She'd change into shorts and a tee shirt and vacuum before dinner. She hadn't had a cleaning woman for four years. There never seemed to be money for that.

Near the top of the stairs she stopped short. From the master bedroom – its door open only a sliver – emerged the sound of muffled voices. Tim *was* home. But who was up here with him?

All at once alarm pulled a rope about her throat. She remembered the break-in last week on the other side of the hill. *Intruders*. Was Tim all right? *He could be so hot-headed sometimes*.

Propelled by fear for Tim's safety, Jan hurried up the last few steps and down the hall to the door of the master bedroom. Her heart pounding, she pushed the door wide.

Tim couldn't see her. Naked on the bed, he was astride an equally naked young redhead with a voluptuous sun-tinted body. She could not have been more than twenty.

"What the devil are you doing?" Jan blazed in shock.

"Fucking," the redhead said coolly.

Tim turned around. His mouth went slack.

"Get that fat bitch out of here!" Jan's voice was shrill.

"Who's fat?" the girl shrieked.

Jan swung away from the door and charged towards the bathroom. Trembling. Her mind in chaos. She slammed the bathroom door behind her and tried to comprehend the situation.

Tim had not expected her home before six. It was just past four. He knew the kids wouldn't be home until he drove down to the pool for them. He was sure he was safe in bringing that young slut into the house. *Into their bed*. How long had this been going on? Did everybody in the neighbourhood know?

While she struggled to overcome her trembling, she heard Tim and the girl – he called her Anita – in low-keyed conversation.

3

Now they were walking downstairs. Moments later a car started up. Tim was driving that little bitch home – or wherever she wanted to go. *This was a soap opera segment.*

Jan forced herself to leave the bathroom and go into the Spanish Mediterranean master bedroom to change clothes. She averted her eyes from the rumpled queen-sized bed, still bearing the imprint of their bodies.

She'd known her sexual life with Tim was out of kilter when he moved a television set into their bedroom four years ago – and left it on while he made love to her. When the re-runs on *M\*A\*S\*H* became tense, the lovemaking halted. Even the national news pre-empted her sexual needs. She'd tried to tell herself this was the way it was after seventeen years of marriage.

Agonizingly conscious of the scene just played out in the nearby bed, Jan reached into a drawer for a tee shirt, went to the closet and pulled down a pair of shorts. With a shudder of distaste for what she had just interrupted, she deserted the bedroom and moved with compulsive haste into the privacy of the bathroom. *This was unreal. Something that happened to other women.*

In a need for ego bolstering Jan stripped to her skin. She minutely inspected her reflection in the full-length door mirror. It astonished her when people told her she was beautiful. When men made passes. But she'd never slept with anybody except Tim. She belonged in the Smithsonian, she jeered silently.

Despite two pregnancies she had a good body. Tim had a martini belly from the three drinks that were his pre-dinner routine. At bedtime he always had a Vodka gimlet.

Was Tim having what other wives called a mid-life crisis? So there were nights he tried to have sex and nothing happened. She never complained; she was sympathetic. On those nights, she rationalized, he didn't want sex. He was testing his macho image.

She remembered what Madge said at the bridge game last week when – as always – the talk turned to husbands. 'So Hank is fifty, and he can only get it up once a month. What's a wife supposed to

4

do?' Ridgefield ladies knew what Madge did. She had a propensity for men younger than her son in medical school.

God, what a birthday present! She might have been less furious if he hadn't brought that little bitch into the house. She paused to consider this. Would it have made any difference if Tim had taken the girl to a motel?

How many others had there been in all those years when Tim was forever dashing off on business trips? She'd been too busy to wonder. An eleven-room house with little or no domestic help, two children to raise, family chauffeuring, the community activities that were essential to keep up the image of corporate wife – and the grinding out of shoddy stories that brought in regular cheques to supplement Tim's income, had isolated her from suspicion.

Jan forced herself to dress. *What am I supposed to say when Tim comes back? Am I supposed to ignore that little romp in the hay? How can I ever sleep with him again without seeing him in bed with that slut? Did it have to be a twenty-year-old girl? We could have had a daughter as old as she.*

Listening for the sound of a car coming up the driveway, Jan went downstairs and out to the kitchen. She had planned the children's perennial favourite: spaghetti and a salad, and after that, watermelon. That was when they'd spring the birthday cake. *Why did it have to happen tonight?*

At regular intervals she made quantities of marinara sauce to be stored in the freezer. Dinner would be easy and fast. As she reached into the freezer to bring out a plastic container of sauce, she heard the car coming up the driveway. Moments later the sound of the children's voices assailed her ears. Tim had picked up the kids. Not to save himself an extra trip but to provide a barrier between himself and her. She almost welcomed the necessity to delay the confrontation.

The birthday cake and small presents from the children were especially endearing tonight. Tim hadn't bothered with a gift. He had the excuse of their financial situation. Jan made the required show of delight over the birthday cake, all the while avoiding any eye contact with Tim. They'd made a tacit agreement to control any explosion until the children were upstairs for the night.

When at last both Lisa and Brian – tired from the hours in the water – retired to their respective rooms, Jan went out to the kitchen to empty the dishwasher and gear herself to face Tim. They could talk out here without their voices carrying up the stairs to the children's rooms. Not that it would matter. Rock music from either Lisa's stereo or from Brian's would drown them out.

"Jan—" Tim's voice spun her around.

"Damn it, Tim! That wasn't what I expected for a birthday present!" When was the last time she had raised her voice to Tim? She was always the gentle one. Tim yelled.

"You didn't have to act like a Nineties melodrama—" He was trying to sound cool.

"Did you expect me to sprinkle the two of you with champagne?"

"I planned to wait until after your birthday to tell you." Tim was staring at her as though he hated her. *He'd never looked at her that way before.* "But I don't have to wait now. I'm leaving you. I've had all I can take of this whole shitty rat race."

Jan gaped in stunned silence. What was Tim talking about? She found her voice and took refuge in anger.

"I don't know how you had the gall to bring that little bitch right into our house—"

"Look, there's no need to talk any more. I want a divorce. I'm sick of this whole way of life. The job pressures. Family pressures. Supporting a lifestyle I hate." *But it was Tim who insisted on living beyond their means. Tim who ran up bills with an abandon that still unnerved her.* "I'll take my car and drive out to Reno. I'll get the divorce out there and—"

"Marry that juvenile delinquent?" When Lisa was angry with

6

her father, she'd say, 'Mom, why don't you divorce him?' But to Jan marriage was forever.

"I'm not marrying anybody." Tim grimaced in rejection. "I want to be free." *How could he be free when they had two children to raise?* "Anita's going out to Reno with me," he admitted. "She's a great cocktail waitress – she'll find a job with no sweat." *He meant for Anita to support him while he played at being free.* "It's more practical for me to get the divorce. I mean to head out west anyway. I want to give the Coast a try. Maybe Big Sur."

"What about Lisa and Brian?" She was trembling. Her throat was tight. How could she manage alone? For seventeen years Tim had always been at her side.

"The children belong with you." He was impatient to be done with this scene. "I'm giving you the house." It was in both their names – the way a house should be. "It's worth a fortune in today's market." With the mortgage paid off it'd be worth a lot. "Sell it and move back to New York." *Move to New York with two kids?* They hadn't lived in New York since the first time she was pregnant. Tim insisted it was impossible to raise kids in the city. "I've already talked to Joe about the settlement." Who else beside their lawyer knew Tim meant to divorce her? "You get everything except what's in the cheque account. I'll need that for legal fees in Reno and expenses getting out there." He'd already cleared out their joint cheque account, she interpreted. They had no stock portfolio. A few hundred in savings. "You have the house and the second car and the furniture."

"A house with an enormous mortgage," she reminded him. How could Tim stand there and talk so cold-bloodedly about walking out on the children and her? "The car wouldn't bring six hundred dollars. We still owe money on the new furniture. Your car has three more years of payments due!" A car loaded with every possible gadget.

Tim shrugged. "You don't have to worry. Your name's not on the loan. Let the bank try to catch me."

7

"I don't believe this." Jan stared at him as though seeing him for the first time in the seventeen years of their marriage.

"Look, you know the divorce statistics. I'm forty-three years old, and I want to be free. I don't want to worry any more about mortgage payments, fuel bills, orthodontia, and the rising cost of a college education. I want out. That's it, Jan."

Jan forced herself to walk into the master bedroom. Standing beside the bed she was assaulted by visions of Tim pushing himself into that little slut. When would she look at a bed again without seeing them?

Clenching her teeth, feeling herself unclean, she stripped the sheets from the bed and rolled them into a bundle. Dropped the bundle on the floor to pull off the pillowcases. Now she took the sheets and the pillowcases downstairs and shoved them into the garbage can on the deck.

Walking back into the house she heard the eleven o'clock TV news seeping from the den. Tim would sleep on the convertible sofa in there until he took off. In two or three days, he'd said. Seventeen years of marriage, and he was taking off in two or three days.

Suddenly exhausted, Jan climbed the flight of stairs to the second floor. She pulled down sheets and pillowcases from a shelf in the linen closet and went into the seldom-used guest room. She could never bring herself to sleep again in the bed she had shared with Tim.

Tim said he would tell the kids tomorrow that he was leaving. How could he make Lisa and Brian understand that their father was walking out of their lives?

The music that belched forth from the children's rooms earlier had been silenced. Feeling a stranger in her own house, as though she was preparing for a night in a motel room, Jan settled herself in bed, vowing not to be mowed down by panic. That was a luxury she could not afford.

She had been so sure she knew Tim. Through the years she

8

had made so many excuses for him. When he was irascible – and this was frequently – she told herself he was upset about things at the office. When he blew up at the kids, she told them Daddy was working too hard; they must understand.

On the nights when he sat down to dinner with the children and her, he griped about his day. Then he made a pretence of listening to the kids' reports of their day. After dinner he settled himself in front of the TV set. Sometimes he fell asleep there. Weekends he religiously disappeared – on the golf course or tennis court or whatever. About one week in five he flew to Houston or Atlanta or San Francisco, or wherever business sent him.

She wouldn't allow herself to believe that Tim was at fault when he was fired after two or three years on any job. When the charisma wore off – she forced herself to admit now. Tim harboured illusions about being destined for great wealth. Becoming Chairman of the Board. Her financial contribution – never amounting to more than seven or eight thousand a year – was 'small change' to Tim.

Was he having an emotional breakdown? Should she urge him to go into therapy, though God knows where they'd find the money? For a precarious moment she clutched at the possibility of bringing their marriage together again. Then reality moved in on her. *No.* Tim had been planning his future for months. He'd even worked out the details with his lawyer. He was coldly and calculatingly cutting himself free from the children and herself.

Lying against the pillows Jan considered her position. She was a thirty-eight-year-old woman with two growing children to raise alone. How much money would be left over from the mortgage when she sold the house?

Now she could distil the essence of their lives with fresh clarity. She had been wife, mother, secretary, housekeeper, valet – and whipping post. Yet in moments of grave decision, Jan analyzed, Tim had leaned on her. She had focused on building up his strength in crisis situations. She had bolstered him, supported him, and propelled him into necessary paths.

9

Why had she failed in pushing him back into the job market after this last fiasco? Why couldn't she make him understand that he wasn't the first over-forty executive to be kicked into a tough job market? But it wasn't just the job, Jan conceded. That would not break up a marriage.

When she married Tim, she envisioned him as a mercurial leader of men. But she made no demands. She had convinced herself that her role in life was to be a supportive wife and mother. Her own ambitions were secondary to the family's needs.

She had been awed when dashing Tim Ransome, so sought after by girls, had chosen to marry her. To her it was a miracle. Her ego had always been a fragile vessel. How could it be otherwise, considering her childhood?

Growing up beside gorgeous Diane, who might have been a top model or a movie star if she had not died on the ski slopes at twenty-two, was not an ego-builder. Mom loved her, but she worshipped Diane. It seemed natural that Diane should go to Bennington, draining what money Mom had held together from Dad's life insurance. A Bennington girl was sure to marry rich, Mom thought. When *she* was ready for college, there was no money. She went to Hunter.

Because she had known the pain of growing up in the shadow of a beautiful sister pampered and spoiled by their mother, she had vowed that Lisa and Brian would never be caught in that trap. She leaned over backward not to show partiality. The only time she stood up and fought Tim was when he favoured Brian over Lisa. Funny, it had been the other way round until Lisa grew feisty and independent.

Diane was gone, and Mom was gone. And in a couple of days Tim would be gone. How could she bring up Lisa and Brian on her own? To make every decision alone? To provide? But she must.

Her mind grappled with what lay ahead. First, the house must be sold. Quickly. She meant to put the children in school in New York when the new term began in September. No money for private schools, she warned herself – and tried to suppress her anxiety about the conditions in New York City public schools. Tomorrow morning she'd have to call the brokers.

The word would be all over the hill in a day or two. Tim and Janet Ransome are splitting up. She wouldn't be one of the Ridgefield wives any more. A divorced woman was a pariah in suburbia. A threat to the wives.

Sleep was elusive. The first pink streaks of dawn were penetrating the greyness of the night before Jan succumbed. She awoke four hours later to hear Lisa and Brian fighting downstairs. As usual Tim was screaming at them. He had no patience with the children.

"All right, I'll drive you down to the pool!" he yelled. "For Chrissake, stop fighting!"

While Jan adjusted her shower spray, she heard the car pull out of the garage. Tim would be calling on Joe this morning. He'd tell Joe to speed up the papers for the settlement. How could a few legal papers wash Tim out of their lives? He might stop being her husband, but he could never stop being Lisa and Brian's father.

She ought to be represented by an attorney. That was accepted procedure in a divorce. But Tim was walking out on his family, disappearing from their lives. What good would it be to have a court order for alimony and child support when Tim was off in space? He was giving her a mortgage-laden house – to him that was ample compensation for the years she'd given him. He'd said something vague about Joe's setting up some child support arrangements at such time as he was working again. If she could catch up with him, Jan thought wryly. Not likely.

All right. Plan the day. Push through one day at a time. First she'd call the brokers. Then Ronnie. A trickle of relief invaded her. Thank God for Ronnie, who had gone through what she was going through now.

She could hear Ronnie's voice, telling her about how *she* walked into her bedroom and found Hank there with another woman:

11

'*It wasn't enough that Hank brought that bitch into the house, into our bedroom – but there she was in my best nightgown, rolled up to her navel!*'

Ronnie emerged from her divorce to rebuild a life for herself and Deedee. She went right to work as an editor at the magazine factory where she still was today. Ronnie fought her way out of rough times, fighting for child support whenever she could locate her ex-husband. But Ronnie and Deedee survived.

She'd ask Ronnie to help her find an apartment. Recalling New York City rentals, she shuddered. How much cash would the house provide? Enough for the kids and her to live on for a year if she was careful? What happened after the money from the house was gone? Even Joe, who insisted on incorporating the child support clause, conceded it would be unwise to count on such funds.

How did a thirty-eight-year-old woman with no skills except writing for sleazy magazines – a field that narrowed yearly – bring up two children in the middle-class manner? In New York City – but where else could she go? That was her job market.

Some wives went back to college for a graduate degree after a divorce. A liberal arts degree had little value in the market place. But she'd been out of school so long. She'd be broke before she could earn a master's. Could she make it as a freelance writer? The Authors Guild bulletins regularly bemoaned the average annual income of writers: under five thousand a year.

Jan turned on the needle spray of the shower so that the water pounded on her tense back. All this craziness of the divorce had been fomenting in Tim's mind. How many women had occupied his hotel beds through the years when she had taken it for granted that she was the only woman in his life?

Where had she failed Tim? She searched her mind in uneasy guilt. What could she have done to save their marriage? She was losing a husband, and Lisa and Brian were losing a father. *Was it her fault? Had she been blind to signals?*

She'd tried to be sympathetic and encouraging. When they

fought, it was because of money. Like last month. How could Tim go out and spend nine hundred dollars on golf clubs when they were already behind in all their bills?

Why did Tim need other women? What was lacking in her? *She* didn't drag a TV set into their bedroom – Tim did that. Even now she could feel her humiliation when TV won out over lovemaking. Did Tim require a perennial twenty-year-old in his bed?

# Chapter Two

Her face strained with the effort not to show her anguish, Jan watched while Tim – in ebullient spirits – went through the business of disposing of personal possessions collected over a lifetime. She waited for him to tell the kids about the divorce, even while she remembered that unpleasant chores had always been shifted to her shoulders. As she anticipated, he dodged this chore.

"I can't tell them," he said with an air of martyrdom the night before he was scheduled to leave. "You explain it," he said and escaped to the den.

How did she tell Lisa and Brian that their father wanted no part of the responsibility of bringing them up? There was no easy route. She sat them down in the kitchen with girl scout cookies and glasses of milk at bedtime and told them.

"I knew it had to be something crazy when you gave us cookies," Lisa said after Jan had delivered the news. This was a household that shunned junk food and sweets. "Is Daddy having a mid-life crisis?"

"Daddy feels he has to do this." *Daddy has rocks in his head.* Where did kids pick up all these sophisticated phrases? Television. "We'll sell the house and my car and move to New York."

"We're going to school in New York City?" Brian was shocked. "That jungle?"

"It's not all jungle." Jan refused to be ruffled.

"Why are you selling the car?" Brian asked. "Will we be poor? I could get a job after school."

"People in New York don't need cars," Jan said. "They have subways and buses."

"Mom, every time you take us down to New York—" Brian began, but Lisa interrupted.

"About twice a year!" Lisa was on a ballet kick. She couldn't understand that the family budget didn't allow for weekly trips to Lincoln Center.

"Every time you take us to New York," Brian reiterated, "you complain about all the traffic. Cars."

"Mostly commuters," Jan insisted. "Native New Yorkers are too smart for the car trap."

"Where will Daddy live?" Brian was uneasy.

"He wants to go out west somewhere. He's not sure just where." But the focal point was Reno. "He'll keep in touch with us," she soothed. A postcard once a month. Maybe he'd remember birthdays. Normally he depended on her for that.

Lisa seemed hostile about the divorce, despite her periodic urging of such action. Brian was unnaturally quiet. How could you ever know what went on inside kids' heads? But soon they'd be involved in the change of schools. That would help take their minds off the divorce. Public schools – there was no way she could pay private school fees.

The kids were sombre when they kissed Tim goodbye. Tim was in great spirits. He sounded like Brian last summer when he went off with a group to hike a chunk of the Appalachian trail. But Brian had been thirteen and Tim was forty-three. How could he just drive away without worrying about the kids and her? How could he be so sure they could survive without him? *She* wasn't.

They dallied in the expensively black-topped driveway. Tim and she and Lisa and Brian. The perfect family as depicted in the movies, on television, and in novels. Now Tim hesitated beside the car, as though not sure if he was expected to kiss her goodbye. For the first time in their marriage she offered no help. He cleared his throat self-consciously, waved a hand in jaunty farewell, and slid behind the wheel.

16

Droplets of rain began to fall from the ominous sky as Tim drove his late model Olds down the driveway, out onto the road, and out of their lives. Jan watched with a feeling of unreality. It would not be so awful, she told herself, if she had been suspicious of Tim. But he had given no clue that he was chasing other women – or, perhaps, she had been too involved in the necessities of living to notice.

"Want to play chess?" Brian asked Lisa after a few moments in which the three had stood in a silent tableau of disbelief. "We can't go swimming this morning." He squinted at the sky with a sombreness that was unrelated to the weather.

"Okay." Lisa was unfamiliarly docile. "Let's go."

Jan stood alone in front of their picture-book house in the 'American dream' community. She stared at the lush peony bush across the driveway without seeing the giant pink velvet flowers. Tim was gone. This insanity was real.

As though her finger was suddenly scorched from the contact, she snatched her wedding band from its familiar resting place. She'd read somewhere that it was traditional for a divorcée to wear her wedding band on the right hand. She'd never wear hers again.

She thrust the ring into the pocket of her jeans while her eyes inspected the house. She couldn't afford to stay here with the children even if she wanted to. Not that she would want to remain here without Tim. It was always *his* house. It had never been a happy house for them, Jan decided in retrospect. But she had been too busy to notice that her marriage was falling apart.

According to the divorce settlement she'd signed at Joe's office yesterday morning, she was waiving alimony in return for full ownership of the house. Tim was committed to pay child support until the children were eighteen. Never mind about the college years, she thought bitterly.

The amount of child support was set at one-third of Tim's after-taxes income. But how would she ever know when Tim

17

was gainfully employed? How could she chase after him in family courts across the country?

Oh yes, Tim was free.

\*　　\*　　\*

It became clear within a matter of two weekends that selling the house would not be a simple matter. The shortage of mortgage money and the high interest rates made this a buyer's market. Jan lowered the price of the house, then lowered it substantially a second time. She must sell, and quickly.

She knew she must find an apartment in the city. This entailed moving costs, two months' rent, and utility deposits. The mortgage payments had to be met until the house was sold. When a couple appeared with an offer that shocked even the affable broker, Jan accepted. The new owners were impatient to be settled in by the time school opened. She knew she must be in a city apartment by the time the city schools opened.

Now life became a twenty-hour a day rat race. The broker was sweating out an early closing date. Jan and the children debated about what furniture would go into the apartment, what must be sold. She tried to explain to them that a city apartment would not have the dimensions of a suburban house.

They held weekend tag sales, learning after the first week that an ad reading '10 a.m. to 6 p.m.' meant that cars would be streaming into the driveway by 8.45 a.m.

Only now did Jan realize how little the house reflected her tastes. Everything had been chosen to please Tim. She loved bright yellows, deep greens, warm earthy tones. Tim fancied beige or grey. The exquisite Royal Doulton china had been bought to be shown off when Tim's boss came to dinner. It would be sold now. She would have no use – or space – for fine china in the New York apartment.

Ronnie spent lunch hours running from one apartment to another with her. Ronnie insisted it was urgent they live in her area, where good schools were still available. Ronnie had lived in the Gramercy Park area for scarcely a year but was a true convert. She could walk to work. No hassle with subways or buses.

"Pray that Brian and Lisa make Stuyvesant High School," Ronnie said. "Then you won't have to worry about a private high school." She sighed. "Deedee didn't make Stuyvesant. But with Hank working here in the city now I know he'll have to come across with the child support cheques each month plus Deedee's fancy tuition."

Ronnie was already worrying about college. How would *she* cope with college? She couldn't count on Tim. *Don't even think about college.*

When she picked up Ronnie today, Ronnie announced she had a great lead on a vacant apartment.

"But first let's run in for a fast hamburger and coffee. I didn't have time for breakfast this morning. I was in another raging battle to get Deedee off to school. They've got a new rule this term. No jeans. Well-pressed slacks with a crease. Deedee's rebelling."

Jan and Ronnie hurried to the coffee shop in the building and found a booth for two. A waitress immediately took their orders.

"Don't look across the room," Ronnie said softly, "but you've got a fan. The guy can't take his eyes off you. Not bad, either."

"He's looking at you," Jan said without turning her head. Ronnie's tall, slim figure made everything she wore look like a designer creation. She was strikingly attractive with her hair lightened to almost silver blonde, in contrast to her perennial rich tan and perfectly made up blue eyes.

"Jan, he doesn't even know I'm sitting here," Ronnie said impatiently. "Surely you must know you're a damned gorgeous woman. You're what men want."

"I haven't time for men." Jan was grim. "I have two kids to raise. That takes precedence over everything."

*Julie Ellis*

"Honey, stop looking so desperate," Ronnie scolded. "You're a survivor."

"Me?" Jan was startled. But Mom, too, had said that.

"You had to be to stay married to Tim for seventeen years. I used to hate him for the things he pulled on you. I would have walked out on him years ago."

"I thought they were things every wife had to put up with," Jan admitted after a moment.

"In marriage you fight every step of the way. I tried to keep my marriage with Hank together. I really worked at it. But he threw it away. I wasn't surprised when he divorced the little bitch he married after me. I won't be surprised when he divorces his third wife."

"One thing I can say with conviction." Jan was resolute. "I'll never marry again. Maybe a relationship under the right circumstances," she conceded, "but I never want to be legally tied to another man. I value my freedom." What she really meant, Jan thought, was that she could never face the trauma of another divorce.

"I'd marry again." Ronnie startled her with this admission. "But he'd have to be rich, and there'd have to be a premarital agreement about what I get in cash if the marriage didn't work out. God, it'd be the ultimate luxury not to have to work for Mannie! I might even write a novel. But in the meantime," she chuckled, "nobody with income tax problems is beating a path to my door." She paused reflectively, sighed. "Some people swear by the personal ads. And some swear at them," she conceded. "For me they never work."

"You've run ads in the personal columns?" Jan was shocked.

"Hey, they make sense. When I run ads, at least I'm going out two or three nights a week. They cut right to the core. They save a lot of time, wasted energy."

"I don't think I could bring myself to do that," Jan admitted.

"Upscale magazines run personals," Ronnie reminded. "Everything from *New York Magazine* to *The Washingtonian* and

20

*Chicago Life* and *Los Angeles Magazine*. And some great marriages have come about through the ads."

"Tell me about this apartment we're going to see," Jan prodded. Talking about marriage brought Tim into her mind. She didn't want to think about him. Even now she worried about him. Habit. One she'd have to break.

They ate without a wasted moment and hurried over to the building with the vacancy. The super gave them the key and sent them upstairs to see it.

"It's just like every other so-called luxury high-rise apartment building," Ronnie conceded, "but it does have two bathrooms. That'll make life easier in the mornings."

"I'll take it," Jan decided. She wouldn't find anything less expensive in Manhattan. "Let's go down and talk to the super."

On the train going home Jan planned on how to handle a two-bedroom apartment. Bookshelves would divide the master bedroom for Lisa and Brian. The smaller bedroom would be hers. Ronnie had told her to pick up copies of *New York Magazine* and the *Village Voice* and to check out neighbourhood bulletin boards. She would find a mover with rates compatible with her budget. This was the first time she had to move without the team sent in by the corporation for whom Tim was working at the time. It would be a traumatic experience.

\* \* \*

Early on a Saturday morning the movers from Manhattan – two out-of-work actors with the necessary brawn and an aspiring and muscular opera star, plucked from a supermarket bulletin board – drove up to the Ridgefield house and started to shift furniture and cartons from house to truck. They stopped for frequent refreshment, but considering the record heat of the day Jan was sympathetic. She was less sympathetic when they broke a favourite lamp.

Nine hours later the movers departed from the mercifully air-conditioned apartment. Brian and Lisa shifted furniture from one position to another at Jan's instructions. They stopped once to resuscitate themselves via the McDonald's bag that Brian had brought up from downstairs. Later they took a frozen yogurt break.

Jan fought panic. Why did pieces that seemed so practical when she had planned the move appear so monstrously large now? But by close to eleven Jan decreed the apartment suitable for living. Later they'd worry about hanging drapes and unpacking cartons. The living-room was informal but cosy.

The beige rug from the family room was almost wall-to-wall here. The hunter green velvet sofa with the attractively slipcovered love seat made a pleasant seating arrangement. The coffee table was too large, but would be practical. The wall of bookcases lent colour to the room.

The dining-room furniture had been sold at a staggering loss, but the round oak table from the breakfast room, with a leaf removed, fitted into the dining area along with three captain's chairs. The fourth chair had been shunted into the children's room. She had brought in Lisa and Brian's twin beds from their old individual bedrooms plus their dressers and matching desks. In her bedroom was a double bed and dresser from the guest room; she had never set foot in the master bedroom after the afternoon she discovered Tim in bed with Anita except for necessary odd moments and packing. Later she would set up a table in a corner for her computer and printer. That would be 'the office'.

\*　　\*　　\*

After four days in the apartment Jan conceded that the divided bedroom for the children was not workable. There was the conflict of stereos that even brought complaints from the neighbour on the other side of the wall. She decided to move Brian into the living-room. He would sleep on the convertible love seat. Instantly the living-room became a disaster area.

A week later Jan moved Brian into her room and took up residence in the living-room. She tried to tell herself it was like living in a studio apartment. In truth, it was a buffer zone.

At uneasy intervals Jan worried about Tim. He drove too fast when he was uptight. He never ate properly away from home. But that wasn't her concern any more, she rebuked herself.

With each rediscovery of city living Jan realized how bored she had been in suburbia. She had existed in suburbia; she lived in New York. It was a joy to be able to send one of the kids down to a supermarket to shop for a container of milk instead of having to get into the car and drive three miles. She marvelled that she could walk almost any place she cared to go. Lisa and Brian walked to school.

Jan scheduled her days to allow for maximum work time. She disciplined herself to turn out a set quantity of pages each week. Ronnie was buying from her with reassuring regularity. When Ronnie's boss started paying on publication rather than acceptance, Ronnie had lost a solid chunk of her regular writers.

Still, Jan knew she must draw on the money from the house each month to keep them afloat. As soon as Lisa and Brian were settled into the new school, she'd have to face the problem of orthodontia. Jan winced each time she considered this. Orthodontia would leave a giant hole in the house money.

On the third Saturday evening of the school term Lisa went off for dinner at a classmate's house. She would be brought home, Lisa promised. Jan was relieved Lisa had found a friend in the neighbourhood. 'Betty's father says public schools are our heritage, and we must use them.'

"Don't worry if I'm late," Lisa said airily. "Betty said her father's new sleep-in girlfriend likes to serve late dinners. Like they do in Europe."

Jan tried not to react to the 'sleep-in-girlfriend' feedback.

Mothers were supposed to be sophisticated about such trends in 1995. She saw Lisa off and went into the kitchen to prepare hamburgers and salad for Brian and herself. Ronnie had invited her to go out to a movie, but Jan felt it wouldn't be right to leave Brian alone on a Saturday night this early in their New York residency.

"Where do you think Dad is now?" Brian asked over the last watermelon of the season.

"San Diego," Jan guessed. They'd received three cards since mid-June plus the legal papers on the divorce. Lisa was furious that he had not remembered to send her a birthday card. "He wrote from there."

"That was three weeks ago," Brian bristled. "I sent you a card five times when I was on that trip last summer, and I called you every time we came near a phone." Collect, naturally. She had been so glad each time he called.

"Darling, we can't concern ourselves with Dad's activities."

"Do you think he'll ever come back?" Brian tried to sound casual.

"He says he hates New York."

When Tim pulled out of their driveway that morning in June, she had hoped for a few painful moments that he would come back. It had seemed unbelievable that he could drive out of their lives like that. Yet each day that passed she recognized fresh holes in their marriage. Tim had always been wrapped up in his own potential happiness. There was no room for the children or her.

For seventeen years he had needed her, leaned on her and used her as a whipping post. Now he decided he didn't need her. He was running after eternal youth. A forty-three-year-old swinging bachelor.

At a quarter to ten Ronnie called. The movie was a dog. Not worth standing in line for thirty-five minutes.

"Come over and have coffee," Jan invited.

"You're about five minutes too late, but thanks anyway. I

just threw off my clothes and pulled on a nightie. My feet are falling off. Saturdays I run around doing all the nonsense things like going to the cleaners and the supermarket and doing the laundry downstairs. Tell you what, get yourself a cup of coffee and I'll make a cup for me. Then call me back and let's yak. I don't feel up to tackling the *Times* crossword puzzle yet."

"Call you back," Jan agreed, pleased to hear an adult voice. "Brian," she said in a surge of enthusiasm for the city, "go down and pick up the Sunday *Times*. In New York it comes out on Saturday night," she forestalled his reminder that this wasn't Sunday.

"You're sure you want me to go down on a Saturday night?" Brian fished for an excuse. "In New York City?"

"Brian, it's not ten o'clock yet, and the newsstand is a block away."

"Okay." Brian was nonchalant. "But if I'm mugged and murdered, remember I went down for you."

Though she was convinced nothing vile would happen to Brian, Jan waited until he returned with the *Times* before she settled herself in a chair by the phone to call Ronnie. Brian disappeared into his room to read a portion of the paper with a rock music background.

"I'm waiting here with my trusty cup of coffee," Ronnie said with a show of high spirits. "What are we doing sitting at home on a Saturday night?"

"You went to a movie," Jan reminded.

"Why do I always feel like a pariah when I walk up to the cashier's booth and ask for one ticket? Who says the world is one big Noah's Ark?"

"We'll do something next Saturday," Jan placated, feeling guilty. "Come over here for dinner first."

"Let's see what develops," Ronnie stipulated. "Maybe my nutrition expert will decide he's not too exhausted from three hours of tennis to take me out next Saturday night. Wouldn't you think that by the time a man reaches fifty-four he'd take

25

it easy on the tennis courts? I hate to have a man yawning in my face when he's making love to me."

Jan recalled that the nutrition expert – a twice-divorced school teacher – was the current man in Ronnie's life. She'd met him at a wine and cheese party several months ago.

"Why don't you invite him over for dinner?" Jan suggested.

"We've been through that scene." Ronnie sighed. "Lenny says he feels more comfortable at his place. I think Deedee upsets him. Anyhow, that's a good excuse. This way he can invite me over to his apartment for dinner – or take me out if he's not in a penny-pinching mood – whenever he's ready for a roll in the hay. If I call him, it's just to talk. I can't say, 'how about taking me out tonight?' I feel like an over-aged call girl." Ronnie's chuckle was wry. "But I go. After forty you pack your pride and take your sex when it comes along. Provided, of course, the man is fairly successful. No woman who's doing well herself can bring herself to go to bed with a guy who's lower on the social and economic ladder."

Jan was shocked. "Ronnie, you're a damned attractive woman." *Hadn't Ronnie said that to her?*

"To some men. Too many of them figure mathematically. A girl has to be half their age before they're ready for bed. Not all," she conceded. "Lenny says he'd feel he was committing incest if he slept with some hot-blooded twenty-four-year-old. His daughter is twenty-five. But I don't believe him. Some men yes, Lenny no. Let's indulge in a moment of truth," she said after momentary cogitation. "To make it after forty in the singles world a woman has to be very attractive. A man only has to be successful."

"You'll meet a better prospect than Lenny." It was depressing to think of vital, attractive Ronnie making herself available on demand.

"I won't go near the bar scene." Ronnie's voice was sharp with distaste. "The 'meat market'. That's not for me. Oh, I tried them for a while when I first came back to New York after the divorce. Half of the guys are married and looking for extra-marital action.

Ninety-five per cent are after one-night stands. Anyhow, the bars are really the 'under thirties' scene."

"What's doing with Deedee?" Jan knew Ronnie was having problems with her daughter.

"She'll be coming home sometime before breakfast." Frustration infiltrated Ronnie's voice. "At least I've got her on the pill and carrying condoms. She won't come home pregnant or with AIDS."

"When did this happen?" Jan felt a kind of relief that Lisa was only twelve.

Ronnie sighed.

"Before she went away for a weekend in August on Fire Island with her girlfriend and the girlfriend's swinging mother. I took her to this dignified late forties gynaecologist with several kids of his own. He looked at Deedee after I explained the situation and said in a fatherly voice, 'Deedee, do you have to do these things?' And she looked him straight in the eyes and said, 'Don't you?' "

"These kids make me feel so old," Jan said.

"Look, plenty of our generation slept around in their teens and twenties," Ronnie tried to rationalize. "Oh, and now she's started pulling last year's number again. She hates school – it makes no sense. And I end up by giving her cab fare because by that time – with me panting to leave for the office – she'd be late for school if she took the bus."

Jan and Ronnie swapped stories about the kids. Jan acknowledged that her problems were minor league compared to Ronnie's. They talked for almost an hour, then closed the phone conversation for the night. Jan rapped on the door to Brian's room and asked for the book review and the magazine section of the *Times*.

Her mind refused to focus on reading. Why wasn't Lisa home by now? It was close to midnight. She tossed aside the newspaper and went to call Betty's apartment. As she began to dial, the doorbell rang. She hurried to the door and pulled it wide.

"Hi!" Lisa glowed. Beside her stood the sexiest twelve-year-old since Brook Shields. She wore shorts so brief Jan was sure an eye-catching swathe of rump was on display. "I told you they'd bring me home early."

'They' included, in addition to Betty, a six-foot male model type who looked no more than twenty-eight.

"I'm Jeff," he introduced himself with a charismatic smile whose value he knew. "Betty's father."

"Jan," she said and extended a hand. "Lisa's mother. Thanks for bringing her home."

"Our pleasure." He seemed reluctant to release her hand. His eyes were taking avid inventory. "Lisa didn't tell us she had such a beautiful mother."

"We had the greatest dinner. Just smashing," Lisa intruded, oblivious to the by-play. "This fancy leg of lamb with apricots and all," Lisa bubbled. "Jeff's girlfriend is the best cook."

Jeff's smile lost some of its sparkle. He released her hand. Had he been about to make a play for her? But he was so young! His marriage to Betty's mother must have been one of those teenage 'have to' deals.

"Let Lisa come over for dinner again soon okay?" he said and swatted Betty on the rear. "Let's beat it, kitten."

Jan sat down to listen to a full report on the evening. Lisa was adapting well to the city, she told herself in relief. Brian, too. Now Lisa rose to her feet and headed to the kitchen for her favourite pre-bedtime diversion. She stood before the refrigerator with both doors flung wide and inspected the interior.

"There's nothing to eat," she complained.

"The refrigerator's loaded," Jan protested. "Besides, do you really want to eat after that late continental dinner?"

"I don't suppose you'd let me run down to buy a slice of pizza?" she asked wistfully.

"I would not." In New York they lived by the city rules. Lisa was not to run around the streets alone at close to midnight.

Lisa settled for a chunk of cheese and an apple and retired

to her room. Jan sat down with the *Times* again, but she didn't read. The conversation with Ronnie ricocheted in her mind. The encounter with Betty's father offered mild gratification. He *was* about to make a pitch. Did he think Lisa and Betty were too young to understand? Betty looked as though she'd read the *Joy of Sex* instead of *Janet and John*.

All at once she was conscious of how long it had been since she'd slept with Tim. She'd told herself that part of her life was packed away. She was too busy, too occupied with keeping her life on an even keel to think about sex. But Betty's father had made her aware of being a woman. He made her remember the wonderful first months of their marriage when Tim had been so eager to please her in bed.

In the first shock of Tim's walking out on her she had convinced herself she could survive very well without a man in her bed. Now she wasn't so confident.

# Chapter Three

Indian summer morning sun spilled into the living-room, warming the array of late tomatoes Jan had placed on the windowsill for ripening. She leaned over her computer. Another two sentences and she'd wrap up the confession story for Ronnie that had hung over from yesterday. Each story was a fresh obstacle course.

She'd proofread later and delay starting the next story until this afternoon. Two loads of laundry had to be done. This morning she welcomed an intrusion on her writing schedule.

Dumping soiled clothes into a shopping cart Jan dissected her distaste for writing confessions. She had been at them for too many years. She was sick of them. And they kept her from throwing all her efforts into a novel. Like every conscientious English major she had long harboured an ambition to write a 'good' novel.

Each time she had begun to work on a novel, she'd been forced to discard the rough pages for another short formula piece that would bring in quick money. Not so quick now that the magazine was paying on publication, but at least she knew the cheques would eventually come in to replace part of what she was pulling out of the house money each week. She still wasn't earning enough to support the three of them. Maybe she could manage if they lived in some rent-controlled South Bronx tenement and depended upon pasta and rice for dinners . . .

Restless this morning, rebelling mentally against her self-imposed treadmill, Jan waited for the elevator. One elevator was tied up on the lobby floor. Somebody must be moving in. There was no service elevator. An economy measure on the part of the builders about which tenants regularly complained. The porters were probably using the other elevator to remove from the stairwells the piles of newspapers not suitable for the compactor. But she couldn't walk to the basement laundry room from the eighth floor.

At last an elevator slid to a stop. The door opened. Jan pushed in her shopping cart, topped by a box of Arm & Hammer laundry detergent. Brian was an environmental knight. Nothing was allowed in the Ransome household that might be a pollutant.

"Hi." A tiny, still pretty, slightly overweight ash blonde in her late forties greeted Jan with an eager smile. "I thought I might have to carry my laundry down ten flights." She spoke in a little girl near-whisper aggravated by a decided Southern accent.

"We'd wear dirty clothes first," Jan laughed. Her fellow passenger pushed 'B' again.

"I'm Peggy Phipps," the blue-jeaned blonde introduced herself while she inspected Jan with lively interest. "I moved here four months ago from Brewster. Right after my divorce," she added after a moment.

"Welcome to the clan." Jan's smile was wry. "I'm Janet Ransome. My two kids and I came into the building in late August. From Connecticut. After my divorce."

"Of course, my divorce won't be final for almost a year," Peggy explained, "but it's the same as gone through. Hal has already found himself a new girlfriend. He didn't waste a minute."

The elevator came to a stop. The two women moved out into the hallway and walked down to the tropic-hot laundry room. Jan was aware of the resentment simmering in Peggy. She was angry at being replaced. Had her husband left her for the new girlfriend? Peggy seemed to read her mind.

"I know I asked for the divorce," she said aggrievedly. "Hal fought against it. But it seems indecent for him to be sleeping with somebody else already. In *my* house. I'm glad my two boys are away at college. They don't have to see that."

32

"It's nice that they're college age." Jan stationed herself between a pair of empty machines. Peggy moved down to the next one. "Mine are twelve and fourteen. But they seem to be adjusting to the divorce." Were they? Sometimes she worried about that.

"I couldn't take any more of suburbia. I hated the whole ugly picture." Peggy grimaced. "I hate driving, and there I was the family chauffeur. Running all of Hal's errands. 'Go to the bank, Peg.' 'Do the shopping, Peg.' 'Take my car in to the garage, Peg.' Before I was married, I was an artist. I could have had a real career if I hadn't been tied down to running that big house and raising two sons. Nobody ever cared about me. About my needs." Peggy was talking with machine-gun rapidity. Jan visualized her spewing out these grievances to a series of psychiatrists. "I always had to cater to my husband and my children. If I tried to work at my painting, somebody was always interrupting. They wouldn't give me any space!" Peggy's hand trembled as she dumped detergent into the tray. "I dragged Hal to a marriage counsellor, but he didn't really cooperate. To him it was a waste of time. For a couple of weeks he took me out to dinner on Fridays. He just sat there and sulked. I asked him why he took me out to dinner, and he said, 'Because I paid a marriage counsellor a hundred dollars a session, and he said to take you out to dinner.' That's when I cut out."

"I think Tim believed he was a Nineties flower child," Jan said wryly.

"Hal thought he'd get off easy because I was anxious to leave. But I got myself a sharp lawyer. I wouldn't let myself be sold short." Jan felt the steel beneath the velvet magnolia. "I've got a base alimony of twenty-five thousand a year, after taxes. Every time Hal's salary goes up, my alimony goes up. He's waiting until he's fifty-five to sell the house – for the tax break. I get half of that. I gave him twenty-four years of my life. I have security coming to me."

"You did better than me," Jan admitted in rare confidence. She talked to no one except Ronnie about her divorce settlement. But then she talked to no one except strangers. Corporate wives moved too often to collect a circle of friends. She talked to people in elevators and in the stores where she shopped and at occasional lunches at the Cafe American Style at Lord and Taylor when she needed an escape from the apartment.

"You should have fought." The wistful helpless quality that seemed to exude from Peggy before had disappeared with chameleon swiftness.

This was a hard, driving woman who would go for the jugular, Jan assessed, discarding her earlier impression. She was startled to meet the second Peggy Phipps. With that kind of drive behind a career she might have made it big in the art world. Even with only a fair amount of talent.

Compassion surged through Jan. How sad to have a talent and not develop it. Though what had she done with her own talent? Writing confessions and soft porn. But she had her head together, Jan thought. She wasn't sure about Peggy Phipps.

The two women opened the doors of their machines, loaded them, deposited the requisite coins, and pulled out the slots. Three more laundries were in work.

"Jan, why don't you come up to my apartment for a quick cup of coffee? I've got half a carafe hot and waiting. We can come down in half an hour to dump the clothes into dryers." This Peggy was vivacious and charming.

"Thanks," Jan accepted. She loathed the suburban coffee klatches, where women were thrown together because of proximity. But Peggy was a kindred soul.

"Do you work or are you independently wealthy?" Peggy bubbled while they waited for an elevator. "Since you say you aren't getting alimony."

"I had a – a limited cash settlement." She recoiled from discussing this aspect of the divorce with anybody other than Ronnie. "And I work," she said after a moment. "I'm a freelance writer." She saw the sudden glint of sistership in Peggy's eyes. "I write garbage," she admitted, "but it brings in cheques. Small ones."

"You're a 'pro'. That's what counts. In the last twenty-four years I've sold maybe a dozen paintings. I never had time to develop as an artist. Until now." All at once her eyes went opaque. "I've fixed up a studio in the bedroom of the apartment. I sleep in the living-room. I haven't got any work done so far. It takes time to get over the emotional pain of a divorce."

"Sure," Jan said gently. "Don't try to rush yourself." *She* had no choice. The landlord and the supermarkets didn't want to know about her emotional pain.

"Tell me about your kids," Peggy said in a surge of warmth.

Jan always felt a kind of happiness when she talked about Lisa and Brian. But she was aware that Peggy retreated into private thoughts after the first few moments. When the elevator stopped on '4' for a nursemaid with an ingratiating pig-tailed two-year-old named Jessica, Jan dropped to her haunches to exchange small talk with the tiny blonde. Jan adored all children, all dogs, all cats.

"Thank God, I'm free of kids," Peggy said frankly when the nurse and Jessica got off on '5' to visit Jessica's friend on that floor. "They should be kept in cold storage until they're twenty."

Peggy's apartment was sparsely furnished. She explained she wanted a minimum of responsibilities. She showed off the studio set-up in the bedroom, where the north light pleased her. Jan saw an abstract hanging on the bedroom wall that faced the door.

"What an interesting painting!" Jan moved forward for a closer scrutiny. Interesting and morbid and devious.

"It's really better if you stand back. I did that one when I went to the first shrink." The furrows on her forehead and about her mouth seemed to intensify. "I hate them all. They're crazier than their patients. Let me pour our coffee," she said abruptly and spun around to walk to the kitchenette.

Jan sat on the Hollywood bed dressed up to look like a sofa. Peggy brought over two ceramic mugs filled to the top with strong black coffee.

"I should have asked if you like cream and sugar," she apologized. "I can spill some off—"

"No need. I take it black with no sugar." Jan's eyes rested on the reading matter scattered across the square marble-topped table. *The Village Voice*, *New York Review of Books*, and something called the *New York Almanac*. She knew the *Voice* and *New York Review*. The other was a stranger to her.

"Do you read the *New York Almanac*?" Excitement under-coated Peggy's voice.

"I've never seen it."

"It lists all kinds of happenings in New York. It's far out. I just learned about it a couple of weeks ago. It was at this one-night seminar I took on how to meet men in New York." Jan realized all at once she was gaping at Peggy. "Look, women have to be realistic. Take me. I've been in the city for four months without meeting a single man I'd like to date. I've gone to church groups and concert socials and all kinds of programmes. Nobody. I'm forty-eight years old. I have a lot to offer the right man. If I ever meet him." She reached for the *Almanac*, turned to the back page, and handed it to Jan. "Read the 'Personals by Women' and the 'Personals by Men'. Mine won't appear until next week. They've set it up great. Once in a while somebody will give a phone number, but most of the time you run an ad with a box number, and the men write in."

With a sense of discomfort Jan began to scan the ads.

"Jewish men are in great demand. They're warm, usually professionals, and good sex partners." Peggy paused. "My husband used to complain I was frigid. I'll tell you the truth – he never turned me on. But I'm not looking for a sex partner. I want a man to take me to the theatre and ballet and good restaurants. Somebody who's a good conversationalist and compassionate. I'm running ads in three magazines. It's a numbers game."

"That could be dangerous." Jan gazed at Peggy in total incomprehension. Ronnie, too, talked about running ads in the personal columns. But Ronnie, she suspected, could handle that scene. Peggy seemed so vulnerable. "What about AIDS?"

"You have to use your head. You screen the letters. There have to be a lot of intelligent men in New York who are just as anxious to meet women as women like me are interested in meeting them. Most of them are professional men. The others don't spend money on ads. They're sensitive and articulate and—"

"Sensual," Jan added, reading an item. "Peggy, wouldn't it be safer to take some courses? At the New School, or NYU night classes?" Ronnie followed this route. '*At the necessary point you talk about "safe sex",' Ronnie had said.*

"You have to sign up for weeks of classes. I don't have time for that. I want to meet somebody right away." A poignant wistfulness replaced the hostility in her eyes. How vulnerable women in their position were, Jan thought uneasily. "It's not as though I'm going out with every guy who answers my ad. I'll be selective. And what can happen if I meet a guy for a drink or a cup of coffee? The woman who taught the class said you're never to make a date for dinner on the first round. Why waste a whole evening if you've pulled in a dog?"

All at once Jan was worried about Peggy. She had no concept of the jungle she was trying to crash. The jungle of divorced or single women in search of divorced or single men. She remembered what Ronnie had said one night:

'Honestly, it's horrendous to see some of these women who have been out of circulation for fifteen or twenty years – or even longer. They don't know the rules have changed. When a man buys a woman dinner, he expects to climb into bed with her later. If not on the first date, then at least on the second.'

No 1990s man would take Peggy Phipps to dinner and the theatre and ballet and wait for her to decide whether or not she wished to sleep with him. Could *she* have sex with a man she had been out with only once or twice? The prospect repelled her. Were Peggy and she misfits? Out of the running?

"I think we'd better go down to the dryers. I hate it when

people take my clothes out of the dryer and dump them on that musty old table in the laundry room," Peggy said. "Not that I mean to rush you."

Jan and Peggy transferred their clothes from washers to dryers. Peggy decided to make a dash to the supermarket while the clothes were in the dryer. Jan guessed that the mail was in the boxes by now. She'd check it out. Until now Tim had sent neither a card nor a birthday present for either Lisa or Brian. She had resurgent hopes that he would remember, even though belatedly.

Jan and Peggy emerged from the elevator into the lobby, which was clogged with incoming furniture. Peggy darted out of the building. Jan detoured to the alcove that contained the mail boxes. She opened their box and pulled forth the usual pleas for donations, catalogues, a telephone bill, and an ad for a computer dating service. Coincidence, or was she on some mailing list of the recently divorced? She filed everything but the telephone bill in the lobby waste basket.

The movers were piling furniture into one elevator. She pushed the 'Up' button and waited for the other one to descend.

"This must be moving-in day." Jan heard a mellow male voice in exchange with George, their drily humorous doorman. "Now I know why the office told me to have my movers arrive after noon."

"You don't have to worry, Mr Tempest," George said. "The elevator will be clear by then."

A tall, quietly good-looking man with a deep tan and rumpled greying hair turned the corner to stand beside Jan. He was somewhere in his late forties, Jan estimated. Startled by this trend of thought, she dropped her eyes to the open carton of books he deposited on the floor while they waited for the elevator.

"Some books I don't trust with movers," he confided, chuckling. "Every time I move, I seem to lose a carton of books."

"Usually the ones you least want to lose," Jan commented with a reminiscent smile. A swift inventory told her that Mr Tempest had eclectic tastes in reading.

"I don't expect to be moving again for a long time." For an instant his face was taut. Was he recently divorced? "I hope they're not entertaining ideas about co-oping this building? Nobody said anything when I signed the lease—"

"I don't believe so." Jan was uneasy for a moment. But she had a two-year lease. She didn't think beyond that. "I haven't heard any rumours."

The elevator door slid open. Jan moved inside. Mr Tempest, grappling with the carton of books, followed her.

"Beautiful weather, isn't it? Autumn's my favourite season of the year."

"Mine, too." Jan's face lighted. "The heat of the summer is over, and there's a promise of good things to come." Normally she felt that way about the fall of the year.

Involuntarily her eyes sought the fourth finger on his left hand. No ring. And he'd said, 'every time *I* move.' She felt her face grow hot. What was the matter with her? Peggy Phipps might react this way to an obviously pleasant new male tenant. Not Janet Ransome.

The elevator stopped at '4'. He moved forward with his carton of books.

"Have a good day."

"Thanks. You, too."

It was absurd to feel this surge of good spirits because she had exchanged a few words with an attractive man. Maybe she could use this kind of a situation in a story for Ronnie. She was forever terrified she might run into a dry spell. So far it hadn't happened.

Jan missed Peggy when she went down to the dryer. She hurried back up to the apartment to fold the clothes. The telephone bill, always larger than expected, was a stern reminder that she'd better get back to the computer.

What was that bit from Andrew Marvell that hit such a

responsive chord in her? 'But at my back I always hear/Time's winged chariot hurrying near—' The time that bothered her was the due date on bills. She wished she could crack a better paying market. Romance was big time now – but she had no time even to try a new genre.

Jan worked through without interruption until close to three, when she realized she had not stopped for lunch. She made herself a cheese sandwich and a pot of tea. She'd had enough coffee for one day. In half an hour the kids would be coming home from school. She always made herself free for them.

She flipped on the radio to WQXR while she ate. It was a quiet parcel of time with the classical music she loved. Later she would be sandwiched between Lisa's stereo and Brian's.

While she ate, Jan thought about Peggy Phipps. Peggy's husband complained she was frigid. But four months out of marriage Peggy was frantic to find another man.

It was not sex that motivated Peggy, Jan decided. She was lonely. Man-lonely. It wouldn't be enough for Peggy to have vital, interesting women friends. She needed a man to make her feel attractive and important.

What about herself, Jan probed. Did she need a man to make her life complete? Did she need a man in her bed? There were nights when she lay sleepless, Jan forced herself to admit. Nights when she was aware of physical stirrings. But she had no time to coddle herself. She could manage her life without a man. The big deal was to raise Lisa and Brian.

With an eye on the clock Jan checked the refrigerator. Once the kids were home from school, she did the necessary grocery shopping. Sometimes she stopped in Cosmos for a cup of tea and carrot cake. Today she'd have to pick up her suit at the cleaner's. When she took stories up to Ronnie's office, she had to make a decent appearance.

Now she remembered to empty the waste baskets in the two bathrooms. She carried them out to the compactor. She spied a cluster of old issues of *Playboy* on the floor. With a smile she bent to retrieve them. Brian might like to have them. At fourteen they were a status symbol.

As she moved out into the hallway, the elevator stopped. Lisa emerged, spilling over with her day's news. At the door to the apartment, left ajar, Lisa stared curiously at the copies of *Playboy* in Jan's arms.

"What are you doing with *Playboy*?" She shot Jan a gamine grin. "*Playgirl* I could understand."

"They're for Brian."

"Mom, that's a waste. You give Brian a copy of *Playboy*, and he'll come running out of his room yelling, 'Hey, Mom, look at this great car!' "

The phone rang as Jan put the second of the waste baskets in the master bathroom.

"Mom, phone," Lisa yelled from the kitchen where she was improvising a sandwich.

The caller was Ronnie.

"Jan, you won't believe who I bumped into on the street at lunchtime. Remember Craig Yarbrough?"

"Atlanta," Jan pinpointed instantly. A lilt in her voice. She'd been very fond of Craig. "I haven't seen Craig since then. Is he living in New York now?" A question in her voice. Craig was gay. Had he escaped the AIDS scourge?

"Craig's fine." Ronnie understood. "He's been here a year. Doing quite well, I gather, except that he's recovering from a bust-up with his boyfriend."

"Craig recovers fast," Jan remembered.

"He's left public relations for paperback book packaging. You know, the romance *schtick* – hopefully with Fabio on the cover. There might be something there for you, Jan—"

"Right now I'm concentrating on a sure thing. You."

"Oh, the real reason for my call," Ronnie said. "We can talk about Craig later. I've just come out of an urgent conference with my boss. Somebody who was due to bring in a 'one shot' next Monday called to say she was way behind, plus she's going

41

into the hospital for emergency surgery today. It's a diet book. You know, magazine type. You can do it in your sleep. But it's a whole book," she emphasized. "And I have to have it in my hands by next Monday."

"Ronnie, a whole magazine?" Jan gasped.

"Sweetie, it'll earn you two thousand."

"I'll do it," Jan said. Ronnie had uttered magic words.

"Can you take a run up to the office now? I'll give you what photos I have plus the stuff the other writer picked up from the PR people. And don't worry. I'll tell you exactly how to handle the magazine."

"I'll grab a cab and come right up."

She knew it wouldn't be as simple as it sounded. But that two thousand dollar cheque was a powerful incentive. Inflation – supposedly slow – was still scaring the hell out of her. She must increase her earnings. She'd bring in this diet book if she had to work twenty hours a day between now and Monday.

Twenty-five minutes later she sat in a chair across from Ronnie and listened while Ronnie briefed her.

"Basically you need some gimmick to tie a bunch of recipes together. Here's a folder of recipes we have on file from other diet books. I'll give you the phone numbers of three PR firms handling food accounts. Call them for more recipes. Work out six diets – one for the characters who can't survive without pasta once a day, one for those who think the only way to diet is to live on citrus fruits and—"

"You mean I make up the diets?" Jan interrupted in shock. "I'm not a doctor!"

"Neither am I." Ronnie grinned. "For the diet books I was Dr Herman Goldsmith, PhD. Just use common sense. For those women who can't live without pasta, tell them they can have one cup once a day. But no rich sauces on it. This is October. It'll be a spring diet book," she pinpointed. "Think along those lines."

"Like, 'Summer is approaching. Be ready with the new You when bikini time arrives'?"

"You got it." Ronnie grinned. "You'll need some break-up features. Hairstyles that'll make the face thinner. Exercises. Oh, and for my own peace of mind, I always preface everything with a warning to check with their doctors before they start a diet or an exercise programme."

Ronnie handed over recipes, photographs, and phone numbers.

"I'll grab a cab home and drop you off on the way. I've got to take work home with me again."

They left the office and snared a cab on the third try. Two more devious men copped the first two cabs. They settled themselves with sighs of relief. Ronnie promptly opened up a folder and dug out a pencil.

"I had to dump a story I'd bought for this issue because a chunk of it was lifted right out of Sidney Sheldon. I'm knocking out a replacement myself," Ronnie explained. "If you weren't tied up with the diet book, I'd ask you to come to my rescue again—" Ronnie was scribbling on sheets of lined paper probably borrowed from Deedee's school supplies, Jan surmised.

"Are you ladies writers?" the cabbie demanded avidly.

"That's right," Ronnie said without looking up.

"You know, I always thought I could write a book. I just never had the time." He took advantage of a red light to turn around. "Watcha doin' now?"

"I'm trying to find another word for 'fuck'," Ronnie told him.

At this point he seemed to lose his voice. Jan expected him to flip over the photographs of the three small children that adorned his windshield.

"We'll have dinner with Craig at my place one night next week," Ronnie said as Jan reached for the door. "After the diet book is in. Right now that's the crucial event."

Lisa and Brian were in for a rush re-education programme. Between now and Monday she'd be available for preparing, serving, and eating dinner with them. She'd be available for

43

any real emergency. Outside of that she *worked on the diet book.* They'd just have to understand.

But already guilt tugged at her. Why did she feel obligated to make herself accessible to her kids at any moment they made a demand? Shouldn't there be a life for her beyond motherhood?

*Was she never to have a time in her life when she took first place?*

# Chapter Four

When the children charged out of the apartment to head for school on Wednesday morning, Jan hung a calendar over the table where she worked. She circled the following Monday in red. The two thousand dollar fee waiting for her when she brought in the book was about the strongest incentive to write she had ever encountered. Lisa and Brian had been briefed about her work schedule. They seemed to understand this was an emergency situation.

Ever disciplined, Jan sat down to chart her day. Even writing a diet magazine was an improvement over the confessions, she told herself in satisfaction. Later in the morning she would call the PR people about new material and photos. She'd bribe Brian to pick them up after school.

Jan worked at top speed, bringing together the format of the magazine. Feeling it take shape with less difficulty than she had anticipated. At regular intervals she turned on the gas beneath her whistling tea kettle. Tea kept her moving.

She was startled when – much later – the doorbell rang. It was past three, she realized in unwary panic. She had not phoned the PR people.

"Who is it?" she asked automatically. One hand on the top lock.

"Me," Brian announced. "Hurry up. I have to take a giant piss."

She opened the door for Brian. He disappeared into the bathroom. Now she dashed to the phone. She made contact with the first name on Ronnie's list. Delighted with the cordial response. She was unable to contact the next two. She hung up the phone in disappointment.

"Oh, shit." She utilized the second most popular word – currently – in Brian's vocabulary. The first was 'gross'.

"Mom," Brian clucked from the bathroom doorway, "I think you had better clean up your language or leave the house. Do you understand?"

"Brian, would you like to make a dollar plus car fare?" She was scribbling the address of the first PR firm on a scrap of paper.

"Do I hear two?" He flashed his charismatic smile.

"You heard one. You ought to do it for nothing," Jan reproached. "This is for you, too."

"I'll take one," he accepted.

With Brian off to make the pick-up Jan flipped on the radio to WQXR. Beethoven filtered into the room. She could listen to Beethoven without slowing up on the diet book. A fringe benefit.

While she was listening to the *Eroica*, Lisa arrived from school. Jan allotted ten minutes to talk, then insisted she had to return to the computer.

"Mom, do you have to listen to that awful music?" Lisa complained.

"It's Beethoven."

"It's depressing," Lisa grimaced.

"Not to me," Jan said firmly. "Lisa, I have to work."

One day blended into another while Jan buried herself in diets, hairstyles, and exercise copy. On Thursday Peggy Phipps rang the doorbell to invite her up for 'afternoon tea'. When Jan explained her situation, Peggy beat an apologetic retreat.

On Friday afternoon Ronnie called to check on her progress and to invite her to come over with any problems she might foresee.

"We'll eat while we talk," she encouraged. "I'll bring up a Chinese take-out."

"Great." Jan was relieved. She could use some reassurance at this point. "I'll throw a chicken in the oven for the kids. They can make a salad to go with it."

Jan spent just an hour with Ronnie. She was exhilarated by Ronnie's approval of what she had accomplished thus far. It was a tremendous boost to her spirits to realize that she could produce something that would pay a more substantial reward. In a burst of exuberance she stopped off at the supermarket for low-fat frozen yogurt.

Lisa was closeted in her room, listening to CDs a classmate had loaned her.

"Lisa, are you doing your homework?" she called automatically through the door. *How did they listen to CDs and do homework?* Though when it came to serious study, the rooms on either side of her area became dead quiet.

"Sure, Ma—"

"Come get Ben and Jerry's Cherry Garcia."

"Coming!"

She turned over the frozen yogurt to Lisa to divide up and went to Brian's door. She knocked. There was no way he could hear her call over the stereo.

"Yeah?"

She opened the door. Brian was sprawled across the textbook-laden bed, writing in his notebook. In addition to the radio the TV was on but silent.

"Brian, why do you have the TV on when you're listening to the radio?" Why did she keep asking him the same question, her mind reproached.

"I like to look at it every now and then," he shrugged. Accustomed to this frustrated inquiry.

"Lisa and you ate?" she asked.

"Lisa had the chicken. I had a dish of nitrites," he reported. Translated, that meant he had made himself franks. "But we both ate a lot of grass," he comforted. Salad.

Jan returned to the computer, fighting yawns. Eighteen hours' work, six hours' sleep, and she wasn't in top condition. If she did a good job on this 'one-shot', maybe there would be more. What was Tim doing now? Was he still travelling with that young slut? But it wasn't her business. He wasn't her husband any more.

\* \* \*

By nine-thirty Monday morning Jan was in the elevator en route to Ronnie's office. She clutched an oversized tote crammed with segments of the diet magazine copy plus photos. She had finished the diet book at four this morning.

Ronnie was elated at her early appearance, though vowing she had known Jan would deliver on time. She'd have a cheque for Jan in two weeks.

"It'll break Mannie's heart, but I told him you wouldn't leave the book with me unless I swore on my mother's life that he'd pay right away."

"Wow, will that cheque look good to me!"

"I'll take you back to the art department now. You'll go over everything with them. You divided the articles into separate folders, didn't you?"

"Like you said," she reassured. "With photos clipped to each. They'll have to come up with a few of their own – I didn't get delivery of everything promised."

"No sweat. Just tell them which should be lead pictures, and make sure the pictures they come up with fit. Mannie will have four or five people working on layout. Go over the whole thing while you're here. It's easier than trying to do it over the phone if they have questions."

"Sure."

"Oh, I spoke with Craig," Ronnie told her while they headed together for the art department. "He's coming over for dinner Friday night. I told him you'd be there, too."

When she had finished conferring with the art department, Jan left the office and headed back home. She was too exhilarated at the moment to collapse from lack of sleep. It would hit her in an hour or two. Passing the stationery store she decided to stop in for a ream of paper for her printer. It would save her a trip later.

She stood at the counter waiting for the paper when a man came up beside her with a warm 'hello'. She turned to face the new tenant on '4'. George had called him Mr Tempest. She had not run into him since that first encounter, but several times she had involuntarily thought about him.

"Hi." Her smile was cordial as they introduced themselves properly. "Are you getting settled in?"

"Trying." He sighed in resignation. "It'll take months to get my books in order." Another clerk approached him. He asked for a ream of printer paper.

"That's popular today," Jan laughed. "That's what I'm buying."

She was conscious of quickened interest in him. Because she owned a computer? she mocked herself.

"Would you like to stop in somewhere for a cup of coffee or breakfast?" he invited. "We can exchange horror stories about our computers."

"That would be lovely." All at once she had forgotten that she was exhausted. There was something charming and unpressured about Dan Tempest.

Jan and Dan Tempest left the stationery store and walked towards the coffee shop on the corner. Jan was aware of a disconcerting pleasure at being in Dan's company. This was a fresh experience, a new feeling for her; she mentally dissected her reactions. She had felt like this at fifteen when a new boy in her English class contrived to walk home with her. But she wasn't fifteen now; she was thirty-eight.

In the coffee shop Dan prodded her towards a cosy private corner. All at once she understood the incomprehensible confidences of Ronnie immediately after *her* divorce. It was like emerging from the Ice Age, she thought with a touch of humour. She was rejoining the world of the unattached. The singles. All the years of marriage were to be stashed away in a memory machine. She was learning to walk again in a strange, unfamiliar world.

For over an hour they sat and talked over pancakes and coffee. While Dan taught English lit. now, he had been in investment banking. Eleven years ago he returned to school, earned his PhD and went into teaching. He taught at a Long Island college.

"The commuting isn't bad because I'm travelling against the traffic," he pointed out. "And I always work on the train. It's my office away from home."

"You enjoy teaching," she decided admiringly. How few people worked in occupations that gave them pleasure! After all the years of Tim's mood swings, his short fuse, his arrogance, Jan appreciated Dan's gentleness. Yet at the same time she sensed a quiet, reassuring strength in him.

"I love teaching," he confirmed. "And it gives me time to indulge in activities that are important in my life. I may complain about the prices," he chuckled, "but I manage to see a lot of theatre and ballet and the opera." He hesitated. "I even manage to write a little poetry." Jan's face lighted. "I'll never make a living at it," he added hastily, "but I'm published at intervals. Small university presses—" His smile was deprecating.

"But you write what you wish," Jan said with respect. "Not the garbage I keep knocking out for the cheques."

"What kind of garbage?" he teased but it was clear his interest was sincere.

Dan listened with flattering attention while she told him about her own writing efforts, dredging up amusing anecdotes that elicited laughter from him. Tim never cared to hear about this side of her life; it was something to be shoved away in a closet except when the cheques came in. He never liked Ronnie, she remembered now.

Peggy complained about how impossible it was to meet an interesting, intelligent man in New York. Here she sat with a delightful man she'd met right in their own building. Instinctively she knew, of course, that this was a rarity. But he was being more than neighbourly, she assessed. He was interested in her as a woman. She had intercepted his covert glance at the right finger of her left hand.

"Do you like theatre?" Dan asked at a fleeting pause in their conversation.

"I love it. I haven't seen much in the past few years," she admitted. "I was squirrelled away up in Connecticut." She had given up on buying theatre tickets. Too often Tim had a change in plans and had to be out of town on business. Or something came into the office at the last minute, and he was tied up for the evening. He'd always *said* he was tied up on business.

"The parents of a student of mine are involved in an off-Broadway production. He gave me a pair of tickets for the performance a week from this coming Friday. I don't know how good it is. It doesn't open until Wednesday evening, so there've been no reviews. But it's Shaw," he said in anticipation. "How far wrong can they go with Shaw? He's almost actor-proof. Would you like to go with me?"

Jan hesitated only an instant.

"I'd love it." Her smile was dazzling.

*She had not gone out with a man other than Tim for seventeen years.* Except for Craig down in Atlanta and other gay friends through the years. What Tim called her fag club. She had never harboured any romantic thoughts about them; they were good friends and convenient escorts. Was she harbouring romantic thoughts about Dan Tempest? She hardly knew him! But why not, she asked herself defiantly. She was divorced and unattached.

Jan and Dan finished their late breakfast and returned to the apartment house. He had no class until late in the afternoon, he explained. In the elevator Jan impulsively invited him to dinner before they went to see the Shaw play.

"I'll fix something simple and quick so we won't be late for the performance," Jan promised. "Dinner about six thirty?"

"Fine." He radiated a pleased anticipation.

"I'm in 8C." She felt like a sixteen-year-old arranging her first date. Nervous and expectant. "Lisa and Brian will clear away so we can leave right after we eat."

"You have a daughter and son?" He seemed pleased.

"Lisa's twelve, Brian's fourteen," Jan told him as the elevator stopped at his floor. "But they both think they're twenty."

"We'll be running into each other before Friday week," he said and made a necessarily hasty exit.

Alone, Jan was beset by doubts. Should she have invited Dan to dinner? Did it look as though she was pursuing him? It seemed the natural thing to do – to ask him up to dinner – if he was taking her to the theatre.

Would the children be upset? But she was divorced – they knew that. She wasn't entering a convent because she was no longer married. Lisa and Brian were with-it kids. They would not be upset.

Dan let himself into his apartment. Right away he realized Keith had awakened and left. When Keith was here, the rooms ricocheted with the abominable rock music that was part of his twenty-year-old lifestyle. In particularly noisy moments he felt inclined to tell Keith to pack up and get out. Yet he knew he would never do that.

The problem, Dan analyzed, was that he was unaccustomed to living with someone so young. It was different to encounter the young in his classrooms. But nobody in this world meant as much to him as Keith.

Dan checked his watch. He didn't have to leave for the Long Island train for another two hours. The apartment was in chaos. He might as well tidy up. Only because Keith was in such a bad emotional state did he refrain from admonishing him about the disorder that had become a constant since he moved into the apartment.

What had possessed him to invite Janet Ransome to go to the

theatre with him? Because Keith had been so arrogant when he mentioned the tickets. Keith knew he'd enjoy a theatre evening with him. 'You go,' Keith had drawled. 'I'll stay home and listen to music.' Why must Keith always try to make him feel he was gauche or stupid?

So he was taking a woman to the theatre, Dan told himself in silent defiance. Knowing he would make sure that Keith was unaware of this. That didn't mean he was having an affair with her.

What about Jan had drawn him to her? He had encountered other bright, beautiful women in his forty-nine years of living. He couldn't afford to complicate his life with a woman.

He was attracted to her, he berated himself, because she was a writer. Who else did he know in this whole city that he could talk to in a serious vein about writing? Writers – and he allowed himself to be included in this category – were notoriously hungry for the companionship of other writers.

He wouldn't see her again, Dan promised himself. He couldn't take chances on messing up his relationship with Keith. Maybe during the Christmas vacation Keith and he could fly out to Arizona for ten days. Keith would like that. Dan felt immeasurably cheered.

*     *     *

By Tuesday Jan was back at the old grind. The two thousand dollar cheque from the diet book was most welcome, but it hardly solved her economic problems. She had to keep busy pumping out the confessions.

Brian was making her very conscious that next September he'd be going into high school. She knew he was a bright competitive student. Would he make Stuyvesant High? Ronnie said she couldn't see Brian or Lisa going to public high schools in Manhattan.

On Wednesday morning Peggy phoned.

"Have you finished that rush assignment?" she asked tentatively.

"Yes," Jan said. "But I'm off again on the confessions."

"I'll just be a minute," Peggy said quickly. "I'm going to a Single Parent meeting tonight. This one is especially for people who have just gone through a divorce and are kind of floundering. It'll discuss – among other things – how adolescents react to divorce and how to help them. Brian's a teenager and Lisa will be soon, so I thought you might like to go with me. It's only four dollars." She was breathless with the effort of persuading Jan to go with her.

"I don't really have the time," Jan stalled. Could she learn something at the meeting? It might be reassuring to hear how other parents were coping. "All right," she decided on impulse. "I'll go with you. What time?"

"I'll pick you up at seven thirty. It starts at eight. It's in a meeting room at a hotel within walking distance. No jeans but you don't have to dress up." Peggy sounded almost blithe.

"I'll be ready," Jan promised. She was surprised that she felt a sense of guilty delight at the prospect of spending an evening away from the apartment.

Over dinner Jan told Lisa and Brian that she was going out to play bridge with Peggy. Both took it for granted that she would play bridge – which she loathed, but it had been part of the suburban picture – with women. She would have felt uncomfortable saying she was attending a meeting of single parents. That would sound as though she was unable to cope.

After dinner the children dashed into their separate rooms to study. The days when they shared chores were past. *Why didn't she insist?* Because she felt a personal guilt that they were deprived of a father. Absurd, she chastised herself; Tim had walked out on them. But rationalizing did nothing to lessen her guilt.

At twelve minutes to eight Jan reached for the phone. Wasn't the meeting tonight? At that moment the doorbell rang. Peggy stood there, bright-eyed and vivacious and spilling over with Southern charm.

"Don't you worry, honey," she soothed. "It's just a brisk ten minute walk to the hotel. We don't want to arrive a year ahead of time. That makes us look so anxious."

"You're looking very pretty," Jan told her, with a suspicion that Peggy needed an ego boost. "That suit is so becoming."

"I've got to start exercising," Peggy sighed. "Next week for sure."

They left the apartment in a convivial mood, Jan thought, for two divorcées headed for what was in truth a kind of therapy. The crisp night air, hinting at the approach of winter, was exhilarating.

"Most of the parents will be younger than me," Peggy said. "Most of them will be younger than you," she added. "Those with real young kids seem the most anxious; but teenage kids have problems adjusting, too. Just on a different level."

"Lisa and Brian seem all right." Were they all right? She wanted so desperately to provide a full life for them. "They saw so little of Tim when he was with us. One week in five he was out of town. He came home so late the last year or two we had dinner in shifts so they could get to their homework. And weekends Tim was always off on the golf course or tennis courts or watching football on television."

"You don't have to tell me." All at once Peggy was grim. "That was Hal for the past ten years."

Jan was aware of a sudden self-consciousness as Peggy and she walked into the small, modest hotel. Peggy went directly to the bulletin board in the lobby to check the locale of the meeting.

"It's the usual room." Peggy had been here before. "We turn right and go down the corridor."

A card table was set up at the door. A thirty-ish blonde with long, straight hair falling down her back and wearing a voluminous skirt and poncho was handing the four dollar 'contribution' to the smartly dressed woman who sat behind the card table.

"Do you expect a big crowd tonight?" she asked with a wistfulness that Jan found touching.

"We never know." The woman at the cash box was cheerful. "It varies from week to week."

Jan and Peggy each paid their four dollars and walked into a well-lighted, rectangular room that was smaller than Jan had expected. Chairs were set up in a semicircle facing a lectern. Six women of varying ages sat at one side, four men on the other side. No one spoke. The atmosphere was oppressive.

Peggy sat next to the cluster of women and Jan sat beside her. As more people arrived, they perpetuated the sexual division; women on one side of the semicircle, men on the other. It was past the time for the meeting to begin. Why didn't they start?

The men were eyeing Peggy and her with an interest that said they were here for something more than advice on handling their children. All they needed here was a piano, Jan thought, to make it look like an 1850s whorehouse. This might be labelled a meeting of 'single parents', but all at once she understood this was a variation of the 'singles social'.

A woman wheeled in a cart with a coffee urn, a container of milk, a sugar bowl, and quantities of paper cups and holders. Instantly a line formed so that the guests could be served. Of the thirty people who had eventually arrived, eight were men. Jan was impressed by the calibre of the women. Socially they towered over the men present.

Some feeble attempts at conversation were made. Peggy was clearly disappointed. She had come here hoping to find an interesting man.

"They're all dogs," she whispered to Jan while they walked off to one side of the room. "The woman who runs these meetings told me they drew professional men with college backgrounds."

"When will the lecture start?" Jan was uncomfortable at being the cynosure of a rather pleasant-looking man of about forty with desperate, dark eyes.

"Not for another fifteen minutes," Peggy said. "Then we'll

have another social period afterwards. But we don't have to stay."

The man who had been staring so hard at Jan came over with a hesitant smile. She understood that he was afraid of rejection.

"How many children do you have?" he asked softly, ignoring Peggy, who shrugged and walked away.

"Two. A girl and a boy." Jan tried to seem matter-of-fact. They were here to listen to a lecture. At least, that was what Peggy had told her. "Brian is fourteen and Lisa is twelve."

"I have three. Six, seven, and nine. My wife just packed up one day and left." His face reflected his anguish. "How does a man raise three little girls without a wife?"

"It's rough," Jan sympathized.

"I don't make a lot of money. I sell insurance." Now his words were tumbling out in his agitation. "But I own a house out in Queens and a car. You look like a very nice woman. Would you consider marrying a man with three little girls?"

"It'll be a long time before I get over my divorce," Jan said gently. Hurting for the man with three little girls to raise. "I doubt that I'll ever marry again."

"You're a nice woman," he repeated slowly and turned around to survey the other women at the meeting.

Jan and Peggy sat through the lecture. Then they fled from the meeting room. Peggy was philosophical. This was better than cruising the singles bars. Any kind of meeting had an aura of respectability. That was important to Peggy.

\*     \*     \*

Jan looked forward to having dinner with Ronnie and Craig on Friday. Ronnie said Craig had not changed a bit since Atlanta. He was forty-three and still looked about twenty-eight. He had come back to New York determined to make it big. He, too, felt Marvell's 'time's winged chariot' at his back.

Ronnie and Craig had been at college together. He was the

only child of a once wealthy and social family. His parents had
little money left but clung to their place in the social register.
Though they were exasperated by Craig's candid homosexuality,
they were supportive and helpful when he needed 'contacts'.

On Fridays both Lisa and Brian went to after-school groups.
They wouldn't be home until five. From habit Jan took a break
at three. She was becoming claustrophobic. She had not been
out of the apartment since yesterday morning. She'd run over
to Cosmos for carrot cake and herb tea, she told herself. Her
inexpensive escape hatch.

In the lobby she met Peggy coming into the building with a
manila envelope clutched in one arm.

"Hi." Peggy was effervescent.

"Hi. I'm running over to Cosmos for a snack. Feel like coming
along?"

"Come up to my place instead," Peggy invited. "I'll make coffee
for us. And I baked brownies this morning. They're yummy."

"Fine," Jan accepted. "How's everything?"

"My ads ran Wednesday in the *Voice* and in the *New York
Almanac*," Peggy said. Her voice was electric with anticipation.
"I told them to hold my replies instead of mailing them out to me.
I said I'd prefer to pick them up in person each Friday." She patted
the manila envelope under her arm. "This is the first batch. Let's
face it. You don't meet men sitting in your apartment and wishing.
I don't want to put down a chunk of money for a computer dating
service or for one of those social participation clubs. Newspaper
ads are the practical answer. Cheap and fast."

"You'll have to be careful," Jan cautioned.

"I will," Peggy promised. She pushed the 'Up' elevator button.
"I was talking to a woman in the supermarket a couple of days
ago. She's been married about four months. She said she met
her husband through one of these ads." Peggy's face tightened.
"I'm not getting married again. I'd lose my alimony. That would
be stupid. But that doesn't mean I can't have a social life." She
hesitated. "The first few weeks after I left Hal, he came over

for dinner once a week and slept over. He even wanted a key to the apartment, but I wouldn't give it to him. Then he went to a church singles dance and met a woman. He didn't come over any more after that."

"I'll never marry again," Jan said slowly. She couldn't expose herself to that kind of hurt a second time. "And I have no alimony to lose."

In Peggy's apartment Jan settled herself on the improvised sofa while Peggy went to put up the coffee and bring out brownies. With the coffee up and the brownies on a plate on the coffee table Peggy reached for the manila envelope.

"Let's see what I pulled in on this first round," she said blithely. Peggy was expecting a knight on a white charger, Jan thought compassionately. "Men keep sending in replies for five to six weeks after an ad appears," she added.

Jan reached for a brownie while Peggy dumped letters from the manila envelope, each one addressed to her assigned box number.

"This one sounds sweet," Peggy said with softness, "but I don't think he's well educated. He can't spell worth a damn."

Jan laughed.

"I know Ivy League graduates who can't spell worth a damn."

"He lives in Brooklyn. That's out." Peggy was definite. She reached for the next letter. "This one's a creep." She grimaced with distaste as she read: 'Dear Fuck-partner, If you have big tits and a good ass, call me.' She ripped the letter to shreds. "My ad made it clear I didn't want that kind of guy. I want a warm, bright, non-smoking professional between forty-five and fifty-five. Well, on to the next one."

Over coffee and brownies Peggy read through fourteen letters. The Bronx, Brooklyn and New Jersey residents were automatically discarded. One man gave two phone numbers and pleaded to be called immediately. Peggy phoned him at his office number. She put a hand over the receiver for a moment.

She seemed impressed. "He's got a receptionist. It's some kind of export firm."

Jan tried not to be uncomfortable while Peggy sparred with the man. Obviously she had no intention of seeing him.

"His diction told me he wasn't for me," she said flatly. "He might call himself a responsible professional, but I could never have a social relationship with him."

Peggy opened another letter.

"Oh, the bastard." She crumpled it in disgust.

"Obscene?"

Peggy considered this.

"Yeah, I'd call it obscene. He wanted to be sure I understand that if we go out together – and he loves theatre, ballet and fine restaurants – it would be understood that I'd pay my own way."

"That's common these days," Jan reminded her. "Women talk about being equal with men. About maintaining their independence." She hadn't offered to pay her share of the cheque when she had breakfast with Dan Tempest, she remembered now. She was sure the thought had never entered his mind that she might. Nor hers.

"That makes my Southern blood boil. The day will never come when I'm out with a man, and I offer to pay my own way." Peggy was emphatic. "If he's interested in my company – and I'm a reasonably attractive, intelligent, sensitive woman – then it's his obligation to pay for that. It has nothing to do with equal pay for equal work or freedom of choice on abortions."

"I was crossing Third Avenue the other day, and there was a girl trying to fix the flat on her bike. A man stopped and offered to help. She turned him down. When he'd walked on, she said to me, 'If I was a boy, he wouldn't have offered to help.' "

"Of course he wouldn't," Peggy snapped. "Is that bad?"

"I think we're sending men mixed signals," Jan admitted. "And they're picking up what they like."

"To some men women are just a body with a chequebook,"

Peggy bristled. "Like the ads asking for an apartment-sharer and an enduring relationship. Somebody to pay half the rent and dish out free sex. That's revolting. I'll never answer that kind of ad."

Peggy picked up another batch of letters and opened them, scanning the contents with a new scepticism. She put aside two letters that seemed possible choices. One was a lawyer, the other a teacher. Both gave evening phone numbers.

"These two sound like solid prospects," Peggy said in satisfaction. "If they gave night numbers, they're not married. But it's like the teacher of that course told us. It's a question of numbers. Oh, I just found another course," she reported with fresh enthusiasm. "It's called 'Fifty Ways to Meet Your Lover.' I may take it if nothing comes of these ads."

"Have you thought of joining a health club?" Jan asked. With her alimony and no children to support she could afford it.

Peggy shuddered.

"Not until I lose two inches on my waist, four inches on my hips, and firm up my bust."

Peggy reported on her other activities. She had tried several church groups without finding anybody who appealed to her. She had gone to one social where the men were all losers. She was scheduled to go to a rap session at the Universalist Church. But she wanted no part of the singles bars.

"I hope you find somebody." Jan harboured little confidence in Peggy's ways of searching.

"What are *you* doing?" Peggy challenged. "You can't just sit around and wait for something to happen."

"I haven't had much time to think about men," Jan dodged. It wouldn't be politic to mention meeting Dan Tempest in the building. "I'm too busy trying to keep ahead of the bills."

"You'll think about it," Peggy predicted. "As soon as the shock of the divorce wears off." All at once her eyes were wistful. "Am I asking so much? Just a nice, comfortable guy to go out with a couple of times a week. He doesn't have to take me to fancy

61

restaurants all the time. I won't mind fixing dinner for him some nights. I need somebody to share my thoughts with, to go to a movie or a museum or just to walk around New York with." She paused. "And after a while to go to bed with. But I can't hop into bed with a man I hardly know." All of Peggy's bravado seemed to evaporate. She was vulnerable and scared.

Jan had splurged on a roast because there had been a sale on in the supermarket. And she wouldn't have to worry about tomorrow night's dinner. She prepared the roast for the oven, slid it inside, and set the timer. Without a timer she'd never remember to drop it from 425° to 375° in twenty minutes. The roast would be ready before she left for Ronnie's. She'd serve the kids and take off.

She went in to shower before Lisa and Brian got home. The hour she had spent with Peggy lingered in her mind. It disturbed her that Peggy – or any woman – would expose herself to the hazards of answering personal ads.

She understood the logic behind Peggy's thinking. Of course there were men out there – bright, sensitive, warm men – who were anxious to meet women. But how could a woman take such a gamble? *Wouldn't it be marvellous material for a novel?*

Jan adjusted the water in the tub and reached for the shower knob. This was a parcel of serenity for her. For a few minutes she was inaccessible to anyone. Even the phone couldn't disturb her. She left it off the hook rather than turning on the answering machine. That way anyone who called knew she was home and would try again.

Her thoughts turned to Ronnie, who was talking about signing up in the spring for half-shares in a house out at the Hamptons. 'Half-shares' would entitle Ronnie to share a bedroom every other weekend during the summer months. First she'd have to go through the 'grouper' parties with the hope of being invited to come back and discuss taking on a share.

Houses made all kinds of stipulations. The so-called choice

ones demanded Manhattan residents. Brooklyn or Bronx people were automatically rejected. The age cut-off in a lot of houses was thirty-five for women and forty for men. Which meant, Ronnie admitted, they might have to settle for a second string house. Even so, most groupers were friendly, intelligent, professional people. And who could afford to rent a house at the Hamptons without sharing, in a city where the great summer escape was essential?

Ronnie said ideally groupers were within a ten-year age span of one another. That this was a great way to meet men. But last summer her house at Westhampton offered an age range from twenty-eight to fifty-eight.

No need for *her* to worry about half-shares at the Hamptons, Jan grimly told herself while the hot shower spray hammered at her arched back like a would-be whirlpool bath. There was no way she could afford it. She worried, instead, about the possibility of summer day camp for Lisa and Brian.

Emerging from the shower Jan remembered that a week from tonight she would be going to the theatre with Dan. She had not run into him since Monday. She realized with a start that she had been hoping to encounter him before their theatre date.

Would Dan expect her to go to bed with him because he was taking her out? No. He wasn't one of the New Men who thought because he spent a few dollars on a woman she owed him an evening of sex.

Or was she being naive, like Peggy?

# Chapter Five

Ronnie loaded her tote bag with work to be done over the weekend. Nothing short of Mannie having a heart attack – which he threatened at crucial moments – would keep her at the office later than 5 p.m. today. She looked forward to the dinner tonight with Jan and Craig.

She would allow herself time for a leisurely soak in a perfumed tub and then meditate for twenty minutes before she started dinner preparations. Deedee was going to Gloria's house straight from school. She'd have dinner there, then the two girls would go to a neighbourhood movie.

She felt a trickle of pleasure. Lenny was springing for dinner and a movie tomorrow night. Afterwards they'd go to his place. If he coaxed, she'd stay over. She had a toothbrush stashed in his medicine chest plus a bottle of moisturizer for those nights she did stay. Lenny was unpredictable. She was never sure when he'd ask her to stay overnight.

She left the office and stopped off at her fish place on Third Avenue. They were having a special on scallops. She'd use that Pierre Franey recipe for scallops in wine. With the scallops bought she went next door to the produce market for salad makings, Idahos, and a melon as an appetizer. No dessert. Craig never ate desserts except when he was having a bad time romantically. He took pride in keeping his body in great condition.

The phone was ringing when she slid the key into the top lock of the apartment door. Damn, she forgot to turn on the answering machine before she left this morning. She hurried inside, willing the caller not to hang up. It was infuriating to pick up a dead phone. Dumping her parcels on the dining table she reached for the phone.

"Hello—"

"Hi, Ronnie." It was Lenny. "I called at the office, and they said you'd left already. You on strike?"

"I'm having a couple of people over for dinner," she explained. "Jan and an old friend who's moved up from Atlanta." She'd talked to Lenny about Jan, but he had never met any of her friends. Because he made a point of not bringing her into his social circles. That was irritating after all the weeks she'd been seeing him.

"Honey, I have to renege on tomorrow night." His voice was regretful. "My mother insists I come out to her place." Lenny's mother lived in Westbury. "She has some legal problem."

"Sure." Ronnie was casual. Was Lenny a lawyer that he could solve his mother's legal problems? Somebody was taking him to a party where he might meet some new woman, she interpreted. Not one of the 'pay' cocktail parties. Lenny was too tight for that more than once a year.

"I'm just a couple of blocks from you." His voice dropped into what Ronnie called his 'early Kevin Costner' pitch. "Is Deedee home?"

"No."

"Why don't I run up for a drink?"

"I'm having people over for dinner," she reminded. Why did she put up with Lenny? Because Lenny was better than nobody, she taunted herself. There were men at the office dying to take her to bed. She never allowed her business and sex life to overlap. But Lenny was comfortable. Already she was aware of arousal.

"Ronnie, it's five thirty," Lenny clucked. "When're your friends showing?"

"Seven thirty. Okay, come over for a drink." A drink meant a glass of wine and a hop into bed.

She rushed into the bathroom for a quick hot shower. She was

66

pulling on a bright red velvet robe when the doorman buzzed to say, "Mr Goldman is coming up." She went to the kitchen and pulled out the bottle of white wine that was always ready in the refrigerator. She brought down two glasses. Lenny had a crazy idea that wine loosened her up for sex. She was always ready.

Ronnie opened the door and waited. The elevator stopped at her floor. Lenny hurried out. Tall, slender, not a touch of grey in his hair. Nobody would think he was fifty-four, she thought with a certain satisfaction. He looked late forties. And he was trim. That was one thing she demanded in a man. She couldn't go to bed with a guy with a pot belly. And he was good, she acknowledged to herself while he strode towards her. Not as good as he thought he was, but a hell of a lot better than most men his age.

"You're looking beautiful as always," he said, his eyes skimming over her. Knowing she wore nothing under the robe. She doubted that he actually saw her. In his mind he was already pumping away.

"Here's your wine." She picked up the two glasses, handed one to Lenny.

What would Lenny say if she threw him out after his wine? But she knew she wouldn't. He'd go to that party tomorrow night in hopes of meeting some gorgeous young thing. But why would a gorgeous young thing want Lenny Goldman? And he'd hop back into her bed.

Lenny drained his wine and pulled her to him.

"Let's take that beautiful body into the bedroom."

His arm about her waist they walked into the darkened bedroom. Lenny would like to have every light in the room on when they made love. She had told him right in the beginning that she considered that unromantic. Maybe if she had a twenty-year-old body it would be romantic. But no, she mentally rejected this. She liked soft lights and shadows. Candlelight. For all her practicality she was a romantic when it came to bed.

She still had a great body, as a stream of men had told her.

The mirror was reassuring. But she knew her breasts and rump were past their prime. Good, but past their prime – and that hurt. The legs, of course, were the last to go.

Lenny kissed her briskly, then released her to strip. With his clothes in a heap beside the bed he lay down beside her.

"I'm thinking about a few ski weekends in January," he said while he slid a hand between her thighs. "Interested?" She knew he meant they'd go Dutch. For a weekend that was okay.

"Provided while you're on the slopes, I stay in the ski lodge," she stipulated. Lenny knew she was terrified of skiing. What happened if she broke a leg and was laid up for months? How would she pay her bills? A husband paid bills. Not a lover.

"That's no fun," he laughed. It could be fun, she considered. Cosy evenings beside a fireplace. Nights in bed together. But Lenny knew she wouldn't go. How much time would he spend on the slopes? He'd be chasing under-thirty ski bunnies. He didn't want her there.

Ronnie murmured reproach when Lenny withdrew his hand. He reached to lift her leg so he could kiss her ankle? Why did so many men think it was macho to kiss a woman's ankle?

His mouth moved upward. She lay back in anticipation. Though she knew Lenny's routine by heart, he still excited her. How could women in their forties say the sex part of their marriage was over? Ronnie repressed a chuckle. She remembered a friend who was a nurse in a home for the aged telling her how many times they pulled an eighty-five-year-old man out of some female contemporary's bed.

"Ronnie?" Lenny sounded wary as he lifted himself above her. "I don't hear any sounds of appreciation."

"You need a hearing aid," she laughed and enveloped him with arms and legs. "Oh, honey, that's great," she soothed. Moments later she forgave Lenny everything. "Oh, Lenny! Lenny!"

Jan glanced at the clock as she collected her purse and coat. It was twenty past seven. She had meant to leave early and enjoy a leisurely window-shopping stroll en route to Ronnie's house. Lisa and Brian were at the table fighting over a bottle of salad dressing.

"Don't forget the potatoes," she ordered while she reached for the door. "They're good for you."

"What time are you coming home?" Lisa asked.

"Oh, I don't know," she teased. "I might stay out all night."

"Call if you do," Lisa giggled. "We don't want to worry about you."

"Bring us something," Brian ordered in the familiar routine. "Cherry Garcia."

At the elevator Jan tapped impatiently with one oval fingernail while she waited for a car to stop. The door opened and she hurried inside. A tall, beautiful girl in a three-piece suit that Jan recognized as an Oscar de la Renta smiled at her. Then the smile turned to a stare of astonishment.

"Excuse me. Aren't you Mrs Ransome?"

"Yes." Jan smiled but with no recognition.

"You don't remember me. I'm Karen Somers. From Houston."

Jan's face lighted.

"I don't believe it!" At seventeen Karen had baby-sat for the kids. Brian had been three, Lisa just beginning to walk. "You've grown up gorgeously!"

"I'm twenty-eight," Karen said wryly. "I came to New York to go into modelling about seven years ago. Then five years ago I got married. I've been divorced eight months."

"Tim and I are divorced, too," Jan told her and saw Karen's surprise.

"How are the kids?" Karen asked.

"Great. You'd never recognize them, of course," Jan laughed. "Do you live here in the building?"

"Yes. I just moved in a few days ago."

The elevator slid to a stop. Jan would have loved to talk to Karen, but she explained she had to rush to an appointment.

"I'm in 8C," she said. "Stop by and let's have a real reunion soon. All right?"

"Wonderful." Karen was pleased at seeing her. "My boy-friend's waiting at the kerb with his car. Can we drop you some place?"

"Thank you, no. I'm just going three blocks. But stop by soon, Karen."

Jan hurried away, but not before she spied the man waiting for Karen. A rather arrogant-appearing, movie-star handsome man of about thirty. What Ronnie would call a prize stud.

Striding through the cool early evening darkness Jan tried to thrust aside the depression that meeting Karen had evoked in her. It was unnerving to know that the children's baby-sitter had grown up, had been married and divorced.

Seeing Karen had catapulted her into the past. In Houston she had been wrapped up in the joys and frustrations of early motherhood. Tim had still been a kind of Wonder Boy to her. Everybody admired Tim, predicted a marvellous future for him. But even then she'd looked around for a way to augment their income. Money seemed to leap out of Tim's hands. No matter how much his salary rose, they were always in debt.

Jan stopped for a red light and checked her watch. She would not be late for Ronnie's small dinner party. She had a compulsion to be on time. Perhaps because Tim was always late.

Karen leaned back against the red leather upholstery of Jason's white Jaguar. It seemed incredible that she had known Jason Campbell only seven weeks. She had gone to Maxwell's Plum with Candy, who kept saying she had to start circulating again. She had been satisfied to go to the office each day, then lounge around the apartment she had been sharing with Candy and try to unwind after the ugliness of the divorce.

The minute Jason walked over and asked if he could buy her a drink she knew he would be somebody important in her life.

She was just about to tell Candy she wanted to leave when she saw Jason heading for her.

Every girl within viewing distance was conscious of his presence. Even before she left the bar with him, she was dying to sleep with Jason. After five years of Howard any fairly good-looking man would be appealing. Jason was sensational.

While Jason fiddled with the radio dial, Karen reviewed her marriage. Howard was in real estate. That was all he ever talked about. Couldn't he understand it made her want to throw up when he talked every night, even in bed, about this latest second mortgage?

Howard could lose a hundred thousand one afternoon and make a quarter million the next. She had looked past his thirty pounds overweight, forty-seven-year-old body, his toupée, his vulgarity, to his impressive bank accounts and stock portfolio. She was sick of the modelling rat race, though she was beginning to get ahead; and she didn't want to go back to Houston. Howard was her 'out', she'd thought.

Howard married her to have a young, beautiful wife to show off. He wasn't even that crazy about sex. The last two years he couldn't do anything three times out of five. He never let her have a cent of cash, though she had charge cards at every good store in town. He didn't seem to care how much she spent on clothes. She came out of the marriage with four fur coats and a designer wardrobe that had cost more than her father earned in the past four years.

If she had not caught Howard with that sleazy garment centre model, she'd never have made such a great settlement. No alimony, but a two hundred thousand settlement plus the jewellery she was allowed to keep was a great consolation. Plenty to take care of her till she was launched on a new career.

A smile touched her expressive face. Listening to Howard talking all the time about real estate, plus the course she took, had landed her a rewarding job. She enjoyed selling property. She had been ambivalent at first.

"We'll eat at the French Shack," Jason broke the comfortable silence between them. "Okay?"

"I love the French Shack," she approved. She liked having Jason ask for her approval. Howard never bothered.

"Afterwards we'll go over to my place and finish up with my packing. The movers are coming at ten. I made it early," he said in response to her raised eyebrows. Normally Jason slept till mid-afternoon on weekends. Some weekends she had appointments to show co-ops or condominiums to prospective clients. She had cleared this weekend. "I'm planning something special." One hand left the wheel to fondle her sleek narrow thigh as they stopped for a red light. "I'm taking you to Connecticut to look at a house somebody at the office told me about this morning. It hasn't been given over to the brokers yet. They'd like to sell direct."

"Why are we looking at a house?" Karen stared at him in bewilderment. He was moving into the new apartment with her. Both of them were wary of marriage at this point. Anyhow, Jason's New York divorce wouldn't be final for another three months.

"It might be fun to have a place to run to on weekends." Jason flashed her the smile that made him a hundred thousand a year ad man at thirty-one.

"I have to work some weekends," she reminded.

"The weekends you don't work, and all the holidays and vacation time. Plus the house would be a business asset for me. We can't do any splashy entertaining in the apartment."

"I thought you loved it." He'd made a big fuss about it, but Karen knew he'd have preferred something in the East Sixties. The rentals up there were too wild.

"It's comfortable for the two of us. But hardly the place to bring accounts. Darling, you're used to having better, too," he said humorously.

"But buying today you'll be hit with such awful interest rates." He was already burdened with the cost of seeing his wife through school to her PhD, as part of the divorce settlement. That was why *she* was paying half the rent of their apartment. "Jason, you're already pressed for cash."

"We'll drive up to Connecticut tomorrow afternoon and take a look at the house," he cajoled. "That doesn't mean I'm buying."

Soft music filtered into the dining-room from Ronnie's stereo. George Gershwin, Cole Porter, Jerome Kern. Red roses in a Waterford vase lent a pleasingly pungent scent to the room. Jan felt herself enveloped in serenity. For a little while she could forget everything except the pleasure of being here with Ronnie and Craig.

"Ronnie, why do you stay in that slave mill?" Craig reproached after they had indulged in bouts of black laughter at Ronnie's stories about Mannie and M & R Enterprises. "You can surely do better. Try the paperback romance market. That's thriving."

"I'll move someday." Ronnie shrugged. "Not yet. Not until Deedee is old enough to fend for herself if I strike out. Maybe she could depend on Hank. I'm not sure."

"Craig, what switched you from public relations to book packaging?" Jan asked. She knew Craig was sensational at promotion.

"I've been looking for twenty years for something that'll make me that first million," Craig said and Ronnie laughed.

"Don't you dare talk about twenty years. You look about twenty-five right now. That's obscene."

"Darling, I live right." He grinned reminiscently, then turned to Jan while Ronnie went into the kitchen for their espresso. "What about you, Jan? Why are you still messing around with the schlock market?" Back in Atlanta he used to try to push her into writing a novel.

"I need the cheques." Jan's sense of serenity evaporated. "No alimony, no child support. I thank God every night that Ronnie's where she is at M & R. I'm not earning enough to keep us moving

73

Julie Ellis

without dipping into my back-up money from the house, but it's a help."

"You might want to take a stab at doing some paperbacks for me," Craig considered. "I've got a terrific set-up beginning to roll. I've tied up with a literary agent who goes out and pushes while I bring the ideas and the books together." He paused. "No," he said abruptly. "That's not what you need. Anybody who can write formula material today can make money, but I've an instinct that tells me you and I together could make millions. What are you doing now beside the confessions? Down in Atlanta you were working on a novel," he recalled. "What happened with it?"

"I could never salvage enough time to finish it. It's been that way ever since." Jan hesitated. "I've got another novel idea floating around in my mind—" Why was she talking about it? She had no time for writing on spec.

"Something commercial?" Craig probed. Jan nodded, feeling a surge of excitement. "Don't try to be the next Steinbeck," Craig exhorted. "Wait till you've banked the first million to coddle yourself that way. Remember, today you have to write something that appeals to women. They're the big buyers. And I don't mean short confession pieces." His smile was joshing. His eyes were dead serious. "And I don't mean what used to be called bodice-rippers. A contemporary, dealing with a vital contemporary problem."

"I think this idea is damn commercial." She had not admitted even to herself until this minute how the book was leaping into shape in her mind. "It's a novel about several women who've been divorced and are looking to put their lives together again. Everybody knows the soaring divorcée rates—"

"Three younger women and one older," Craig pounced. "That's a saleable formula."

Ronnie appeared with the espresso tray.

"Let's have our espresso in the living-room," she suggested. Jan and Craig followed her to the comfortable conversation pit

74

provided by her brown velvet sectionals. "Okay," she urged, "go on with this novel."

"I was thinking about a 'women's book' in the Nineties scene," Jan continued compulsively. "*I'm part of that scene. I'm meeting these women. I'm learning every minute.*"

"Go on," Craig urged.

"I want to zero in on the singles scene." Jan's mind charged ahead. "Not the young singles – the over-forties divorced women. The 'second-time around' women. It should be intriguing, poignant – a strong page-turner—"

"And sexy as hell," Craig finished for her in triumph. "It's the kind of book that's made for today's market." He leaned forward transfixed. "Jan, it's hot! You have a lot of writing behind you, plus – like you said – you're living this book!" He leaned forward, glowing with zeal. "When can you start writing?"

Reality slapped a lid on Jan's excitement. She had allowed Craig's enthusiasm to sweep her along into fantasy land.

"I can't," she said flatly. "I can't take a year or two off to write a novel on spec."

"You can knock this book out in six months." Craig exuded confidence. "It'll just pour out of you."

"A book in six months?" Jan gaped in disbelief.

"Craig's right," Ronnie backed him up. "You can do it. You know this material. You've been sopping it up. Be logical, Jan. You're the best and fastest confession writer I know. You're equally good – and fast – with the men's stuff. How many times have you saved my hide when another writer missed a deadline?"

"You can turn out the women's stuff plus steamy sex. That's the pair of ingredients that'll make this book a sure-fire bestseller. With your background it'll be a snap." Craig's smile was contagious. His enthusiasm was contagious.

"This is your turf," Ronnie emphasized. "And we're living the book."

"But not in six months," Jan protested. "How can I do it in

75

six months? I'll have to do a lot of research before I even sit down to write." Why was she even talking about it with Craig and Ronnie? Time was money. She couldn't gamble on money with two kids to raise.

"You're not researching for a scientific tome," Craig brushed this aside. "It's the now scene, and you're in it. You've been plotting the book in the back of your mind," he pinpointed. "Pick up the single scenes magazines. Tune into the personal columns. Go to some one-night seminars. Go to some of the over-forties' socials," Ronnie said. "I'll go with you. We'll go to the Friday night movies at the New School. We'll go wherever unattached women go who're looking for men. Sharp as you are, you'll pick up all you need to know in three weeks.

"Meanwhile, you'll dig in on characterization and plot. Jan, bestsellers aren't born. They're made. Together we can make a bestseller. If you just listen to me," Craig exhorted. Riding high. "I'll start laying the groundwork before you've put the first paragraph on paper. Before the book even hits the stands we'll tie up guarantees. Movie rights, paperback rights, condensations. Even foreign sales and book clubs. You start the ball rolling right, and it rolls ahead on its own momentum. Of course," he conceded, "you have to deliver – but I know you can do that."

Jan was stunned by Craig's convictions. But he was a former public relations man. He could sell skate boards to octogenarians. *Could he sell a novel onto the bestseller list?*

"Jan, it happens all the time. I'm not bullshitting. The big blockbusters are package deals. You've come up with the right idea at the right time. I can give it the right push. You know my father and I don't always agree—" Craig grinned.

"That may be the understatement of the year," Ronnie laughed.

"Still, he's my old man. He'll go to bat for me. He has a buddy who's an important Los Angeles banker. His bank is always into film packages. He owes my father. I'll ask Dad to call in a favour. Have the guy leak to the newspapers that his bank is negotiating with a company who want to buy the film rights to the book for a quarter million. It doesn't have to be true," he conceded, chuckling. "With that, Gail – the agent who's part of my operation – will make multiple submissions to the hardcover houses. We'll try for a huge hardcover/softcover deal. The highest advance ever paid for a first novel. That in itself is worth a hundred thousand bucks in publicity."

"Craig, I can't afford to take the time off," Jan stammered. Yet she visualized everything Craig was declaiming. She yearned to be part of that kind of action. But how did she know she could produce the kind of book Craig envisioned? *How could she gamble?*

"Jan, you can't afford *not* to take the time off. This is the once-in-a-lifetime deal," Craig insisted. "You don't have to write a literary masterpiece. You write a book that's an easy, compulsive read – with the sure-fire ingredients of a bestseller. I *know* the market. I'll work with you every step of the way. Six months," he pinpointed. "You've got enough of a financial backlog to carry you for that much time?"

"And if it doesn't work?" Jan countered.

"It'll work. I'll lay out an advance for a top book promotion woman. A *woman*," he specified, "because that fits in with the whole picture. I know exactly whom to approach." His face glowed. "Paula King. We'll have to cut her in for a piece of the book. Pity, but Paula is too expensive for my bank balance—"

"Will she go along?" Ronnie seemed sceptical.

"I'll sell her," Craig promised. "Paula is sharp. She'll see this book the way I see it. She knows she'll wind up with a killing. Every little piece fits together. Jan's a natural for the talk shows. It's hard as hell to get a novelist on a talk show without a gimmick. Even a beautiful woman." He turned to Jan. "You're a beautiful divorced forty-year-old woman with a lot to say about the singles scene—"

"Craig, don't rush me. I'm thirty-eight," Jan said wryly.

"By the time the book comes out you'll be thirty-nine and

*Julie Ellis*

facing forty. You'll have a lot to talk about on TV and radio. The over-forties singles scene in New York and how women cope – or don't cope – with it. Every woman over forty will be dying to read the book because the characters could be her. The women under forty will want to read it because they see forty coming on. Women on buses and subways, planes and trains will be reading—" He paused. "What's the title?"

"I haven't got that far," Jan confessed.

"Hey, I've got it!" Craig was on his feet. "*The Second Time Around.* The mating season that goes on 365 days a year."

"I like it," Ronnie approved.

"It's good—" Jan hung in limbo.

"Okay, Jan." Craig dropped his voice to dramatic quietness. "When do you start writing the book?"

Jan wavered – knowing the whole deal could bomb. The room ricocheted with tension.

"At eight thirty tomorrow morning," Jan decided with reckless determination.

78

# Chapter Six

At six o'clock, too restless to sleep, her mind chasing after characters for the novel, Jan left her bed and dug out a legal-sized yellow note pad. Make notes in longhand first.

Was she being bitchy to utilize the women she was meeting in New York? Ronnie was candid. "Use anything you like about me as long as you don't use names." Jan catalogued the women she had been encountering during these weeks in New York. She'd disguise, use composites. On the practical side she considered the possibility of law suits. No chance of their being sued if characters were unidentifiable. And the plot would be the writer's invention.

Actually, Peggy had sent her headlong into this. The ex-Mississippi belle. Ronnie, she thought, had administered another shove. Even Karen, she thought with regret. And Ronnie's friend, Marianne Marlowe. The 'older woman'. Only now did she realize how women dominated her new life.

Jan knew she had the discipline to see her through the writing. But six months was the absolute maximum she could allow herself to stay with it. Each time she had to take money out of the bank, knowing there was no sure replacement for even part of it, she'd be tormented by fresh doubts.

By mid-afternoon she was beset by questions only Craig could answer. She caught up with him by phone and summoned him to an emergency conference. She had left Ronnie's apartment last night on a real high – but without certain concrete information.

How long should the novel be? Working on her outline she had to know this. How many pages would Craig need to start making his pitch? It seemed incomprehensible, once she was removed from Craig's charismatic presence, that he could sell without a chunk of the novel in hand.

Craig rushed over with reassurances and specific instructions. He had not been idle himself. He showed her the rough layout of the presentation he was preparing.

"Look at the statistics!" He pulled out clippings, spread them across the coffee table. "One marriage in two ends in divorce. A lot of them after many years. There're a lot of women out there that this book will touch. They're hurting – and you let them realize they're not alone. It's a huge sisterhood."

After an hour of high-powered discussion with Craig, Jan went into the kitchen to put up coffee, then returned to the living-room.

"I'm phoning Gail to come over and meet you." Craig was at the phone. "She lives ten minutes away." He frowned, stiffened to attention. "She's got her damn answering machine on." He was about to put the phone down without bothering to leave a message when something apparently captured his attention. He clamped the receiver to his ear again. "How could you put the answering machine on when you're waiting for the man in your life to call?" he joshed. He listened for a moment. "Yeah. I know. All men are sons-of-bitches. Listen, beautiful. Get your tail over to Janet Ransome's apartment. You have the address." He sighed with exaggerated patience. "So leave word on the machine that you're over here. Carlos can phone you at this number." He repeated Jan's phone number and hung up. "Gail's got a thing going with this over-heated married guy from Westchester who runs a men's shop on Third Avenue. He pays her charge at Saks as long as she keeps it down to five hundred a month, and she thinks that's love. It's cheaper – and safer – than getting his sex from a call girl." Craig shrugged. "At sixty it's tough to get it for free."

"Craig," Jan scolded, "you're such a gossip."

Craig giggled.

"And everybody loves me for it." He was thoughtful for a moment. "You should socialize with Gail. She'll be a great character for the book."

"Is that why you're bringing her over?" Jan felt uncomfortable.

"Jan," he reproached. "You're so cynical. I called Gail because I want her to get a feeling of the book. She'll have to start talking about it right away. Not much yet. Just a helluva lot of enthusiasm about 'the new book Craig and I are packaging', plus vague hints of film interest." Craig's smile was complacent. "She'll drop the word over lunches. It'll spread fast. There are no secrets in publishing. And enthusiasm is contagious."

"You know you're scaring me to death," Jan sighed, yet she was exhilarated by what Craig was planting in her mind.

"You haven't got time to be scared. Plot and write. Next week," he pursued, "I'll call Paula King and ask her to lunch at The Four Seasons. I'll tell her I'm interested in promotion for a new package. She's busy as hell. Even if she isn't busy, she'll make a point of pushing me off. She 'lunches' every day at either The Four Seasons or Le Perigord. I'll have to wait until she has an open date, even if I fan her with my chequebook. But let's get back to the book." He was on his feet. Prepared to pace. "Let's go over its direction again—"

Jan was exhausted from being pummelled into mental action by Craig when the doorman buzzed.

"Miss Mitchell coming up," he reported.

Jan pulled the door wide and waited for Gail to emerge from the elevator. A tall, slim, mid-fifties woman in a flamboyant plaid cape walked out into the hall and hesitated until she spied Jan at the open door. She hurried towards the apartment. Shoulder-length teased black hair framed a face that managed to be attractive. But time had not been kind. Gail Mitchell looked like a black-wigged, over-aged Barbie doll, Jan thought involuntarily.

Julie Ellis

"You have to be Jan," Gail trilled with stage diction that Jan suspected replaced an earlier Brooklynese or Bronx accent.

"Yes." Jan smiled with warmth because all at once she felt pangs of sympathy for this heavily made-up woman whose love life was wrapped around a sixty-year-old married man. Craig said that Gail was a smart woman. Business-smart, Jan surmised. Not men-smart.

For a while conversation revolved around the book. Like Craig, Gail was extravagantly enthusiastic. She and Craig had clearly discussed the campaign in depth. It was their major project. Then Craig prepared to leave. He was having dinner with his social register parents tonight.

"If I'm going to ask a favour of the old man, I figure it's time to lay the groundwork." Craig was unabashed. "Mother will help as long as she's sober." Cynicism masked the unhappiness he'd revealed in the Atlanta days about his mother's 'drinking problems'.

"I should go, too." Gail seemed reluctant to leave. She was lonely, Jan thought with compassion. "Of course, Carlos knows where to reach me—"

"Why don't you stay for dinner?" Jan invited. Lisa was spending the day and sleeping over at Betty's apartment. The two girls would be alone with Blackie, Betty's dog of undetermined origin. Betty's father and girlfriend were off to the country. She didn't dare admit to Lisa that she was uncomfortable, even though Blackie was with them. That wasn't cool. Brian had gone off on a hike with a school group. Afterwards they'd go out for pizza. She'd be alone this evening anyway. She could throw together pasta and a salad with no difficulty. There was always garlic bread in the freezer. She'd make a fruit salad for dessert. "It won't be fancy," she apologized.

"I'd love it," Gail said instantly. "I hate spending Saturday night alone."

"I'll call Ronnie Ames and ask her, if she's free, to come over." Lenny was unpredictable, Jan recalled. Why did she suddenly feel

82

self-conscious about being home alone on a Saturday evening? Should she worry at thirty-eight about Saturday night dates? "Ronnie's delightful."

"That sounds like fun." Gail seemed to relax.

Jan dialled Ronnie's number.

"Hello." Ronnie was always crisp and cheerful on the phone.

"Hi. Gail Mitchell is over here – you know, Craig's partner. We're having a pasta dinner. Are you seeing Lenny tonight?"

"Didn't I tell you last night? He called up and begged off. He dropped by before Craig and you arrived." She chuckled. "For a glass of wine 'and'."

"Would you like to come over and join us?" Belatedly Jan realized she'd planned on working tonight. With both kids away she could be sure of no interruptions.

"I have a kind of problem," Ronnie said. "You know Marianne Marlowe?"

"The gal you said we should have lunch with one day soon," Jan recalled. "The one who just came back from Natchez."

"She's terribly depressed. I told her to come over and cry on my shoulder while we have dinner. I wouldn't bring her over to you when she's in this state." Ronnie was candid. "When Marianne starts having one of her fits, she'd frighten you to death. But she'll get over it," Ronnie said cheerfully. "She always does."

"If you decide to come over later, we'll be here." Jan noticed that Gail was restless. She was afraid her 'boyfriend' might be trying to reach her. "*Bon appétit.*"

"I've had two husbands," Gail said with a shrug when Jan released the phone. "I don't know why I don't just give up on men."

"Sometimes they're nice to have around." She looked forward to having Dan up for dinner on Friday, going with him to the Shaw play. She wouldn't think beyond that.

"Carlos should have taken me out to dinner tonight and stayed over. That's not really too much to ask of a man you're sleeping with, is it?" A vein was distended in Gail's neck. She churned with rage. "Everything always has to be their way. I don't care if he is married. He said all his wife cares about are her four grandchildren. She's a fat pig who bores him to death. Why must he always dance to her tune just because she has a bad heart?"

Over pasta and salad Gail told Jan about her alcoholic parents who had made her childhood a nightmare. A special bond between Craig and her, she acknowledged. Her parents were retired and living in Florida. When her mother called up from down there, Gail refused to talk to her.

"I wish the two of them were dead," Gail said with a heat that was as fresh as yesterday. "They're pickled in alcohol. Wouldn't you think they'd be dead by now?"

Jan tried not to reveal her shock. Peggy, too, hated her mother. Her father died when she was tiny. After his death, alone with her mother, she became a battered child. Marriage had been an escape. *Don't let me be the kind of mother my children will hate.*

She listened with sympathy while Gail poured out the ever-present resentment towards her parents, who were falling-down drunks. She cringed for the little girl who walked into a house stinking from vomit, who at five had to wash her own underthings if she was to have clean ones. But Gail had fought her way out of that nightmare, for which she should be proud. Or was she out of it?

By ten o'clock Gail decided it was time to leave. She was sure that by now Carlos would not call.

"I ought to send his wife the letters he wrote me." Gail moved from hurt to vindictiveness, startling Jan again. " 'Darling Gail, I can't wait to see you. I wish I could be with you every night of the week.' Of course, he has no intention of divorcing her."

"You'll find somebody else," Jan tried to sound optimistic. "Someone not tied to a wife." *It wasn't that easy.* For twenty-two and very pretty it might be easy.

Jan saw Gail off and went to the computer to make notes.

Gail's love life might be a mess, but Craig said she was great as an agent. Doubts pursued Jan about the commitment she'd made to Craig. Was she out of her mind to gamble six months on what was really a game of Russian roulette?

\* \* \*

With the concentration built up over a period of years Jan threw herself into the novel. She told herself that every available moment must be utilized. She must believe she could pull off her share of this project. The selling and promotion was Craig's job. That was as important as the writing.

She was relieved that Brian and Lisa were involved in after-school activities. Dinner was their time together. Lisa and Brian vied for her attention, waiting impatiently for the other to take a pause. They didn't complain any longer because she refused to allow TV during dinner. The closeness of the television set to the dining area had been a powerful temptation their first weeks in the apartment. After dinner they focused on homework and she returned to the computer. At errant moments she remembered that Dan Tempest was coming for dinner on Friday and taking her to the Shaw play. It unnerved her to realize how much she looked forward to a social evening with a charming man.

Thursday evening at dinner she casually mentioned to Lisa and Brian that they would have a guest for dinner tomorrow night.

"Peggy?" Lisa asked. Lisa had heard her talking on the phone with Peggy.

"No. Dan Tempest." She was conscious of two pairs of eyes focused on her with fresh intentness. "He lives here in the house. He had theatre tickets and invited me to go with him. I thought it would be pleasant to have him over for dinner before the performance."

Relief swept through her when she realized Lisa and Brian were not upset that she was seeing a man. It was absurd to believe they might be, she scolded herself. She was a divorced woman. Divorced women went out with men. '*When they're so lucky,*' she could hear Ronnie commenting.

Late in the morning Jan went to the supermarket for dinner makings. Hurry with the shopping, she exhorted herself. She was taking the evening off from work. But she'd be at the computer over the whole weekend. That would make up.

Craig would be at the apartment on Sunday to go over what she had finished and to discuss the coming week's output. Apprehension was always close to the surface in her. Could she bring this off?

She'd just returned to the apartment when Peggy called.

"I know you're working, but I'll just be a minute. I'm having lunch with the corporation lawyer." Her Southern accent was more pronounced than usual in the bubbly excitement. She sounded like a Mississippi debutante about to be named 'Debutante of the Year'. "He's a nonsmoker." This seemed to be a frequent requisite in the personal ads. "I told him he couldn't miss me. I'll be wearing a lilac suit. He's five feet ten and slim, he says. And he'll be wearing a grey suit and a blue tie. I'll let you know what happens! Oh, and I'm having coffee tomorrow morning with the teacher."

"Good luck, Peggy." Jan tried to sound enthusiastic. Wouldn't it be something if this *did* work out? Despite the formidable odds?

Jan returned to work. After an hour she stopped to put up a pot of tea. She was fighting yawns. The book had taken such hold of her, and she was so aware of her deadline, that sleep eluded her each night. Too many nights, she suspected, she'd be awakening to find her mind charging into the book. The sure road to insomnia.

Jan started when the doorbell rang in the early afternoon. Peggy, she guessed. The doorman had not rung up.

"I won't hold you but a minute," Peggy apologized. She was radiant.

"I'm taking time out for tea," Jan told her. "Come in and

have a cup with me." Like her, Peggy was always ready for a cup of tea or coffee.

"He's good-looking," Peggy reported, following her to the kitchen entrance. "Sort of shy. He looked relieved when he saw me." She laughed. "I think he was scared I'd be a real dog. Anyhow, he took me to lunch at a great place. He's really sweet. When we were walking out of the restaurant, he offered to walk me home. But you were right," Peggy giggled. "He wanted me to stop off with him at his apartment – he lives right near us, across from Gramercy Park – so he could pick up some papers he'd forgotten to take to the office this morning." But Peggy was pleased that he had made a pass. "I said I didn't think so, but I invited him for dinner at my place tomorrow night."

"Peggy, that's an open invitation."

"Not really. My older boy, Eddie, is coming tonight to stay for the weekend. It's his birthday," Peggy explained. "He won't bother us. He'll be holed up in the bedroom working on a paper for school." She smiled with the dreaminess of a romantic seventeen-year-old. "His name is Paul. He held my hand all the way back to the apartment. I don't think Hal held my hand in the last twenty years."

"Did you tell him Eddie would be there for dinner?"

"No," Peggy admitted. "But dinner will give me a chance to get to know him better. Eddie won't be in the way." But in the next room to eliminate any hanky-panky.

Brian arrived just as Peggy left. He was unfamiliarly sombre.

"No after-school activities?" Right now he was deep in the organizing of a chess team.

"I wasn't in the mood." He hesitated. "You know that article on melanoma in that magazine in the bathroom?"

"What were you doing reading that?" She lifted one eyebrow in mock astonishment.

"You don't keep the bathroom literature up to date," he admonished, then lapsed again into sombreness. "I've been worrying. They talked about black spots. I've got one."

87

"Where?" Her heart began to pound.

"Right on my penis," he said in indignation.

"Let me see it," she ordered.

"I will not!" He was firm. Normally Brian walked around the apartment as though it was a certified nudist colony. "Believe me, it's there."

"It's nothing," she insisted. "But I'll make an appointment for you with a doctor." They didn't have a Manhattan doctor. She'd call Ronnie.

As always Ronnie came through. She herself phoned the doctor, explained the situation, and set up an appointment for the following morning. A non-school day.

"Brian, you don't have melanoma," Jan insisted. But the doctor had been sufficiently concerned to squeeze him in before his scheduled patients arrived. "You'll see Dr Lambert in the morning."

Brian recovered sufficiently to go down to Baskin & Robbins for a double-scoop cone of mint chocolate chip. Jan put up the eye-round roast and baking potatoes, which she could forget about while she showered and dressed. But first she made a green salad and brought out the Sara Lee cheesecake to defrost. At unwary intervals she worried about Brian's 'black spot'. Too conscious that every human being lived a breath away from tragedy.

With Lisa and Brian admonished to prepare themselves for dinner, Jan felt a flurry of misgivings. Had Dan forgotten about tonight? She hadn't seen him since the day they'd met in the stationery store and had breakfast together. *Did he expect this to be a quiet dinner for two*? He knew she had a son and daughter.

Lisa and Brian were sprawled on the floor before the TV when Dan arrived. Punctual, she noted with approval. She struggled not to be self-conscious when she introduced him to Lisa and Brian.

While Dan taught at college level, he seemed to have a fine rapport with the younger age group as well. Over dinner Brian

88

and he became involved in a lively discussion about environmental problems.

Brian cleared the table. Lisa agreed to stack the dishes in the dishwasher. They had finished dinner in comfortable time to go to the theatre.

"We have plenty of time to walk to the theatre," Jan remarked while Dan and she headed for the elevator.

"Fine," Dan approved. "I'm a walker."

They moved briskly through the crisp autumnal night, caught up in discussion of their favourite playwrights of the century. Jan was exhilarated that Dan shared her eclectic tastes.

The play was well-acted and well-directed. Despite her anxiety over Brian she found herself relaxing, laughing, enjoying the evening. Dan and she were *simpatico*, she decided with pleasure. Walking home they sought out a restaurant where they might linger over coffee in further discussion.

While they waited for an elevator in their building, Dan asked her to go with him to a concert the following Saturday. This time, he decreed, he'd take *her* out to dinner. He made no effort to invite her to his apartment, for which Jan was grateful. She insisted there was no need for him to see her to her door.

Her first date since her divorce, she thought whimsically while she unlocked the door. And the man had made no effort to drag her to bed. Was Ronnie wrong about the intent of the average American male? She couldn't believe that Dan didn't find her pleasing. She knew he enjoyed her companionship.

"Did you bring us something?" Lisa asked when she walked into the apartment.

"Lisa, that's gauche," Brian reprimanded. "She can do that when she goes out alone." He paused with an air of self-consciousness. A new emotion for Brian. "Mom, you don't have to go to the doctor with me. I'm fourteen."

"But Dr Lambert doesn't know us. He'll expect to be paid right then."

"Make out a cheque to him. I'll fill in the amount and tell

89

you." Brian was anxious to show he was old enough to handle whatever situation arose.

"All right, darling." She understood. Brian was taking his stand as the man in the family. Her going out tonight with Dan had brought the divorce home to him. "But call me the minute you leave the office."

Jan thrashed about her bed in persistent insomnia tonight. Secretly, before going to bed, she had reread the article that had brought on Brian's appointment with Dr Lambert.

She ought to be there with Brian. Last year, when a freak school accident had sent him into the hospital with an eye injury, she had sat holding his hand in the emergency room. She'd spent every possible hour with him during his five days in the hospital. But now Brian looked upon himself as the man in the family.

At moments like this she knew how completely she loved her children. She'd thought she loved Tim. When had she stopped loving him? When she saw him for what he really was. Selfish, concerned only for himself. Walking out on Brian and Lisa. Not caring if she would be able to manage their lives alone.

Had Dan ever been married? Did he have children? Somehow she couldn't visualize Dan Tempest walking out on such an obligation as children. He'd spoken little about himself, she realized as she lay sleepless. Only about his love of theatre, his poetry writing, his teaching. When he walked out of investment banking, Jan was convinced, he had not walked out on parental responsibilities.

At long last Jan fell asleep. The alarm jangled in her ear at shortly past seven. She must get Brian up and over to the doctor's office. Would the doctor think she was an unfeeling mother not to come with Brian? But that was the way Brian wanted it.

She remembered a friend of her mother's who had discovered a black spot on her chest. Mom's friend was sure she was going to die. That was twenty years ago. She was alive and well.

*Nothing was wrong with Brian.* That was something she couldn't have handled.

# Chapter Seven

Jan waited for a call from Brian. She had taken up her position by the phone fifteen minutes after he left the apartment, though logic told her she could not hear from him for at least an hour. But it was impossible to work with her mind in turmoil.

She was pouring her third cup of coffee when the phone rang. She put down the carafe and raced to the phone.

"Hello—"

"It's me," Brian said. "You can stop worrying about where to put the urn with my ashes. It was a blackhead."

"You see?" Jan was buoyant with relief. "Come on home and have breakfast." Brian had rejected food before the appointment. "Hungry?"

"I'm starving. Pancakes, low-fat sausages, and a pumpernickel bagel," he ordered. "I'll be home in twenty minutes. Have it ready."

She would have served him caviar and champagne if he had asked for it this morning. The whole world seemed right again because Brian had nothing more serious than a blackhead. She timed the pancakes and sausages so that breakfast was ready as he walked into the apartment.

Brian ate with a relish that filled her with pleasure, then went to his room to sleep again. Jan settled down to work. Ten minutes later the phone rang again. It was Ronnie.

"What's with Brian?" she asked solicitously.

"He's fine. It was just a blackhead. I should have called you," Jan apologized, "but I thought you might be sleeping late."

"For a blackhead you should have sent him to Elizabeth Arden," Ronnie laughed. "But thank God that's all it was. Look, there's a Cole Porter concert tonight. Would you like to go?"

"You're not seeing Lenny?" Jan hedged. She felt guilty at the prospect of taking an evening off for a concert when the book lay heavy over her head.

"All of a sudden Lenny is busy on Saturday nights. The bastard." Frustration lurked in Ronnie's voice. "We're having brunch tomorrow and watching football at his place. But the concert is business." She sensed – and understood – Jan's reluctance. "It's one of those singles things. Seven bucks' worth of research. I may decide to do something on it for the magazine. And we both love Cole Porter," she reminded. "For that I'll spend seven bucks even though I don't expect to find the man of my dreams there."

"Okay, let's go," Jan approved. "Come over for dinner first. My meat loaf special. What time is the concert?"

"The social is seven thirty. The concert starts an hour later. Will the kids rebel if we have dinner at six on a Saturday night?"

"They'll eat whenever it's put on the table. We'll sit down to dinner at six sharp."

Jan bribed Lisa to shop at the supermarket and Brian to do the laundry. Afterwards, fortified by their 'wages', they took off for Saturday socializing. Jan worked without interruption – not bothering to stop for lunch, until Peggy phoned.

"I just made a mess of red beans and rice," she said. "Why don't you come up and have some with me? You can eat and run." She was familiar with Jan's frenetic schedule. "But I always cook too much. It'd be a shame to throw it away. It never tastes right when I try to freeze it."

"Don't throw it away. I'm on my way up," Jan said, conscious of hunger. "But I will have to eat and run."

"No problem. Come."

While they ate Peggy's superb red beans and rice and

sipped peppermint tea, Peggy brought Jan up to date on her romantic life.

"Paul's just too much," she sighed. Paul, Jan recalled, was the corporation attorney. "Of course," she said with momentary pleasure, "he's been phoning me every day. But he got mad when I said I'd come to dinner at his place and backed out. Then he told me he was busy when I invited him for Tuesday dinner but said he could come on Thursday night." Rancour seeped into Peggy's voice and marred the prettiness of her face. "But I had to call him up on Thursday morning and cancel. I just wasn't in the mood to entertain. He yelled and said I didn't know what the hell I wanted, so let's just forget the whole thing."

"What about the teacher?" Jan asked.

"I had brunch with him last Saturday. Didn't I tell you?"

"No, we've just talked briefly on the phone." Peggy had been on another of her shopping sprees all week, Jan recalled.

"He had a beard." Peggy grimaced. "Men with beards turn me off. I'm running two more ads. Somewhere along the line I'll find a guy that's right for me. Like the teacher in that course said," Peggy clung to the instructor's words, "it's a matter of numbers. You have to be in touch with a lot of men." Now her face lighted. "I've discovered a fantastic new magazine that's been coming out once a month since July." She leapt to her feet and headed towards the 'studio'. "It has pages and pages of personals, most of them from Southern California; but they're starting a special East Coast edition." She disappeared for a moment in the rarely utilized studio to emerge with a magazine.

Jan concealed her professional interest in the magazine, which Craig should include in his sales promotion for the book. While she scanned a few of the personals, Peggy rambled on about singles weekends coming up at resort hotels and about the full page ad in the *New York Times* run by an organization – obviously well-financed – that offered a more expensive but also quick route to meeting other singles.

"But I'm sticking with the personals," Peggy reiterated.

"Screen carefully," Jan reminded automatically.

"It's lots better than the singles bars," Peggy said with a new edge of defiance that warned Jan to play down her exhortations. "Look, you can meet a guy on a plane, or a train or a cruise ship, and nobody worries about dating under those circumstances. We're living in fast times, Jan," she said crisply. "Today a woman doesn't ask for a dossier before she goes out with a man." She paused. "Sure, if it comes down to sex, I'll expect him to wear a condom."

Jan was in a sombre mood when she returned to her apartment. How sad that a forty-eight-year-old woman should be on such a desperate search for love. At forty-eight a woman's life should be set. How many women like Peggy led frightened empty lives? Maybe women's lib had brought women a long way, but why were so many running a frantic race in the singles scene?

Belatedly Jan remembered she had not picked up the mail. Not that she was expecting anything except bills. The kids had stopped asking if there was mail from their father. Tim had not written in weeks. When he did write, it was just a touristy postcard.

Jan reached for her keys and headed for the elevator. When the elevator stopped at '4', Dan got on.

"Hi." He seemed delighted with this chance encounter. "I'm still euphoric over last night's play. One of the pleasures of living in the Big Apple."

"It was a marvellous production," Jan agreed. "I never want to move away from New York again."

"I have to run up to the country to my sister's house," he said. His eyes told her he wished he could dally with her. "It's Lynne's twenty-fifth wedding anniversary. Quite a record these days." His smile was both tender and cynical. "Her husband's arranged a surprise dinner party for her."

"How lovely." In eight years Tim and she would have celebrated their twenty-fifth anniversary. In one year Peggy and her husband would have celebrated theirs.

"I'm looking forward to the concert next Saturday," Dan told

94

her. "I'll call you Friday, and we can decide where we'll have dinner. Do you like French food?"

"I like anything I don't cook," Jan laughed. She was looking forward to spending an evening in Dan's company.

The elevator stopped at '1'. They emerged into the lobby. A sharp wind intruded as George pulled the door open for an arriving delivery man.

"It's cold out there," Dan said, and Jan restrained herself from suggesting that he go back to his apartment for a coat.

"Stay warm." She smiled and turned away from him towards the bank of mail boxes.

Peggy stood there flipping through letters and dumping junk mail into the trash container. She was staring at Dan as he exchanged pleasantries with George before he walked out into the street.

"Such a nice looking guy," Peggy commented. "What a shame he's gay."

"Dan Tempest?" Jan gazed at her in disbelief.

"Is that his name? It sounds like an actor's name," Peggy decided. "Of course, everybody knows showbiz is full of gays."

"He's a college professor," Jan said. "And I doubt that he's gay."

"He's gay." Peggy was emphatic. "Some gorgeous twenty-year-old boy just moved in with him. And already, his next door neighbour told me, they've had a wingding of a fight. They were yelling at each other until one in the morning. She had to bang on the wall to shut them up. Of course, he did apologize next morning for disturbing them." Peggy was determined to be conscientious in her report.

Letting herself into her apartment again Jan told herself this was gossip. Why would Dan Tempest be taking her out if he was gay? Sure, she'd gone out with Craig; but it was clear right from the beginning that theirs was a friendship deal. If Dan was gay, she'd know it. *Wouldn't she?*

Ronnie and Jan decided to split a cab to the hotel where the concert was being held. The wind was penetrating. The temperature had plunged twenty degrees.

"The concert is in a hotel auditorium that's used for large business conferences," Ronnie said when they were seated in the taxi. "This is really the cream of the singles scene. But you'll get a solid picture of what goes on."

"It can't be as bad as that single parents meeting," Jan said with an shudder.

She was conscious of an uncomfortable sense of guilt when they walked into the hotel lobby. She was here under false pretences.

"Have you been here before?" she asked Ronnie. Remembering that there were few facets of the singles scene that Ronnie had not explored.

"No," Ronnie said. "I've been to other concert socials, though."

"Are you looking for the theatre?" the young man at the Information Desk called out to them. "It's right downstairs." Jan remembered now that the hotel housed an off-Broadway playhouse.

"No," she said quickly, aborting a sudden urge to change their destination. "The concert."

"Down the hall and to the right," he directed them. But he was surprised that they were headed for what Ronnie sometimes called a 'singles jamboree'.

"We don't have the right aura," Jan whispered to Ronnie. Unexpectedly convivial.

"Oh my God," Ronnie swore under her breath and stared ahead.

"What's the matter?"

"The tall blonde just ahead. I know her. She's an editor for a competitor of Mannie's. She's been divorced about a dozen years." But Ronnie brushed aside her initial shock. "So we're both looking for men. So what else is new?"

Ronnie introduced Jan to Laura, a pleasant looking fifty-ish and obviously bright woman. The three of them lined up to pay their 'contribution', which eliminated New York City amusement tax. Laura had obviously attended the concerts on earlier occasions. Faintly self-conscious about being caught at a singles concert, she served as their tour guide.

The three women walked together into the auditorium. A room off to one side was designated for the pre-concert socializing. A long narrow table was set up with a coffee urn, a tea urn and trays of hors d'oeuvres. Small, white, old-fashioned ice-cream tables were scattered about the area.

"We split up and circulate," Laura said briskly and headed for the refreshment table. Jan watched while Laura accepted a cup of coffee and settled herself at a table. Some of the tables were flanked by a pair of chairs. At others three chairs managed to circle the table area.

"Let's go get ourselves coffee," Ronnie said. "Essential props. And relax," she coaxed.

With coffee in tow Jan and Ronnie veered towards the wall of bookshelves, somewhat removed from the arriving patrons.

"I suppose we should mingle." Ronnie seemed doubtful. Jan sensed she had inspected the men present and found nobody interesting thus far. She'd said earlier if she did meet somebody tonight it would be a fringe benefit.

"Let's just observe," Jan hedged.

She was unnerved by the candid sweep of male eyes. The unmistakable aura of men shopping for women, and vice-versa. She thought, absurdly, of female slaves on the auction block in the pre-Civil War South. Instantly she was aware of the necessity of avoiding eye contact with the men who slowly circled about them.

The atmosphere here was somewhat less tense than at the single parents meeting she had attended with Peggy. Yet she felt the quiet desperation of the men and women – equal in numbers tonight – who came into the room. Most of them well-dressed. Only an occasional man seemed blue-collar. Several young secretaries were in pairs, but most of those here came alone. The ages ranged from late twenties to late sixties.

Laura sat at a table alone, like other solitary women. A uniform grimness on their faces. Jan was conscious of male eyes that sought for some sign that they would not be rejected if they approached their quarry. Divorced men, she surmised, who felt themselves once rejected and were fearful of repetition. Ronnie said people always feel that a divorced man or woman without a companion is the rejected one. Perhaps some of those here had walked out themselves on a bad marriage. Peggy walked out – she had not been rejected.

Here and there Jan noticed a woman making an attempt at conversation with a man who stood alone and uncertain. In most cases the woman sat or stood in waiting.

"Nobody's smiling," Jan whispered to Ronnie. "They ought to make a pretense, at least, of enjoying themselves."

"That's why the guy at the Information Desk thought we were looking for the theatre," Ronnie said. "We didn't look as though we were headed for a torture chamber." For a moment her eyes left Jan's to inspect a newcomer, then returned. "All losers tonight. Let's keep talking. I always feel guilty when I have to brush off a man. But there isn't one here tonight I'd care to leave with after the concert." She shrugged philosophically. "It's that way at any singles deal. Sometimes you see somebody you click with, sometimes you don't. I met Lenny at a wine and cheese singles for over forties. Ronnie grinned. "I wouldn't object to turning in one fifty-four for two twenty-sevens. Even for one twenty-seven."

"They all look so anxious." Jan wished she had the nerve to bring out her notebook and scribble down the reactions that surged through her mind. This was weird; she was one of these, and yet she wasn't. But Ronnie was right. Here was rich material for the book.

"A lot of men just want to get laid." Ronnie was blunt. "Some of the women are after one-night stands, too. Some of both are looking for a lasting relationship. Face it, honey. This is a grim operation. Why do you think I put up with Lenny?"

Jan's attention was drawn to a tall, lean, voluminously skirted woman in her late twenties, who held on to the hand of a seven-year-old little girl with a winsome face. Someone whose babysitter had stood her up, Jan analysed, but who was so desperate to come here tonight that she'd brought her child with her.

In her mind Jan envisioned the younger woman's frantic daily existence. A job by day, with the little girl having to be picked up after school by a part-time sitter. Rushing home from work to prepare dinner for herself and her daughter. Caught up in the evenings in the myriad details a working woman must leave for the non-working hours. *How little time to be a woman.*

What would she do if she picked up a man tonight? Would she take him home along with her little girl?

"That's tough," Ronnie said softly, following her gaze. "She was probably going stir crazy at home."

"Suppose she meets somebody?" Jan questioned.

"She'll take him home, put the kid to sleep in the bedroom," Ronnie constructed the woman's evening, "then make it with the guy on the convertible sofa in the living-room. Look, she's young and probably hot." Ronnie was silent for a moment. "There was a four month period when I was shacked up with a guy I met at a party. Deedee, Clark, and I were in a tiny one-bedroom apartment. Thank God, Deedee's a heavy sleeper," she said humorously. "Until the night Clark got smashed and made the mistake of hitting me. Deedee came crying out of the bedroom, and I told Clark to pack up his gear and get the hell out. The next morning I had the lock on the door changed. But for four months," she said wistfully, "I had a sex life like I've never had before or since."

"At least the coffee here is great," Jan said after a moment.

"So it's not a total loss," Ronnie flipped. Her eyes were quizzical. "Are you soaking up material, baby?"

"Oh God, am I!"

"We'll stay for the social after the concert," Ronnie reminded. "For seven bucks we're entitled."

Jan's gaze left Ronnie fleetingly. Two other women were seated with Laura. They were seeking mutual comfort in companionship. How long could a woman sit alone without being in agony? For the most part the women were standing about the room and clutching paper cups. The women alone. The men alone. Only a handful of couples exchanged muted conversations.

Jan was relieved when the lights flickered, indicating the concert was about to begin. Ronnie and she made a point of stalling on going into the auditorium, lest Laura should feel obligated to sit with them.

With the crowd thinning out Jan and Ronnie took seats near the rear, beside a young couple. Jan thought they were together – probably friends of the musicians – until she heard the man ask the girl her name. They seemed so right together, she decided with unexpected sentiment. How lovely if tonight brought them into a permanent relationship or marriage.

The Cole Porter music, presented by a trio, was delightful. Jan found herself caught up in remembered show tunes. Then Ronnie slyly poked her and pointed. She followed Ronnie's gaze. A man sat reading a book in the dim light of the auditorium. It appeared to be a textbook. Then minutes later, at the conclusion of a number, he shoved the book into his jacket pocket and walked out of the concert. It was Saturday night and early. He was headed for another 'meet market'. Not long after his departure the woman with the little girl left. She seemed disappointed and frustrated. The little girl was tired and sulky.

At intervals during the concert, with the Cole Porter music predisposing her to this, Jan thought about Dan. She could not believe that he was gay. She didn't *want* to believe it. She remembered that she had been relieved that he had made no romantic overtures – yet. But that didn't mean he was gay.

She found it difficult to accept Ronnie's theory that every man expected a woman to sleep with him on their first date. Yet

Peggy's experience with the attorney sneaked into her mind. He had tried after a short phone conversation and lunch.

How could a man expect to enter into a relationship of any substance with a woman he hardly knew? Or was uncomplicated sex with a faceless body all these men wanted, despite their talk about an 'enduring relationship'?

Was it an ego trip for men to pick up a woman and jump right into bed with her? A salve for their damaged psyches? Dan wasn't like that. And he wasn't gay.

At the brief intermission Jan and Ronnie went out into the social area. Most of the patrons remained seated. Jan was astonished to discover that about a dozen men had not even bothered to go inside to the concert. A pair of women stood at the refreshment table and waited to be served coffee. The men were clustered about the tables in pairs or alone. Satisfied for now to drink coffee and wait for the resumption of socializing. One tall, quite handsome man sat alone and grim. Avoiding conversation, even with other men. Doing research like herself, Jan guessed. Probably for an article.

"They're out of their minds to stay out here," Jan whispered while Ronnie and she waited for coffee.

Ronnie shrugged.

"They hear it without going inside. Besides, they didn't come for the music. They hope there may be some action if some women show up late and don't bother to go into the auditorium."

In a few minutes a flickering of lights sent Jan and Ronnie back into the auditorium. While they seated themselves, Jan felt the weight of several pairs of eyes. She hoped none of the men would approach them after the concert.

When the programme was completed, Jan and Ronnie moved out into the socializing area with the others. Trays of attractively arranged strips of coffee cake, crackers and cheese spreads, and miniature bagels were brought out and set up on tables.

Here and there Jan spied couples in conversation. She overheard one mid-fifties man invite a woman twenty years his junior to go out for a drink. They left with a show of conviviality; yet as they passed her, Jan saw glints of reservations in the eyes of each. These comings together were fraught with suspicions and doubts.

Laura came over to join them.

"There's nobody here I want to talk with," she said candidly. "All losers."

Ronnie and Laura launched into shop talk. The three of them were an island apart from the rest, Jan thought. She left for a moment to collect a cup of coffee.

"It was a lovely concert, wasn't it?" a male voice asked, and she turned to face a hesitant man about her own age.

"It was lovely," she agreed and reached for the cup of coffee extended by the woman at the urn. She hurried back to Ronnie and Laura. Without turning around she could sense the disappointment of the man she'd left behind. A nice enough man, she guessed. But not a Dan Tempest.

For a while she was absorbed in conversation with Ronnie and Laura. They were discussing the business end of publishing, Laura knew only that Jan was a long-time writer in the confessions and men's market field.

"Try me sometime," Laura urged. "I always need good writers."

It was almost eleven when the lights flickered again. Belatedly Jan dragged her attention back to the business that had brought her here. A handful of couples had left. The other patrons had remained to the bitter end. Her writer's mind was rushing off on plot twists for the novel. She was glad Ronnie had suggested their coming here tonight.

Jan and Ronnie decided to walk home despite the coldness of the night. At Forty-Second Street, already chilled to the bone, they detoured into Howard Johnson's for more coffee and to warm up.

"We'll take a cab the rest of the way," Ronnie said when the waitress had taken their orders.

"I felt so sorry for that woman with the little girl. She didn't look as though she had much money. That seven dollars must have been a major investment," Jan sympathized.

"It's better for a woman alone in the city than in suburbia," Ronnie reminded. "The only singles action out there is the church scene."

"So many women alone are terrified of New York. All they hear about are the rapes and the muggings and the murders."

"There are rapes and muggings and murders in suburbia," Ronnie said drily. "They don't make much of a splash. Besides, it's a question of numbers." Jan tensed, hearing in her mind Peggy's voice quoting the teacher of the seminar on finding a lover. *It's a question of numbers.* There must have been two hundred people at the concert, equally divided as to sex: one hundred chances, Peggy would say. "Consider the size of New York's population," Ronnie pursued. "I'll bet statistics would show that we're no heavier into crime than the suburbs. God knows, there's plenty of juvenile delinquency and drugs out there."

"Jan?" A male voice startled her. "Hey, it is you!" Jubilance in the disconcertingly familiar voice, out of its familiar environment.

"Mike!" Recognition lent a lilt to her own voice. "Mike Blume! How are you?" Mike and Cecile Blume had lived across the road from them in Ridgefield. Mike usually interrupted his jogging – morning or early evening, depending upon the season – to exchange good-humoured jibes with her while she planted or weeded or raked the leaves. Though divorces were common enough in their community, he had avoided discussing the subject when word circulated around the hill that Tim had left her.

Jan introduced Mike and Ronnie, aware of Ronnie's approval of him. Mike was slim and muscular, with sandy hair lightly sprinkled with grey. His features were pleasant. He had a sense of humour. A quality missing in Tim.

Mike joined them for coffee, though he kept a close watch on

103

the time. He had to take the twelve thirty to Katonah. The last train out on Saturday evening.

Mike asked about Lisa and Brian, talked about his own two teenage daughters. Cecile was into health foods these days, he reported. That and patchwork quilts. She was on half a dozen local committees, as usual. Jan remembered that Mike said, a long time ago, that Cecile went her way and he went his. They had a comfortable relationship, which Jan had long ago gathered did not include sex.

Jan was startled to realize the time when Mike rose to leave. Ronnie and she left with him. While they paused for goodbyes on the sidewalk, Mike suggested Jan meet him for lunch one day.

"I'll call you next week," he said warmly. "We have to keep in touch."

"Lunch sounds like fun."

Mike reached for his address book and wrote down her phone number and address. She could afford to take off a couple of hours for lunch, Jan told herself. She'd make up the time somewhere along the road. That was one of the fringe benefits of working freelance. Forget about the ulcers brought on by its insecurity.

Mike headed for Grand Central. Jan and Ronnie, shoulders hunched against the cold, sought a taxi on Lexington Avenue. It was a short wait, for which Jan was grateful.

"Mike has a thing for you," Ronnie said softly when they were settled in the taxi.

"Mike?" Jan's eyes widened in surprise.

"Darling, he's not a eunuch. And he's not gay. In fact, I'll bet if I wasn't there, he'd have tried to lure you into bed tonight."

"Ronnie, you have sex on the brain!" Jan jeered. "Mike and I are going to have an affair in the waiting room at Grand Central?"

"In a hotel," Ronnie chuckled. "You have heard of such places?"

"Not Mike." Jan was resolute. "Mike's always good for a few laughs. He's always trying to make a fast million. The company he works for made a fortune on some invention he came up with some years ago. He's still cursing himself for bringing it in on the job."

"He'll make a pass." Ronnie was complacent. "You could have a fun affair with him."

"Ronnie, he's married," Jan objected.

"It's a marriage that lets him off the hook sexually," Ronnie pinpointed. "What's he doing in New York at this hour on a Saturday night? I'm not saying it'll be the grand love of your life. But obviously you two are very compatible. You enjoyed running into him," she pursued. "It's possible to enjoy sex with a guy you aren't in love with but like a lot. It can be a comfortable, healthy relationship."

"Mike Blume won't make a pass at me," Jan insisted. "I'm an old neighbour who's recently been divorced, and he's being nice. That's all it is."

"He's smart. He may not make a pass when you have lunch with him. But the next time he'll take you to dinner. Then it'll be to a hotel. You've got something better lined up?" Ronnie flipped. Her eyes were searching. "Your college professor?"

"I'm seeing him Saturday night," Jan acknowledged. Not even to Ronnie would she admit how strongly she was drawn to Dan. It was absurd. She hardly knew him. And Dan showed no indication of rushing her into a relationship. *Would* she, she asked herself with a new candour. "Dan's just seeking casual companionship," she improvised because Ronnie's smile was knowing. "He enjoys talking with another writer. Shop talk."

She could not accept Peggy's second-hand gossip about Dan's sharing of his apartment with a 'gorgeous young boy'. She could not believe Dan was gay. Not the way he looked at her in unguarded moments. He'd been through a bad marriage, she surmised; he wouldn't rush into a relationship. Like her he meant to be careful.

*Julie Ellis*

She'd see Mike for lunch next week. He wasn't about to make a pass. Ronnie was all wrong. Yet she wondered, like Ronnie, what Mike was doing in Manhattan on a Saturday night – without his wife.

# Chapter Eight

Jan was putting in longer hours than she had ever worked in her life. The novel was becoming a compulsive effort. The singles concert had fired her imagination to a height that jarred her awake at three or four in the morning. Now she kept a notebook on a table beside her bed so that every fresh thought could be put on paper lest it be lost.

Craig came over almost daily to go over the rough draft of the latest pages. Jan and he talked, dissected, argued in heat. Sometimes Craig conceded to her. Sometimes she deferred to him. They shared a deep mutual respect that was promising.

On Thursday morning Mike phoned and suggested lunch the next day.

"Somewhere mid-town if it's all right with you. That way I won't have to waste time travelling. Do you have a favourite place in the area?"

"You're in the high East Fifties," Jan recalled. "Would you like Michael's?" Ronnie and she had lunched at Michael's on Ronnie's birthday back in April. "Outrageous desserts," she warned, feeling lighthearted. It would be pleasant to break her routine to have luncheon with Mike. And then she remembered guiltily that she'd be running away from the computer on Saturday evening. The concert with Dan.

"Michael's," Mike agreed and groaned. "I'll have to jog around the hill twice on Saturday morning."

"If you talk like that, Mike, I won't let you have dessert," she flipped.

"When I have luncheon with a beautiful woman, I expect dessert. I don't care what they say about chic people turning it down."

"What time?" Jan asked.

"One o'clock. I'll make a reservation."

Jan felt a special warmth through the next hours. She could afford to take time off for lunch, she reiterated. She would come back refreshed and raring to get back to the book.

As always these days she was startled when the children arrived home from school. Time rushed by with astonishing speed. Today Brian came home first. He always announced himself as he emerged from the elevator.

"Ma!" His voice echoed down the hall with a zest for living that Jan cherished.

Her face alight, she hurried to unlock the door.

"Hi, darling."

Brian kissed her, dumped his knapsack on the sofa, and collapsed on the recliner.

"Life is a bowl of chicken shit," he said profoundly.

"Why, Brian?" She enjoyed these brief moments alone with him, as she did similar moments with Lisa.

"Questions plague me, Mom." He sighed. "Will I make Stuyvesant High? Will I crack 1400 on my PSATs? Will my college interviews go well? Will I be a success in college? Will I be a successful lawyer? Will I save the world? Will the world collapse before I'm twenty?"

"Would you like broiled flounder for dinner?" Jan was unperturbed. "The world will surely be around for that."

"Why not have my share of mercury tonight?" Brian accepted, arising from a prone position with the alacrity of the young. "How's the book doing?" He went into the kitchen to take his familiar stance before the open refrigerator.

"I've got a long way to go," she warned. She was still uncomfortable in the gamble she was taking. Each trip to the

bank to withdraw household money was a knife at her throat.
*Was she good enough to bring off this book?*

"I think it's great." Brian's voice was muffled by a chunk of cheese. "You're a sharp lady to take a chance. How do you think the Rockefellers got so rich?"

"By being born into the right family." But she was astonished to know how much of the mechanics of her efforts was being absorbed by Brian and Lisa. Of course, they both knew that she was working on a novel, that Craig was helping, and that both Craig and she had heady expectations – though her own expectations were sometimes drowned out by fears.

A series of quick, short rings indicated that Lisa was at the door. Moments later Jan went into her referee act. Times like this she was convinced that Lisa and Brian were mortal enemies. With the battle quieted down she returned to the computer. A few minutes later she swore under her breath when the phone rang.

*Why don't I turn on the answering machine?*

She knew she wouldn't ever do that. First, there was always the chance the children might be trying to reach her. Secondly, even when Lisa and Brian were home and there could be no dire emergency on their part, she had a built-in compulsion to answer the telephone.

"Hello—" If it was Peggy, she'd get right off. Peggy understood.

"Hi." Craig always sounded ebullient.

"I was able to incorporate that idea you came up with last night for the singles cruise," she reported. "It's working out great."

"It'll add glamour." Craig was pleased. "And speaking of glamour, I want you to make an appointment within the next week or two at Margrith of Switzerland. Make the appointment with Margrith."

"What am I doing at Margrith of Switzerland?"

"Adding some zip to your hair. Talk to Margrith about adding a touch of red. She'll come up with just the right formula. There's nobody in the city who's better. After the tint job, consult with her about a short, easy-to-handle hairdo. When you're on the talk show circuit, you won't have time for hairdressers."

"Craig, I've done about a quarter of the book!" she protested. "In rough draft!" All at once she was terrified. This was moving too fast.

"Relax, baby. I want you to become comfortable with the new look. Nothing will happen for months. I'm having lunch with Paula King in ten days. I told you she'd keep me waiting. When you meet her, I want you to look smart. Invest in one absolutely smashing designer outfit."

"Craig," Jan moaned, "do you know what designer clothes cost?"

"Go down to Orchard Street," he said. "I'll get an address for you." All at once Jan remembered the marvellous suit Karen Somers had been wearing when they encountered each other in the elevator. Oscar de la Renta for sure. The look she herself loved. Feminine yet ultra smart. "It's a business investment, Jan." He hesitated. "I'll split the cost with you. We'll write it off later."

"I'll ask Ronnie to go with me," Jan decided. "She has a marvellous sense of style."

"My old man is flying out to Palm Springs with my mother next week. She's scheduled for drying out in a sanatorium, though I'm not supposed to know. Dad'll stay with his banker friend, who has a cottage there. Dad likes a free crash pad; the banker hopes Dad will push him into the social register. Dad will set it up for the word to start circulating. The bank has a client hot for a new novel in work on a highly commercial subject."

"Craig, you're scaring the hell out of me." That was becoming her theme song these days.

"Sweetie, you concentrate on the writing. Let me plot the selling. Remember, call Margrith's for an appointment, and buy yourself a designer outfit for lunch with Paula. Probably the beginning of December."

"I have a beige cashmere coat. That'll be all right, won't it?" she asked anxiously. Luckily she never gained an ounce. She still weighed in at 105 to 108. "It's smart and almost new." She'd worn it twice a year for the past six years. She bought it at Tim's insistence when she went with him – at his boss's orders – to a convention in Las Vegas. She'd adored beautiful clothes since she was a little girl. But beautiful clothes had been for her sister Diane. And when Tim and she were married, the house always came first – except when there was a company dinner. For the last twelve years she'd alternated between the Balenciaga and the Oscar de la Renta that had cost more each than her annual wardrobe. They were still knockouts. Why couldn't the meeting with Paula be at a formal dinner, she asked herself wryly.

"Splurge on an expensive bag. A Judith Leiber or a Morris Moskowitz. I'll get the address on Orchard Street where they're off thirty-five per cent. I want you to meet Paula King looking like you're used to a lot of money."

"A condition I would enjoy," she murmured.

Jan returned to the computer determined to finish up a difficult scene before dinner. Conscious that tomorrow she was having lunch with Mike Blume. And on Saturday attending a concert with Dan Tempest. She must make up for all those wasted hours. Not wasted, she coddled herself. Relaxation time. Most necessary.

She sat immobile at the computer for a moment. Her mind darting away into other areas. Forty was breathing down her neck. What was it Mom used to say? *Why do we have to be ready to die before we learn how to live?*

It was impossible to work every hour she was awake. Actually she was slightly ahead of the schedule she had set up for herself. Even so, she worried that some emergency might arise that would eat away at the precious working hours.

111

*Julie Ellis*

The novel had to be wrapped up, from her angle, by late January. Craig had set a deadline of mid-March. What she was straining to do was to squeeze a year of work into four and a half months.

Friday was crisp and cold but sunny. Jan worked until mid-morning, ever conscious that she was to meet Mike for luncheon at one o'clock. With work piled on a corner of her work table, she focused on what to wear. Her beige cashmere coat over the wool tweed skirt and the beige silk blouse bought at a sale in Saks, she decided, and strode into the bathroom to shower.

Relaxing under the hot spray she thought about Dan. With astonishing frequency he filtered into her thoughts. It upset her that Peggy persisted in saying that he was gay. Instinct told her Peggy was wrong. Still, she was uneasy.

*What do I know about Dan? I know he hated business and loves teaching. I know he's concerned about the environment, about world peace, about poverty in developing countries. I know he has a passion for theatre and ballet and fine books. He never talks about his past.*

Enough, Jan reproached herself. Dress and go meet Mike for lunch. Don't try to make more of her friendship with Dan than he meant it to be. She could survive without a man in her life. She had the children. She had her work. God, that was sufficient to keep any woman busy.

Because there was ample time she spent special efforts today on her make-up and was pleased with the results. She left the apartment in a festive mood, determined to enjoy this respite from the computer.

She walked with small, swift steps across to the bus stop, conscious of admiring glances. The bus pulled to a stop on Third Avenue just as she arrived, made faster progress than she had anticipated.

On impulse she left the bus at Fifty-Third Street. She was

112

ahead of schedule. It would be pleasant to walk the rest of the way to Michael's. After all these weeks in New York the city was still a joyous revelation to her.

She cut through the Citicorp, bustling with lunchtime crowds. The tables at the atrium were ricocheting with the multilingual accents of tourists, who quickly discovered the charm of the restaurants and shops housed here. Coming out on Lexington she continued west to Park, pleasantly aware of the smartly dressed women, the well-tailored men who traversed the area. So much of the city was beautiful.

Mike was waiting for her in front of the restaurant. His face lighted at the sight of her.

"You're looking beautiful." He inspected her with admiration as he pulled the door wide for her.

"Thank you." Compliments always amazed her. Diane had been the beautiful one. She was the sister who graduated at the top of her classes. Mom had been proud of her scholastic achievements, but she gloried in Diane's loveliness.

Jan and Mike were seated at a cosy corner table. For a few moments they concentrated on ordering. Then Mike leaned back with an air of quiet satisfaction.

"I needed an escape hatch today. I'm on shaky ground. I refused a transfer to San Francisco. I'm fifty-three years old," he said with candour. "I'm tired of pulling up roots every four or five years and moving somewhere else."

"Time and I lived in six states in seventeen years," she recalled. "I hated every move."

"Except the move back to New York," he guessed. "City living agrees with you."

"I love being back in the city." She lowered her eyes before the questions in his. He was concerned about how she was surviving the divorce. It must have been all over the hill that Tim left her for that twenty-year-old slut. There were no secrets in suburbia. "How's Cecile?"

Mike reported with humorous comments on Cecile's latest

113

*Julie Ellis*

involvement with local committees. He filled her in on happenings on the hill, told her about the people who had bought her house.

"They repainted the whole bloody house in sea green. I get seasick just thinking about it."

Jan was astonished to discover that it was past two thirty when they left Michael's. Luncheon had been superb. She had relaxed in Mike's company. For a little while the pressures of the book receded.

"We'll have to do this soon again," Mike said, raising a hand to flag down a cab for her. "I'll call you."

"It was fun seeing you," Jan said affectionately. "And lunch was lovely. Give my best to Cecile," she added hastily as a cab pulled up at the curb.

She felt guilty about taking a cab, but time was important. Emerging from the cab she encountered Karen talking to George about a closet door that wasn't functioning.

"Hi, Mrs Ransome," Karen greeted her with warmth. "I've been dying to talk to you, but time just seemed to evaporate. Why don't we go in now for coffee and to yak a bit? Right around here somewhere."

"Let's," Jan accepted. "The coffee shop on the corner all right?" They wouldn't be long. Karen was probably busy, too. "And after all these years why don't we drop the 'Mrs Ransome'? You make me feel ancient."

"Jan," Karen laughed as they headed towards Cosmos. Both walking with quick, small strides. "I just couldn't get over running into you right in the same house." She hesitated. "I'm sorry about your divorce."

"It was a long time coming." Had Tim been playing around even in Houston? Did Karen know? That was the most humiliating part. "At least you got out of your marriage fast."

"It was a horror." Karen shuddered in retrospect. "I thought being married to a rich man would be marvellous. Howard was a pig. I got to the point where I wanted to scream every time he

114

touched me. I'll think a lot before I marry again. I'm living with somebody now. Jason's awfully good-looking. He's close to my age. We have fun together. Right now he's in a bind financially because he has to see his ex-wife through her PhD. Then he'll be off the hook." She paused. "Maybe we'll get married then."

"Where did you meet him?" Jan asked with sudden curiosity.

"At Maxwell's Plum," Karen said. She wasn't self-conscious about it. That was a normal routine, Jan rationalized. "I was there with a girlfriend. Right away Jason and I felt the chemistry bubbling up. He's a terrific lover. To me that's important."

Jan and Karen spent twenty minutes over coffee. Each aware of the need to move on. Karen had come home from the office to change because Jason was taking her out to dinner with some special friends and wanted her to look high fashion. She made a point of dressing super-conservative at the office.

"Come up and have a drink with us soon," Karen urged. "I'd love to have you meet Jason."

"I'll call you," Jan promised. Instinct told her she would not like Jason.

Karen said goodbye to Jan and hailed a cab. She didn't like walking around with a cheque for twelve thousand dollars in her Judith Leiber handbag. Not even a bank cheque. She had meant to roll over her CDs – though interest rates were disgustingly low. But Jason was so upset about losing out on that house in Connecticut because he was short twelve thousand towards the down-payment. He wouldn't see his Christmas bonus until February. He'd pay her back then, he said.

Nobody excited her the way Jason did. Not ever. All he had to do was to put a hand on her, and she was ready to hop into bed. She knew that the first night he took her up to his apartment.

He had champagne chilling in the refrigerator, glasses on a table in the living-room. She knew the stage was set for whomever he picked up that night at Maxwell's Plum. While they sipped the champagne, he slipped Beethoven's Fifth into the CD player.

Not until they'd been together a dozen times did he admit he liked jazz better than Beethoven.

She wasn't going straight back to the office. She was taking the cheque to Jason at his office on Madison and Fifty-Third. He was probably wondering what was taking her so long. She'd called from the apartment before she changed to let him know she'd been to the bank.

She had gone for coffee with Jan because she had meant to tell her it was time she had divorced Tim. Everybody in their community had known he was a chaser. If he had not been scared, he would have made a pass at her. But she couldn't bring herself to tell Jan. Why would a man who had a beautiful wife at home go chasing after other women?

Was Jason seeing other women? He'd picked her up at a singles bar. No, Karen decided. Jason was mad about her. Some nights he left her alone to go to sporting events with a client, but that was business. Jason wasn't sleeping with anybody else.

# Chapter Nine

Third Avenue was lively with people despite the threat of rain or unseasonably early snow. Jan liked the sense of purposefulness that permeated Third Avenue in the twenties and low thirties at this hour of the night. People hurrying home from offices and shops, darting into stores for last-minute dinner shopping. Others en route to early dinners at one of the many restaurants that dotted the area, before heading on to the myriad diversions offered by the city. An air of vitality here that was stimulating.

"Cold?" Dan asked solicitously because the dampness lent a chill to the air below what the temperature indicated.

"No." Jan smiled in reassurance.

"It'll be warm in Emilio's," he promised. "We could try for a cab—" His eyes turned to survey the still heavy flow of early evening traffic.

"No need, Dan. It's only Thirty-Third. Just eight more short blocks."

"You're my kind of woman," he chuckled. "A walker."

"When I walked in Ridgefield, everybody thought I was a health nut," Jan reminisced. "Being able to walk to so many places is one of the delights of living in Manhattan."

"Tell me if I'm walking too fast," Dan said. "Sometimes I forget your strides are little compared to mine." There was a protectiveness in his voice that evoked unexpected pleasure in her.

In the delicious warmth of the restaurant they were seated at a table Dan had specifically requested. He was a regular patron,

Jan deduced. Involuntarily she speculated about other women Dan had brought here.

For a few minutes they concentrated on ordering. The soft piano music – Noel Coward at the moment – lent a disarming air of romance to the room. Jan felt herself relaxing after the tension of the day's writing. She sensed that Dan was uptight. Caught up in the enjoyment of being in his company while they walked to Emilio's, she had not recognized this.

"Rough week at school?" she asked when an unfamiliar silence fell between them.

"I'm being dull company," he apologized.

"No," she rejected quickly.

"This is a date I'd like to forget," Dan said after a moment. "If my wife and I had not been divorced eleven years ago, it would have been our twenty-first wedding anniversary." His jaw tightened. His eyes were opaque now. "It was an ugly, sordid divorce."

"No divorce is pretty," Jan sympathized. She had been right. Dan was divorced. Peggy was so wrong.

"My marriage was ugly and sordid," he said with uncharacteristic harshness. "But let's not spoil our evening thinking about past mistakes. How's the writing coming?"

"Moving along." She hadn't told Dan about the book. He thought she was still batting out confessions. "And yours?"

Dan sighed.

"I don't have a writer's block exactly. But I'm running behind schedule on this collection of poetry. I've never missed any kind of deadline. I might on this one." Frustration crept into his voice.

"I'd love to read some of your poetry," Jan said impulsively. "Will you give me some names so I can look up the books?"

"I'll loan them to you," he offered. His smile was wry. "Not too many stores stock Dan Tempest."

She suspected he made a habit of not discussing his marriage and divorce. That he had mentioned it to her lent a new closeness to their friendship. Friendship should precede a relationship, she reminded herself. On that Peggy and she agreed.

Their conversation roamed with ease from one subject to another. Dan always amazed her with his store of knowledge. Yet despite his efforts Jan was aware that part of his mind was not with her. Was Dan still in love with his wife despite the 'ugly and sordid' marriage? The supposition was disturbing.

Jan's enjoyment of the concert was marred by mental conflict about Dan. After eleven years of divorce was he still in love with his ex-wife? Why was that so important to her? Dan had not so much as kissed her goodnight.

She knew what Ronnie would say if they discussed the situation: *'He's gone through an ugly marriage. He's jumped to the other side of the fence.'* Yet she trusted her intuition. Dan was not gay.

After the concert she waited for Dan to suggest their going in somewhere for coffee. When he didn't and they were emerging from the home-bound taxi, she waited for him to suggest going to his apartment for coffee. He seemed distracted, taciturn now.

Walking to the elevator Jan debated about asking Dan up to her apartment for coffee. No, she decided. Dan was in no mood to prolong the evening.

"I'll see you to your apartment," he said and pushed the '8' button.

"No need, Dan," she said and pushed '4' for him. "It was a lovely evening." He wasn't suggesting another meeting.

"I'm sorry I seem to be out of it tonight." His eyes were sombre. "You're a special lady, Jan." She was startled when he leaned down to kiss her lightly on the mouth as the elevator stopped at his floor. "Thanks for putting up with me."

The door opened before Jan could reply. Her heart pounded. Why had the touch of his lips evoked such a surge of passion in her? She'd had breakfast with him, had gone with him to the theatre and to a concert. *She hardly knew him.*

Dan let himself into his apartment. Relieved that Keith had taken off for the weekend. Two days without fights and recriminations. Just peace and quiet. He'd be able to go over the papers from his Shakespeare Survey class. Maybe even have a go at the poetry.

He switched on a lamp and dropped into the olive green club chair. Why was he so confoundedly upset this year about the date? That nightmare was long past.

Being with Jan had made him more aware of the fiasco of his marriage, he realized. She had looked at him as though she couldn't figure out what was going on in his mind. She had expected him to ask her up to his place for coffee. That was the normal routine.

They'd been out together three times. They obviously enjoyed each other's company. He could have asked her up. They could have made love. Keith wouldn't be back until Sunday night.

He was aching to make love to her. But he couldn't go into that scene now. He had other obligations. Why the hell was he seeing her? There was no space in his life for a woman. *Not now.*

He went into the kitchen and put up coffee, feeling guilty at having disappointed Jan. She was beautiful and exciting. A fine human being. Not like Fern, who meant to use him for her own sick purposes. He closed his eyes and remembered their heated romance.

Fern was small and slight, like Jan. But that was where the resemblance ended, he thought bitterly. He had met Fern at a cocktail party given by his boss's wife. Right away Fern let it be known that she was in pursuit of him. He was amused and intrigued. She was attractive and charming. The daughter of a wealthy banker, who was eager to throw her into marriage.

Five weeks after they met they were married at City Hall. Fern rejected the fancy wedding her mother futilely tried to foist on them. Instead of a fancy wedding Fern insisted on a two-month tour of Europe, which entailed her father's arranging two months' leave for him.

120

Fern and he made love constantly, in some of the finest hotel suites in Europe. She devoted herself to keeping him passionate. She shopped for the most seductive nightgowns and negligées, though she stayed in them briefly.

Dan's face tightened as he remembered the house they'd rented on a mountainside near Geneva for the final two weeks of their honeymoon. The unpretentious but cosy house sat high among the vineyards in a tiny village called Bougy Villars, midway between Geneva and Lausanne. Below lay Lake Geneva. Across the lake rose magnificent Mont Blanc. That first night, when they had unpacked, they walked out unsuspectingly on the tiny terrace. Unprepared for the splendour that greeted them.

"God, Fern, did you ever see anything like that?" He gazed in rapt admiration at the dazzling array of lights that shone through the night darkness. From the houses down the mountainside. From Geneva to Lausanne and from towns across the lake. The auto-route below a gleaming diamond necklace.

"Dan, I want to make love," Fern murmured.

"On the terrace?" he asked humorously.

"In the house." An edge of sharpness in her voice. "I don't mean to waste a moment of these last two weeks before we fly home."

"We can make love in New York," he laughed, dropping an arm about her waist as they walked into the house. He had not expected Fern to be a virgin at twenty-six. But in Paris she had shocked him when she suggested that they hire a prostitute to join in their lovemaking. Sex *à trois* was not his cup of tea. "If I have any strength left."

"I'll make you strong." She paused to lift her face to his when he had locked the door behind them.

While he kissed her, Fern was already undoing the buttons that travelled from neck to hem on her frock. He tried to tell himself that this was their honeymoon. Fern meant to make it memorable for both of them. He felt guilty in his involuntary wish that they might see more of Europe and less of beds.

*Julie Ellis*

"I bought a bottle of champagne. It's already in the refrigerator," she told him while he removed the strip of a bra that barely concealed her huge nippled but adolescent breasts. No matter how tired he was from plane-hopping, she could always arouse him. "If you need encouragement," she needled him. Her hands were tugging at the elastic at her hips. Dan helped her.

"What makes you think I need help?" he countered. He searched his mind for any memory of his failure as a lover.

"I'm not pregnant yet," she pouted.

"Fern, what's the rush?" He was startled.

"I want your baby in me," she whispered. "But meanwhile just you will be enough."

Her mouth closed in on his left nipple while her fingers stroked the other. How little she was without her heels, he thought in sudden tenderness. Little and headstrong. Sex was a game with her. He ought to pick her up, carry her upstairs, and throw her on her back. But indulgently he waited.

Her mouth slid down his chest to his lean, flat belly. She dropped to her knees. Her hands closed in about his rump and fondled. A sound escaped as her mouth closed in on its quarry.

"Don't bite," he cautioned while his hands cradled her head.

No woman had ever excited him this way. He was a body encased in passion. It had nothing to do with love.

She drew away her mouth and, clinging to his arms for anchorage, pulled herself erect.

"Lie down, Dan."

"Here?" he objected. "On the floor? Let's go upstairs."

"Lie down." It was an irritated command.

"Fern, we have three bedrooms."

"Damn it, Dan, lie on the rug." She was furious.

"All right," he soothed. This was not the honeymoon he had envisioned; but he could hardly complain, could he? So his wife had some far-out notions.

He dropped to the foyer rug and held up his arms to her.

122

Fern lowered herself to him, drawing him within her.
"Give me a baby, Dan! Give me a baby!"

That was the only reason Fern married him. She wanted – just
once – to carry a child. She wanted no part of lovemaking. His
wife detested men. But she had an obsession to prove that she
could bear a child.

# Chapter Ten

Jan ordered herself to block Dan out of her mind. Whatever was to be for them would be. She wouldn't allow herself to think beyond the book. That was the crucial issue in her life at this point.

Each time she withdrew money from the bank, she felt fresh pain. How did she know that she could bring off this book? She was gambling with a huge chunk of money. The children's security and hers.

At other moments she charged ahead with exhilaration. Believing everything Craig promised – because she wanted to believe. Working harder than she had ever worked in her life.

No more socializing, she ordered herself. She could not afford distractions. Not now. Concentrate on work to the exclusion of everything else.

Now she encountered a segment of plot that wasn't right. Craig recognized it, too, without knowing how to change it. At last, at the point of panic – because she was exhausted, she solved the situation and moved ahead. But she would put Dan out of her mind. She wouldn't see him again. Wryly she remembered he'd made no suggestions about their doing something else.

Peggy could afford to socialize; she had alimony cheques coming in regularly. Ronnie could socialize; she had her steady paycheque. She, Janet Ransome, had to turn herself inside out to make this book into a potential bestseller.

On Wednesday morning Mike called. He explained he was

125

staying in town for the evening for a late meeting with a business associate.

"Take pity and have dinner with me tonight?" he invited. "I'll die of boredom if you don't. I've already read today's *Times*."

Jan hesitated. She'd vowed to stay with the book; no socializing. But how long would she spend with Mike before his appointment?

"What time and where?" she asked. The kids could have Chinese sent in. Dinner out would relax her. She was so ragged around the edges she'd almost had a fight with Craig last night.

To save time she met Mike at the Indian restaurant he had chosen. She suspected he felt uncomfortable at the prospect of picking her up at the apartment when Lisa and Brian knew he was married, knew Cecile and their daughters. Even though this was a totally innocent evening. Mike was killing time before he met his business associate. He'd go home and tell Cecile what they'd talked about over dinner.

Mike was a bright pause in her day, she thought while she laughed – with sympathy – at his stories of aborted attempts to make his first million. Yet Mike's optimism about the future never completely petered out.

"So I'm fifty-three and still trying," he chuckled. "I don't feel like fifty-three. I feel like thirty-three."

Only now did Jan confide in Mike about her efforts with Craig. It seemed less of a fantasy when she discussed it with Mike. She was astonished that Mike guessed she was a closet writer.

"Nobody's computer goes as many hours a day as yours did," he pointed out, "just to write complaint letters to department stores. The women figured you were trying to be another Margaret Mitchell, spending ten years on some historical novel."

"Me?" She'd thought they'd considered her mired down in cleaning that eleven-room house with no domestic help.

"You were always taking history books out of the library," he said. "The women noticed."

"I'm a history buff," she laughed. "It's my bedtime reading.

126

If this novels falls on its face, I'll probably be writing historical novels," she conceded. "That's basically what Craig is packaging now."

"What does a book packager do when he's not trying to bring in a bestseller?" Mike asked curiously. At odd intervals, Jan recalled, Mike talked about giving up his steady substantial income to become some sort of entrepreneur. The inclination never materialized; Mike had a household to support, two daughters soon to be heading for college. Unlike Tim, Mike had a strong sense of familial responsibility. She nurtured increasing respect for this inclination. "Is there any kind of security in packaging books?"

"A packager is basically an ideas man, a salesman, a promoter." Jan parroted Craig. "A couple of them have built up businesses that bring in high stakes. They sell a paperback house on a series, guarantee to deliver manuscripts ready to go to press. Then they go out and hire writers. Usually through agents. It becomes a factory. Writers are given tip sheets on how to handle the material. Sometimes they're even given outlines and research material."

"Next somebody will invent a computer that'll do the writing," Mike ribbed her. "Maybe that's a project for me. But why do paperback houses want these deals? It sounds to me like they're relinquishing a major function."

"They can cut down on staff, fringe benefits, even exist in smaller quarters. That's what Craig claims." She hesitated. "If our deal doesn't work out, Craig will throw me assignments. If I don't dry up after this book—" That was a frequent nightmare.

"I have great faith in you," Mike said confidently. "I've always known you were somebody special. You'll make it, baby. One way or another."

They dawdled over coffee. Mike had to meet a client arriving on an eight o'clock flight. He figured the client would be registering at the hotel shortly after nine. Then they'd closet themselves in a hotel room over drinks and do business.

"Don't miss the last train back to Katonah," Jan warned. She knew Mike left his car at the Katonah station. Tim had preferred to drive to New Canaan.

"I'm staying in town," Mike told her. "The corporation maintains an apartment on 38th Street off Third Avenue." He sighed. "The way they're looking for budget cuts, I don't know how long they'll keep the apartment."

She insisted Mike put her on the Lexington Avenue bus rather than into a taxi. The taxi habit was one to break until there was money coming in.

"Sure you'll be all right?" He was solicitous.

"Mike, it's only nine o'clock. You out-of-towners have a terrible concept of the city at night."

"I'll call you soon," he said as the bus came into view. "Thanks for keeping me company while I waited for my conference."

On the bus Jan debated about whether it was too late to go down to the basement to do the laundry. If she did the laundry tonight, she could work straight through tomorrow without a break. Groceries were on hand. Whatever was at the cleaner's could wait. Whenever she took off a couple of hours for pleasure, she felt a need to make up time on the book.

She left the bus at her stop and walked leisurely towards the apartment. Revelling tonight in being in the city. No place could be as stimulating as New York, even when she was on too tight a budget for the ballet or theatre or the opera. No time for museums. But just knowing they were within reach was reassuring.

Why had Tim insisted they always live in suburbia, in whatever city they happened to be? Because his wife and children were tucked conveniently away? She had been married to Tim for seventeen years, but she hardly knew him.

Her face brightened as she spied Dan emerge from a coffee shop twenty feet ahead of her. Her first instinct was to quicken her steps and call out to him. But he wasn't alone. He was with another man. From profile and attire Jan guessed that Dan's companion was quite young.

128

Jan slowed rather than accelerated her pace. Her writer's eye observed the tension in Dan's body; intuitively she knew this was a private moment between Dan and the tall, slight young man beside him.

Dan was talking earnestly. Jan saw him reach out a hand to the young man's arm. His companion pulled away. They continued to walk together, Dan absorbed in some point he was trying to make, his companion silent, with hands thrust into the pockets of his jacket, shoulders hunched in rejection of what Dan had said to him.

Her heart pounding Jan turned into the coffee shop from which Dan had just emerged. A sprinkling of patrons sat at the counter. A party of four women sat at a booth flanking the steamed-over window. She hesitated, abandoned her initial thought of sitting at the counter, which she always loathed doing. She slid into a small booth.

She was hardly hungry after dinner with Mike, but she ordered toasted pound cake and tea. Her ticket of admission to a few private moments. It was ridiculous for her to be so upset at seeing Dan with what Peggy called 'his gorgeous young boy'. She had misinterpreted Dan's interest in her. Like too many women alone she was vulnerable. She saw what didn't exist.

Did Dan think she was seeking a relationship with him? This humiliating possibility lent colour to her face. Last Saturday night he had kissed her and said she was a 'special lady'. But he had not asked her out again.

The conversation between the four women in the booth captured her attention. Two of them had been to a singles concert last week. One of them had left with a man. She was seeing him again on Friday.

"He's been divorced six years," a fifty-ish member of the quartet reported to the others. "He has a nice apartment. He says he's an accountant with a big firm. But he's been alone six years. If he's serious about getting married again, wouldn't you think he'd have found somebody by now?"

129

Always suspicions, Jan thought wryly. The second time around every woman – and man – was wary. Even while her mind rejected the presumption that Dan was gay, she couldn't brush the possibility from her thoughts.

She could have a pleasant friendship with Dan. Like with Craig. She valued Craig's friendship. Dan was drawn to her because he knew so few writers. That's all she was to Dan. A fellow writer with whom he could share stimulating shop talk. Writing was a lonely profession, though Dan was frank about saying his main profession was teaching. But he could hardly discuss his writing hurdles with his students.

She didn't have to stop seeing Dan. As long as it didn't interfere with her work. *If* he wished to see her again. But now she understood on what level their friendship was based.

Jan finished her cake and tea and headed home. Before she went to sleep, she'd do some revisions on that last scene. And tomorrow for sure she'd call Margrith of Switzerland and make an appointment to have her hair tinted and styled. Sometime next week she'd have it done, she stalled.

She was increasingly conscious that demands on her time would not be over when she handed over the completed manuscript to Craig. Once they had a book contract – and she prayed this would be fast – she'd be swallowed up in doing revisions.

She had to cut down on the money she was pulling out of the bank each month. Every time she walked into a supermarket she was conscious of how much more everything cost than she had anticipated. Even the price of jeans and sneakers was shocking.

Lisa and Brian were due for dental check-ups, harrowingly expensive these days. Thank God, they didn't need orthodontia, as she'd feared.

Had she jumped headlong into fantasy land with Craig? It was too late now to reverse her decision.

# Chapter Eleven

Jan was working on momentum. Pages were piling up, to Craig's vocal delight. She was so enmeshed in the novel that each day blended into another. She emerged from the apartment only to re-stock the refrigerator.

When Dan stopped by the apartment to bring her copies of his three collections of poetry, she invited him in for coffee, feeling this was obligatory.

"Another time," he said in gentle understanding. "I know you're in the middle of work." He hesitated. "Would you like to go to a gallery showing on Thursday evening? A friend of my sister's is having her first show at fifty-four. I don't know how good she is," he admitted, "but there are some interesting restaurants in SoHo."

"I haven't been down to SoHo since it became an 'in' place," she said. "It sounds like fun." *Where was her stern resolution to avoiding socializing until she was further along on the book*? But she was on schedule, she assuaged her guilt. And tomorrow was her appointment with Margrith. She'd try out the 'new look' on Dan.

Exhausted from her day's work but too stimulated to fall asleep immediately, Jan allotted herself a half hour's reading in bed. Settled for the night she reached for one of Dan's poetry collections. She was delighted with what she read, pushed the half hour to a full hour. Reluctantly she put aside the first of the three slim volumes. The alarm would be going off in seven hours. Without a decent night's sleep her production would suffer.

The next afternoon at two sharp – with four hours of writing behind her – she arrived at Margrith of Switzerland. She was enthralled by the attention and care given to choosing the proper tint for her hair. The same attention would be given to the styling. The cut, as Craig had ordered, must be one that she could manage without care.

Once the colour had been applied, she sat with a cup of coffee in hand and enjoyed this small segment of time when her sole concern was with her appearance. The whole deal was for business, yet she felt deliciously feminine and carefree.

"Jan?" Marianne Marlowe hovered before her. "I thought I saw you before, but you know my eyes. I have to be on top of somebody to recognize him." Marianne refused to wear glasses or contacts. Her 'eye lady' prescribed exercises. In addition to her eye lady she was in the care of a homeopathic physician who supplied her with a chest of pills, an aura lady, and an astrologist.

"Are you becoming acclimatized to New York again?" Jan asked. After eight months in Natchez, Brooklyn-born Marianne had acquired a Louisiana accent and mourned over the absence of black-eyed peas, pralines, and jambalaya.

"My apartment is a disaster." Marianne sighed and sat in the chair beside Jan. "I brought back trunks of books on Natchez and New Orleans. I want to write an historical set in pre-Civil War Louisiana. I'll have to unload a lot of things in my closets to make room. I've got some gorgeous dinner dresses I bought when I was living in Paris. I can't get into them now. You could," she decided triumphantly. "You're the only woman I know right now who's slim enough in the waist to get into them: I'm done—" She tentatively touched her freshly tinted near-black hair cut in an Edith Piaf hairstyle. "Run over to the apartment when you're finished here. I'll make you a cup of real New Orleans coffee." Marianne spilled over a potent charm. In her young days, before she allowed herself to acquire forty superfluous pounds and before her face began to droop, Marianne must have been a beautiful woman.

"I should go straight back to the computer," Jan said doubt-
fully. Marianne knew she was on a book. An as-yet-uncontracted
book, her mind mercilessly pinpointed.

"Another half hour won't put you off schedule." Marianne's
smile was dazzling. "Coffee from fresh ground beans," she
rhapsodized, "and laced with chicory."

"I'll come," Jan capitulated.

Marianne lived in Turtle Bay – a shabby, long and narrow
fifth-floor walk-up studio, overloaded with massive pieces of
furniture. Over the convertible sofa hung a huge painting, which
Jan did not immediately identify as a portrait of Marianne.

"That was done in Paris when I was living with him," Marianne
said casually and pointed to the signature. Jan's eyes widened.
The portrait must be worth a small fortune. "Of course, that
was twenty-eight years ago." Marianne's face reflected an inner
bewilderment and wistfulness.

Jan could read her thoughts. *Where had the years gone?* Two
bad marriages, two divorces. But most of the time Marianne
displayed a *joie de vivre* that was ingratiating. Despite being in
her mid-fifties, Jan thought, Marianne would not find a shortage
of men. Women like Marianne were born with built-in antennae.
Something not to be bought in a shop.

Marianne moved about the painfully cluttered apartment.
Putting up the coffee. Bringing out cups and saucers bought
at Tiffany's. A Waterford sugar bowl and creamer. Sterling that
glittered from earnest polishing. She had gathered together in
one sweep a collection of clothes scattered about the backs of
chairs and on the sofa, but not before Jan had noticed in surprise
the prestigious labels. Bill Blass, Oscar de la Renta, Giorgio,
Armani. In astonishing contrast to the meanness of her living
quarters.

Marianne and Jan were seated at the small antique table in
the dining corner and sipping their superb coffee when a knock
on the door intruded.

"Cornell?" Marianne asked with one hand on the top lock.

"Who else would come calling in the midst of the afternoon?" a musical male voice demanded, and Marianne opened the door with a welcoming smile.

"I know," she drawled and posed melodramatically. "You came to see how beautiful they made me at Margrith's."

Marianne drew Cornell into the room. He was a slim, aesthetic man of about thirty with a mass of auburn hair and striking blue eyes. Exactly Marianne's height, he appeared much taller. He was gay, Jan knew instantly.

Cornell posed before Marianne and inspected her hair in detail.

"Good," he approved, "but darling, I told you. With breasts like yours no bra!"

"I'm not wearing a bra," Marianne protested. "I stopped before I went down to Natchez." She made a pretence of pouting.

"Then unbutton the blouse," he clucked and reached to undo one button, then another. The silk blouse parted almost down to Marianne's naval.

Jan was uncomfortable while Marianne and Cornell sparred vocally. She was relieved when he took off for his own apartment.

"Cornell's an artist," Marianne confided. "He's into packaging right now. He's terribly talented. You wouldn't believe what he's done with his own apartment. Of course, I loathe his roommate," she said candidly. "He torments Cornell. He's bad for him. Before he took up with this creep, I had Cornell thinking in terms of going straight." Marianne was wistful. "That marvellous body. We made passionate love twice. Up to but not including penetration." Marianne was honest. "But since that asshole moved in, Cornell won't touch me." She shot a gamine grin at Jan. "Do I shock you?"

"No," Jan said quickly. She had listened often to Craig's tales of woe about his current lover without any self-consciousness, but Cornell and Marianne's romantic play disturbed her.

With Cornell gone Marianne made a foray into her wall of

closets. She pulled a grey satin and lace gown from a hanger and brought it to Jan.

"I could never get into it now," Marianne sighed. "It was a Schaparelli original."

"It's lovely," Jan said while Marianne held it against her ample body. The height of fashion, no doubt, in the early 1960s. "But that's about a twenty-two inch waist. Mine's almost twenty-five."

Marianne seemed startled, then pleased.

"Yes, I suppose it would be too small for you, too."

They talked for a while, Jan conscious of the passage of time. Then with a sense of guilt because she suspected Marianne wished her to stay longer, she excused herself and left.

Walking down the stark concrete stairs she heard Cornell's distinctive voice behind a second-floor door. He was talking to his roommate about 'Marianne's lovely new friend'. Needling him, Jan surmised, and hastened her steps.

Sitting on a south-bound bus Jan tried not to think of Dan with his 'gorgeous young boy'. To her it was still inconceivable that Dan was gay. Yet Peggy's friend in the building heard battles between Dan and the roommate he never mentioned. The intimacy between them when, unnoticed, she had come upon them on Third Avenue after having dinner with Mike, had been blatant.

Had Dan plummeted into a homosexual situation as a repercussion from his divorce? After all these years was he making an effort to go straight? All at once her head ached from these conjectures. She was fighting against believing that Dan was gay because, in a shockingly brief span of time, she could visualize herself in a lasting relationship with him.

\*    \*    \*

On Thursday evening Jan went for dinner with Dan to a restaurant in SoHo. He was taken aback when she insisted on paying her share.

"I invited you to have dinner with me." He stared at her in dismay.

"Dan, this is 1995." She strived for casualness. "Women pay their own way." Should she have paid her share of the cab fare?

"There are some aspects of women's lib that are foreign to me," he said after a moment. His smile was wry.

Except for the brief incident over the bill Jan enjoyed the evening. Dan was delighted that she praised his poetry with obvious sincerity. His face was incandescent when she quoted several favourite lines. She didn't have to lose Dan's friendship, she told herself. She must put it in its proper perspective.

They talked about the approaching Thanksgiving holidays. Jan debated inwardly about inviting him to Thanksgiving dinner at the apartment. How could she do it without inviting his friend? But Dan never mentioned having a roommate. On those times when they ran into each other at the elevator or on the street, Dan was always alone.

Then Dan told her he was spending the long holiday weekend with his sister and her family up in the country. Involuntarily she wondered if his friend would go with him. But that was none of her business. Dan and she were friends – not lovers. And she valued his friendship.

The approaching holiday made her conscious of Tim's absence. During the seventeen years of their marriage, Thanksgiving had always been a big day in the traditional manner. So that Lisa and Brian would be less conscious of their father's absence, she invited Ronnie, Deedee, and Peggy for Thanksgiving dinner.

Peggy was frank; it would be fun to have dinner with them, but Thanksgiving hardly turned her on. The whole deal was a bore, meant to keep wives in the kitchen. Hal was having dinner with his new girlfriend and her children. Her own sons were going home with college roommates.

Craig wasn't coming for dinner as expected. He had reconciled with his lover. They would have Thanksgiving with Oliver's parents. Belatedly Jan thought of Gail. She would phone Gail and invite her.

"Jan, you're a darling," Gail said with a rush of gratitude when Jan explained her mission. "But I'm having dinner with old friends up in Chappaqua."

Jan sat back and listened to Gail's current tale of woe. Carlos was reluctant to tie himself down to being with her on weekends.

"I don't need a boyfriend who's only available on Wednesdays. I could live without sex forever," she admitted. "I'm doing him a favour to sleep with him. But I detest being alone on weekends and holidays. I want a man around to take me out."

Gail and Peggy were sisters under the skin, Jan thought. Probably a lot of women were not hung up on sex. They needed companionship. For Gail and Peggy male companionship made them feel important.

In the initial shock of her own divorce she had convinced herself that sex was unimportant to her. For years now sex with Tim had been disappointing and frustrating. But in these past few weeks she was conscious of the lack of sex in her life. Even with the pace of her working days and evenings she felt the disturbing lack of a man in her bed.

\*     \*     \*

Jan awoke to the spectre of a cold and gloomy Thanksgiving day. But heat rose cosily in the radiators. Soon the apartment would be filled with the aromas of pumpkin pie and yams in the oven. By the time they were done – to be warmed up later – the turkey would be prepared for the oven.

First she went into Lisa's room, then Brian's to give them a ten minute wake-up warning, after which they were slated to help with dinner. She was determined they would not miss their father's presence today. Lisa was entrusted with the making of the pumpkin pie. Brian would help her with the tossed green salad and the buttermilk dressing.

Where was Tim spending the holiday? Despite her hurt and resentment she was concerned for his well-being. The habit of worrying about a man didn't die swiftly. But some day – not now – she would think dispassionately about Tim.

Jan was touched by nostalgia when she brought the turkey out of the oven. She remembered her first Thanksgiving as Tim's wife. She'd bought a turkey large enough for a small army because Tim kept adding to their list of guests. That year he could do anything he liked. God, she was in love with him then.

Dinner was a huge success, though Ronnie was irritated that Deedee insisted on eating and running. Peggy reported that she was having dinner the following evening with a man she had met through one of her personal ads. He had gone upstate to spend Thanksgiving with his elderly mother and two unmarried sisters.

"He used to be an alcoholic, but he's past that now," Peggy told them. "I had coffee with him yesterday. He had such sad eyes. I don't know what drove him into drinking. I know that he's suffered. There's something *nice* about this guy." She was in one of her effervescent moods. "He adores films and walking about the city and eating in good restaurants. Like me. I think this will work."

In the evening Jan returned to the computer. This was a good day, she congratulated herself. She had been oddly apprehensive about their first Thanksgiving away from Tim. Now the realization that Christmas was creeping up on them highlighted the passage of time. Already the shops were garbed for the Christmas season. Christmas would be tougher to survive than Thanksgiving. Let Tim remember to send gifts for the children.

Tim had always insisted on buying Lisa and Brian an avalanche of presents, most of which were broken within forty-eight hours.

Their bills in January were always stupefying. Not this coming January, she promised herself grimly. Lisa and Brian would have to understand.

On Monday morning Craig phoned to tell her that the two of them were to meet with Paula King for lunch on Wednesday. The deal was arranged. He was paying Paula a five thousand dollar advance – meagre for her.

"Plus a percentage," Craig reminded Jan. "She knows we've got a hot property. She loves the pages I showed her."

"Craig, you laid out five thousand dollars?" Jan was shaken. Craig was gambling on her bringing in a book that would make it big. A blockbuster. The pressure was suddenly suffocating.

"I'm seeing a lawyer about our incorporating. For this one book, since Paula's cut in for a share. But after this book she'll be on a straight fee basis."

"Craig, let's don't talk beyond this book. I can't cope." She shook her head in disbelief. Craig was light years ahead of her in his thinking.

"Unless my radar is shot, you can write a shopping list after this book, and it'll make the bestseller lists. Baby, sit down and take a look at the lists in the *New York Times Book Review* and in *Publisher's Weekly*. Once a writer makes the list, he's got a preferred place in the future. Check it out," he urged. "How many newcomers do you see each week? In most cases it's the oldies back for reruns."

"I'll have to make that trip down to Orchard Street with Ronnie tomorrow. To shop for an outfit." She was fighting off a bad attack of nerves. "Ronnie said she'd take a morning off to go with me unless her boards are shipping."

"Spend money," Craig exhorted. "When you walk into Le Perigord on Wednesday, I want Paula King to be impressed with your talk show potential."

At a few minutes past nine the next morning Jan and Ronnie boarded a Second Avenue bus and travelled down to Orchard Street. They located the unimpressive little store, where they had

139

to buzz for admission. As Craig's source instructed, they walked downstairs to the designer section.

Clothes hung on starkly plain racks. The coldness of the day was alleviated somewhat by an electric heater in the centre of the long, narrow room. No dressing rooms were provided. Already a tall, smartly coiffed woman in her fifties was trying on a Calvin Klein two-piece silk outfit.

Ronnie went to a line-up of suits and began to check the size fours. Sensing that Jan and Ronnie meant business, a saleswoman came over to tell them that a box of suits would be brought downstairs in just a few minutes.

"They're Oscar de la Renta," she confided. "Beautiful."

"I saw a gorgeous Oscar de la Renta suit in Saks," Jan remembered. "But it was a fortune. Anyhow, it was black. I can't wear black. I need something that'll fit in with my beige cashmere coat."

"Let's see what comes downstairs." Ronnie refused to be perturbed.

In a few minutes the saleswoman came downstairs with a brown kraft box in tow. She deposited it on the table near the stairs, pulled off the rope, and began to bring out the several suits neatly packed in the box.

"Ronnie, that's the suit I saw in Saks!" Jan's voice was electric. She could envision herself walking into Le Perigord wearing the black Oscar de la Renta! "But it'd be crazy for me to buy black."

"Try it on," Ronnie ordered.

Except for a need to shorten the skirt the suit was perfect. It could be worn with or without a blouse. Without, Jan decided. Her pearls – an unexpectedly extravagant Christmas present from Tim ten years ago – would be perfect.

"In late April I can wear it," Jan said in despair. "But not to Le Perigord tomorrow."

"I have an idea." Ronnie turned to the saleswoman. "Is there a phone in the store that I can use?"

"A pay phone," the saleswoman said. "Right at the top of the stairs."

"Ronnie, who are you calling?" Jan was bewildered.

"My ex-sister-in-law. I like her even though her brother's a heel. I'll borrow her chinchilla cape for you to wear to lunch with Paula King."

"Ronnie, fur?" Jan flinched. "You know I never wear fur!"

"You will, just this once," Ronnie wheedled. "It's for a good cause."

Jan and Ronnie left the store in ten minutes with the suit in tow. They pushed through the narrow crowded street, where merchandise was set up outside the stores to entice passers-by. They threaded their way to the purse shop. Jan paled at the price – even here – of the Judith Leiber purses she admired, but immediately discovered a smart black karung Morris Moskowitz she could handle. The chinchilla cape would be collected tonight and returned tomorrow afternoon.

*     *     *

Jan was a nervous wreck as she waited for Craig to pick her up for the luncheon date with Paula King. She inspected her reflection in the mirror a dozen times. With the cape. Without the cape. Either way, she conceded, she looked accustomed to money. It was a reassuring recognition.

Craig buzzed from downstairs. He was holding a taxi. She hurried to join him. They would shoot right up First Avenue to Le Perigord on East 52nd, Craig told her. They'd be there in a few minutes.

While they rode up First Avenue, Craig refreshed Jan's memory of Paula's background. She was the doyenne of women publicists specializing in the book field. Her own husband was a novelist whom she had lifted out of oblivion into the top ranks of commercial fiction.

"She's probably castrated the old boy," Craig guessed, "but

141

he's rich and castrated. Six months before he has a book coming out no wise author will hire her. She's a dynamo with one direction at that time. Happily he writes only one book in five years. She's clear for the next three."

Paula King was waiting for them at a secluded corner table. Craig had said she'd be there first. That was part of her image: to be enthroned when her luncheon partner or partners arrived. It was as though, Jan thought, she was granting an audience.

Although Paula was sitting, Jan knew that she was tall and pencil slim. She wore a black crêpe designer dress and half a dozen gold chains. Her features were sharply chiselled, her hair elegantly frosted.

Paula King poured forth charm with a generous hand. She spoke in superlatives, name-dropped with a machine-gun rapidity that made Jan dizzy. She was also a gossip. Jan suspected Paula King had nothing good to say about any writer other than her husband. Despite her aura of sophistication, she told stories about past and present clients with a lack of subtlety that disturbed Jan. What could Paula King spread around town about her once their deal was over?

Jan guessed that the smart professional woman exterior that Paula King presented to the public was a facade for a woman who was more comfortable in jeans and sweatshirt. That rather than dining at Le Perigord or The Four Seasons, she would prefer to sprawl in front of a TV set watching baseball with a six-pack of Budweiser close at hand.

Not until their chocolate mousses arrived did Paula settle down to business.

"You'll do fine, sweetie," she assured Jan. "You're damned attractive. You're bright. And you've got lots of energy. Starting next week I want you to spend an hour a week with this woman coach who works with some of my clients." Jan tensed; more money would go out. But Craig signalled that she was not to worry. "She'll teach you how to modulate your voice. How to give punch to key points on the talk show circuit. She'll even teach you how to apply TV make-up because a lot of times you'll be on your own. I like to start early with this so you're in condition when the time comes. It saves a lot of wear and tear on the nerves. Later I'll work with you. We'll set up anecdotes to use in the interviews. Background material about yourself that will interest women viewers or listeners. Remember, everything must sound spontaneous. But don't worry yet, Jan," she soothed because Jan looked stricken at the prospect of having to become a showbiz personality. "We won't get down to that for at least another six months. The book can't possibly be on the shelves for another sixteen months. You just keep writing. This may be a novel, but it's promotable. You've got something to say that millions of women – and men – want to hear."

*   *   *

All at once Christmas was breathing down Jan's neck. Again she was determined that Lisa and Brian would not feel the loss of a father in the household. Damn Tim! Why couldn't he at least let them know where he was living? If need be, she'd send him money to shop for presents for the children.

The week after her luncheon with Paula – whom Ronnie referred to as The Presence – Jan began the coaching with Anne Raynor. She was learning to breathe from the diaphragm and to practice meditation. At Anne's stern orders she began a wake-up programme of setting-up exercises that fascinated Lisa and Brian. But not sufficiently for them to accept her invitation to make it a three-person programme.

Two weeks in a row she met Mike for lunch. Occasionally she encountered Dan in the building or on the street. Once they went to Cosmos for carrot cake and coffee. He was distracted and apologetic. She told herself she must stop feeling like a sixteen-year-old on the threshold of first love each time she was in Dan's presence.

She allowed herself no other socializing. The way the work was

143

going she expected to finish the book by the end of January. She wrote by day, revised by night. Already, Craig reported jubilantly, the ball was rolling. His father's friend had 'leaked' word that the bank was involved with a possible package on a first novel called *The Second Time Around*.

Ten days before Christmas Craig phoned to say that his father's banker friend had been approached by an independent film producer who asked to see the material. If it was right for a star he had under contract, they might have a movie sale even before the novel was finished.

"Oh, Craig!" Jan was awed.

"Don't expect this to go through overnight," Craig warned. "They could keep us dangling for four or five months and then drop it. But the momentum has started. That's what counts, darling."

Jan was trembling when she put down the phone. But everything was 'iffy', she reminded herself. Her stomach churning she went into the kitchen to put up water for tea. How could she sit right down to work after what Craig had just told her?

While she waited for the water to boil, she was jarred by another telephone intrusion. Mornings like this she wished she had the guts to turn on the answering machine.

"Hello."

"You sound uptight," Mike sympathized.

"I am," she admitted. "This whole crazy scene is sending me up the wall."

"Have dinner with me tonight and let's talk about it. Seven o'clock okay?"

"Fine," Jan said. "But expect me to be in a vile mood."

They talked a few minutes more. Then she went back into the kitchen to prepare a pot of tea. Days like this she drank non-stop. She was just pouring a cup for herself when the doorbell rang. It had to be Peggy; George was unfailing about announcing visitors. She went to the door and pulled it open.

144

"Can you take off a few minutes?" Peggy was agitated. "I know you're working—"

"I'm taking a tea break. Come on in." Jan smiled in reassurance. She knew Peggy would stay only a few minutes. Peggy was conscientious about not intruding on her working hours. What did Peggy do with her days? She wasn't painting. She admitted to being a slapdash housekeeper. How many hours a day could she shop? "How's the great outside world?" Jan crossed to the kitchen.

"I'm so upset." Peggy hovered at the door to the kitchen. "I've been seeing this guy, you know. Arnold." She frowned. "I never call him Arnie – we both hate that. He's the one who's made it off the booze," she reminded. "He's fifty and nice looking. He teaches at some posh private school uptown. I know he doesn't make a lot of money so he takes me out one night and I make dinner for us the next time we see each other. And he knows I can't stand being rushed into bed. I saw him six times – twice at my apartment – before I said I'd sleep with him."

"How was it?" Jan asked gently. Was Peggy upset at sleeping with somebody other than her husband?

"He couldn't," Peggy blurted out. "He broke down and cried. And then he said we shouldn't see each other again. My God, Jan, he's only fifty!"

"He was humiliated." The years were rough on a man in the singles scene, too, after a certain age.

"I was sympathetic. I told him it wasn't the end of the world. But he didn't want to hear. I didn't honestly care," Peggy said. "I liked it when he kissed me and held me. It was enough to think that he cared for me. But you know what he said? 'All women care about is a stiff prick.' "

"Write him off," Jan urged. "You'll never change his thinking."

"I'll keep on running the ads," Peggy said vigorously. "And there was an overnight Party Cruise advertised in the *Times* again. A group for 18–35 and one for 35 plus." There must be

145

*Julie Ellis*

a total absence of thirty-five-year-olds on the singles scene, Jan thought with a flicker of humour. How would they decide which way to go? "They have planned activities on the cruises so everybody gets to meet one another. They even have the seating broken down by age groups. Sounds like it could be fun." Already Peggy was bouncing back.

"Be careful," Jan pleaded. Probably most of the men Peggy met would be lonely and searching like herself – but there was always the chance that there would be one psychotic.

Jan served an early dinner to Lisa and Brian and hurried to shower and dress. She enjoyed the brief private time under the hot spray, where thoughts of the book were pushed aside; and she looked forward to dinner with Mike. He must have another of those late conferences. He said he'd be staying over at the corporate apartment.

Tonight she spent a shockingly long time on her make-up. She couldn't go right out after a shower on a cold night like this, she excused her dawdling. The restaurant Mike had chosen was a charmingly informal neighbourhood place – she wouldn't have to dress. She chose a black wool skirt and a frilly lilac blouse that Anne Raynor said made her eyes look more green than hazel.

When she bought the skirt two years ago, it was faintly tight at the waist. But for a Calvin Klein skirt on sale for one-third its normal price she would put up with minor discomfort. Now the skirt fit perfectly. She still marvelled that her fifteen-minute-a-morning exercise programme had lessened her waist dimensions, tightened her tummy.

With time on her hands before she was to meet Mike she decided to walk. In her down coat bought three years ago she would be warm enough despite the sharp drop in temperature. The cold night air would be invigorating.

She walked swiftly up Third Avenue with a pleased awareness of the festive, close-to-Christmas mood. The shop windows were colourful in Yuletide garb. She was glad that she had shopped

146

early for Lisa and Brian's modest Christmas gifts. She pretended not to intercept their furtive conferences about gifts for her. They would have a plastic tree because the three of them were appalled at the cutting down of live trees for such a purpose. She had brought in a box of tree trimmings from the house.

*Where was Tim? Why didn't he write to Lisa and Brian? Would he send presents for the kids?*

Jan arrived at the restaurant with her usual punctuality. Mike, who relished the cold, was waiting outside for her. Taking her hand he walked into the restaurant with her. He asked the hostess to seat them at a private corner table.

Jan liked the restaurant for its ambience as well as its food. To dine here amidst the huge pots and hanging baskets of greenery was like dining in a gazebo. She admired the summery air of the cane-backed chairs, the light woods of chairs and tables and floors. It was the kind of place where Mike seemed to relax.

He was a quiet, comfortable man with whom to share an evening. She had recognized that long ago. She felt no pressures in Mike, though God only knew the demons he kept locked within himself. A man with his creative energy could hardly be phlegmatic.

Mike ordered glasses of sherry for them. Then they concentrated on choosing dinner. Jan settled for the carrot soup and a spinach quiche, which she knew from past experience would be excellent. Tonight Mike was content to order the carrot soup, on Jan's advice, along with a hamburger and salad.

"We'll worry about dessert later," he decided with a grin. Jan knew his penchant for sweets.

While they waited to be served, Jan brought Mike up to date on what she called the Ransome-Yarbrough Circus. He surprised her with his comprehension of what happened in publishing.

"Look, they're selling a product. The days of Maxwell Perkins are long gone. It's the bottom line that counts. Do you know what it costs to run a full-page ad in the *New York Times Book Review*? A publisher can ship an author on a ten-city tour for less." He grinned. "I'll have to bring in a small TV to the office so I can catch you on daytime shows."

"Mike, this whole thing could fall apart." For a moment Jan was weighed down by depression. "It's a total gamble."

"You've got some sharp characters on your team," he consoled. "And I'm rooting for you." His hand reached out to close over hers. For an instant she saw arousal in his eyes and was startled. "It'll work, honey."

"I keep telling myself that."

She was unnerved by the sudden erotic feeling that bound them together at this moment. Relief brushed her when she saw the waiter approaching their table. Mike withdrew his hand and leaned back in his chair.

Over dinner Mike talked about office problems. There was some heat on because of his refusal to move to the San Francisco offices. He didn't like the prospect of switching the girls to another high school. Next year his older daughter would be a senior, the younger a junior.

"I don't want to leave New York," Mike said. His eyes held hers. The message was unmistakable. He didn't want to put three thousand miles between them.

Jan lowered her eyes in sudden confusion. Up till now Mike and she had enjoyed a feeling of camaraderie. This was new. *But Mike was married.* Yet from subtle hints that she had, up till now, ignored, she knew Mike and Cecile shared an open marriage. She was sure Mike had been in and out of affairs for years. Why had she been so naive as not to understand where he was leading her?

Over coffee and dessert Mike seemed to grow tense. He was gearing himself for his meeting, she supposed.

"What time is your evening appointment?" she asked.

"I have no appointment tonight." His hand reached across the table for hers. "Just us."

She hesitated. In this split second their relationship was changing.

"Mike, are you making a pass at me?" she asked unsteadily.

"I'm sure trying." His smile was lopsided. "I haven't rushed you. This hasn't been a singles bar pick-up. Jan, I want to make love to you so bad." His eyes pleaded with her.

"I must have been so dense—" Conflicting emotions chased through her. She knew that she would enjoy making love with Mike. It was something they both needed. "But Cecile—"

"I figured you knew. Cecile goes her way, I go mine. She has her part of the house, I have mine. We're solid friends, but that's all there's been between us for years."

"I wouldn't want anybody to get hurt, Mike," she said.

All at once Mike's face was incandescent.

"Nobody," he vowed, squeezing her hand.

"Where?" she asked after a moment. She recoiled from the prospect of going with Mike to a hotel. They couldn't go to her apartment.

"I have the keys to a place right here in the neighbourhood." He was looking around for their waiter. Impatient now to leave the restaurant.

"That corporate apartment?" *What am I doing? I'm out of my mind! But why shouldn't I have an affair with Mike if nobody is hurt?*

"The company dropped the apartment," Mike explained. "I have the key to an apartment that belongs to an old friend who's away. It's been sublet, but the new tenant won't move in until the first of January." He smiled in satisfaction. "It's ours till then."

Jan was cold despite the warmth of the restaurant. Waiting for Mike to pull a credit card from his wallet to pay the cheque, all at once the mechanics of the situation were unnerving. Mike and she would go into a strange apartment, make love in a strange bed. But it wasn't as though Mike was some man she had picked up at that singles concert or through an ad. She'd known Mike for years, talked to him almost every day.

She had never in her life slept with anybody but Tim. She'd

feel self-conscious admitting that to anybody. She was an anachronism.

"Let's go," Mike said softly and rose from his chair.

His arousal was contagious. She was conscious of a response within herself as they walked from the restaurant. She was a divorced woman. She had a right to make love with Mike. Then why did she feel so splashed with guilt?

While Mike talked about casual office happenings, making them sound humorous, Jan remembered what Ronnie said that night they had encountered Mike in Howard Johnson's. *'Mike has a thing for you.'* And then when they were in the taxi. *'He's going to make a pass. You could have a fun affair with him.'*

For some absurd reason Jan was glad this was a building without a doorman or a manned elevator. They sped up to the sixth floor one-bedroom apartment, which was a replica of thousands in so-called luxury buildings scattered around Manhattan. The furnishings were casually attractive.

A glance into the small bedroom showed a queen-sized bed, a chest of drawers, and a dressing table. A woman's bedroom, Jan recognized.

"Let me take your coat, Jan."

"Why not if we plan to stay a while," she laughed. Trying to sound cool and sophisticated. She was here with Mike in a borrowed apartment, where they meant to make love. Why did it seem so tawdry?

Mike had been here often. It was an apartment that belonged to a woman with whom he'd had an affair. There was never a corporate apartment. Now the woman had been transferred to another city, and Mike had turned to her.

"I've waited a long time for tonight." Mike pulled her into his arms and kissed her.

Jan's arms closed in about his shoulders as he poured his mouth into hers. She responded with a passion she had feared was dead in her. This wasn't Janet Ransome; this was some woman in a

150

novel she was writing. For an instant she considered running out on this unfamiliar scene.

Mike's mouth left hers to brush her throat while his hands familiarized themselves with her slender yet curvaceous frame. She closed her eyes. Giving herself up to sensual emotions. Refusing to think.

"We don't have to stay out here," he murmured, holding her tightly against him.

"No," she agreed. Aware of the hardness of him that clamoured to be within her. "No," she said forcefully.

Hand in hand they walked into the bedroom. She would not allow herself to dwell on the knowledge that Mike and the woman who'd lived here had shared that bed. The faint scent of a perfume she could not identify still lingered in the room.

Mike switched on a lamp beside the bed. Why couldn't he leave the room in darkness?

"You're beautiful," he said. "I used to look forward to seeing you each morning when I jogged. It was my beautiful sight for the morning." His hands were fumbling with the tiny buttons of her blouse.

"I'll do them," she said because he was having difficulty.

How weird to be standing here with Mike and taking off her clothes. She slid the blouse from her shoulders. All at once self-conscious at standing here in her lilac satin bra while Mike stripped down to shorts without allowing his eyes to leave her. She unzipped her skirt and stepped out of it. Her heart was pounding now.

She stood uncertainly in her sheer black pantyhose over the lilac satin hiphuggers that Lisa had given her on her last birthday because they looked 'so sexy'. *This was unreal*. Mike ripped off his jockey shorts that had not masked his readiness for bed. Seeing him stand there – tall, lean, and ready – she tensed with anticipation. Mike wouldn't stop in the middle of making love to watch TV.

151

"You look like a poster for a very sexy movie," he commented and pulled her to him.

For a moment they were content to sway together cheek to cheek. Savouring the feel of each other. Then his hands reached for the hooks of her bra. He pulled the straps down from her shoulders and tossed the scrap of lilac satin across to the chest of drawers.

Mike's mouth sought hers again while his hands caught the lush spill of her breasts. He caressed them with a sensuous, searching movement that evoked a surge of passion in her. In seventeen years of marriage Tim had never realized how much this excited her.

"You're overdressed," Mike chided after a few moments.

She stood with her head thrown back, lost in exquisite emotions too long quiescent while he peeled away her pantyhose along with the hiphuggers. Yet a tiny crevice of her mind insisted on being an observer. That part could not totally accept her being in a strange room alone with Mike Blume. This woman was a character in a novel she was reading – or writing.

Then Mike pulled a curtain against the observer. She murmured approval as his mouth burrowed first at one nipple, then the other; and his hands rippled over her warm, responsive body. She wasn't thirty-eight and blasé about sex tonight; she was seventeen and wildly passionate.

In one swift gesture he lifted her from her feet and deposited her on the bed. What woman – from the time of Eve until the present – did not respond to this act of love? Her arms reached up to him as he lowered himself above her. By now her earlier self-consciousness had evaporated. She couldn't wait to receive Mike within her.

Mike probed between her thighs. How long it had been since she felt this way! Now he drove within her with eager, impatient thrusts. A low sound of excitement escaped her and was echoed in him. They clung together. Moved together. The room reverberated with the sounds of their pleasure.

152

"Oh, God," he gasped when they touched and exploded in a final, simultaneous climax. "Oh, God, that was wonderful!"

Afterwards Jan lay with her head on Mike's chest. One slender leg thrown across his. His arm about her.

"I feel great," he said complacently. "I could stay like this forever."

Mike made her feel like a woman again. She wouldn't think about where they were headed. They would take one day at a time.

153

# Chapter Twelve

Not until the children were off to school and she was sitting down with the second cup of coffee that always preceded her morning's stint at the computer did Jan allow her thoughts to focus on last evening. It had been good for both Mike and her. And nobody would be hurt, she assuaged her puritanical conscience. Neither of them would allow that to happen.

She went into the kitchen to rinse the cup that would serve her for the day's intake of coffee, alternating with tea, when the phone jarred the comfortable oasis of silence. She hurried into the living-room. At this hour of the morning the caller could be only Craig or Peggy.

From habit her voice was cheery, though she felt subconsciously harried. She nurtured every minute of her working time at this period in the book.

"Hello—"

"Merry Christmas, Jan."

Tim's confident, charismatic voice jolted her into the past. All the intervening months seemed to disappear. Her mind was a kaleidoscope of images. Tim and that girl naked on the bed. Tim behind the wheel of his car that morning when he drove out of their lives.

"Merry Christmas, Tim." Her heart pounded. They had not received even a card from Tim for weeks. Why hadn't he called later in the day, when the children would be home? In California it was 5.30 a.m., she computed with a start. "How are you?" She recoiled from the need to make small talk with Tim.

*Julie Ellis*

"Good." He was irritatingly casual. "How are the kids?"

"They're fine. Counting the days till school holidays." Playing the civilized divorced wife when her instinct was to scream at him: *"Why don't you write to the kids? Then you'd know how they are."* Had he sent Christmas presents? This was Tuesday already. Only three more days for presents to arrive. "They're at school now, of course." Why had he called? Because it was easier than sending a Christmas card? They had not sent him a card – they had no permanent address.

"I've been in LA for a month. The weather's gorgeous out here. I have a tan you wouldn't believe." He hadn't called three thousand miles to talk about his tan. Did he want to come back? The involuntary question jolted her. Did she want Tim to come back to them?

"We've had some early snow." Her throat went dry as her mind tried to deal with this situation. *No.* She didn't want Tim to come back into their lives. It wouldn't be good even for the kids.

"I've got a great deal coming up." Tim was ebullient. "Top job with lots of perks. The kind of set-up I've always been after." How many times he had made this same pronouncement!

"That's marvellous, Tim." Don't let him say he wants to come back. I don't want him back. "Is the job in California?"

"Up in San Francisco. Wonderful city. Cosmopolitan. Casual. My kind of town." He cleared his throat. Jan stiffened. She knew that little sound so well. He was working himself up to say something she would hate. "Only problem, I have to fly up there and see this guy. I may have to do some entertaining. You know how it goes. Jan, I need a fast five hundred. I can get it back to you by the middle of February. But I have to have it right away."

"You know what the mails are like this time of year." Relief surged through her; he wasn't trying to come back into their lives. "But frankly, Tim," she forced herself to continue, "I did badly with the house. Money is tight—"

"I'll get it back to you in six weeks." He was trying to sound

156

matter-of-fact, but she heard the impatience seeping into his voice. "Hell, Jan, you can't have gone through all the house money. I went out and bought presents for the kids – I didn't realize I'd have to make this trip. You know, air fare, two or three nights at a decent hotel, and taking the guy out to dinner. I need that extra five hundred for a cushion." He must have sensed her indecision. "Get a bank cheque and send it Express Mail. I'll have it first thing in the morning. I'll take an early afternoon flight. I have to sew this up before Christmas."

Angry with herself for capitulating, Jan agreed to send Tim the cheque. She still had not broken the habit of worrying about him. A seventeen year habit didn't die easily.

Maybe she'd see that five hundred again. If he did land a substantial job, she could ask for child support, she excused her parting with the money. *But this would be the only time.*

With a triumphant grin Tim set down the phone. Tomorrow morning this time he'd have five hundred dollars to blow. He'd buy Anita that sequined jumpsuit she saw over on Rodeo Drive. She'd really flipped for it. When she knew that would be under her little Christmas tree, she'd stop making cracks about his looking for a job.

He rose to his feet and started to strip. Glancing with pride at his trim, tanned body – the pot belly gone now. He was whistling when he opened the bathroom door. Anita was still under the shower.

"Hey, baby, you staying in there all day?"

"It's night for me," she reminded. "I just got home from work an hour ago."

"Move over," he ordered and reached to slide the glass door to allow his entry. "You know that sequined jumpsuit you're so mad about?" he said, stepping into the tub, reaching with one hand to fondle her curvaceous wet rump. "The one in that boutique on Rodeo Drive—"

"What about it?" Anita swivelled her head towards him.

"I'm buying it for you for Christmas," he drawled.

Anita leaned forward to turn off the spray. The water gushed into the tub, almost drowning out her voice as she spun around to face him.

"Tim, it cost four hundred dollars!"

"Shall I pick it up blind, or do you want to go over and try it on?" Later today he'd drive over to Magnin's and pick up some stuff for the kids. Something small that could be shipped out Express Mail at the minimum rate and arrive in time.

"Honey, I'll try it on." Anita slid her wet arms about his shoulders and nuzzled her hips to his. "But first, let me try on something else—" Her hand moved between them and found its quarry. Tim grunted appreciatively.

"Let's get out of here first before we slide and break our necks." Anita might look sometimes at those twenty-year-old beach characters who swaggered about in crotch-huggers, but he knew how to keep her happy. It wasn't how many times a night they did it. It was *how*. Tim Ransome was a master.

Today Jan was having difficulty piling up the normal amount of pages. Talking to Tim had upset her. Her whole life had been turned upside down in these last six months. When had she stopped loving Tim? Today, talking with him over the phone, she was certain that she didn't love him.

She wasn't in love with Mike. But Mike was great for her morale. It was fun to be with him. With Mike she could ignore – or pretend to ignore – her feelings for Dan. What was going to be with Dan? She didn't dare dwell on this.

Dan never invited her down to his apartment. She had never encountered the boy that lived with him, except for that one night on the street. Dan never mentioned him. But she never said no when Dan phoned and suggested coffee.

And he didn't say no the twice she had impulsively asked him up for dinner with Lisa and herself when Brian was off at a friend's house. Lisa enjoyed his gentle teasing, his interest in her school activities.

Were the others right – and she wrong – about Dan? Was he trying to go straight? Sometimes he looked at her as though he was dying to make love to her. He never made a move.

She felt a warmth and a tenderness in Dan that was beautiful. Some men who played the gay scene for a while went straight again. It did happen. He said his divorce was ugly; that could have sent him in the other direction. If he was gay now and wanted to go straight again, could she accept that? It was a disturbing question. *Was he all right*? The AIDS situation was scary.

Impatient with herself and restless, Jan left the computer and crossed to the wide picture window. She spied Dan emerging from a taxi. He was staring at his watch. He was supposed to leave on an afternoon flight to Phoenix, she remembered. He was spending three weeks with his parents. Those brief periods – almost daily now – when she had coffee with him had become astonishingly important. She felt a sense of loss at his prospective absence.

The ringing of the phone brought her back from the window. Gail was calling. Ostensibly on business. Actually Gail wanted a listening ear. She had broken off with Carlos. Jan suspected Carlos had called off the deal. Gail's demands turned him off. Now Gail was seeing a sixty-ish stockbroker with an eighty-four-year-old mother in Queens. Jerry's mother expected to be called daily and taken to dinner every Sunday evening.

"His mother is a bitch," Gail said. "Like Wednesday night. We're in the middle of sex, and all of a sudden he says, 'Oh, God, I forgot to call my mother!' As though the world would collapse if he forgot one night."

"He knows she depends on him," Jan soothed.

"I'm tired of wives and mothers who take precedence over me. He's been married and divorced twice. All right, his last wife died when they'd been married just three months," Gail conceded. "But this old bitch wants him dancing attendance on her all the time. Why can't I see him on some Sundays?"

"Talk to him," Jan encouraged. "Maybe he can switch nights." She was uptight at being tied to the phone when she should be at the computer, but she remembered the terrified little girl who spent a childhood with constantly zonked parents. Gail was still pathetically looking for love.

Dan moved about the apartment, making the necessary last minute checks. The refrigerator was turned off and the door ajar. He'd taken the contents to Jan, though she insisted she'd hold the frozen stuff pending his return. Lisa would come down to water the plants. The gas was turned off. The windows closed. The blinds partially drawn.

"Keith?" He tried not to sound annoyed at Keith's dawdling. "Remember, we have a plane to catch."

"I'll be right there," Keith called back in that calm, deliberately detached fashion that was more upsetting than his outbursts of anger.

In a few moments they were at the elevator with their luggage. Maybe in Arizona Keith – and he – would unwind. Maybe they could fight their way out of this mire of silent hostility that threatened to pull them into unbearable depths.

In the cab en route to JFK for their four thirty flight to Phoenix, Keith buried himself in a paperback. Dan leaned back, stared out at the passing streets without seeing them, visualizing instead Jan's lovely, expressive face. Through the years he thought he had convinced himself he didn't need a woman in his life. In the first eighteen months after the divorce he had had two casual affairs with women in his academic world. Then he'd shied away from any but the most casual relationship.

What was it that made Jan so irresistibly attractive to him? It wasn't just that she was beautiful. He'd met other beautiful women. She was completely feminine, he analysed, yet he felt she could take whatever knocks life threw in her path and not knuckle under – and that was an admirable combination. She was a writer, therefore creative. That drew him to her. She was warm and tender. And she had guts. No crying about having to support herself and two kids. Janet Ransome was a rare woman. But there was no room in his life for a woman.

Dan was relieved when they were at last airborne – the plane lightly populated. The hours in flight were always, for him, a period of release. He allowed his thoughts to dwell on Sedona, a hundred miles above Phoenix, where his parents had retired twelve years ago.

Dan's face softened in recall. Once a year he made the trek to Sedona. This year he was sandwiching in this second trip in hopes that Sedona and Grey Creek Canyon – nature's mammoth sculpture in magnificent shades of terracotta, gold, and silver – might do for Keith what it always did for him in times of stress. Sitting on the deck of his parents' small house that nestled into the red earth so that it was hardly visible, he gazed at the awesome beauty wrought over 280 million years, and his problems seemed minuscule and fleeting. There he became, like the Canyon, timeless.

"When do we reach Phoenix?" Keith interrupted his reverie.

"Seven thirty Phoenix time," Dan told him. "If you're not starving, we'll have dinner at The Hideaway in Sedona. You've always liked eating there," Dan cajoled. "Lasagna, an antipasto, a garden salad, and wine," he tempted. "This time you're old enough to have wine," he chuckled. "We'll eat by candlelight on the balcony." With a breathtaking view of Grey Creek Canyon on display before them.

"I haven't been in Sedona these last two summers," Keith reminded, and stared quizzically at him. "I never understood how you let Mother get away with that."

"How could I deprive you of two summers in Europe?" Dan said wryly. "You don't know how I missed our usual summers with your grandparents. They missed you, too."

161

Keith avoided his eyes.

"I thought you were glad to be off the hook."

"Keith, how could you think that?" Dan fought to keep his voice low lest other passengers – though seated rows away from them – should overhear their suddenly personal conversation. He had never given Keith any reason to believe that!

"You didn't fight for custody when Mom and you were divorced," Keith shot at him. Keith thought he had been content to walk out of his life? Keith didn't know what a wrench that had been. "You gave me up except for summers. Mom said you didn't fight."

"Your mother wasn't entirely truthful. I fought for custody until she convinced me that a child belongs with its mother. I wanted you with me, Keith. I wanted that in the worst way. But it was the natural thing to allow you to remain with your mother."

"Knowing what you knew about Mom?" Keith shot back. A vein throbbed in his forehead. His dark eyes, so like Dan's, were pained. "When I picked up the newspaper and saw that story—" Keith paused, shook his head as though to brush away the memory. "I left the campus and flew home. I was sure the newspapers were lying. But Mom didn't deny it!"

Dan winced. He would never wash from his memory that night last October when Keith burst into his apartment and thrust that newspaper headline before him: 'WOMAN PSYCHOLOGIST SUED BY PATIENT'S HUSBAND'. Two columns had spewed forth the sordid details of Fern's love affair with a young wife who had come to her for treatment. Neither Fern nor her patient denied the allegations.

"All right, Keith. I'll tell you how it was." For the first time he was being completely honest with his son. "I made a deal with your mother. She promised that if I let her have custody of you, she'd be silent about her sexual inclinations." He was perspiring, though the temperature in the cabin was comfortable. "She agreed not to share the house with her lover. The relationship would be kept under wraps. Remember, she asked for the divorce eleven years ago – at a time when a lot of gay people were coming out of the closet. She was determined to do the same. I was terrified of your being exposed to that kind of trauma. It frightened the hell out of me. How could a sensitive nine-year-old child cope?"

"You shouldn't have let her take me!" Keith reiterated.

"Keep your voice low," Dan admonished. Why did Keith pick this moment for a confrontation? All these weeks they had dodged the real issue. He had fought with Keith to return to college. Keith kept refusing. He sat around the apartment and seethed in silence. After the first few days of ugly recriminations against his mother, he retreated into that frightening, stubborn silence. "I did what I was sure was best for you. I was buying you a normal childhood. Your mother always provided a good home for you. In all the years you never suspected she – was a lesbian. She gave you a normal upbringing – that was our deal. Maybe I was wrong." Dan felt drained. "Maybe I had no right to keep your mother in the closet. Maybe it wasn't fair to her. But it seemed to me that the well-being of our child took precedence over what was right for us."

Keith's eyes were bitter and accusing.

"She never should have had a child."

"Don't ever think that, Keith," Dan objected gently. "Your mother gave me the greatest gift of my life. My son."

The stewardesses were coming down the aisles with dinner trays. Of necessity their conversation was silenced. But Dan was relieved that he had been able to speak honestly with Keith.

He had never suspected that Keith resented being left with his mother except for Christmas holidays and summer vacations. He had phoned every week, flew out for Keith's birthday. How awful that his son had felt himself abandoned by his father.

Maybe in Sedona he could convince Keith to go back to school. Keith had planned since he was twelve on going to law school. Somehow, he must help Keith through this period and back to the normal path.

Through the years – while he could never totally erase from his mind the ugliness of his marriage – he had come to respect Fern. She knew what way of life was right for her. When Keith entered school, she had gone back to acquire her Master's and then her PhD in psychology. She'd fought to get ahead professionally, but she had been a good mother, too. Now, God knows, she had earned the right to live openly as she wished. It would be difficult, but he prayed that Keith would come to understand. Until he did, there would be no peace for Keith or himself.

# Chapter Thirteen

Jan was impatient for Christmas to be out of the way. She had told Lisa and Brian that their father had phoned from California. Then she was sorry she had told them. They were disappointed and hurt that he had not thought to phone when they would be in the apartment. She had refrained from explaining that the call had been motivated by his request for money.

When two inexpensive gifts for the children arrived – the Express Mail charge was almost as expensive as each gift – she understood they had been bought after she had agreed to send Tim the five hundred. But that was the end of the line, she reiterated. Any further calls for money would be rejected.

On Christmas Eve the children and she decorated the plastic tree that Lisa and Brian had chosen at Woolworth. Ronnie and Deedee, along with Peggy and Gail, came over for Christmas dinner. The apartment ricocheted with laughter and holiday spirits, but Jan sensed that Lisa and Brian were comparing this Christmas with earlier ones and found this one lacking.

Why was it that holidays emphasized Tim's absence from their lives? But she would not spend the rest of her life feeling guilty because Lisa and Brian were deprived of a father in their home. Tim made the choice. Perhaps her guilt was enhanced because she knew the change – for her – was for the better.

In the evening Marianne, spilling over with her usual charm, dropped in with presents for Lisa and Brian.

"Nothing fancy, sugar," she told Jan while the two kids

unwrapped the whimsical gifts. "Just some things I've picked up along the road."

"You're just in time for left-over-from-dinner turkey and plum pudding," Jan said with obvious welcome. Ronnie, too, had brightened at Marianne's appearance from a day with her sister. Gail and Peggy had been taking slightly veiled pot shots at each other since their respective arrivals.

Now an air of conviviality permeated the apartment. Only Peggy remained grim. It took Jan aback to realize that Peggy was irritated to comprehend the possible returns if Craig was right about *The Second Time Around.*

Lisa and Brian disappeared with Deedee into Lisa's room to listen to CDs. Gail was the first to leave. She was hoping Jerry would call before the evening was over.

"He might remember when he gets back from Queens. He took his mother to spend Christmas day with family." Her heavily mascara'd eyes were resentful. "Wouldn't you think he would have invited me, too? His family wouldn't have objected if he brought a girl along." Involuntarily Jan flinched. She recoiled each time Gail referred to herself as a girl.

"Men have a way of keeping their love life apart from 'old friends'," Ronnie pointed out. "I haven't met one of Lenny's friends yet. He told me about his birthday. I even bought him a birthday present. But I didn't see him that day." Her smile was wry. "I probably won't even see him for New Year's Eve. He'll be spending it with his 'old crowd'. Sometimes I feel like saying, 'So sleep with your old crowd'. But I don't," Ronnie said philosophically. "It's the old story. Half a loaf is better than none."

When Gail had left, Marianne kicked off her shoes and stretched out on the love seat. Peggy explained again why she had not gone to spend Christmas day with her two sons, home from college, and her ex-husband.

"Even though Hal's girlfriend took her kids home to her parents' house, I couldn't bear spending a whole day out there.

It's too depressing. I'm so glad I'm out of that." But Peggy wasn't happy. She still hadn't found a man. Or fame. She seethed over her lost career as an artist.

"Marianne, I made an appointment for you with Dr Swan," Ronnie reminded. "Next Tuesday at three. Don't you dare forget."

Marianne sighed.

"I'm only doing this because you're holding a knife at my throat. I've got my vitamin man, and my aura lady and—"

"And now you've got Dr Swan," Ronnie interrupted with a warning glint in her eyes. "You can't take care of your health with quacks and astrological charts."

The sound of the phone startled Jan. She crossed the room to pick up the receiver. Lisa darted out of her bedroom and peered inquiringly.

"Merry Christmas!" Dan's voice was a beautiful intrusion.

"Hi! Are you back in the city?" She shook her head at Lisa. She saw Lisa's face drop. Lisa had thought her father was phoning from California. For all her hostilities towards Tim, he was her father. She had expected to hear from her father on Christmas Day.

"I'm calling from Sedona," Dan surprised her. "I couldn't let the day go by without calling to wish you a Merry Christmas and Happy New Year. Who else have I got to keep me pushing into the poetry?" he chuckled. Putting their relationship in its proper position, Jan tormented herself.

"Enjoying Arizona?" she asked, conscious of Peggy's curiosity. Ronnie and Marianne were busy dissecting a new film.

"Jan, there's no way I could describe Sedona and Grey Creek Canyon and do them justice." Dan's voice was deep with enjoyment. "Someday you'll have to see it."

"I'm sure I'd love it." For a moment the silence between them was loaded with unspoken emotions. "Store up on those views and bring them back to me." Jan laughed, all at once self-conscious.

"I miss our talks," Dan said quietly. "You're a very special lady." Jan heard a woman's voice in the background. "My mother's ordering me out to see the Arizona moon," Dan reported. "She insists that out here it's special. Keep well. I'll see you soon."

Jan returned to the others. She was exhilarated by Dan's call. All the way out there he had thought of her.

"That was a friend who's out in Arizona," Jan said in response to Peggy's look of inquiry. She didn't mention Dan by name. She had never talked about Dan to Peggy except in the most casual fashion. Despite her own encounter with Dan and his young friend, part of her mind refused to accept Peggy's insistence that Dan was gay. Yet she knew she must be realistic. Dan was drawn to her because they shared interests important to both of them. But there was no effort on his part to move their relationship beyond friendship.

"One of your literary friends?" Peggy's query was laced with sarcasm – which Jan tried to ignore.

"Yes," Jan told her. "Who's in the mood for hot apple cider with a stick of cinnamon?"

Dan leaned back in the car while his father drove the family group up the tree-lined road to the village of Strawberry, 6,407 feet above sea level on the Mogollon Rim. They'd stop at Strawberry Lodge to have superb hamburgers and matching coffee before a woodburning fireplace. He was glad that the heavy snows that sometimes closed the roads in the higher altitudes had not yet descended.

"Keith, we'll have to drive up to Jerome before you go back," his grandmother said persuasively. Dan knew she didn't dare say 'before you go back to school', but that was what they were hoping. The three of them were trying to encircle Keith with love, but until he accepted his mother, Keith would have no inner peace. "You know about Jerome, don't you?"

"No." Keith remained imprisoned behind a private wall that admitted no one.

"You'll love it, Keith," his grandfather picked up enthusiastically. "It was once a booming mining town propped up on old Mingus Mountain. Now it's the world's largest ghost town. But it's been restored."

"I keep my eyes shut on the drive up there," Mrs Tempest laughed. "To me it's almost perpendicular!"

When would Keith come out of his shock and anger? Not until Keith was back on keel would *he* feel he could begin living again. Jan would love it up here. Involuntarily his thoughts focused on her. He had never expected to fall in love when he was staring at fifty. He had never expected to discover a woman like Jan.

"Tomorrow we'll go up to the Chapel of Holy Cross," Dan decided, and his mother nodded in approval.

Though not a religious man he experienced an exquisite serenity within that tiny jewel-like masterpiece set into the red rock monoliths. Someday he meant to write a collection of poems about Grey Creek Canyon. He wished with a startling intensity that Jan was here to share this with him.

Somehow, between now and their return to Manhattan – which seemed a million miles away – he must convince Keith to return to school. That was the first major step. It would be possible for Keith to register for the spring term. He had contacts. If he explained the situation, the administration would understand. A wry smile touched his sensitive mouth. Keith would balk – at first – at the fact that he was using his contacts. The young had not yet learned to deal with realities.

\*   \*   \*

The days were running past for Jan with a frightening speed. Sometimes she felt as though she were a computer. A book-writing machine. New Year's Eve was particularly unnerving. Here they were on the threshold of a new year. The old one was running out. She should be grateful for that, she told herself as she sat in the living-room with the cluster of women who made up her life today: Ronnie, Gail, Marianne and Peggy.

Lisa was closeted in her bedroom with Betty, who was sleeping over. Brian had gone cross-country skiing with three school friends and the father of one.

"It really pisses me off that Lenny has to go out to the Poconos to ski just this weekend," Ronnie complained. "I think my New Year's resolution will be to dump the bastard."

"Jerry's with his mother at Grossinger's." Gail was bitter. "Her birthday is on New Year's. They always celebrate it at Grossinger's. With or without his wife of the moment. A girlfriend doesn't count, of course."

"I'm dying to know what Hal's bonus is this year. He won't see it till February, but he ought to call and tell me how much it is. I get a third of it," Peggy announced with a touch of triumph. "He's being bitchy not to let me know."

Jan went out to bring in the glasses and the bottle of champagne, chilling in the refrigerator, that Ronnie had brought over to welcome in the New Year. She struggled with the cork, finally succeeded. For a moment, with the champagne poured in readiness, the women generated an aura of genuine high spirits as they watched on TV for the five foot diameter ball – studded with 180 lightbulbs – to descend at the twenty-four-storey building at 1 Times Square. From time immemorial, it seemed, New Yorkers had welcomed the New Year in this fashion. From time immemorial – it had seemed – she had been Tim's wife, Jan thought. Now she wasn't.

She was grateful for freedom, Jan analysed. With Tim she had existed in a vacuum. She had been a non-person. But now she lived in another kind of vacuum, her mind taunted. Her life revolved around a game of roulette. What if it failed?

They had heard nothing yet from the Coast. Craig insisted he wasn't concerned; he was convinced they had a winner. Gail was sure. It was comforting that Paula King – The

Presence – was sure. For her it was still a game of Russian roulette.

Craig's packaging business was moving ahead with gratifying success, even while he was tying up money and time with *The Second Time Around*. But if the book bombed, she was out of months of earnings from aborted confession stories, Jan remembered at painful intervals. And the confessions market was not enough to support the kids and herself. Her precarious financial situation was unnerving.

The Monday after New Year's, Craig called her late in the afternoon. When he spoke, his voice was guarded. Giving her no clue to his mood.

"I just got off the phone with Sam Martin," he reported. Martin was the independent producer who was reading the first hundred pages of *The Second Time Around*.

"What did he say?" Jan demanded, her throat tightening.

"He wants to see more. He likes what he's seen so far. Now that doesn't mean a thing," Craig warned. "He can love it this week and hate it next week. But it's promising. As soon as he has the full manuscript – and if it holds up to the first hundred pages – he's sending it to Donna Warren." Craig had hoped they could land a movie commitment from Sam Martin on the partial plus the outline she'd worked out to accompany it. "Donna's perfect for the lead. And she's one of the most bankable women stars in Hollywood."

"When did you tell him we'd have it?" Panic was moving in again.

"I didn't give him a date." Anticipation replaced his undertone of disappointment. "How does all this make you feel?"

"Marvellous," Jan laughed. "And scared." She hesitated, her mind trying to cope. "I'll wrap the book up sometime during the last two weeks of February," she committed herself.

"Good enough," Craig approved. "Then we'll go over the manuscript. The four of us. Gail, Paula, you, and I. A month ought to take care of revisions." Jan shuddered at the way Craig apportioned time. Money was rushing from her bank account. "We won't waste time with individual submissions. A multiple deal. With Donna Warren we'll be on strong ground."

"If Donna likes it," Jan reminded.

"Donna will love it," Craig predicted. "Get back to the salt mine, baby."

Jan discovered it was impossible to concentrate after the conversation with Craig. She struggled at the computer for half an hour, then decided to take a tea break. Brian charged into the apartment as she settled down with a cup of mint tea.

Teacup in hand she trailed to the door of the kitchen while he made his routine survey of the refrigerator's contents, both doors opened simultaneously. He reached inside for an apple, took a swig of milk from the container between chomping into the apple.

"Do you like the pyjamas I bought you?" Jan asked. At first the children were outraged to find clothes were included in the Christmas loot. But they were understanding when she reminded them of the financial situation. Guiltily she remembered the five hundred she had sent Tim. She was convinced now he had conned her. "The print is attractive."

"Yeah, they're okay," Brian conceded.

"Then I'll buy you another pair," she decided. She meant to be sure Brian liked them before she bought a second pair. "Your other pyjamas are falling apart."

"Mom, no," Brian objected. "I've got another pair. There's something fascistic about having more than two pairs of pyjamas."

The doorbell rang with a frenzy that could only mean Lisa was on the other side. Jan pulled the door wide and Lisa rushed in.

"I'm starving," she announced, dumped her knapsack on the sofa, and headed for the kitchen.

"Have a bagel and cheese," Jan urged. "That's nourishing."

"Mom, will you stop telling me what to eat? If I want a bagel and cheese, I'll eat it." But after skimming the refrigerator she settled for bagel and cheese. The door to Brian's room slammed shut. While he denounced soap operas, he was addicted to whatever he could comfortably catch of *General Hospital.*

"Mom, the milk's almost gone," Lisa complained. "And Brian's been drinking out of the container again!" she discovered in outrage. "There's apple on it."

"Darling, run down to the supermarket and pick up some milk," Jan urged. "Not right away," she cajoled diplomatically. "Just sometime between now and dinner."

"Mom," Lisa wailed, "make Brian go. That'll take me forty-five minutes."

"So it'll take you forty-five minutes." Jan was grim. It was time she made the kids do their share of the running to the supermarket.

"That's one and a half sessions of *M\*A\*S\*H.*" Bagel in hand Lisa dashed into her room and slammed the door. *General Hospital* now echoed on both sides.

Ten minutes later, while Jan was feeling like a down-trodden mother, Mike called.

"How was your New Year's weekend?" he asked.

"Passable. How was yours?"

"It was nice and quiet. I did a lot of sleeping. I know this is last minute, but how about dinner tonight? I'm depressed. No bonus this year."

"You said the firm was retrenching." Lots of firms had forgotten about bonuses this year.

"Console me tonight," Mike urged.

"You don't have the apartment any more," she reminded after a moment's hesitation. "The sub-tenants moved in over the weekend."

"I found a little hotel that has special provisions." Jan knew that Mike was concerned about the high costs of New York hotel rooms. "Special rates for 'short-stay' guests. That's us," he chuckled. "If I don't make the ten fifteen to Katonah, I'll be

173

useless at the office tomorrow." Meaning, Jan interpreted, that 'short stay' did not extend to overnight. "I can get away from the office for an early dinner."

"What time, Mike?" She'd have dinner ready to be served. Neither Lisa nor Brian questioned her when she went off for dinner and an evening with Mike. They assumed she was seeing Craig about the book.

"I can be there by six," Mike said. "Maybe a little earlier."

"Six is fine," she agreed. She was so tense – it'd relax her to spend a few hours with Mike. He was standing in for Dan, she thought with dark humour. So quickly Dan had filled a void in her life – but she was in New York and he was in Arizona.

Though she was early, Mike was already at the restaurant. She listened sympathetically while he griped about the job, then told him about the phone call from Sam Martin, quick to point out that everything about the book was 'iffy'.

Tonight they didn't dawdle over dinner. Mike was anxious to check in at the hotel. He'd phoned to make a reservation. They explained that with short stay guests it was first come, first served.

Jan and Mike walked through the brisk cold to the small hotel. It was absurd to feel so self-conscious about going to a hotel. Women did this all the time. Mike pulled open the door to the small lobby, and they walked inside. His hand moved protectively to her elbow when they spied their predecessors waiting to register.

Half a dozen couples of widely varied ages waited. A pretty blonde in her early twenties could not suppress a giggle. Everybody knew their common destination was bed. For the fussy there were even water beds.

Jan suspected that the smartly dressed woman in her forties, wearing a hat and dark glasses, had been here before. Obviously she was with the bearded professorial type clutching an attaché case with one hand while he signed the registration card with the other.

"Christ, I didn't know it would be like this," Mike whispered apologetically. "I wonder what the rooms are like?"

In turn Mike signed in, paid for their room. They headed for the tiny elevator – empty except for themselves.

"How did you sign in?" Jan asked with sudden curiosity. "Smith or Jones?"

"Ernest Hemingway," he said. "Why not travel in style?"

The halls were clean but shabby. Mike struggled with the door. They both realized this was not the comfortable apartment they had occupied on other such occasions.

Finally Mike unlocked the door and pushed it wide.

"Oh, God," he gasped as he prodded Jan inside.

The room was a tiny, square cubicle with bed, dresser, colour TV, washbasin, and a minuscule tinny shower. The only illumination was from a red bulb in a bedside lamp. Mike checked the other lamp; it was bulbless.

"Jan, I'm sorry," Mike apologized again. "I didn't expect this."

"At least it's clean," Jan comforted. Trying not to show her revulsion.

"Maybe we can get some good music." Mike crossed to the TV, switched it to 'On'. The colour TV showed porno films.

"That we don't need," Jan said quickly, but Mike had already switched off the sex à trois tableau on the screen.

"Forgive me?" Mike reached for her without taking off his coat.

"How could you have known?"

Mike's mouth was warm and hungry as it found hers in the red-tinted darkness. They'd forget this creepy place, Jan promised herself. Afterwards they'd laugh about it.

\* \* \*

A week later Jan was stunned when Mike talked over dinner about finding himself an apartment in the city.

*Julie Ellis*

"What about Cecile?" she stammered. This was moving into waters too deep for her.

"She'll stay at the house with the kids," Mike said. "She loves it up there."

"Mike, apartments in New York are impossibly expensive. Don't even bother looking," she said more forcefully.

"I could drop by your place while the kids are at school," he offered after a second's cogitation.

"No!" A nightmarish vision of Lisa or Brian walking in at an inappropriate moment flashed across her mind. "It would be impractical." Suppose Dan dropped by unexpectedly? She'd die.

"I could pick up a studio and split my week between the house up there and the city. We'd have a chance to see some theatre," he tried again.

"Mike, have you any idea what apartments cost in New York today? You'd have to pay close to a thousand – at least – for a studio."

"Without the bonus I couldn't swing that much. Not with college coming up for the kids. It's back to the red-bulb motel," he said with a grin. "Can you take that awful place again?"

"It's not the place. It's the people," she said. But she, too, loathed that cheap, shoddy hotel.

*She must stop seeing Mike. This whole scene was getting out of hand.*

176

# Chapter Fourteen

Jan watched the calendar for the day of Dan's return from Arizona. She had known she would miss him. She had not realized how intensely she would miss him. She had not comprehended the extent to which he had woven himself into the tapestry of her life.

In his absence she read from Dan's poems each night before she went to sleep. Feeling his closeness as she read. Conscious of the deep emotional hurt in him. Trying to understand the conflicts that had pushed him – if gossiping neighbours were correct – into homosexuality.

In her heart she still didn't accept the house gossip. Or was it that she didn't wish to accept it? If Dan was fighting his way out of homosexuality and turned to her, could she block his past from her mind?

Most importantly, Jan cautioned herself, she must make no move that would influence whatever battle Dan was fighting within himself. She must give no inkling that she was in love with him.

How could she even be sure her love for Dan was real? It could be a typical post-divorce rebound. It could have happened with Mike, she reasoned, except that she knew Mike was married and was subconsciously governed by this.

Dan and she were warm friends. That was the way their relationship must remain. For now. It was possible for a man and a woman to be close friends without sexual involvement.

She had promised herself that she would not see Mike again.

Yet when he called and suggested dinner and a movie, and she knew they would find their way to a hotel afterwards, she acquiesced. She was too uptight to reject him, she excused. She relaxed with Mike. She needed that right now with the deadline of the book hovering over her.

Ronnie was right. Sex without love – if there was a feeling of real compatibility – could be satisfying. Didn't everybody know that life was a series of compromises? Ronnie was still seeing Lenny because he represented sex on a fairly regular basis. Lenny saved her from seminars, courses, and lectures that, she admitted, usually bored her to death. Yet with increasing regularity she vowed to find a replacement for him.

"Sometimes I feel like a woman in a Fanny Hurst novel," Ronnie complained one night. "In 1995! Why don't I ever meet Lenny's friends? Why do we exist in a vacuum?" Then her face brightened. "The grouper parties for the Hamptons 'shares' start in a couple of weeks. Maybe some sensational male on my wavelength will show up."

When Dan phoned early one afternoon late in the week to say he was back, Jan struggled to conceal her elation.

"Let's go out for dinner, and I'll fill your ears with stories about wonderful Sedona and Grey Creek Canyon," he tempted her. "I feel like a new man after three weeks out there."

"I'm dying to hear," she accepted.

"Tonight?" he asked eagerly.

"Fine." She pushed down her guilty realization that this would be the second night within a week that she was socializing. "Seven thirty all right? So I can give the kids dinner before we go out?"

"Seven thirty is fine. Pick you up then."

Jan returned to the computer with renewed enthusiasm. Tonight, she decided, she'd tell Dan about the book. She was ashamed that she had not confided in him thus far. She was deep into work again when the ringing of the phone shattered her concentration.

Impatiently she crossed to the phone. These interruptions drove her out of her mind. *What I really need is a cabin up at Yaddo or the McDowell colony – away from everything – until I finish the book!*

"Hello." Jan strained to be polite.

"I know you're working," Marianne's voice soothed, "but I figure the kids would never forgive either of us if I didn't make this call. You remember when I did that article for Ronnie on special icecream desserts? Well, the PR department over at Louis Sherry just sent me a wagonload of icecream bombs. Bring an insulated bag or two so you can take some of it home. I can't get it all into my freezing unit. Grab a cab, come up and collect the icecream, and go," she said. "I promise not to hold you up."

"I'll be right there," Jan laughed. "The kids would kill me if I passed this up."

In the cab en route to Marianne's apartment Jan thought about Marianne's new affair with an actor almost thirty years her junior. He was working in some off-off-Broadway play – without payment but with the hope that some agent would see him and send him out to read for a part. Marianne was supplying food and sex.

"No future in it," Marianne had confided blithely, "but it's a hell of a lot of fun while it lasts."

Marianne confessed in depressed moments that her first husband had been the real love of her life. But there was no way, she declared, that they could live together. When he'd fallen ill with cancer two years ago, she had been with him constantly up until the day he died in New York Hospital.

*She* had been sure she'd never marry again. Yet now she could envision sharing the rest of her life with Dan. Had his marriage turned him away from thoughts of a permanent woman in his life? God, she wished she could see into Dan's mind.

True to her word Marianne didn't coax Jan to stay. With Louis Sherry icecream crammed into the two insulated bags, Jan cabbed home again. While she paid the driver, she spied Dan and a young

179

man walking into the building. She could feel her heart begin to pound, but by the time she reached the elevators, Dan and his companion were gone.

Dan was still living with that boy. Disappointment chipped away at her anticipation of seeing him tonight. Why had she expected three weeks away from the city to make a difference?

Was there some logical explanation for that boy's presence in Dan's apartment? Could he be a young student that Dan had taken in? No, her mind rejected. Dan would have talked about him. Dan said nothing about a room-mate.

They discussed so much that was personal. Childhoods, their adolescent years, college. But except for that brief moment when he had told her about his bad marriage – not going into detail, Dan was silent about the past twenty years of his life. He'd told her about leaving the corporate structure to go into teaching. He never delved into the really personal aspects of these past years.

Dan arrived punctually at seven thirty, with gifts for the three of them. Lisa squealed delightedly when she unwrapped the box that contained a turquoise and silver bracelet. More reticent but obviously pleased, Brian inspected what Dan explained was a 'bolo tie', – the Western version of a tie. It was a handsome oval of petrified wood, glazed and hung by a segment of silken rope.

"It's great," Brian chortled, sliding it over his head and adjusting it to a tie position. "But I'd better not wear it on the subway," he decided. "It's a lethal weapon." He pulled the cord in mock demonstration.

For Jan, Dan had brought a pair of charming turquoise and silver earrings.

"Dan, they're beautiful," she thanked him. She was startled when Lisa rushed forward to plant a kiss on Dan's face.

"You're two beautiful ladies," Dan smiled, "and a handsome gentleman," he nodded to Brian. "All right, let's go eat so I can do my travelogue on Arizona."

Dan was in a festive mood. The trip had been good for him,

Jan decided. But she kept a tight rein on her emotions. Let Dan discover no evidence of how she felt about him. *He was still sharing his apartment with that boy.*

Over chocolate mousse and espresso Jan told Dan about the book, warmed by his obvious interest and his conviction that she could bring this off. He was working again on his collection of poetry and hoped to bring it in close to deadline.

"Of course, that's small potatoes compared to your venture," he said with a wry smile.

"Mine's a promotion piece," she said. "Russian roulette," she pulled out her favourite phrase for this effort. But God, the rewards could be stupendous. Ivy League colleges for the kids, a lifetime of security if she invested wisely. But first she had to finish the book. Then they'd see where they would go with it.

A light snow began to fall as they walked home, sticking to the tops of parked cars. She loved the early hours of a snowfall in Manhattan. Snow seemed to bring a sense of peace to the city. A lovely serenity.

Jan glanced at a clock in a shop window. It was early. Should she ask Dan up for more coffee? She knew he would not invite her to his apartment. Could not, her mind jeered, but she thrust this aside for an instant.

Why did Dan never mention his room-mate? Didn't he trust her to understand? Then she remembered the way he looked at her in unguarded moments. He wasn't sure of himself. He still fought some inner battle.

"Come up for coffee?" she asked lightly while they waited for the elevator, propelled by a wistful eagerness to prolong the evening.

"I think not," he said with a glint of regret. "With school reopening in a few days, I have to allot time to work on the poetry. We're both slaves to the computer. But I'll be less harried when I hand in the manuscript," he promised.

Dan let himself into the apartment. Keith had already opened up the sofa bed and was sprawled out with a book.

"Feel like coffee?" he asked. He was still wary with Keith. He had been pleased when Keith, while they were still out in Sedona, had agreed to try for re-admission to school. A few phone calls seemed to have settled the matter; but until the official letter came through, neither Keith nor he would relax. "We ought to try that new French roast your grandmother sent back with us."

"Okay." Keith shut the book and laid it aside. "I'll put up the coffee."

Dan went into the bedroom and changed into pyjamas. He'd have enjoyed going up to Jan's apartment. He'd missed her those weeks out in Sedona, much as he relished being with his parents.

Jan couldn't figure him out, he thought sombrely. She couldn't know that he had Keith living with him, could she? Not likely. For weeks at a time Keith never went out except for a midnight walk around the neighbourhood. Probably people on their floor didn't even know Keith lived with him now.

Through all these months he had never made a move to touch Jan. There had been moments when he was sure that all he had to do was reach out – but something always held him back. Though he was aching to make love to her, he didn't trust himself to become emotionally involved until Keith was straightened out.

Dad kept saying he ought to write to Fern and ask what was happening about the trial. Yet he felt that to contact Fern would seem a sign of disloyalty to Keith. It would be a long time before Keith recovered from discovering the truth about his mother.

Perhaps the suit was being settled out of court, he thought hopefully. That would be the end of the whole ugly scene. Or would it? He couldn't talk to Keith about his mother since that confrontation on the plane. At any effort to talk about her, Keith froze.

He owed Keith all his attention at this point in his life. How could he tell his son he was in love with Jan? To Keith that would seem yet another desertion. When he went out, like tonight, Keith thought he was seeing colleagues from the campus.

"Dad," Keith called. "Coffee's ready."

\*　　\*　　\*

Jan was working compulsively, begrudging every hour that she was away from the computer. She knew Craig was disappointed that Sam Martin wasn't ready to move on the strength of a partial manuscript. It was crucial for Craig to hold the auction with movie rights already tied up. That was the gimmick that would allow him to establish a six-figure floor. With a seven figure grand total.

She vowed to finish up the first draft on schedule. By the end of February – no matter what happened – she would have to start writing the confessions again. That would be easier for her than taking on the assignment of a paperback romance novel, which Craig promised her the minute the first draft was in his hands. She could do the confessions with her brain in low gear. She'd work on them by day, and in the evenings Craig and she would work together on the revisions.

Dan understood she was in a crisis situation. They met briefly for coffee each day, when she reported on her progress on the book. He was supportive and encouraging. Back on campus now he was managing to sandwich in enough hours of writing to feel he would complete his own book close enough to deadline to keep his editor happy.

In mid-February, after begging off seeing Mike for two weeks, she agreed to meet him for dinner. He sounded depressed. Serious problems had developed at the office, he told her over the phone. But not until they were seated at their favourite corner table at what Mike liked to call their 'big-splurge' restaurant, did he confide what was disturbing him.

"You know how I've been refusing that transfer to San Francisco? They've cornered me now," he said tiredly. "It's a matter of accepting or leaving the firm. At my age I don't feel like chasing after a new job. I hate like hell to leave New York.

For several reasons." A hand reached across the table to cover hers. "Would you consider relocating to San Francisco?"

"Mike, I couldn't." She would miss Mike, she acknowledged to herself. Yet she was relieved that the relationship, which she found so difficult to end, would be aborted. "I'll miss you," she admitted.

"I wish you'd think about it," he pushed. "San Francisco is a beautiful city." Unexpectedly he grinned. "Unless you're afraid of all those gloomy predictions about California falling into the ocean."

"I'm not," she laughed, though her eyes were serious. "But it wouldn't work."

"I used to tell myself there could be a future for us." His eyes were resigned, though. "But I don't think Cecile could manage on her own."

"It wasn't meant to be," Jan said firmly. "But it has been fun. You saw me through a very rough period."

Mike sighed.

"I think I need a drink." He signalled the waiter.

After tonight she would not see Mike again. It was the end of an era.

\*     \*     \*

Days blended into one another as Jan put in what amounted to double shifts at the computer. Now each day's work was picked up on the following morning by Craig's secretary. Martin would be sent this version, which included Jan's initial revisions, as soon as she finished up the final chapters. When this was out of the way, Jan and Craig would settle down to final revisions before submissions to the publishers.

Craig's packaging firm was taking off so successfully that he had enlarged his staff. Still, he had not lost his excitement over *The Second Time Around*. Craig had a compulsion to bring in a 'million dollar first novel'. To make a real killing on one book.

Jan knew that Peggy was annoyed that she was unavailable for hours-long sessions of soul searching. "*You don't have time for your friends any more,*" Peggy accused. Dan and Ronnie worried that she was driving herself too hard.

Jan took time out one afternoon for coffee with Karen because she sensed Karen was distraught. They met at Cosmos just after two, when the luncheon rush was over. Always fashion model thin, Karen looked gaunt now. Dark half-circles emphasized her violet eyes.

"How's the house coming?" Jan asked, suspecting Karen was exhausted from racing back and forth to the place in Connecticut. Jason and she were going up mid-week as well as weekends, Karen had confided on an encounter in the elevator, in an effort to redecorate in time for a house party Jason planned to give for a client.

"We're climbing the walls trying to get painters and plumbers and electricians organized. I hadn't realized how much work needed to be done." She sighed. "But Jason adores the house."

"Holding down a demanding job and chasing back and forth up to Connecticut is rough," Jan sympathized.

Karen hesitated.

"I know you're working your tail off, but there's nobody else I can talk to," Karen said when the waiter had taken their orders and left them. "Even if Mom or my sister was in town, I couldn't talk to either of them about this. I'm worried about Jason. God knows, I'm not narrow in my thinking. I'm living with the guy." She managed a shaky laugh. "But I can't buy the drug scene. I don't know if you remember my kid brother, Johnny?"

"Yes!" Jan was startled that she did. "He was an adorable little boy."

"That adorable little boy is now a vegetable," Karen said bitterly. "He was on something – we're not sure what – and then he freaked out. He's been in an institution for almost five years. There was irreparable brain damage."

"Karen, I'm sorry." Jan was cold with shock.

185

"Maybe that's why I'm reacting this way with Jason. I know he's into drugs. It frightens the hell out of me."

"Have you talked to him about it?"

"He just gets sore and yells. So he sniffs coke at a party now and then, he says. But I know it's more than that. He's losing weight. He has awful mood swings. I don't want to lose him." Karen was honest. "Except for this business with drugs, everything is great with us."

"Karen, make him understand how you feel about this," Jan urged. "If he realizes he might lose you, then maybe he'll get himself off drugs."

Jan and Karen talked a little while longer, both conscious of the need to be otherwise engaged.

"Do you hear from Tim?" Karen asked curiously as they rose to leave the coffee shop.

"Not since Christmas," Jan said. "He's out on the Coast. Los Angeles. Enjoying the beach bit," she said with involuntary sarcasm. For a moment she thought Karen was about to say something about Tim. Whatever it was, Karen decided to allow it to remain unsaid.

By early afternoon Jan pulled the final page of the manuscript from the printer. *It was finished.* She reached for the phone to call Craig. He was not in the office. She left word for him to call her, then settled down to revise the final dozen pages.

When Brian barged in with three friends, she waved to them and continued with the revisions, vaguely aware that they had raided the refrigerator and then retired to Brian's room. She didn't even stop at a fourteen-year-old voice leaping perilously high to say, "Jesus, Brian, your mother will kill us!" Later she'd kill them.

Why wouldn't Sam Martin make a commitment on what he had of the script? But she knew that was expecting too much. Donna Warren would insist on seeing the whole book before she would agree to do the film. Craig said Donna could be

186

difficult, but she was committed to Sam for a picture and this was far enough ahead to fit into her schedule. Sam loved what he had seen so far. Jan hugged this to her.

As she finished with the revisions, Jan was aware of a furtive departure on the part of Brian and his friends.

"Be sure you're back by seven," she called automatically. At seven sharp dinner went on the table. That cleared the rest of the evening – normally – for revisions. Tonight she anticipated an after-dinner conference with Craig. If she had champagne in the house, she would have put it in the refrigerator to chill.

Restlessly she straightened up her work table, and in sudden disquietude walked to the door of Brian's room. Now that nervous comment that emerged earlier was evoking unease in her. She looked into Brian's bedroom. On one wall, in bright red paint, were scrawled two words, 'Fuck you'.

"Oh, God," Jan muttered and strode into the room.

The can of paint bore the legend, 'Invisible Paint'. Invisible to a blind man. She'd make Brian buy a can of paint out of his own money and redo the whole wall, she vowed.

The doorbell sounded. That would be Lisa. She left Brian's room and slammed the door closed behind her. She would deal with him later.

"Mom, could we talk about planned parenthood?" Lisa asked.

"Isn't that a little premature?" Jan countered.

"I figured if we discuss it in our sex education class, I'd like to be a little ahead," Lisa shrugged. "But if you're too busy—"

"I'm not too busy," Jan said. Lisa and Brian knew exactly how to handle her, she thought, with a mixture of exasperation and tenderness. "You know I'm never too busy for you." That was born of her single parenthood, Jan thought grimly. Guilt always rode on her back. "Sit down, darling."

At Lisa's insistence they retired to her room for their conference. Jan worried that Betty, Lisa's best friend, might be sophisticated beyond the norm for twelve. She remembered the twelve-year-old

187

at Deedee's posh private school who was pregnant. But the most infamous disgrace was to appear 'uncool' before your twelve-year-old daughter. Handle this with care.

Jan and Lisa were concluding their conference to Lisa's satisfaction when the phone rang. It was Craig.

"You've finished the manuscript," he guessed jubilantly.

"I've printed out the last pages," she told him.

"I'll be over about ten. Is that too late?"

"No."

"I'll have xeroxes made tomorrow morning." Craig was contemplative. "I'll Express Mail a copy to Sam in California."

Jan's heart was doing flip-flops.

"Do you think it's ready? Without final revisions?"

"If these last pages are up to the rest, sure it's ready. So later we'll polish here and there. Donna Warren won't know the difference. All she'll read is her part. That's splashy – and sexy – enough to satisfy her. Congratulations, sweetie!"

"Craig, I'm scared." How many times had she said that in these last months?

"We're on our way, Jan. I'll mail it out to Sam, then call him on Monday evening. He'll start reading the minute he has the manuscript in his hands. He's dying for a great role for Donna. This is it."

"Suppose Donna doesn't like it?" Panic threatened to set in yet again. "Where are we then?"

"We'll bluff," Craig said with a show of confidence – which Jan didn't share, "until we sew up a movie deal."

Jan sat still in a corner of the sofa. This whole deal was orchestrated around their coming up with movie interest. The publishing market was rough as hell now, Craig had conceded several days ago. Neither hardcover nor paperback houses were springing for big deals unless there was strong indication they were buying a winner. *What did they have so far?*

The doorbell rang. Didn't anybody in this house except her ever unlock a door, she grumbled silently while she walked to the door. Brian stood there with a sheepish grin on his face. He guessed she had seen the artwork on his bedroom wall.

"You look cold," she fretted. "Where's your cap?"

"In my pocket. It's beginning to snow. Snow," he said rhapsodically. "God's way of quieting down the earth."

"I'll start dinner." She headed for the kitchen. Later she'd lace into Brian for messing up the wall with bathroom literature.

For half an hour it was an escape to focus on dinner. It had become a hard-and-fast rule that she remain in the kitchen while preparing a meal. She could win prizes for burning pots.

Jan fought down an urge to phone Dan to share the news that she had wrapped up the book. She made a point of not phoning him. She was fearful of who might answer the phone. If Dan had not mentioned his apartment-sharer, she didn't wish to know about him.

With dinner on the table she knocked on Lisa's door, then went to Brian's. She knocked and opened the door, intent on reminding him that he had a chore to perform. He'd already made temporary repairs. A poster, salvaged from an earlier school assignment, hung over the latrine language. It bore a legend other than what had been designed for class:

'The irrelevance of school is measured by the disasters of society.'

"That'll do for now." She suppressed a grin. "But the paint to redo that wall comes out of your money."

Brian and Lisa – both with Friday evening socializing ahead – rushed through dinner. Jan was grateful to be alone for a while. The book was finished except for frills. Now doubts assaulted her. They used to laugh and say that Craig was the con artist of the century. Had *she* been conned into squandering all these months on a bad gamble? It wasn't Craig's livelihood. To him it was a sweepstakes ticket.

Promptly at ten Craig arrived. He was in exuberant spirits despite his irritation that Sam Martin wouldn't commit himself on the basis of a partial manuscript.

"Let me read," he ordered, holding out one hand as he collapsed into a corner of the sofa.

"Here it is." Jan handed him the sheaf of pages that was the final chapter of *The Second Time Around*. Why did she feel so apprehensive? Craig would find no surprises in this last segment. They'd discussed it in detail. "I'll put up coffee." She needed to be busy.

Subconsciously she was watching the clock for the children's return. Betty's father would bring Lisa back to the house. Jan had made it clear that it was sufficient to accompany Lisa to the elevator. Jeff made her uncomfortable when he lingered at their apartment door with that 'So why don't we jump into the sack' look on his face.

Brian would probably bring a mob home. It was a comfortable supposition. That meant Brian wasn't floating around the city streets alone. He had been told – over and over – if he was ever approached by a mugger, he must hand over whatever was requested. Material items could be replaced; his life could not. It was tough to justify this attitude, she thought with a sigh. What happened to the old ideals of standing up for what was right? But they lived in a society today where animals roamed the streets.

Jan dawdled in the kitchen with coffee preparations. She was keyed high with the knowledge that now, except for minor revisions, they were ready to play ball.

"Jan!" Craig's voice was electric.

"Be right there—" Her heart was doing flip-flops again. She poured coffee, reached into the silver drawer for spoons, and headed for the living-room with the coffee tray.

"It's terrific," Craig said with relish. "I want Paula to start with some column items. You'll need photos right away," he decided. "A hundred glossies for starters. From a theatrical photographer with a good make-up person on tap. I'll ask Paula who to use. Let the son-of-a-bitch start earning some of that money I gave her."

"You can't use Donna Warren's name until she's read the manuscript," Jan warned. She knew that Craig sometimes displayed an over-supply of *chutzpah*.

"Don't worry, baby. Paula will know what to do. She always has favours to call in. All we need now is that one push. A phone call from Sam Martin saying he's offering the lead in *The Second Time Around* to Donna Warren. The rest will make publishing history."

# Chapter Fifteen

Monday evening Jan waited nervously for Craig to show up at the apartment. Tonight they'd settle down to discuss revisions. All day she'd kept hoping there would be a call from Craig saying he'd spoken with Sam Martin. Glancing at the clock – a compulsive action today – she reminded herself again of the three hour time difference. It was a few minutes past eight in New York. In California it was a few minutes past five.

When the phone rang, she tripped en route to the phone table in her rush to answer.

"Hello—" Her voice was breathy with anxiety.

"Sam loves it," Craig said. "He's Fedexing it to Donna in Rome. She'll have it tomorrow."

"Rome?" Jan was startled.

"Donna's over there doing a film. Sam's sure she'll love the part." There was a hint of special excitement in his voice now. "She's making headlines in Rome with her new lover. And you know the *paparazzi* – they love Donna. She'll be headlining all the scandal sheets. Perfect timing for us."

"When will Sam hear from her?" Jan refused to be swept along on the impetus of Craig's confidence.

"A week or two," Craig judged. "Don't forget, she's in the midst of a film and a hot love affair. Somewhere in between," he chuckled, "she'll find time to read the script. I'll be over in about an hour," he updated their schedule. "I was up till five this morning rereading the book. I don't think we have to worry much about rewrites. I gave Gail a xerox to read, so we'll

193

listen to her ideas, too. She'll be over with us tonight. Tomorrow we'll spend some time with Paula. A xerox went over to her this morning."

Sitting down with Craig and Gail, Jan discovered it was difficult not to be caught up in Craig's excitement. She was fearful of an awful let-down if Donna Warren rejected the book. But she sensed an ambivalence in Gail tonight that was new. And disturbing.

Gail sat tense and unsmiling while Craig paced the length of the floor and tossed out ideas about minor revisions or additions. Craig was sharp, Jan thought, pleased with what he offered. Gail's complaints were picayune, even ridiculous. Craig brushed them aside. Yet Gail's lack of enthusiasm was unnerving. Were Craig and she wrong? They were much closer to the book than Gail. Could she see what they couldn't?

Yet instinct told Jan that Craig was right about the book's commerciality. And like Craig she saw Gail's comments as nit-picking or non-professional.

"How long do you think it'll take you to do the revisions?" Craig asked when they'd gone through to the final pages.

"Oh, a few days. A week at the most," Jan guessed. "It's a piece of cake." She hesitated. "Unless Paula comes up with some glaring holes we've overlooked."

"I doubt it." Craig remained optimistic. "We'll know tomorrow."

"What do you expect for the film option?" Gail asked. A certain scepticism in her normally ebullient voice. "If Sam goes ahead with the book—"

Craig's expression was sheepish.

"I promised Sam the option for five thousand," he admitted. "But that's against a purchase price of two hundred thousand – with the usual escalation deals."

Jan was giddy. Wow, the figures Craig threw around! Even with splits and commissions the figures were fabulous. *If* Craig could swing this. She was not forgetting the old domino theory. If Donna Warren said no – despite

Sam's approval of the book – the whole deal would collapse.

"Craig, you're being damn greedy." Gail was sharp. "Sam won't buy that deal – not for a piece of shit like this."

All at once the atmosphere was tense with hostility. Jan was pale as she watched an unspoken battle between Craig and Gail.

"This is the kind of operation I've planned from the beginning." He stared at Gail. "What's come along to change the situation?"

Gail frowned exasperatedly.

"Craig, we're doing so well with the packaging. Don't go off the deep end about this one book." The taint of contempt in her voice grated on Jan's nerves like a wrong note in a Beethoven sonata.

Craig's jaw tightened. Jan sensed that he read more into Gail's complaint than she did.

"My package set-up," he said with definite emphasis on the 'my', "is a pushcart operation. I buy cheap and sell cheap, in volume. My best writer on the packaged books earns ten thousand. Maybe another five or ten, with a lot of luck when royalty time comes around. You should know. You're collecting commissions on each and every one."

"I'm not collecting on this one." Gail was supercilious.

"This is my own package," Craig pointed out. "You didn't bring in this writer. I'm letting you work with me on this one – as you asked," he emphasized, "so you could say to the publishing world that you'd handled a million dollar book. I'm doing this as a favour to you."

"It's not all going into one pocket—" Jan was defensive. *If it came to pass.* "Craig, Paula, and I all share – and the expenses Craig piles up come off the top. We don't know how much we'll eventually net." *Why was she apologizing to Gail?* "We may be lucky to end up with a hundred thousand each."

"I think it's outrageous that you could make a hundred thousand dollars on a book! Some corporate executives don't earn that much." Resentment poured forth from her like lava

195

from an erupting volcano. "I think it's outrageous that you might make a million!"

"We'll consider your part in this operation over, Gail." Craig was ominously calm. "You can continue to bring in writers for the packages. I'll handle this on my own."

Gail stumbled to her feet and reached for her coat.

"That suits me fine. I don't need to waste my evenings hand-holding Jan."

Jan stared in dismay as Gail flounced to the door and left. She recalled the endless hours she had forced herself to listen to Gail's outpourings of woe. Feeling compassion for Gail's lifetime of unhappiness. And now Gail talked about hand-holding *her*.

"Don't look so upset," Craig soothed when the door had slammed behind Gail.

"After that I need more coffee." Jan managed a shaky laugh. "Will this cause you problems?"

"None," Craig assured her. "That little bitch is dying of jealousy. We haven't even made a cent yet, but she can't bear the thought that we will. I'll keep working with her on the packaging," he said candidly. "For now. I need her. She keeps me supplied with formula writers. That's a great time-saver. Packaging has to operate on an assembly line basis. But I'll never trust her again."

"What about the auction?"

"Darling, I don't need Gail to handle that for me. I knew I'd have to step in somewhere along the line. She's small-time. This is way out of her league." Craig was on his feet now. Pacing in the familiar pattern. "The minute we get word from Sam that Donna's given him the go-ahead, I send out multiple submissions. We'll set a date for the auction. With the six-figure floor," he emphasized. "Donna Warren's signature on the film commitment will earn that with no sweat. A major motion picture starring Donna Warren," he said with relish.

Jan tossed sleeplessly until dawn. The future of *The Second*

*Time Around* rode on the whim of a temperamental film star in Rome and in the throes of a new film and a new love affair. *What happened if Donna said no?* Sam Martin was the only independent film producer who had displayed any interest in the book, she forced herself to acknowledge. In the normal course of events she was just another first novelist – and everybody in the business knew how few first novels sold more than three or four thousand copies.

At three the next afternoon Jan and Craig were in the lush reception room of Paula's office suite, waiting for her to return from a three-hour lunch at The Four Seasons. Jan compulsively inspected the array of blockbuster bestsellers lined up behind glass doors in a wall grouping of floor-to-ceiling bookcases. Titles that Paula had helped thrust into that position over the past sixteen years.

Jan tried to appear impassive when Naomi – Paula's stunning thirty-ish assistant – paused at the switchboard and accepted a call that dealt with a Paula King novel just celebrating its twenty-sixth week on the major bestseller lists. They were discussing an autograph session at Barnes & Noble in conjunction with a full-page ad in the *New York Times*. Jan remembered that Craig said Naomi was Paula's hatchet woman, performing with the charm and grace of a career diplomat.

Naomi smiled at them and disappeared into one of the collection of private offices that housed the Paula King staff. A moment later Paula – tall, pencil-slim, and dressed by Isaac Mizrahi – strode into the reception room. She had the presence of a fine stage actress of fifty years earlier, Jan thought admiringly. But she'd never want to cross Paula King. She could be lethal.

Jan and Craig were greeted with warmth and ushered into Paula's private office that might have been the living-room in a posh Park Avenue apartment, except for the huge work-table laden with manuscript boxes, folders, memos and book jackets that sat at one side of the room.

"You're looking beautiful, Jan. That dress is a marvellous

colour for you." Jan knew, also, that it was part of Paula's routine to compliment her clients. When they were in her good graces, Craig had warned her. If a client tried to wiggle out of some promotion Paula had set up, she could be a devastating bitch.

Paula announced that she had read the manuscript from cover to cover. Jan suspected she had skimmed. When Paula dug out her notes and offered her suggestions for revisions, Jan was stunned. She was grateful when Craig rushed in to back her up when she fought against revising three crucial scenes into cliché situations, though she diplomatically went along with some slight revisions that would cause no upheaval. But Paula retreated fast, Jan discovered with relief. And she was still enthusiastic about the potential of *The Second Time Around*.

Jan finished the revisions within four days. It was frustrating to know that the manuscript was word processed, xeroxed – and waiting to be sent out to the publishing houses.

With the manuscript off her hands Jan tried to get back to writing the confessions. It was rough going when her whole future – the children's future – hung in the balance. Dan was sympathetic and supportive, insisting on taking her out to dinner twice within one week. The following week she asked him up to dinner with the children and herself. After dinner Dan persuaded her to go with him to a neighbourhood movie, while Brian and Lisa disappeared into their rooms to study.

Peggy had reported that Dan's room-mate was no longer in his apartment, according to gossipy neighbours. Still, he never invited her to his apartment, Jan taunted herself. He wasn't sure of his destination, she tried to rationalize. With her he felt safe. No demands. Companionship and good conversation. They could enjoy being together without going to bed. Yet she was ever conscious of a pull in that direction which – sometimes – she felt reflected in him.

She wondered what the children thought about her seeing so much of Dan. They enjoyed having him in the apartment, she told herself with bittersweet pleasure. They considered Dan to be a close friend, like Craig, she ultimately decided. The category that was comfortable for Dan.

Craig was involved now in launching another series for a paperback house. Ronnie had finally dumped Lenny. She was seeing a top-management executive in his late forties in the process of getting a divorce. He had married a stunning model sixteen years his junior and – he discovered after marriage – with nymphomaniac inclinations.

"She was between more sheets than bedbugs in a fleabag hotel," Ronnie reported. "Steve was a nervous wreck. He finally figured he'd better buy himself a divorce before he landed in a mental institution." Ronnie sighed as she transferred Chinese take-out food from container to plates for Jan and herself on a rainy, dank Friday evening in her apartment. "So now he's in London for two weeks."

"I spent six days in London the summer of my junior year at college. As a nursemaid to a seven-year-old," Jan recalled humorously.

"Honey, when the book gets moving, you'll be able to travel all you like." Ronnie's eyes softened. "It was sweet of Steve to invite me to go with him. London, Paris, Zurich. It could have been a ball. I could have gone sightseeing during the day when Steve was busy, then we'd spend the evenings together. His office was willing to spring for his wife's expenses. They don't know yet that he's in the middle of a divorce." She squinted in thought. "He arrived at Heathrow yesterday morning. Damn Mannie for keeping me tied to the office. I don't dare to have a twenty-four hour virus, much less a two week holiday in Europe."

"Anyhow, you'd be nervous about leaving Deedee for that long," Jan comforted. Ronnie was shaken to discover Deedee taking a crash course in sex education via one-night stands she picked up at Third Avenue bars. "Though I told you, Deedee could have stayed with us. The kids could have taken turns sleeping on the sofa or in Brian's sleeping bag."

"You'd have been a wreck," Ronnie laughed. "But you know

199

what I'm going to do? I'm throwing a buffet dinner Friday night. I need some cheering up."

"That's short notice," Jan worried.

"I can swing it," Ronnie promised confidently. For a moment she was pensive. "You know, I can't get a handle on Deedee. I can't lock her up. I'd be scared to death she'd run away at the first chance. So I put her on the pill – and that's a licence to fuck. But if I didn't put her on the pill, she'd come home pregnant. And instead of candy, I keep condoms in that Waterford crystal deal in my bedroom. What am I supposed to do? Damn her father! He's home free. No headaches except paying child support."

The phone rang. Ronnie pushed back her chair and rose to her feet.

"That's Marianne," she guessed, en route to the phone. "She's been having one anxiety attack after another since she saw Dr Swan last week. He told her that her blood pressure is way out of control. But when she got out of his office, she just ripped up the prescription he gave her and went to see her aura lady. She'll call and break the appointment Dr Swan set up for her next month." Ronnie picked up the phone. "Hello." Her face brightened. "Steve, how are you?" She listened attentively. Now her mouth was agape with shock. "Oh my God, Steve!" Jan looked up in concern. Ronnie was ashen. "Okay. I'll take care of it right away," she promised. "No, don't panic." They spoke briefly, and Ronnie put down the phone.

"Ronnie, what is it?"

"That bitch of a wife Steve's divorcing!" Now colour returned to Ronnie's face. "She came by the apartment about a month ago. He'd had a few drinks and was feeling sorry for himself. Anyhow – even with the divorce in motion – they hopped into bed. Without a condom. Afterwards they had a winging of a fight, and Steve told her to get out and stay out. But she left a present behind." Ronnie's face was grim. "Steve was having a problem. Finally he went to a London doctor this morning. It's VD. Not AIDS," she emphasized, her smile wry. "At least he realized it wasn't me. He wanted me to know so I could get myself checked out right away." She shuddered. "VD in 1995?"

"Call Dr Swan," Jan urged. "You know him well enough to call at this hour."

"I'll ask him to see me first thing in the morning. He has Saturday office hours." Ronnie reached for the phone. "You know what they say about these new strains of VD. They're very resistant to treatment. God, at my age!"

Dr Swan agreed to see Ronnie at eight o'clock the next morning. He sensed Ronnie's panic and tried to soothe her. Jan, too, was shaken.

"Poor guy." Ronnie chuckled now. "He said, 'Honey, I don't know how to tell you this.' And then he blurted it out. I'm supposed to be a bright, sophisticated woman. How the hell did I get caught like this?"

Jan awoke early next morning. She moved nervously about the apartment – staying close to the phone. Finally Ronnie called.

"It looks like I'm clear," Ronnie reported. "But Dr Swan gave me a shot, and I have to follow through on a whole series." She sighed. "And I can't even say, 'Damn men!' because Steve's bitch of a wife is responsible."

\*     \*     \*

Dan was delighted that Keith was back in school. Still, he worried about Fern's case coming to trial, and Keith's reaction to the notoriety that was sure to ensue. He could not bring himself to write to Fern to learn if an out-of-court settlement had been reached. He prayed that it had.

Several times in the past three weeks he had tried to gear himself to tell Jan about his divorce, about Keith, and about the suit against Fern. Each time he shied away at the opportune moment. It was illogical not to tell Jan. God knows, she wouldn't censure him for Fern's way of life.

Jan would be the last person on earth to be intolerant of any

201

human being. If that was the way Fern wished to live, that was her business, Jan would say. Normally his own reaction to friends and colleagues in the gay scene. Why, after all these years, did he still cringe at the memory of his marriage?

It still upset him to know that Fern had used him to have a child. Had used Keith. No matter how many times he reminded himself that Fern had been a fine mother, he was furious with her because Keith was in such emotional torment since he discovered the truth. And deep within himself he knew that the scars from that first marriage, plus the responsibilities towards Keith that marriage laid upon him, were what separated him from Jan. Until Keith was clear of this ugliness, *he* was not a free man. He owed all his loyalties to his son.

Dan arrived home today with a pleasant awareness that tomorrow was the last day of school before the spring recess. Keith's recess began a day later. He'd be flying back here for the holiday period.

Jan ought to know, Dan told himself guiltily. He'd have little time to see her while Keith was here. He meant to fill the ten days that Keith would be in New York with sightseeing. To make sure Keith had little time to worry about the trial. He'd take Keith to museums, the theatre, maybe for a couple of days of cross-country skiing upstate. A couple of days at Beth's house. She was eager to see him.

Dan went into the kitchen to put up coffee. While he was fishing in the refrigerator for something to accompany the coffee, the phone rang. It was Keith. Right away he realized Keith was distraught.

"The trial starts Monday!" Keith's voice was shrill with rage. "Those goddamn newspapers! You don't know how rotten they make it sound. She's already told the reporters she's been married and has a son. *At this school.* She didn't mention me by name, but they'll find out soon enough on campus. I'm her Great Experiment," he said bitterly. "Proof that a lesbian can be a successful mother."

"Keith, listen to me." Dan battled to remain calm. "I'm taking the next flight out. You finish with classes tomorrow afternoon, right?"

"I won't go to classes," Keith lashed out. "You're out there in New York. Maybe the newspapers there aren't running the story, but here it's big local news. Everybody on campus will read every lurid detail that comes out at the trial. It makes me feel like throwing up!"

"We're not the only family named Tempest," Dan stalled. But already he feared that the weekly scandal sheets would make much of the trial. It was a natural for those rags. He flinched at prospective headlines that raced across his mind. "Nobody will—"

"Dad, she talked about her son at this college. How many students named Tempest are enrolled here? By tonight everybody on campus will know my mother is a bull dyke!"

"Keith, I don't want to hear talk like that from you," Dan shot back. "You'll go to class tomorrow. I'll meet you, and we'll fly out to Sedona for the spring recess." With luck he'd keep Keith away from the newspapers. The scandal sheets. In Sedona, Keith would hear nothing about next week's trial. How long could it drag out? "Keith, you've got some growing up to do. Go to classes tomorrow," he reiterated. "You don't have to explain your mother's way of life to anybody. You're only responsible for your own."

Dan called the airlines for a reservation to the closest city to Keith's college. Simultaneously he made reservations for the flight to Phoenix the next evening. He'd have to phone Mom and Dad, he plotted while he waited for the reservation clerk to come through with the necessary information. He'd put everything on his charge card. It was too late to go to the bank to transfer funds into his cheque account. *Why in hell couldn't Fern have been more discreet*? How could Keith not be upset? For all his liberal upbringing Keith had not been prepared for a mother who defied conventions. Lesbian mothers fought to rear their

203

children in a normal fashion, but the world was not yet ready to understand.

Dan phoned Jan. There was no answer. He remembered now that she had her weekly session with Ann Raynor this afternoon. He scribbled a hasty note explaining that he'd been called out of town on family business, then went to Jan's apartment to slide it under her door.

Back in the apartment he threw clothes together into a valise, watching the time. He couldn't afford to miss the flight. He wanted to sit down with Keith at dinner tonight. They had a lot of talking to do.

Jan hurried home from Ann Raynor's apartment, remembering when she was a block from home that they were low on milk. Hating the rush-hour confusion in the supermarket she detoured to a convenience store where she might pay a nickel more for a container of milk, but she would not have to battle lines at a check-out counter.

With the milk in tow she walked towards the house, conscious of how much later night was descending on the city these days. It was mid-March already. She wasn't turning out the confessions with her normal speed. Money was leaving the bank account with inexorable regularity. She wished with recurrent frustration that Sam Martin would push Donna Warren into a commitment. *Why was it taking so long? Would it ever happen?*

Emerging from the elevator Jan sought in the jungle of her purse for the house keys. Both Lisa and Brian were involved in after-school activities. She'd prepare a fast dinner so she could settle down afterwards to finish off that last story for Ronnie. She was determined to have Friday clear for Ronnie's party.

With the door open she spied an envelope on the floor and bent to pick it up. From Peggy, she guessed. Tickets for the opening night of the play by that off-off-Broadway company for which Peggy was designing programmes and throwaways.

Jan ripped open the envelope and pulled out the sheet of paper inside. She read, then reread the note from Dan. It sounded so cold and brief. Couldn't he have said where he was going and why?

Had Dan reconciled with the boy who used to live with him? Had they gone off together for a big make-up scene? She must be more realistic about Dan. He was a cherished friend – no more. It was stupid of her to sit around waiting for him. Hadn't he made it clear he was not interested in her romantically? She kept misreading glances, glints in his eyes when they rested on her, because she was so anxious to believe he was in love with her. *Forget Dan.*

# Chapter Sixteen

Jan stood before the opened doors of her closet off the living-room and debated about what to wear at Ronnie's party tonight. Fleetingly she considered the black Oscar de la Renta. She dismissed this. That must be kept for important business meetings. Also, with Ronnie's apartment – like most New York apartments – heated to a facsimile of a tropical forest, she'd be uncomfortable in wool.

She settled for a grey velvet Ralph Lauren skirt topped with a full-sleeved grey silk blouse, both four years old but still smart and fresh. With wardrobe decided she took a quick shower and settled down to a careful make-up job. Ronnie expected a commendable sprinkling of men tonight. Divorced, widowed or single men chosen with Ronnie's determination to make this a most successful party.

Focusing on her eye make-up Jan remembered that four of the men were signed up for shares in the same Hampton house where Ronnie was on half-shares. Ronnie was shipping Deedee off to a summer camp in Switzerland, courtesy of Deedee's father, who had been alarmed by Ronnie's blunt explanation of why it was necessary to remove Deedee from the hot Manhattan scene when summer arrived.

En route to the apartment, planning to arrive slightly ahead of the other guests, Jan stopped to shop for early spring daffodils. Wordsworth's words danced across her mind:

'I wandered lonely as a cloud

That floats on high o'er vales and hills,
When all at once I saw a crowd,
A host of golden daffodils.'

Where was Dan tonight? With whom? What had pulled him away from the city during his spring recess? He had seemed distracted these last two or three weeks. She had been so wrapped up in waiting for word on Donna Warren that she had pushed this out of her mind.

She arrived at Ronnie's apartment just as Deedee was darting out to a friend's birthday party. Deedee would be sleeping over at a girlfriend's house tonight, Jan recalled. Deedee exchanged a fast hug with Jan, admired the daffodils, and confided that she was into transcendental meditation.

Looking dramatic in high fashion make-up recently applied, but still in a robe, Ronnie was setting up the dining table as a buffet and bar. A dozen stack tables, eight borrowed from neighbours, were set off in a corner until they'd be required.

"I'm on schedule," Ronnie announced with pleasure as she brought out a dozen silver-rimmed plates to put down beside the silverware and napkins. "I just finished putting up the *coq au vin*. It'll be ready in an hour. The wild rice is washed and ready to go. I'll put a light under it in twenty minutes. The salad is ready to be tossed whenever I'm ready. And for dessert I played it easy and safe," she giggled convivially. "A Black Forest cake from the bakery."

"No last minute cancellations?" Jan asked. Ronnie was determined that there would be a sufficient supply of men tonight.

"Not one," Ronnie said with satisfaction. "Six men, six women. Plus Craig. He's coming alone. Oliver has to go to his parents' house for the evening. It's their wedding anniversary. Four of the men are from the groupers at the house at the Hamptons this coming summer," she reminded. She squinted in contemplation. "Of course, I've always said

208

I'd never have a relationship with a man sharing in the same house—"

"Why?" Jan was curious.

"If you two have a fight in the middle of the summer, then everybody's uncomfortable. But there's this one guy – Burt Spencer – who's kind of interesting." She checked her watch. "I'd better fall into clothes. Will you be a darling and put a Cole Porter CD into the player?"

Within ten minutes Ronnie emerged in a red velvet hostess gown cut to display her slim figure to its ultimate advantage.

"You look marvellous," Jan approved.

"So do you," Ronnie said. "So why aren't we sweeping away men?"

The intercom buzzed. Ronnie rushed to respond.

"I told the evening doorman to buzz for the first guest, then just send the others up."

Craig was the first to arrive.

"I'm your bartender," Craig announced. "Show me to the supplies."

Guests arrived in clusters. With her usual vivacity and thoroughness Ronnie introduced everybody. Muted Cole Porter was a pleasing background for conversation. Within fifteen minutes the party was fully launched.

The guests scattered about the room with drinks in hand. Jan found herself in a corner with Burt Spencer. He was almost as tall as Mike, with restless blue eyes and thick greying hair. Handsome in an unassuming fashion, appearing younger than his age. Ronnie had told her he was forty-five.

"Are you in publishing like Ronnie?" he asked. Not just party talk, Jan decided. He was genuinely interested.

"Sort of. I'm a freelance writer." Why didn't Ronnie stop circulating and come over to talk to Burt? Ronnie said he was the one man among tonight's guests that she thought could be exciting. Nice, Jan evaluated, though not the kind of man whom

209

*she* would pursue. But when had she pursued any man? Besides, Dan monopolized her thoughts.

"You're divorced," Burt said, his gaze fastened to her ringless fingers. Assuming that she couldn't be thirty-eight and still single.

"Isn't everybody?" Jan laughed. In her current world, at least.

"My wife and I split up eight years ago," Burt said sombrely. "I couldn't take another day of our marriage. My parents and my sisters were furious. They thought I ought to keep the marriage together for the sake of the kids." His eyes searched hers. "Do you have children?"

"Two," Jan told him. "Brian's fourteen. Lisa's twelve." There was no chance of keeping her marriage together. Would the kids have been happier if she had?

"My two boys are twelve and seventeen." His face was wistful. "I never really got to know the younger one."

"All right, everybody," Ronnie sang out. "Chow time."

The conversation became general. Except for Ronnie and herself the women were in their late twenties or early thirties. Women Ronnie knew from business. The men were all somewhere in their forties, in varied professions. All bright, unattached, and – except for Craig – straight.

Marianne had refused to come to the party. She complained that all the youthful competition would be depressing. Ronnie candidly said she had not invited Peggy because she would not fit in.

The evening was festive, rich in light conversation and laughter. Jan felt herself relaxing in the party atmosphere. Ronnie, too, appeared to be enjoying herself.

When Craig left shortly before one a.m. the others prepared to depart, also. It had been a good party, Jan judged. A stimulating evening. Burt offered to see her home. She thanked him, but explained she was staying to help Ronnie straighten up and would sleep over.

While they were loading the dishwasher for the first round, Ronnie told Jan that Burt had cornered her and asked for Jan's phone number. Jan was disconcerted.

"Why didn't he ask me?"

"That was his coy way of getting off the hook with me," Ronnie pointed out. "He tried to get me into bed after the grouper party. I stalled him. When I invited him tonight, he made noises about seeing me again. So tonight he asked for your phone number," she elaborated with a cynical smile. "That was to let me know he'd crossed me off his list."

"I won't see him," Jan said.

"Look, if you're in the mood, give it a whirl." Ronnie shrugged. "You might have a ball." Her eyes were compassionate. "You need a new man in your life, baby. It might as well be Burt Spencer."

*       *       *

On Sunday afternoon Burt phoned. He solicited her help in buying a birthday present for his teenage niece. She agreed to meet him for lunch next day and to go shopping at Saks for the birthday gift. They talked on the phone for half an hour. Jan said goodbye with a conviction that Burt Spencer, despite his casualness at the party, was shy. Today he was tense and self-conscious. She was sure the birthday gift was an excuse to call her.

Over a marvellous lunch next day his shyness did not stop him from inviting her to dinner at his apartment the following evening. Gently she rejected this. He revised the invitation to dinner at an East Side restaurant in his neighbourhood. His eagerness to see her coddled her shaky ego. Almost in defiance, remembering Dan's precipitate departure with only a vague, impersonal note, she accepted.

Over dinner the next night, at a delightful and expensive French restaurant, Jan knew that Burt would try to take her to bed that

211

night. It was months since she'd slept with Mike. Dan had not
so much as touched her beyond a goodnight kiss on the cheek
after they'd been out somewhere.

*She needed to make love.*

Could she handle sex in the casual way that Ronnie accepted
it? She had felt a closeness to Mike. He wasn't a man she had
known four days. Yet she felt drawn to Burt. Was it because she
still hurt from Tim's rejection? Though she knew now that she
had stopped loving Tim a long time ago, it hurt to be pushed
aside for a girl half her age. And in a way Dan was rejecting
her. Her ego – never strong – had been damaged.

Over coffee Burt suggested going up to his apartment when
they left the restaurant. He lived just three blocks away.

"For me this is awfully fast," she stalled.

"Why must we play games?" he countered, reaching across
the table for her hand. "You're beautiful. I'm dying to make
love to you."

"I've been divorced less than a year. I'm new to this scene,"
she said with candour. "It's scary."

He squeezed her hand reassuringly.

"I have a great bottle of champagne in the refrigerator. I've
been saving it for something special. Our first evening together."
His eyes made love to her. She was conscious of a stirring low
within her.

"More than one glass of champagne puts me to sleep," she
warned.

"One glass is all you'll get." His smile was inviting.

They left the restaurant and walked hand in hand to his
apartment. She remembered how pleased Peggy had been
when one of the men who replied to her ad had liked
to hold hands. It was a warm, ingenuous experience. Tim
had always considered himself too sophisticated for such a
gesture.

Burt lived in a small, well-cared-for building on an expensive
block. He must be successful as an architect, Jan surmised. He was

a bright man. She respected success and intelligence. Admirable virtues in a man, Mom always said.

While they rode up in the tiny elevator, Burt talked about his current assignment. When he left his wife, he had resigned from a large, prestigious firm to open up his own office. Obviously he enjoyed working for himself.

His arm about her waist, he piloted her towards his apartment door.

"I was lucky to find this apartment last year when my old building was torn down. I can walk to my office. It's on East Sixtieth Street," he explained while he unlocked the door.

"That's a pleasure, isn't it?" Ronnie, too, walked to work on pleasant days. Increasingly New Yorkers walked to work, even when it entailed a mile or two each way. One of the delights of living in Manhattan was being able to walk to so many destinations.

Burt drew Jan into the narrow, dark hallway of his apartment. Closing the door behind them he pulled her close for a moment before he flipped on the light switch. He was warm and sweet and bright. This could be good. Why did she feel like a character she had written into the novel?

Because she knew so little about Burt Spencer, her mind snidely intruded. She knew he had been divorced for eight years. He lived with a woman lawyer for three years. He was an architect, he was graduated *magna cum laude*, and he phoned his mother out in California once a week.

"I'll hang away your coat." His voice was a caress.

She let Burt help her out of her coat and walked into the living-room. Burt stopped to slide a CD into the CD player. Why did she know before the first strains of the orchestra infiltrated the room that it would be Beethoven?

Burt went into the kitchenette. She heard the refrigerator door open. He was bringing out the bottle of champagne, taking glasses down from a shelf. The classic seduction scene. Was it seduction when the woman was willing?

213

"I plan on redoing the apartment soon," he said. "It's not what I like for myself." He came towards her with the filled glasses.

"It's pleasant and comfortable." Jan knew he was anxious to impress her with his worth. Why was he so insecure?

Burt gave her a glass of champagne and sat down beside her with his glass.

"You're beautiful," he said again. A hand fondling her arm.

"Keep telling me that," she laughed. "I lap up compliments." He was going to make love to her. It was crazy to make love with a man she'd seen twice before tonight. That was what Peggy kept saying.

Burt held his glass to hers.

"To us," he murmured and slid an arm about her waist while they sipped champagne. And then he put his glass on the coffee table and took hers from her.

When he kissed her, he was gentle but thorough. Not rushing. It could be good with Burt, she told herself.

"We'd be more comfortable in the bedroom," he said after a few moments and pulled her to her feet.

Burt's bedroom was small, dominated by a queen-sized bed covered with a paisley throw. He didn't bother turning on a lamp. A faint light spilled into the area from the living-room. She stood immobile while Burt fumbled with the buttons down the front of her lilac silk shirtdress.

"Let me," she offered and reached for the next button.

Naked they moved together beside the bed. He was broad-shouldered, flat-bellied, muscular. A man who made a point of keeping his body in shape. While he familiarized himself with the high thrust of her breasts, her slender hips, the delicate swell of her pelvis, his mouth filled hers to the background of Beethoven's Fifth.

Burt was a much less conventional lover than Mike had been. He reminded her of Tim in their first year – except that Tim had been plagued by youthful impetuousness. Burt was mature and practiced. Unrushed. He made an art of sex.

Afterwards they lay tangled together for a while. When Jan went in to shower, Burt put up coffee for them.

"Don't get dressed," he reproached when she emerged in a towel and headed for the heap of her clothes. "The evening is young. I'll bring our coffee to the bed."

Lying in her own bed later, too stimulated by the evening with Burt to sleep, Jan tried to analyse her feelings for him. He was gentle and sweet and solicitous. Actually quite good-looking, though at first she had not been impressed by this aspect of him. In bed he was marvellous.

Why had he been so obvious in asking Ronnie for her phone number? Was Ronnie right in thinking that was his way of brushing her off? Why should she allow that to disturb her? It had not disturbed Ronnie.

Burt said he would call her tomorrow. Should she see him again? Why not? She had no commitments to anyone. She was a divorced woman with no man of her own. Why should she not have a relationship with Burt Spencer?

Jan turned on her side with a determination to fall asleep. In five hours her alarm clock would be ringing. Why didn't they hear from Sam? Why was he taking so long to get back to them? She remembered now that she had an appointment with the photographer at eleven tomorrow morning. She'd look rotten on short sleep.

In three months she'd be thirty-nine. Staring at forty. Why did that seem so grim now?

She awoke with a frown when the alarm jangled in her ear, and staggered out of bed to wake Lisa and Brian. When they were off to school, she'd stay under a hot shower for half an hour. That would take away some of the tension that tied up her shoulder muscles.

It was important that she look good in the photos. Thank

God for make-up men and studio lights. Craig said he didn't want one of those photographers who popped into the subject's apartment with three cameras and no lights, concerned only for photographic artistry. Craig and Paula meant for her to look as much like a movie star as was humanly possible.

The phone rang while she was in the shower. With the blinds fortuitously drawn she was able to dart from bathroom to phone.

"Hello—"

"Do you always sound so sexy this early in the morning?" Burt chuckled.

"I just jumped out of the shower," she explained. "I can't bear not to answer a telephone."

"If I didn't have to see a client in twenty minutes, I'd run right over," he murmured. "How are you, honey?"

He said he was swamped with work. He sounded self-conscious again, she thought tenderly. Why didn't he relax? He didn't say anything about when he'd see her, but he did promise to call tomorrow. The 'call waiting' on his side intruded.

She was putting on make-up, which the make-up man at the photographer's studio would shortly remove, when the phone rang again. This time the caller was Craig.

"I'm pissed off with all these delays," he complained. "I've called Sam three times in the past five days. He ought to be able to get some word from Donna. The minute your photos come through, I'm having Paula plant a story that Donna Warren is excited about playing the lead in *The Second Time Around*. I want Paula to try to plant your photo along with the item."

"Without hearing from Donna?" Jan was dismayed.

"We'll chance it. We can't waste any more time. Donna's over in Rome being screwed six times a day. Between that and shooting the film she won't be reading American newspapers. As soon as the item appears, I'll make a multiple submission. We'll set the auction for April 12th," he improvised. "By then Sam will have Donna set for the film."

"We have no guarantee." Jan was alarmed. "Suppose she reads the manuscript and hates it?"

"In this business we have to be opportunists. Donna's grabbing off space in the scandal sheets like no other star. We can't afford to waste such sensational publicity."

"Will Sam go along with this?"

"All we're saying is that she's excited about the book," Craig stressed. "We won't say she's signed."

Jan went back to finish her make-up. She wished she shared Craig's convictions that everything would move according to his master plan. She'd talk to him about doing an assignment through his packaging set-up, she promised herself. She'd written a complete novel. She had proved she could write a novel under pressure. Fast. She could knock out a historical for Craig. She'd earn more with that than with the confessions.

How could she know when she'd see money from *The Second Time Around*? *If she'd ever see it?*

Dan sat on the deck of his parents' house in the pink-tinged sunset and watched while his mother consulted with Keith about the painting on which he had been labouring for the past four days. It was a miracle the way Mom had conned Keith into painting along with her. She had started with the painting after being out here only a few months. Neither Keith nor she was intent on becoming a professional. It was a release from the tensions of life.

He was glad he had brought Keith out here again, even though it was so soon after their Christmas visit. Keith was unwinding in this beautiful solitude. He wished they might have yet another week here, rather than flying back the day after tomorrow. He hoped Keith would return to school. Since they left the plane at the Phoenix airport, Keith had closed his mind – mercifully – to the imminent trial.

"Dan, have a mug of hot apple cider with me," his father disrupted his introspection. "It's cool sitting out here this time

217

of day." He chuckled as he smiled down at his wife and grandson on the incline below. "Those two wouldn't know if a snowstorm came up."

"Thanks, Dad." Dan accepted the mug of cider, toyed for a moment with the cinnamon stick stirrer. "I think it's time I tried to put a call through to Fern." Last night Dad and he had talked far into the night about how to help Keith come to peace with himself. He had capitulated and agreed to phone Fern out in Ohio. If the case had been dismissed or settled, then he would have this news to give Keith.

"Go inside while they're still painting," his father urged, his eyes sombre. Like himself, Dan knew, his mother and father had been keenly aware that as of Monday, Fern was presumably in court. The three of them dreaded picking up each morning's newspaper lest the trial had become national news.

They had a pact to keep Keith out of supermarkets and newspaper stores. On Wednesday, while Keith and Mom were exploring the art galleries at Tlaquepaque, Sedona's Spanish-colonial arts and crafts village, Dad and he had come face to face with a lurid headline above blurred photographs of Fern and her lover: LESBIAN MOTHER STEALS BEAUTIFUL YOUNG WIFE.

Dan shut himself into the den and reached for the phone. His verbal contacts with Fern since the divorce had been brief and impersonal, concerning only his picking up Keith for routine visits and returning Keith to his mother. But to talk to Fern about the trial was to thrust himself back into the painful years of his marriage and the divorce.

Dan reached for the phone and dialled information. With the number on hand he geared himself for the call. Let Fern be home. Let him have something good to report to Keith. Surely Fern must know that Keith was still shaken from the last encounter with her.

Dan turned cold when Fern picked up the phone.

"It's Dan," he said. "I'm out in Sedona with Keith."

"How is he?" Her voice was uneven with anxiety. No matter

218

what tripe the newspapers dug up, Fern had been a good mother.

"He's upset," Dan told her. Their one communication since Keith's confrontation with his mother had been Dan's brief note reporting that Keith was with him. "I got him back to school, but then the story about the trial broke in the newspapers in his college area, and he panicked. That's why I brought him out here for spring recess." He dreaded to tally up the costs of their flights back and forth, but it was a necessary expenditure. "How's the trial going?" he forced himself to ask.

"We settled out of court on Monday morning." Fern was trying to sound casual. "I called you in New York and there was no answer. I tried to reach Keith on campus. I didn't realize this was spring recess. And you know me with addresses," she apologized. "I was never sure what town your folks were in out there. I tried Flagstaff. That wasn't it. And it wasn't Prescott. So I gave up."

"Fern, don't give out any interviews. No more publicity, for Keith's sake." Despite his efforts his voice was reproachful.

"No publicity," Fern promised. "I'm carrying on with my practice. I lost a few patients," she conceded, "but I've picked up new ones. I mean to be happy," she said with conviction. "Please, try to make Keith understand."

"I'm trying," Dan said. "With the trial off it'll be lots easier."

Keith said nothing when Dan told him about the out-of-court settlement. But he was relieved, Dan decided. No question now about his going back to school. As for himself, all at once Dan felt able to talk to Jan about Fern.

Keith was going to be all right. Now was the time for him to have a life of his own. With Jan.

# Chapter Seventeen

Jan settled a major battle between Lisa and Brian and went into the bathroom to dress. She was having dinner again tonight with Burt. She had not seen him since Tuesday, but he phoned daily. She looked forward to picking up the phone and hearing his voice. Amidst his hectic working schedule he thought of her. Took time out to call.

She remembered her anxious adolescence, when she was so shy and insecure. When the phone rang in those days, the call was inevitably for beautiful, extrovert Diane. Not until years later did she understand that her reclusive shyness drove away boys who had been eager to pursue her. But in her marriage she emerged from behind that wall of shyness. That much Tim had given her. That and Lisa and Brian. She could never say her marriage was a stretch of wasted years. It had given her the children.

Lisa had offered to make pasta tonight for Brian and herself. The battle had been over whether or not to put Chianti into the sauce. Lisa was in a stage where she liked to put wine into everything from spaghetti sauce to chocolate pudding.

While she dressed, Jan remembered that Burt had said nothing about doing something tomorrow night. Ronnie suspected he had a steady Saturday night woman. Was it true? She was uncomfortable at this possibility.

Tonight Burt was preparing dinner for them at his apartment. Afterwards they would watch some movie he was eager to see on Home Box Office. She would stop by a florist and pick up a bunch of daffodils, she decided, and was pleased by this decision.

In slacks and a sweater, because Burt had warned her that his landlord was remiss about supplying sufficient heat in the current cold spell, Jan emerged from the bathroom and went to bring her thinsulate jacket from the closet. Brian was sprawled on the floor watching the six o'clock news. Lisa was in the kitchen, feeling important at being entrusted with dinner preparations.

"I made baked apples this morning," Jan reported to Brian while she pulled on the jacket. "Lisa," she raised her voice, "there are two of those huge baked apples you like, wrapped in aluminium foil in the fridge."

"Great," Lisa yelled back.

"With honey and cinnamon and nutmeg?" Brian asked hopefully.

"All that," Jan assured him.

Brian looked ceilingward.

"Thank you, God."

"Mom," Lisa called again from the kitchen. "We don't have any garlic bread in the freezer."

"You'll survive without it."

"Are you having dinner with Craig?" Lisa emerged into the dining area.

"No. With Burt Spencer." Jan leaned forward to kiss her.

"Why didn't he pick you up?" Lisa clucked.

Jan hesitated, startled that Lisa would notice.

"This time I'm meeting Burt at the restaurant," she improvised. She'd be uncomfortable in telling the kids she was having dinner at Burt's apartment.

On the corner of Third Avenue she spied a man selling early daffodils from a paper carton and bought a bunch. A bus pulled up at the stop. Crammed with humanity and taking on even more. Jan hesitated. She was reluctant to spend money on a taxi. But there were three more buses right behind. One was sure to be half empty. Today she was glad that Manhattan buses seemed to travel in schools, like fish.

Burt had timed dinner perfectly. What he called his 'drunken' pot roast would be ready in half an hour, at the same time as the potatoes baking in the oven. He would toss the salad when they were ready to sit down.

Jan put the daffodils in water while Burt poured white wine for them. Tonight the landlord was generous. There was adequate heat. They sat on the sofa to sip their wine.

"Oh, something's missing," Burt said with his slightly lopsided, endearing smile. "Let's have *My Fair Lady* with dinner."

With the music suitably muted Burt told her about an assignment he was handling. He was genuinely sensitive to the needs of his clients, she thought with admiration.

"The woman's an actress," Burt went on. "She's in one of the soaps. She told me how hard they work on those things. Her husband and she have bought a brownstone; but the small, cramped rooms are all wrong for her needs. I'm ripping out walls, putting in skylights. Designing a greenhouse off the kitchen. It's a fun assignment," he acknowledged. "You may know her," he surmised after a moment.

"I doubt it," Jan smiled. "I never watch the soaps. I'm more attuned to public broadcasting. And of course, I love the theatre. Have you seen any new plays lately?"

"No." Burt was strangely terse. "Though I see most plays that come to Broadway in the course of the season. I make sure I do."

All at once Burt seemed a stranger. Cold and forbidding. She was bewildered. Did he think she was asking him to take her to the theatre? She hadn't meant that at all. But she would expect more of a relationship than dinner and bed.

"There's the timer." Burt was smiling again. It was like Ronnie said. Those who had been divorced were super-sensitive and suspicious. She mustn't be that way.

"Let me help." She was on her feet instantly.

"I'll slice the pot roast." He slipped an arm about her waist while they walked to the kitchen. "You check out the potatoes."

The potatoes were done. She anticipated spending the evening with Burt. Watching Home Box Office, even if the movie should be a dog. *She didn't need Dan.*

They ate dinner at the small round table by the dining area window, overlooking a neighbour's attractive terrace ablaze with golden forsythia. For coffee they transferred themselves into the living-room.

"This sofa is beat up." Burt frowned at the terracotta hobnail cotton velvet upholstery. "I had to buy the furniture to get the apartment. But every stick goes out as soon as I find time to go out and shop for replacements."

"Burt, it's fine," Jan protested.

"It's a comfortable apartment," he conceded and put down his coffee cup. "You're comfortable to be with. That's a compliment," he pointed out.

His mouth reached for hers. His hands moved erotically about her body, eliciting instant arousal. Anxieties fled from her as she abandoned herself to Burt's lovemaking. No reservations in her any more.

"I'm going to give you a hickey," he warned and burrowed at her throat.

Jan laughed.

"I haven't heard that phrase since high school."

"Let's go into the bedroom," he said after a moment.

Burt fell asleep during the final twenty minutes of the film. With an unexpected surge of tenderness she awakened him. He opened his eyes and smiled.

"Stay over tonight," he coaxed.

"I can't," she said gently. "The kids expect me home."

"You could phone them."

"Not tonight," she demurred.

"When?" he asked. "The kids are old enough to realize you have a right to a life of your own."

"Soon," she hedged, uncomfortable at the prospect of Lisa and Brian's knowing that she was sleeping over at a man's apartment. They were too young to have to deal with that. "But you don't have to take me home."

"Of course I do." He frowned.

"Put me in a taxi," she soothed. "No problem."

"Okay," he agreed but with reluctance. "Let me splash some cold water on my face."

They walked together to the most likely corner for a taxi. Hand in hand. Her hair brushing his shoulders at intervals because they walked with touching closeness.

"There's a cab." He lifted a hand. "Do you have cab fare?"

"Sure."

He pulled open the door, kissed her, and helped her into the cab. Jan guessed he would fall asleep the minute he hit the pillow tonight. He had dozed for a few minutes after they had made love.

When she unlocked the apartment door, Brian stuck his head out of his bedroom.

"Craig called," he reported. "He said to phone him no matter how late you got in."

"Okay, darling. I'll do it right now."

Craig picked up on the first ring.

"Hello." He sounded irritated. Had something gone wrong?

"Brian said you called." Craig had heard from Donna, she tensed in alarm. Donna didn't like the book?

"When are you picking up your photos?" Craig asked.

"Monday morning. I'll take them right to—"

"No," Craig interrupted. "Bring them to me. I know a place that will give us copies the same day. Paula is getting an item in either Tuesday or Wednesday's paper. She has it all worked out, but it'll be better if she can swing a photo along with the item. I want to get it to her first thing Monday morning, when she comes in from her long weekend at the beach. The manuscripts will go out to the publishers on Thursday morning. I'll set the auction exactly as we planned. We won't wait any longer for Donna." But he sounded apprehensive.

"But without a movie deal, we're nowhere—" Jan's throat constricted with anxiety.

"We're going to put this across." Craig sounded defiant rather than confident. "We've got a hot property. Sam admits that. Between now and auction day he'll see to it that Donna signs on for the film."

"Did you see that bit about her boyfriend – what's his name?" Jan searched her mind.

"Gino Armani," Craig said and chuckled. "Yeah, I saw it. Great for Donna's film. Great for us because she's as hot as a pistol now. I just hope Gino doesn't pull something so way out they'll spirit him off to a sanitarium."

"You're sure it's all right to say Donna's excited about the book?"

"Why should Donna object? It's something else about her in the newspapers. She feeds on publicity. Anyhow, she won't see it for weeks. Not until her clipping service gets the item to her. Sam's phoning her again over the weekend. Maybe we'll get lucky and have some word on Monday morning."

"Craig, I'm moving so slowly with the confessions," she said on impulse. "Could you feed me an assignment? I won't be bored with a book—"

"We're in a slow period. I've got nothing new on hand." He was apologetic. "You know how it is. Feast or famine. Right now the paperback houses are issuing against inventory and what's scheduled to come in. You know how crazy the economy is. Besides," he said encouragingly, "how can you get yourself involved in another book at a time like this?"

"My money keeps sliding downward. I look at that receding balance, and it scares the hell out of me."

"Don't be scared," he soothed. "Great times are coming."

Now he was brisk. "I'll be at the office by ten. I'll wait for you to bring over the photos. You won't be there before ten?"

"No. The studio doesn't open until ten. But I'll come over as soon as I've made the pick-up."

Later Jan lay in bed and thought about the column item Paula was planting. With her photograph. This was something that was happening to a stranger. Not to her, Janet Ransome. How would the kids react? Would they be excited?

She turned over on her stomach and burrowed her face into the pillow. Burt had not said anything about tomorrow night. What did he do with his Saturday evenings? Why was she so hung up on this?

Burt wasn't seeing his sons on Saturday evenings. He was unhappy about his relationship with them. He felt that his ex-wife's new husband had usurped his place with the children. He carried a mammoth guilt for having walked out on his marriage. *Was* there some other woman he saw on weekends? That woman with whom he used to live?

Did Burt think of her as a featherweight intellectually? She would resent that. It wasn't enough to be a passionate body to a man. She could never survive in that kind of a relationship.

Dan wouldn't be that way. But Dan wasn't aware of her passionate body, she mocked herself. Though there had been times she'd been sure he was dying to take her to bed.

Don't think about Dan, she exhorted herself for the hundredth time. Keep him in his proper place in her life. *Oh, damn, I'll never get to sleep tonight.*

She fell asleep unconscionably late, awoke unconscionably early. She moved quietly about the apartment so as not to awaken Lisa and Brian. They'd sleep till noon if they were not disturbed.

She forced herself to eat breakfast after a quick shower, then decided to make a fast run to the bagel store before it was time to leave to pick up her photos.

In the elevator she encountered Peggy, en route to the

227

supermarket because she was out of milk for her morning coffee.

"To hell with the milk. Let's run in for coffee somewhere," Peggy suggested. "I can't function properly without two cups in the morning. I don't want to wait until I get back from the supermarket."

"All right," Jan accepted, "though I'll have to make it fast. I have to be at the photographer's to pick up pictures when he opens at ten." She was sympathetic to Peggy's need to talk.

"Why do you need pictures when you haven't sold the book yet?" Peggy seemed irritated. "Is Craig making you spend more money?" Peggy had never met Craig, but she knew Jan's financial situation.

"Craig's paying," Jan soothed. "Or rather, he's laying out the money against hopeful income."

"Let's go in here for coffee since you're so rushed." Peggy prodded her into an unprepossessing coffee shop they normally avoided.

"How's the play coming along?" Jan asked when they'd squeezed themselves into a tiny booth for two.

"I dropped out of the company last week." Peggy grimaced. "They expected me to break my back when I wasn't even being paid. But I met somebody there." All at once she was simultaneously self-conscious and radiant. "Not a man in my life," she pointed out conscientiously. "A friend. I'm not like Marianne. I can't have a thing with somebody twenty-two years younger than me. But he's lonely and needs a friend – and he's terribly talented. Someday he'll be a famous artist if he can make his way through the insane rat race in the art world. But there's nothing wrong with my having a friend who's younger than me. Women *can* have close men friends. And Ralph isn't gay," she said with conviction. "But we can still be friends."

"Of course." What she had with Dan was friendship. Forget that she wished it were more.

"You've built up a real friendship with that college professor

228

on the fourth floor," Peggy said, and Jan started. Peggy was inspecting her curiously. "You still think he's not gay?"

"I've had no occasion to find out," Jan parried. "But no, I don't think he's gay." She hesitated. "He was married. Now he's divorced."

"What does that mean?" Peggy pounced. "Lots of gay men have been married. I suppose he's somebody to spend time with." Jan knew Peggy was fishing. "But what's the future in seeing a gay guy? As soon as he finds a new lover, you'll be out of his life."

"Peggy, I'm not in his life." Jan tried to conceal her annoyance. "Dan's a friend. We have a lot of common interests. I've spent some time with him the past few months, but I don't pry into his personal life."

"His next door neighbour says that boy has been gone for weeks. They must have split up."

"Dan and I never discuss his personal life." Why did she allow herself to be upset at this discussion? When he dashed off that way with only a brief note, he had told her clearly where she stood. *Why did it hurt this way?*

She didn't need Dan. She had Burt. She lifted a hand to summon their waitress. "Peg, I really must get back to the apartment."

"Why is it so urgent to have photographs right now?" Peggy pressed again.

"For publicity," Jan explained. "Craig's publicity woman expects to get a column item on the book. She hopes they'll run my photo along with it. It's part of the build-up." She shrugged cynically. But Peggy was staring at her in shock.

In Peggy's eyes Jan saw the same look as in Gail's on the last occasion when they had been together. All at once Peggy understood the potential that lay ahead if the novel made it big. *Peggy churned with resentment.*

Jan was conscious of Peggy's inner hostility as they drank their coffee. But Peggy and Gail would resent any woman's success. And what success had she acquired so far, Jan jeered at herself. Craig and she were having nightmares about Donna turning down the book.

Still, Jan was all at once more aware of what a complete turn-about in her life might be ahead. Up till now she had been so involved in finishing the manuscript she'd had no real time to consider the future except in an overall picture. Now she could fill in the details. Exciting and enthralling. *If* it happened.

When they left the coffee shop, Peggy went to the supermarket. Jan decided to forget about bagels this morning. The kids would have to rough it; they'd have toast with their Saturday morning bacon and eggs.

She went to the photographer's studio, picked up the photos, and took them to Craig. His assistant, Sally, had come in this morning to get out some letters. A rarity on Saturdays. He pulled Sally off that detail and sent her to the copy store.

"I had a call at four this morning from Sam," Craig reported when Jan and he were alone. "Donna's laid up in the hospital after some accident on the ski slopes."

"Is it bad?" Jan asked anxiously.

"Sam thinks not. She had demanded they shoot around her so she could have a three-day weekend. Now the picture will be held up until they know the extent of her injuries. The doctors think she's just shaken up, but they won't be sure until they've checked out x-rays and run tests. One bright aspect of this," Craig pointed out, "is that if Donna's going to be laid up in the hospital, she'll have plenty of time to read the manuscript."

Needing to clear her head, Jan walked home from Craig's office. By the time she reached her door, the phone was ringing. She sought for her keys. Why hadn't she turned on the answering machine? Lisa and Brian would pull the pillows over their heads and ignore the summons.

She unlocked the door and dashed across the room to pick up the phone.

"Hello—" Her voice was hoarse from exertion.

"Did I wake you?" Burt was solicitous.

"No," Jan laughed. "I've been all the way uptown already."

"On a Saturday morning?"

Jan remembered how little Burt knew about the book extravaganza. She settled herself on the sofa – still in its night-time form – and told Burt about the novel and their hopes for its future.

"You'll be a rich lady," he said and chuckled. "Congratulations."

"It's still a big gamble," she cautioned. "The whole thing could blow up in our faces."

"Feel like coming over about five and watching a foreign film on HBO with me? Afterwards we'll go out for dinner."

"Fine. That'll give me time to finish up the confession story I'm working on. If I can get my head together."

"I think you're a very together human being," he approved.

"See you at five." It was Saturday night and he was free, Jan thought with a kind of vindication. He wasn't seeing somebody else.

Dan collected his luggage from the conveyor belt at bay three of JFK and made his way outdoors. His original intent was to take the Cary bus into New York. But tonight he was eager to get into the city. To see Jan. He spied a free taxi and climbed inside.

The taxi moved swiftly out of the airport area and onto the highway. The city was garbed in night. What a contrast to Sedona, he thought whimsically. Still, the city had a beauty of its own. A vitality that he enjoyed. He was glad to be home. At last he was free to sit down and be honest with Jan. To answer all the unvoiced questions he read in her eyes. To tell her he loved her as he never loved any other woman.

He allowed his mind to wander back to the lengthy discussion he had shared with Keith last night. Keith was no longer a boy; in a brief few weeks he had become a man. It would be a long time before he could think of his mother without hurting, but he understood she had a right to live her own life. He admitted that, until he saw that first sordid headline and had been able to wring no denial from his mother, he had loved and cherished her. In time Keith and his mother would be reconciled.

All at once Dan was aware that they were travelling on a route unfamiliar to him. He took it for granted they'd drive into Manhattan via the Midtown Tunnel. They were on a bridge. Not the Queensborough Bridge. Not with the skyline that was rushing past him now.

Dan leaned forward.

"Where are we?"

"Triboro Bridge," the driver told him.

"To go to the Gramercy Park area? That'll take us up to about 116th Street!"

"It's faster than going over the Queensborough Bridge or through the tunnel tonight." The driver refused to be ruffled. "You heard the news. Traffic's heavy."

"Going out it's heavy," Dan pinpointed. He leaned back in his seat. It was futile to argue now.

"We'll shoot down the East River Drive," the cabbie placated. "You'll be home in no time."

At last they left the bridge and headed south on the East River Drive. By the time they were down to the Nineties, they were crawling. There was some kind of tie-up ahead.

"I'll get off at the next exit," the cabbie promised, knowing Dan was fuming. Irate passengers were light on tips.

At last they were driving south on Second Avenue. The Saturday night traffic caused them to lose light after light. Dan searched for a street sign. They were still in the Sixties.

Suddenly he spied a familiar figure on the sidewalk. That was Jan! Her walk. Her way of holding her body erect as though reaching for the clouds. He'd missed her these past ten days in Sedona. He'd missed her the three weeks of the earlier trip.

Now the taxi sat motionless while horns blared behind them and ahead blared in reproach. Instinctively he leaned towards the window and lowered it, intending to call out to Jan. Then he realized she was not alone. She was with a man. They were holding hands.

What the hell was the matter with him? Had he expected Jan to wait around until he got his act together? Masochistically he focused on the man beside Jan while the taxi sat without moving. Pleasant looking. Tall. Younger than he, Dan punished himself. Probably about forty. Maybe only thirty-five.

Here he was staring at fifty. How old was Jan? Thirty-four? Thirty-five? He could never judge a woman's age. How could he have deluded himself into believing Jan might care for him? He was a friend. Somebody with whom she could relax and unwind. Somebody comfortable and handy. And undemanding.

*What kind of a fairy tale had he been constructing in his mind?* There was no future for Jan and him. She was walking along the street there holding hands with another man. Irrationally Dan hated the other man without ever having exchanged a word with him.

# Chapter Eighteen

Jan sprawled on the length of the love seat with a pair of pillows at her back while she read the *Times Book Review* section. She had been too stimulated when Burt brought her home last night to settle down to read. She smiled in retrospect. Burt was sleepy after sex. She was relaxed. Her mind active and clear.

But even this morning her mind veered away from reading. She was acutely conscious that Dan was to return today. He had Monday morning classes scheduled to be resumed.

When the phone disturbed the morning silence, she reached for it eagerly, guessing that the caller would be Dan.

"Hello—"

"Hi. I'm back in the rat race," Dan said. "How has the city held up in my absence?"

"We're still here," Jan laughed, enjoying the sound of his voice. "No earthquakes, tornadoes, or other major disasters. How was your trip?" He had not told her where he was going.

"You know how I feel about Sedona. And it's always great to spend time with my parents."

They talked for a few minutes about Dan's love affair with Grey Creek Canyon, then Dan told her with satisfaction that out in Sedona he had finished the final two poems for his collection.

"Happy about them?" she asked. Waiting for him to offer to read them to her.

"Pretty much," he acknowledged. "I'm on schedule. Of course, it'll be a year before the book comes out."

Jan was on the verge of inviting him up for dinner. But

suppose Burt called while Dan was here? That would be awkward. While she hesitated, Dan veered off into a discussion of school politics. He was acting department head, which he took most seriously. There was conflict about who would become permanent department head. Dan shied away from fighting for the position, though several of his colleagues were convinced it should be his.

"I have to leave for my sister's house in Westchester in about an hour," he reported. "I've been commissioned to deliver a painting my mother did for her birthday next week." He paused a moment. "See you soon, Jan."

At intervals through the day Jan replayed in her mind the brief telephone conversation with Dan. In retrospect she realized he had been strangely reserved. *So unlike himself.* He had not offered to read her the two new poems. Normally he was eager for her reaction. He said nothing about meeting for coffee or for dinner. But why should she be anxious to have coffee or dinner with Dan? Burt had moved into her life.

On Monday morning Burt phoned from his office to suggest dinner the following evening. A new restaurant had opened around the corner from his apartment.

"I hear it's terrific. Let's give it a whirl," he said casually. "Meet me there?"

"Yes." Why drag Burt all the way down here when they'd be having dinner near his apartment. Which would be their ultimate destination. "Give me the address."

She said goodbye to Burt, sat pensively by the phone. Her dates with Burt were always dinner and bed. How many women she'd heard complain about this arrangement! As soon as money was more available, she'd buy a pair of theatre tickets, invite Burt over for dinner and an evening at the theatre. She must remember to be sure it was something he hadn't seen.

Mid-morning on Tuesday, when she was at the computer, Craig called.

"Run downstairs to the newsstand," he ordered. "Paula came through. The item about Donna's interest in the book is in the column. Along with your photo."

"I'll pick the paper up right away." *This was unreal.* She was moving into a strange new world.

"Tomorrow the manuscripts go out. No need to wait another day. I just pray we get an okay from Donna before the auction," he admitted. "That's crucial."

"Craig, suppose she doesn't read it by then?" Suppose she didn't like it?

"Jannie, positive thinking," Craig exhorted. "She'll read it. She'll love it. I'm calling Sam to check on her condition as soon as it's a respectable hour in California. The tests ought to be in by now."

"You'll call me?" Jan asked. Knowing the answer.

"Honey, relax. We're on our way."

Twenty minutes later Marianne phoned.

"Sugar, you're famous."

"Hardly," Jan laughed, but she knew what Marianne meant. It surprised her that Marianne read the gossip columns. "Craig's scheduling the book auction." How could she talk so calmly about it?

"Let's go out for lunch and celebrate," Marianne said. "I'll call Ronnie, too. It's about time somebody in this clique made it out of the bull pen."

Before she left to meet Marianne and Ronnie for lunch, she phoned Craig's office to see if he had spoken to Sam. Sally reported that he was at that moment on the phone to California. Jan explained she was going out for lunch. But she'd call back in about ten minutes.

At the restaurant she immediately sought out the public phones. Craig was free. He had talked to Sam. Except for bruises, Donna was fine. She'd been released from the hospital. She promised to read the manuscript within a few days. Jan returned to the table in an aura of shaky optimism.

237

Leaving the apartment building to go to the restaurant where she was to meet Burt for dinner, Jan spied Karen pulling out of the garage. She was behind the wheel of Jason's white Jaguar.

"Can I drop you off somewhere, Jan?" Karen asked with a warm smile.

"If you're headed for the East Sixties," Jan said.

"I can go out that way. I'm driving up to the house in Connecticut. Jason's spending a few vacation days up there supervising the workmen who're putting in the Jacuzzi and the sauna."

"Great." Jan climbed in beside Karen. "How've you been?"

"Okay, I guess." Karen was focusing on traffic. "The kids and you?"

"Fine. Except that I'm in the midst of a deal that's keeping me awake nights. If it goes through, it's bigger than anything I ever dreamed about. But I'm scared even to talk about it." She wouldn't let herself think that it might fall through. She'd be right back to square one.

"Jason tells me he's off the coke scene," Karen said after a moment. "I'm not sure I believe him. And he's seeing this girl for lunch quite often. He claims it's business. It could be," she conceded, "but this crazy little voice inside tells me it's more than that. If I find out Jason's sleeping with somebody else, that's it. We're finished."

"Don't jump, Karen," Jan said softly. She knew that Karen was mad about Jason. "Make absolutely sure before you take any action."

"I'll make sure," Karen promised. "But I couldn't sleep with him if I knew he was running around with other women. I know some women just close their eyes and enjoy. Some women don't want to know. I'm not like that."

"Nor me," Jan said. Was Burt having a thing with somebody else? Maybe he'd just broken off with someone, she reasoned. He said he had a hectic work schedule. When he was seeing her this often, how could he find time for another woman?

Karen deposited her in front of the restaurant. She went inside. Burt was right; it was a charming place. She spied him being seated at a table.

"Perfect timing." His smile was effervescent. "You manage your life well."

"Right now I'm not sure I know what I'm doing," she confessed, and reported on the column item and Donna's promise to read the manuscript in a few days. "It had better be in a few days." She frowned worriedly. "The auction is already scheduled."

"It will be." Burt meant to be reassuring. "This man you're working with sounds as though he knows what he's doing." Burt had guessed right off that this was not a romantic attachment. "You'll be raking in money soon," he prophesied. "You can send the kids away to great boarding schools."

Jan stared at him in astonishment.

"Why should I do that?"

"It would be the sensible approach if you're going to be dashing around on the talk show circuits, doing the usual bestselling author bit."

"I would never send the kids away to school." Even the idea unnerved her. She worried about the thirteen-city tour Craig was counting on, though Ronnie said that Deedee and she would stay with Lisa and Brian if she had to be away. Thirteen cities could be covered in fifteen or twenty days, she consoled herself. "Anyhow, I don't have to concern myself with all that yet. Everything is still up in the air."

"I'll bring a TV set into the office," he mused, "to try to catch you on air." His hand moved across the table to hers. "I'd rather catch you in bed."

Dinner was perfect. The food superb and elegantly served. The ambience delightful. Burt dropped into a reminiscent mood, telling her amusing stories about clients of his. She knew that the lovemaking that followed would be equally perfect. With all the tensions that imprisoned her these days she needed that. She needed Burt in her life, she told herself – and almost believed it.

After they made love and she had emerged from the shower, she discovered Burt was sound asleep. She stretched out on the bed beside him, wrapped in his paisley dressing gown, which she had found hanging on the bathroom door.

He was sweet and passionate – why did she feel that she was not getting through to the real man? He kept a wall between himself and the world, played some private, disturbing game. Could he make her forget Dan Tempest?

On impulse she went into the kitchen to put up coffee. When she was pouring it into cups, Burt appeared in the doorway.

"You should have awakened me," he chided.

"You looked too comfortable. Put some clothes on, have some coffee, and put me into a taxi."

Even after coffee Burt seemed sleepy. But he walked with her to the taxi, kissed her soundly while the driver waited, and said, "I'll call you tomorrow, honey."

Knowing that the manuscript was being read by half a dozen publishers Jan was uptight at the lack of communication from Donna Warren. She was terrified that Sam would back out of the deal since Donna was being so difficult.

On Wednesday Burt phoned. He was flying to Chicago on business. He'd return over the weekend.

"I'll buzz you the minute I get back," he promised.

Jan tried again to involve herself in the confessions. It was still an impossible situation. Her whole future lay hanging in the balance. And she was miserably conscious of the silence from Dan. Was it something she had said or done?

She searched her mind for a reason for Dan's silence. Peggy said that his apartment-sharer – whoever he was – was not with Dan any more. Had Dan found some other woman? Why should it concern her? She could never have a relationship with two men at the same time.

On Thursday Jan had lunch with Ronnie, then headed for Craig's office. Since the first time she had been here, Craig had made notable changes. A wall had been broken down to add an adjacent suite to his modest quarters. He had hired two editors in addition to his assistant.

Jan walked into his private office. Craig was hunched over his desk, focused on figures.

"I jumped too fast in building up the staff," he moaned. "Do you know how much I'm paying out in salaries each week? Plus the additional rent for increasing the office space?"

"I can imagine," Jan sympathized. "But this is a temporary lull, isn't it?"

"My mind says it is. But I look at my bank balance, and I get paranoid."

"I know." Her bank balance gave her nightmares.

"I called Sam half an hour ago. He talked with Donna last night. She's been too busy to read the manuscript. She's having battles with the director on the film. Sam says it isn't Donna's fault. The director thinks he's Svengali. Donna may be flaky in some ways, but she knows what's right for her acting-wise. Damn it, that's why she should read the script!" He banged on his desk with one fist.

"Donna's right for the starring role." While she had followed Craig's formula of three younger divorcées plus an older one, she had focused on the character they hoped Donna would play. It was the pivotal role. A dynamic thirty-year-old divorcée emerging from the suburban cocoon and fighting to raise two small children and to restructure her life in the singles jungle.

Craig rose to his feet, began to pace. Jan waited for him to verbalize whatever was fomenting in his mind.

"I've scheduled the auction for Monday. Ideally I'd fly to Rome tonight, talk to Donna tomorrow, and fly back with a signed contract on Sunday. But the timing is too tight. I can't take that chance. I have to be here for the auction," he emphasized. He paused for an instant. "I'll fly to Rome next Friday evening. Whatever happens at the auction, it's urgent to tie up Donna fast."

"Can you manage the trip?" Jan was concerned about the financial aspect.

"I have to manage it." Craig seemed relieved that he had arrived at this decision. He leaned over the desk to buzz for his assistant. "Sally," he spoke into the intercom, "book me a flight to Rome on next Friday evening with a return seat on the following Monday. As late in the afternoon as possible. And Sally," he called after her, "economy class."

On Saturday morning shortly past nine Burt phoned.

"I didn't wake you, did I?" he asked.

"Goodness no," Jan laughed. "This is my day to do nonsense things like laundry and grocery shopping and vacuuming. I try to do them early."

"The weather report says tomorrow will be a glorious spring day. Would you like to drive up to the country? Or better still," he said with a lilt in his voice, "why don't we drive out to the Hamptons? The beach will be empty. We can walk for a mile without seeing a soul. And there are some great restaurants out there."

"I'd love it." Jan glowed. Walking along an empty stretch of beach was like a private exploration of heaven.

"I'll show you the house where I have half-shares," he promised. "Later in the summer you'll come out to spend a weekend there."

"Lovely." It was an intriguing prospect.

"I'll pick you up around ten thirty tomorrow morning. If I can't find a parking place, I'll ask the doorman to buzz and tell you I'm waiting. Okay?"

"Fine. I'll be ready."

Jan put down the phone and leaned back to savour the vision of a whole day away from the city. With Burt. She had not been out of the city since the kids and she had moved into the apartment over seven months ago. She was glad Burt had suggested a day at the Hamptons. The kids had their weekend days tightly scheduled – she'd have no problem being away.

On Saturday evening Jan, Ronnie, and Peggy – like thousands of unattached women – went to a neighbourhood movie. Jan was conscious of the women – in twos and threes, who waited along with them in the line at the movie house. Here and there she saw a man alone, or with a male companion. Why did women look at a pair of men together and assume they were gay?

For a while Jan was able to lose herself in the film. When they emerged at the end, Ronnie led them towards a coffee shop rather than accepting Peggy's suggestion that they go to her apartment for tea.

Over hot apple strudel and tea Ronnie reported on Deedee's latest bizarre activity.

"Everybody says all teenagers go through this craziness, that it'll pass. The question is, will I survive?"

Peggy rarely talked about her two sons. Tonight she was upset at not having an absolute guarantee that her financial situation would not change.

"I've got my alimony as long as Hal keeps working. What happens if he's sick? I'll be stranded." If Hal died, she was the beneficiary of a huge insurance policy that was part of the divorce settlement. She'd be safe. It was the possibility of his becoming ill that terrified her.

"Honey, you'll survive," Ronnie said calmly. Less than sympathetic to Peggy's neuroses. "At worst you'll get a job."

"Do you know the unemployment rate in this country?" Peggy was indignant. "I have no skills to sell. I spent the years when I should have been building a career raising two kids and running a house I hated. There's this woman in the apartment next to me. She doesn't lift a finger. Her husband cooks and cleans. Her mother takes care of the baby. She's not even pretty, and her husband lets her get away with that crap."

243

"It's like Marianne said once," Ronnie reminisced. "We were talking about women like that, who rake their men over the coals; and she said, 'Some men love being kicked in the balls.' That's the way it is."

"Peg, why don't you settle down seriously to the painting?" Jan encouraged. Even if Peggy didn't sell, it ought to be good therapy.

"It's not easy after what I've been through." Peggy's stock lament. "Though Ralph believes I have a lot of talent. I showed him some of my things." Ralph, Jan recalled, was the artist Peggy had met at the off-off-Broadway company.

Ronnie yawned. "I don't know why I'm so damn tired on a Saturday night." She grinned. "Show me some gorgeous stud, of course; and I'll wake up fast."

"You don't see Lenny any more?" Peggy asked curiously.

"No. He got around to trying to start up again, but I told him I didn't see any future in it. He's little better than a one-night stand."

"Let's go home," Peggy said, her face etched with irritation. "Being out on a Saturday night with two other women is so damn depressing."

While the children watched TV, Jan scanned the book review section, then settled down to read back issues of *Publishers Weekly* that Craig had passed on to her. She couldn't go to sleep until Lisa and Brian called a halt to TV and went to their rooms. While each had a small-screen TV for personal use, neither Lisa nor Brian liked watching old movies on their own sets. If the book clicked, they could afford a three-bedroom apartment, Jan thought with glorious anticipation. How marvellous to have a room of her own again. They might even be able to buy a beach house.

Shortly past one the children were persuaded to call it a night. Jan went to bed. She expected to fall asleep instantly. It didn't happen. She worried about the auction on Monday. She was concerned over Dan's coolness since his return.

Once last week she ran into Dan at the supermarket. They'd

gone for coffee and exchanged reports on their prospective books. But she was hurt by the new reserve she sensed in him.

So there was to be no emotional involvement between them. That didn't mean they must abandon their friendship. She was startled by the depth of her disappointment at this unexpected estrangement between Dan and herself.

At last she fell asleep, to awaken hours later to the sound of a harsh ring. She reached to silence the alarm clock. It wasn't the clock. The phone was ringing.

"Hello—" She glanced at the clock. It was a few minutes before eight.

"Jan, did I wake you?" Burt sounded apologetic.

"You're up bright and early." She pulled herself into a sitting position at the corner of the sofa-bed. At once fully awake.

"We'll have to call off the trip to the beach. I just got a phone call. One of my kids took a bad fall off a horse this morning. He's in the hospital."

"Oh, Burt, how awful! But maybe he's just shaken up."

"He's in x-ray now. I'm driving out there to the hospital." Burt was grave. "He's been riding Sunday mornings for the past year. This is the first accident he's had."

"Which of the boys was hurt?" she asked, trying to remember their names. Had Burt ever mentioned them by name?

"The older one. Paul. Jan, I have to run now—"

"Of course. But remember, kids heal fast," she comforted.

"If I get back early, I'll call you," he promised, and hung up.

Jan went into the kitchen and put up water for tea. Why did she have this ridiculous suspicion that nothing had happened to Burt's son? That he was involved in something that interested him more than a day at the beach with her.

She should be ashamed to be such a sceptic, Jan upbraided herself. But it was like Ronnie said. Divorced people were always suspicious of partners in a relationship.

All through the day and into the evening Jan waited for the

phone to ring. Hoping for a call from Burt. Alternately anxious about his son and cynical about her concern. At one point she pondered over the wisdom of calling the local hospital – there'd be only one in the Long Island suburban neighbourhood where Burt's ex-wife lived. She could phone and inquire about the condition of Paul Spencer. No, she mustn't do that.

*Was she afraid she'd discover that Burt was lying to her?*

Monday morning Jan awoke to the immediate realization that this was auction day. Burt phoned as she was dressing to leave for Craig's office. His son was doing fine, though a bad cut had entailed a blood transfusion.

"I had to give blood," Burt said. "I nearly passed out."

They talked briefly because Burt was due at a client's office. Jan took it for granted that he would call her tomorrow. She didn't mention the auction. He had sufficient worries on his mind today. How rotten of her to be suspicious about the accident to his son.

Jan and Craig closeted themselves in his office to await phone calls from the six publishers who had read the manuscript and were expected to make offers. The morning swept past without a call. Craig sent out for lunch for Jan and himself. While they ate, Craig rehashed their situation.

"I couldn't set a floor – the way I orchestrated this deal originally – because we have no firm commitment from Donna. And we're not talking hard/soft." Which meant the hardcover house would share in paperback rights – a situation Craig had meant to avoid. "I explained I'm flying to Rome on Friday to meet with her. They've all seen the correspondence from Sam saying he loves the book and wants to do the film. But not having Donna signed up is a big drawback."

The phone rang. Craig lunged for the receiver. Jan put down her sandwich. Right away she realized the caller was a publisher. Craig looked less than elated.

"Remember, this is just the first bid," Craig cautioned when he put down the phone. He sighed. "Ten thousand. They'll go along with the option deals."

Ten thousand was a long way from a million, Jan thought while the part of the roast beef sandwich she had consumed churned in her stomach. Craig's silence told her that he, too, was involved in soul searching.

"Let's be realistic." His optimism resurfaced. "The day isn't over. Christ, why can't Sam call up and say he's scheduling the film?" Craig was on his feet again. Pacing. "But I'm making sure the book doesn't go out for a paperback sale – for any subsidiary sale – until we've got Donna signed. I've stipulated that no subsidiary rights deal can be solicited for a minimum of three months from signing."

"We're accepting ten thousand?" Jan was aghast.

"The auction isn't over," Craig pointed out. "We won't know the top bid until six o'clock. And remember, whatever deal we accept, there are option clauses that can shoot the money way up. Don't look so dejected. This is just the first round in a big sweepstakes." His joviality was meant to lift her spirits.

Craig paced about the room again, dissecting recent blockbuster novels and the deals surrounding them. Focusing on their own paperback prospects.

"Friday night I'll be on that flight to Rome, I swear to you, Jan. I'm coming home with Donna Warren's name on the contract. She owes Sam a film. He wants her to do this book." Jan knew Craig had received a Fedexed copy of the contract to be signed between Sam and Donna this morning. Sam, too, was growing anxious. "I'll push her into reading the manuscript. I'll get her signature on the contract."

By four in the afternoon they had received another offer for ten thousand, two offers for fifteen, and one for twelve five. All accepted the escalator clauses and stipulations. At five minutes to six the last of the publishers called in. Her offer was for twenty-five thousand.

"That's a big up-front price for a first novel," Marilyn Kahn, executive editor for Satlof Publishing, said while Jan listened in on an extension, "but we're excited about the book."

"Excited would be a hundred thousand advance," Craig countered.

"Not that excited," she said. "Twenty-five thousand is our top offer."

"You agree to the escalation terms and the stipulations?" Craig pinned Marilyn now.

"We agree," Marilyn said.

"No paperback action in less than three months?"

"We agree." Marilyn chuckled. "Craig, we want that movie deal as badly as you. When do you expect Donna Warren's okay to come through?"

"I'm flying to Rome on Friday," he told her. "I mean to come back with the movie sewed up."

Craig and Marilyn talked for another few moments. The deal was set.

"Satlof has a lot of new blood over there. And Marilyn is one very sharp lady. They'll fight with us," he prophesied. For a moment he was contemplative. "Okay. So we didn't get a hundred thousand or more. We're readjusting to the situation. We wouldn't have got the twenty-five thousand if it wasn't for that item Paula planted. They don't entirely buy it, but Satlof is guessing we can pull it off. And we will."

"Suppose Donna turns down the film?" Jan insisted on being realistic.

"Then we fight like hell for another star. We have to have a movie deal to pull off a fat paperback sale. With the right manoeuvring we'll get it. I'm calling Paula right now. You'll have lunch with her at The Four Seasons tomorrow. Nobody lunches with Paula at The Four Seasons unless something big is up. The next day you and I will have lunch there with Marilyn. If I can swing it, she'll bring Satlof himself with her. We've got the ball in our hands, baby. We have to run with it."

# Chapter Nineteen

Jan tried to be philosophical about the twenty-five thousand advance from Satlof Publishing. This was a large advance for a first novel – and one without any substantial subsidiary sales as yet. They had done this well only because of Sam's interest in the book as a movie vehicle for Donna Warren.

Marilyn Kahn had persuaded the publishing house that it was a hot property. That a huge movie sale and a big paperback sale would be acquired. They were playing along on her hunch.

Jan was also aware that the twenty-five thousand advance, to be split between Craig and herself, would first be subject to expenses laid out by Craig. The five thousand advance to Paula. All the typing and xeroxing expenses. Messenger services. The endless long-distance calls to California. And now Craig's rush trip to Rome.

She would not allow herself to believe that this could be the end of the line financially. They had Marilyn and Satlof Publishing fighting on their team now. As Craig said, their position was strengthening.

Craig cursed colourfully when Paula insisted she could not have lunch with Jan and him until Friday. Craig set it up for Paula and Jan alone. He would be too tied up on Friday, with an early evening flight to Rome, to squeeze in the luncheon.

When Burt phoned Jan on Thursday, she told him about the sale. He was impressed. They'd have dinner tonight to celebrate.

"I haven't seen you for a while," he reminded, his voice amorous.

"Are you having dinner with Dan?" Lisa asked interestedly when she learned that her mother was going out for the evening.

"No. With Burt Spencer," Jan said.

"Why don't you bring Dan up for dinner?" Lisa encouraged. "He's fun."

"I will soon," Jan said self-consciously. "He's busy at school right now."

At truant intervals through dinner Dan's face invaded her mind. Each time she ordered herself to forget about him. It was clear he meant to put their friendship on ice. She had been weaving fantasies when she thought he might be a little bit in love with her.

A heavy reader of current glitzy bestsellers, Burt was intrigued by the possibilities of *The Second Time Around.* He respected money and success despite his pride in having walked out of an important executive position for the insecurities of a freelance architect. He was knowledgeable about what was currently selling in the publishing field.

"I wish I had the time to read as much as you." Jan managed a light laugh. But a man who read so heavily from the bestseller list, she thought, was a man seeking escape.

After dinner Jan and Burt retreated to his apartment. His lovemaking was always arousing. Always the same pattern. She realized suddenly that he needed this whole production to perform. Again he coaxed her to stay over. Again she pointed out that, at this point, it would be awkward for her. But she would stay over some night, she promised.

"When?" he pressed.

"Some night when the kids are sleeping over at their friends' homes," she said. "They're both talking about sleep-overs soon." But that would be on a Saturday night. It was rare that she saw Burt on a Saturday. Where did he go?

Tonight, in a mood for fresh air and exercise, Burt walked her halfway home before putting her into a taxi. He would walk back to his own apartment, he said, as he kissed her goodnight. Last winter he had skied up at Stowe at least two weekends a month. This winter he'd had little exercise. He wanted to get into shape before summer.

"Maybe I'll sign up at a gym," he threw at her as she settled back in the taxi. "I like to keep in trim."

Away from Burt her thoughts focused on the luncheon tomorrow with Paula. She'd wear the black suit again but with a frilly white blouse. Ronnie had already arranged to borrow the chinchilla cape from her ex-sister-in-law. If the weather was unseasonably warm, she would wear the suit without the cape.

When Jan arrived home, Lisa reported that Craig had phoned. She pulled off her coat and reached to dial his number. He expected to be leaving the office for the airport shortly before four tomorrow afternoon. He would have dinner at JFK. He was in a sweat about missing the flight because of rush-hour traffic if he waited until later to leave for the airport.

"Hello." Craig's voice was harried.

"I just got in," Jan reported. "Did you hear something?"

"I spent two hours with Marilyn today. She expects to begin editing in about ten days. She'll want to work closely with you. I've been pushing them into a rush on the book. I'd like it to be on the shelves by November. To be a Christmas item."

"That's awfully fast." All at once she was assaulted by visions of a frenetic publicity campaign. Seeing herself dashing on and off planes. Racing from interview to interview. "What did Marilyn say?"

"We're at an impasse," he admitted. "Marilyn says she can persuade the firm on a fast deal like that only if we have either a major movie or a high paperback sale. Which puts the ball in our court." Craig sounded abnormally testy. "We have to sew up the movie before we're sure of a fat paperback sale. I may have to stay in Rome beyond Monday," he warned. "I've told Sally that you'll be in the office. If a call comes from Sam, you're to take it. You'll have to play this whole thing by ear."

251

*Julie Ellis*

"Then you want me to stand by at the office on Monday?"

"Monday and till I return," Craig said grimly. "Oh, more news. I'm flying to Paris instead of Rome. Sally managed to get me a seat on a Paris flight."

"Why Paris?" Jan was bewildered.

"Sam just called. These time differences are getting me crazy, but it all breaks down to Donna's flying to Paris at seven p.m. Rome time for a weekend in Paris. Sam told her I'd see her for lunch tomorrow at the Hotel Plaza-Athénée, where she's staying with Gino. If I can get her out of bed," he groaned.

"How does Sam feel about the situation?"

"Anxious." Craig sighed. "I don't want him to give up on the film because Donna's such a tough nut to crack."

"Does he sound like he might?"

"He's sold on the book, but Donna's driving him up the wall. If I don't get a chance to talk to you before I leave, look beautiful when you meet Paula. It's at The Four Seasons," he told her.

"I know," she said gently.

*     *     *

Despite the hardcover sale, Jan was nervous – conscious of all the past months when she had not earned a cent. She brushed aside thoughts of taking a taxi to The Four Seasons and settled for the Third Avenue bus.

She wished Craig was coming with her to the luncheon with Paula. This business of being seen with a high-powered public relations woman in the hunting grounds of high echelon publishing was unnerving. She was being shown off in a display case. Up for sale.

Yesterday morning the checker at the supermarket asked her if she was a writer and was that her picture in the story about Donna Warren's next movie? If *The Second Time Around* was to become a blockbuster, she'd have to become a full-time promotion woman. Other writers had managed to do it, from Jacqueline Susann to

252

Judith Krantz. Why not Janet Ransome? It went with the job. They knew they were not writing literature; they were writing entertainment.

Considering the potential rewards, she admonished herself, she would be ungrateful even to consider the promotion rat race a painful chore. Whatever Paula lined up for her – short of stripping in Saks' windows – she'd do.

Jan left the bus at Fifty-First Street. She was glad she had worn the chinchilla cape. The air crackled with a sharpness that reminded New Yorkers that winter had not yet departed. She walked up to Fifty-Second and cut west. Walking with compulsive swiftness though she had ample time.

Tension gripped her at the sight of The Four Seasons canopy. Paula would be waiting for her. The few times she had sat down with Paula, she'd felt ill at ease with her. Paula played a game. She doubted that anybody ever saw the real Paula King – except, perhaps, her husband.

Burt played a game, too. She suspected that his pursuit of her was a carbon copy of what every woman in his life these past eight years since his divorce had experienced. Why was it necessary for people to assume roles? Paula did it to make huge sums of money. Why did Burt? Was the real man he saw so unacceptable to him? He carried a lot of guilt for having walked out on his wife and kids. But he never dodged child support payments – unlike Tim – and Ronnie's husband, on occasion.

Jan opened the door and walked into the expansive entrance to the restaurant. For a moment she hesitated before the cloakroom at her right. No. Take the chinchilla cape with her. It was on loan. She crossed to the wide carpeted stairs at the left that led to the upper floor. Clearly the dining rooms were upstairs.

She followed a party of three to the reservation desk, admiring the pots of magnificent azaleas that sat close by. Aware of the potted trees that, someone had told her, were changed four times a year to match the current season. Waiting behind earlier arrivals to ask for Paula's table, she approved of the quiet elegance of the high-ceilinged room, dining balconies on either side.

She was surprised when she was led upstairs to the balcony area to the east. She would have expected Paula to be seated in the large square section, thus far lightly populated. On the balcony, tables for four lined the railing. Cosy tables for two were set against the attractive burnished wood-panelled wall. Paula sat at a particularly private table at the far end.

"Hello, Jan." Paula lifted her face for the conventional kiss on the cheek. "You're looking beautiful, as always. And that blouse is exquisite."

"Thank you." Jan knew compliments were part of the Paula King routine.

Jan slid into the chair opposite Paula. They went through the usual chit-chat until the waiter arrived. Paula ordered a martini. Jan settled for Perrier and a twist of lime. With Paula she needed a clear head. Sometimes it was difficult to follow her conversation.

Paula reported that she had talked with Craig this morning. Jan thought she detected a slight aura of condescension towards Craig. He was a newcomer in publishing, and Paula was the doyenne of book publicists. But Paula had accepted this deal, Jan reminded herself defensively. For a five thousand advance and a percentage of the profits.

"I hope Craig ties up this movie deal." Paula frowned in mild reproof that it had not already been accomplished. "The subsidiary rights people at Satlof need that to go after a big paperback sale. We can't lose sight of a serious complication. The contract that Craig worked out with the publisher ties in the amount of money they put up for promotion to the size of the subsidiary sales. Of course, I can set up local TV and radio guest shots, column items, all the usual local scene without their laying out a cent. But New York promotion alone won't put the book on the bestseller lists. We need at least a thirteen-city national tour. For that," Paula added pointedly, "Satlof has to pay."

"Sam seems confident that Donna will sign," Jan said uneasily. "He thinks it's just a matter of pinning her down to read the manuscript. He says she always goes along with scripts he approves."

"Let's hope so." Paula was unexpectedly acerbic. Now she embarked on a monologue about what she expected of Jan. No show was too small to appear on. In fact, she pointed out, before Jan went on tour she'd appear on every small local show – regular and cable TV and radio – within commuting distance. "That will break you in for the big time. You'll learn how to handle yourself. We can check on your make-up. There'll be stations where they won't have make-up people, and you must learn to do your own. Ann Raynor has been giving you great training, but these small shows are equivalent to an out-of-town run for a Broadway play. And you never show up at an appearance – no matter where it is – *without a copy of your book in your hand.*"

Paula paused briefly when the waiter appeared with their drinks and again when he came to take their orders. Much of what she said she had covered earlier. Clearly she was determined that it all be etched on Jan's brain.

"Remember, Jan. Authors don't just write books today. They must go out and sell them. You have to become a showbiz personality, pitching every minute. You have to think quickly, be prepared for whatever comes up. I know you're ambitious, and that's important." Her smile was disarmingly sweet.

"Paula, I'll do whatever you think is necessary," Jan promised.

"Never forget how much coverage you get through TV and radio," Paula pursued. "Publishers realize how much more they get for their promotion dollar through media appearances." Even Mike had pointed that out to her, and he knew little about publishing.

"Once the subsidiary sales are in, I'll lay the groundwork for the hardcover tour," Paula emphasized. "A year later you'll make a repeat run for the paperback release. But let's get back

*Julie Ellis*

to the hardcover tour." Mercifully months away, Jan comforted herself. "You'll need a smart, TV oriented wardrobe. You wear clothes beautifully." Paula's voice dropped into softness. "I'll help you select what to take on tour."

"Things that pack well," Jan reasoned. Why were they talking about this now? She remembered the prime object of this luncheon was for her to be seen with Paula King. Though it was unlike Paula to settle for a table off the beaten track this way. "Trying to iron a dress or a blouse in a hotel room can be deadly."

All at once she tensed as she talked. Paula's knee was pressing hers under the table. No! It was ridiculous to think Paula was making a pass. Probably she was so involved in their discussion she didn't realize it. "I'm the world's worst ironer anyway." Jan tried to sound humorous. But the pressure of the knee against her own was more insistent. Disturbingly eloquent. "But the tour's months ahead—" She was imagining this. Paula was *not* making a pass at her.

"We must plan everything well ahead," Paula said warmly. "It becomes so damn hectic later."

The waiter approached with their luncheon tray. Paula leaned back in her chair. The pressure of her knee against Jan's ceased. When the waiter left, Paula launched on reminiscences about her husband's last tour.

"I didn't see him for months, of course. But then we live fairly independent lives. At the beach house he has his wing, and I have mine."

Paula was charming, amusing, poised. And the errant knee resumed its pressure against Jan's. Jan didn't dare withdraw. She'd pretend she didn't understand, she decided, fighting panic. *She couldn't antagonize Paula.* She must not destroy their business relationship. Paula could be a lethal enemy.

A few minutes later, while Paula ladled out her customary gossip denigrating her earlier clients, Jan felt the slow withdrawal of Paula's knee from hers. What had led Paula to believe she would be receptive to a lesbian pitch? Because she had told

256

Paula she would do anything that was necessary? That didn't include accepting Paula as her lover.

Jan was relieved when at last the luncheon was over. Paula was rushing back to her office by cab. Jan murmured an excuse about having to run over to Saks to pick up something for Lisa. She needed to walk in the fresh air. She needed to clear her head.

She paused before a public telephone, debating whether to call Craig. He had probably left the office by now. He would be home packing. Why upset him when he was rushing off on such an urgent trip? She would have to tell him later about what happened at the luncheon with Paula. Somehow, her mind warned, Paula would seek to get back at them for this rejection.

Jan walked another few blocks, then paused at another public phone. She had to talk to Ronnie about Paula. The adjacent phone was not in use. Few people walked along the sidewalk, she noted. She'd keep her voice low – nobody would hear.

Ronnie listened without interruptions.

"I can't say I'm surprised," Ronnie admitted. "You know how people gossip."

"You've heard somebody say that Paula's a lesbian?" Jan was astonished. Not censuring – astonished.

"I've heard it, but then I've heard it about straight women, too. You know how people jump to conclusions. I imagine Craig knows."

"Why didn't he tell me?" Jan said in a burst of anger, feeling gauche that she had been unaware. "And why make a pass at me?"

"Maybe she thought you were so hungry for success you'd play along," Ronnie surmised. "Me," she laughed, "for the amount of money Paula King generates, I'd fuck a moose."

"I didn't try to catch up with Craig and tell him."

"Time enough when he gets back. Look, I think you need some cheering up," Ronnie pursued. "I'm taking you out to dinner tonight. Somewhere fancy. We'll dress. I just convinced Hank he should raise the child support cheques by a hundred a

257

month. He agreed because he's scared I'll take him into court again to have it raised even more. The bastard's making so much money it makes me sick. Pick me up at the apartment at seven. Okay?"

Jan walked the rest of the way home with a determination to wash from her mind the unnerving encounter with Paula King. It was Friday night. The kids would be happy to settle for pizza and a salad for dinner. She'd wash her hair and take a leisurely shower when she got home. Spend time on her make-up. That would ease away some of the awful tension. Recurrently she worried about having antagonized Paula.

Unlocking the apartment door she knew Brian was home. She heard the sound of the toilet seat making contact with the tank. She and Lisa had finally convinced him that toilet seats belonged down when not in male use. From Lisa's room came the roar of rock.

"Can I sleep over at Betty's?" Lisa asked before she was inside the door. "I'm invited over for dinner, too."

"May I," Jan corrected automatically.

"Okay, may I?"

"Why don't you sleep over here once in a while?" Jan complained.

"Betty comes over sometimes," Lisa said virtuously. "But it's more fun over there. She's got a whole floor for herself."

"All right," Jan capitulated. "But check in with me tomorrow morning."

"Okay." Lisa was the patient martyr now. "But don't expect me to call early."

"Ma?" Brian called from the bathroom doorway. "I'm sleeping over at Howie's. We're working on a project together for school. Okay?"

"Does his mother know about it?" Jan questioned.

"Sure. She says that keeps Howie home on Friday night. Then when the man on TV asks, 'Do you know where your children are?' she can say yes."

258

Within an hour both children were gone. Jan went in to shampoo her hair and shower. Tonight she could have slept over at Burt's place. Now she realized he had not called today. But then she'd been away for the long lunch with Paula.

For all the talk of women's lib, most women still waited for the man to take the lead. Burt had not said anything about their getting together tonight. She was glad Ronnie had suggested dinner. Don't think about Burt, she exhorted herself. But when she was with Burt, she could push Dan out of her thoughts.

Out of the shower and drying her hair Jan focused on what to wear for dinner. Ronnie said they'd dress. The turquoise silk, she decided. With the turquoise earrings Dan had brought back for her from Sedona.

Pleased with her decision, she laid out the dress and brought out black sling pumps. Now she went to her jewellery box, a Christmas present from Lisa and Brian, and reached inside for the turquoise earrings. They were missing. Where could they be? She was anguished at the thought that she might have lost the earrings Dan had given her.

She stood immobile before the jewellery box and tried to reconstruct the last occasion when she had worn the earrings. Dinner with Burt last night. Her face brightened. She had taken them off when they made love. They were on the table beside Burt's bed.

She must call and alert Burt about the earrings, her mind ordered. It was so easy for a pair of earrings to be brushed aside, perhaps caught up in a carpet sweeper or vacuum cleaner. She'd ask Burt to put them in some safe place.

Jan hurried to the phone and dialled Burt's number.

"Hello." He picked up on the third ring. *Was it Burt?* He sounded odd.

"Am I calling at a bad time?" she asked.

"Yes." He was terse.

"I'm sorry," she stammered. "Goodnight."

Her heart pounding, she put down the receiver. Burt had a

woman in his apartment. Probably she had interrupted their lovemaking. The phone was right beside the bed.

*I won't see him again. Not ever. This is the end of the line.*

All at once she felt shaken. She wanted no more of Burt. Dan had put their friendship on ice. Mike was long gone to San Francisco. She was without a man in her life again. *But she could survive.*

Painful laughter welled in her throat. In months to come – if everything went well with the book – she'd be on talk shows. Talking about the hazards of being single and unattached. Particularly single and unattached over forty. God, could she speak with conviction!

# Chapter Twenty

Suppressing a yawn because he had slept little during the flight between JFK and Orly, Craig paid the taxi driver and sprinted in the morning drizzle to the entrance to a relatively inexpensive hotel on Rue Richelieu. This was where his parents stayed on their now infrequent trips to Paris. At least, he thought with satisfaction, it was on the Right Bank.

Within minutes he was settled in a tiny but immaculate room with a private bath. He gazed longingly for a moment at the bed. No – he aborted this trend of thought – no time for a nap. A fast shave, a clean shirt, and he'd have to taxi over to fashionable Avenue Montaigne and the Hotel Plaza-Athénée.

While he shaved, he ran through his mind what he had read in the columns about Gino Armani. It was said there was not a woman in Rome who would not happily lie down for Gino. His films were automatic successes. Gino Armani was the quintessential male sex symbol.

Any set that must accommodate Gino Armani and Donna Warren must be as highly charged as a summit meeting between Israel and the Arab states. Particularly when the director and Donna were on a constant battlefield. But Donna was a hell of an actress, with just the right personal appeal for the role of Lori. Sam, too, saw that right off.

By the time a taxi deposited him before the Hotel Plaza-Athénée, Craig was conscious of having acquired his second wind. He was 'on'. He could handle Donna Warren.

Where would they have luncheon, he wondered. In the Régence

restaurant that looked onto the centre garden courtyard – which his mother had favoured in more affluent times – or in the Relais Plaza, which was the trendy place to be?

Stepping out of the taxi he was conscious of the line-up of Rollses, Ferraris, and Bentleys lined up at the curb. What else? Here was the haven of the ultra-rich. He admired the tiny garden and goldfish pond next to the entrance. With a special spring to his step he walked across the domed turquoise and gold lobby.

At the desk he was told that Mademoiselle Warren was expecting him. He was to go directly to her suite. Waiting for the elevator he was conscious of the elaborate livery of the help, who must outnumber the guests three to one. He remembered that the Plaza-Athénée was said to spend more money on flowers than on electricity, and already Craig believed this.

Involuntarily he stared for an instant at the woman who joined him in waiting for the elevator. The Hotel Plaza-Athénée was obviously the haunt of American celebrities as well as those from every country in Europe.

Donna herself greeted him at the door.

"Darling, has jet lag devastated you?" she crooned.

"I come from hearty stock," Craig laughed, accepting her hand. At the same time he admired the Louis XV decor of the suite's sitting-room, the chairs and sofas delicately carved and gilded, the upholstery in early eighteenth-century tapestries.

"I don't know why Sam insisted you fly over to talk to me about the book," Donna pouted. "I would have gotten around to reading it in a few days."

"Donna, we'll have lunch in the suite," a masculine voice called in English barely touched by an Italian accent. Gino Armani. A tall, virile man with rumpled dark hair and sardonic eyes strode into the sitting-room. His eyes passed over Craig. Not missing an inch. "I'm Gino," he announced superfluously with a warm caressing smile that disturbed Craig. You never knew what the man behind that kind of smile was thinking.

"Craig." He was receiving other vibrations now. But he must

be wrong. Gino was the prime Italian stud, catering to the great beauties of the world.

"Show Craig the view," Gino ordered. "I'll call room service and order lunch."

Donna drew Craig out onto the balcony that faced Avenue Montaigne and a montage of elegant shops. She was talking with a machine-gun rapidity about the minefield that was their movie set in Rome.

"I've never worked with a director so insane as this maniac! All he cares about are camera angles, atmosphere. Fuck it! The audience wants to see Gino make love to me in glorious technicolour. They don't care about light and shadows — they want to see as much skin as we dare to show. Every woman out in the audience wants to feel Gino pushing himself into her – and every man wants to have his hands all over me. He's Italian. He's hot-blooded. Why can't he understand?"

"You're director-proof," Craig soothed. "The audiences will love you."

"I've had enough of these foreign locales." Donna's voice dropped low. "I can't wait to get back to Hollywood."

"Donna!" Gino yelled from the sitting-room. "Champagne with lunch?"

"What else?" she demanded. "Seltzer?"

Lunch was a masterpiece, as Craig had anticipated. *Sole farcie*, which was boned and stuffed with mushrooms and topped with a champagne sauce and served with fresh asparagus. *Dom Perignon*, which Donna had adopted as her standard drink.

Donna talked non-stop – mostly invectives aimed at their director. Gino ate with the seriousness of a true gourmet, though at intervals Craig was aware of furtive inspections. He knew he'd have to wait for the right moment to launch into a campaign on the book.

"God, I'm bushed." Donna yawned expansively when luncheon was consumed and they were alternating champagne with espresso. "Gino and I haven't slept since Thursday night. Why

*Julie Ellis*

don't we all sack out for a while. Later," she decided with a
transitory burst of vitality, "we'll show you Maxim's. Do you
know Maxim's?" she probed.

"No," Craig lied diplomatically. It had been years, of course,
but he still remembered the Belle Epoque murals, the ornate
mirrors, the stained glass and polished brass of Maxim's. "But
I'd adore to go."

It seemed to Craig that within seconds of stretching out on
the bed in the second bedroom of the suite, he was sound
asleep. He awoke hours later to hear the sounds of a battle
emerging from the bedroom shared by Donna and Gino. Lying
still, eyes shut, he comprehended that Gino was having difficulty
performing. What man didn't on some occasion, Craig thought
sympathetically. Visualizing Gino – that marvellous body – he
felt himself becoming aroused.

"Gino, fuck me!" Donna screamed. "You said it would be all
right in Paris! Away from the set. Get it up!"

"Donna, make me hot," he coaxed. "Then we'll do it."

"Damn you, I've done everything! Nothing happens. You look
like an over-fried sausage!"

"Maybe your friend from New York," Gino said with insidious
casualness, catapulting Craig into total wakefulness. "Together
the three of us could have a wonderful time. Really special,
darling. You'll go out of your mind."

Craig lay immobile, eyes closed, face towards the windows while
the other two left their bedroom and crossed the sitting-room to
the bedroom where he lay. God, he had not expected anything
like this. Yet remembering Gino's eyes when they first met, he
cursed himself for not being prepared. How could he play coy
with Donna and Gino? He had to get Donna's signature on that
contract. If he didn't Sam would chuck the whole deal.

"Hi, sweetie—" Gently Donna shook him by one shoulder.
"You don't want to sleep away a whole weekend in Paris."

Craig forced himself to pry his eyelids apart. Donna and Gino,
both *au natural*, hovered beside the bed. He managed a sleepy

264

smile when he felt Gino's hands on him. In a few minutes Gino would be passionate. Donna would be happy. She'd sign the contract.

Oliver would kill him if he ever found out . . .

Jan knew the weekend would be an obstacle course painful to endure. On Saturday morning she awoke at seven despite a night of broken sleep. Instantly aware, as her eyes focused on the clock beside the sofa bed, that it was one p.m. in Paris. Was Craig sitting down to lunch with Donna yet? Were they talking about the book?

When would she hear from him? He would phone from Paris as soon as he knew where they stood. Whether the news was good or bad. Craig knew she'd die of impatience if she had to wait until he arrived back in New York on Tuesday evening. What would he say when she told him about the luncheon with Paula? But what could Paula do in reprisal? She strived to be realistic. If Donna signed, they didn't need Paula.

Early in the afternoon Ronnie came over. Jan told her about the phone call to Burt, and her reaction.

"Look, Jan, if you're getting emotionally involved with the guy, drop him fast," Ronnie advised. "On the other hand, if you can categorize him as good casual sex, then he can fill a basic need."

"I'm dropping him." Jan was firm. She had been able to have casual sex with Mike and enjoy it. She knew it wouldn't work that way with Burt.

"I'm driving out to East Hampton early tomorrow morning with two of the women and one guy from our house. The guy has a car. He offered to take us out so we can see the house before we start going out in June. We'll have breakfast on the road, lunch in East Hampton, and then drive back. It'll be pleasant," Ronnie predicted dreamily. "Great to see things turning green after a long, hard winter. Daffodils in bloom. If I call Jeff and ask him if he has room for one more in the car, would you come along?"

265

"Thanks, Ronnie," Jan's gaze settled on the phone, "but I'm not budging from the apartment today."

After several hours of courageous efforts to divert Jan from the Paris scene Ronnie left for her own apartment. She meant to be in bed by ten. Jeff was scheduled to pick her up at seven sharp.

Jan sprawled out with the Sunday *Times* when Brian brought it up from downstairs. She knew it would be hours before she fell asleep. *Would* she fall asleep tonight?

She was glad she had made that impulsive phone call to Burt. Now it was over with him. Why didn't she hear from Dan? Why was he being so distant since he came back from Sedona? She could survive even a disaster with the book if Dan was in her life. But he wasn't, and she didn't know how to deal with that.

In the morning Jan was relieved when first Brian and then Lisa dashed off for Sunday social activities. She put up coffee. Tea was for relaxation. Coffee was for emotional emergencies. She remembered her mother's cliché consolation: No news is good news.

By early afternoon she wished Lisa and Brian were back in the apartment. The silence was oppressive. Yet when she tried to watch television, she recoiled from this intrusion.

Ronnie was out at the Hamptons. She decided to call Peggy and invite her down for tea. But Peggy reported that Ralph and she were off to some exhibit in Soho.

Between five-forty and six o'clock the apartment became alive again. First Lisa, then Brian, then Ronnie arrived. After a fast raid on the refrigerator and an acknowledgement that dinner would be on the table within an hour, Lisa and Brian disappeared into their respective rooms. While Jan prepared a casserole for the oven, Ronnie fixed a salad. Then, with mugs of coffee in tow, the two women retired to the living-room.

"I gather the trip to East Hampton was a success," Jan surmised. Ronnie glowed.

"The house has the usual drawbacks," Ronnie admitted. "It's not first string. The bedrooms are small. The house is a drive

from the ocean unless you feel like a half-hour hike each way.
But something happened," she confided smugly.

"What happened?" Jan pounced. She had attributed Ronnie's
ebullient spirits to a day out of the city.

"The car conked out as we headed for lunch. Jeff tracked down
a garage that was open on Sundays, and they told him it would be
eight o'clock tonight before he could pick up the car. The others
were satisfied to hang around town until the car was ready. I was
restless." Ronnie smiled dazzlingly. "Somebody up there must
be plotting my life. I decided to take the Hampton Jitney back
into Manhattan. And on the Jitney I met Todd Stuart."

"Interesting man?"

"We clicked right off. As if we'd been matched through some
computer dating deal. Look, I'm almost always aware of being
part of the singles scene. Prospecting for a man. But I wasn't
even thinking of it today. And there he was."

"Tell me about him." It was a delight to see Ronnie so
enthusiastic about a man.

"He's not Tom Cruise," Ronnie admitted. "And I'm not Nicole
Kidman. Todd will be fifty in September. He's been divorced for
four years. A few days before their silver wedding anniversary
his wife told him she was packing it in. It hadn't been a working
marriage for years. His wife's main concern in life was her garden
club and social activities in suburbia. The usual problem. They
were married at college graduation and spent the next twenty-five
years growing apart."

"What does he do?"

"Right now he's a stockbroker. He's retiring in a year, and he
plans to work at what has been his avocation for years. In some
field to do with improving the environment. Jan, he doesn't play
games. I feel comfortable with him."

"Does he live out in the Hamptons?"

"No, in Manhattan. He was out at Montauk for what he calls
his once-a-month rejuvenation programme. He goes to Gurney's,
walks hours every day on the beach, swims in the saltwater pool,

relaxes in the sauna or steambath. Sleeps well, eats well and comes back ready for the rat race again."

"So there's hope for all of us." Jan laughed affectionately. "There are men out there."

They talked about men–women relationships until the timer went off. Jan hurried to take the casserole from the oven before it was burnt. Over dinner Lisa and Brian vied with each other in reporting their day's activities.

After dinner Lisa and Brian went to their rooms for the customary last-minute Sunday night hassle with homework. Jan stacked the dishes in the dishwasher. Ronnie put up more coffee,

"Baby, relax," Ronnie exhorted when they settled in the living-room with second rounds of coffee. Despite the diversion of conversation Jan was constantly aware of the crucial meeting being acted out now between Craig and Donna.

"If I was a pill-popper, I'd have been through half a bottle of Valium since Friday." Jan shook her head in frustration. "Craig's in Paris trying to sell Donna on signing the contract and meanwhile back on the farm I've screwed up things with Paula."

"You didn't screw," Ronnie reminded. Her chuckle was compassionate.

"Bad choice of words," Jan conceded.

When the phone rang, she rushed to pick up the receiver. *Craig?*

"Hello," she said eagerly.

"Hi, Jan. It's Cornell." Marianne's friend. "I couldn't reach Ronnie at her place so I figured she might be with you." He was clearly agitated.

"Yes, she is," Jan said, but Cornell rushed ahead.

"Something awful has happened! I went down to Marianne's apartment this afternoon. She had *Tosca* blaring on the stereo – you know she's mad about opera—"

"Yes—" Jan beckoned to Ronnie, but Cornell surged on.

"When she didn't answer the bell, I got terribly upset. I ran down and insisted the super unlock the door. We found Marianne unconscious on the floor. She's had a stroke."

"Oh, God!" Jan turned to Ronnie. "It's Cornell. Marianne's had a stroke."

Ronnie grabbed the phone and talked to Cornell while Jan hovered over her.

"Marianne's in the ICU at St Vincent's," Ronnie relayed. "Nobody is allowed to see her except her sister. She's on her way into Manhattan."

Ronnie agreed to come right over and stay with Cornell for a while.

"He's devoted to Marianne," Ronnie said when she put down the phone. "He's out of his mind with worry. They won't know for forty-eight hours just how bad she is. Damn those quacks!" Ronnie's voice crackled. "Why didn't she listen to Dr Swan and go on medication? Marianne didn't have to have a stroke!" Neither of them allowed themselves to consider that Marianne might not survive.

"Shall I go with you?" Jan offered while Ronnie pulled on her coat.

"No point. Cornell just needs some sisterly handholding. As soon as we know anything, I'll call you."

Jan walked with Ronnie to the door, then collected the still half-filled mugs and took them into the kitchen. So much was happening over one long weekend. Recurrently she remembered the turquoise earrings she had left in Burt's apartment. Somehow she would get them back, she promised herself.

She was too tense to read. She switched on the television and promptly switched it off again. She glanced at the clock. Not yet eight thirty. She flinched at the prospect of the empty hours ahead.

Was Dan home? Peggy insisted he was living alone now. She had not seen him since he returned from Sedona. Despite her

269

Julie Ellis

determination to push Dan from her mind, too often she found herself thinking about him.

She wasn't in love with Burt. She had tried to convince herself that there was another man inside Burt, whom she could learn to love. She needed to be in love to wash Dan out of her heart.

She could defrost that Black Forest cake in the freezer and invite Dan up for coffee. *Could she?* Women took the initiative these days. Why not, she challenged herself. She wasn't asking Dan to come up here to make love to her. He'd know that. With the kids in the apartment that would be impossible.

All at once warm with anticipation, her heart pounding, Jan reached for the phone.

"Hello." The familiar mellow voice elicited a surge of tenderness from her.

"I'm defrosting a Black Forest cake." She was faintly breathless in her effort to sound casual. "I thought maybe you'd like to run up and have some with me." How awful to be eating Black Forest cake when Marianne lay unconscious in the ICU, she thought guiltily. But Marianne was one of the reasons she needed to be with Dan tonight.

"How can I resist?" There was a lilt in his voice. "Shall I come right up?"

"The coffee's brewing already," she tempted.

"I'm on my way."

Five minutes later she heard Dan at the door. Her face lighted. It had been such a long time since she had seen him. She had not even encountered him in the elevator or the lobby since he came back from Sedona. She pulled the door wide with a welcoming smile.

"Hi." The softness of her eyes told him she had missed him. She was learning to take the initiative, she congratulated herself. The theme song of today's woman.

"I've missed seeing you," he told her.

"Don't be such a stranger," she admonished lightly, closing the door behind him.

270

"Mom?" Lisa peeked out of her room. "Hi, Dan!" She was vibrant with welcome. "We haven't seen you since forever."

"I've been away," he explained. Seeming self-conscious. "How's school?"

"Oh, I hate math," Lisa moaned. "Would you help me with this assignment?" Her face brightened. Dan had given her several assists with homework in the past.

"How can I say no when you smile at me like that?" he chuckled. "Lead me to it."

"I'll check on the coffee." Jan turned towards the kitchen. It pleased her that the children liked Dan.

"If there's coffee, there's cake," Lisa calculated. "Me, too!"

"You, too," Jan assured her.

All at once the apartment seemed a warm and cosy place to be. Jan busied herself in the kitchen while Dan helped Lisa with her math. When the coffee was ready and the cake sufficiently defrosted to serve, Jan summoned Brian to join them. Complacent in the knowledge that once the kids had demolished their cake and polished off their milk they would return to their rooms.

She waited until Dan and she were alone to tell him about Marianne. Dan was encouraging.

"She received quick medical attention," he pointed out. "That's important. With today's medical miracles many stroke victims return to normal lives."

Now she briefed him on the auction and Craig's rush trip to Paris. She said nothing about Paula. It was so good to be able to talk with Dan again. To be in his company.

Then Dan read the last two poems in his collection for her. They were close again, she rejoiced. He talked about his poetry and about Grey Creek Canyon, which seemed so important in his life. Then at last he reluctantly admitted he must be leaving.

"I have an early class on Mondays," he reminded, just as the phone rang.

"That's Ronnie with word about Marianne," she guessed and rushed to pick up the phone. "Hello—"

*Julie Ellis*

"It's Craig," he said. Why did he identify himself? When had she not recognized his voice?

"You're back already?" Alarm made her voice sharp.

"I'm in Paris. In Donna's suite." Now she understood.

"You can't talk freely."

"That's right."

"Does she like the book?"

"Possibly. I'm flying to Rome in a few hours. Will you explain to the office staff and follow through?"

"She hasn't read it yet, but she will when you get to Rome," Jan interpreted, simultaneously waving a hand in farewell to Dan.

"Right. Paris is always beautiful in April. Like they say in the song."

"Do you know when you'll be flying home?"

"I've reserved a seat on the afternoon flight out of Rome on Tuesday. I should be able to keep to that schedule."

"Craig, be persuasive," Jan urged, knowing this was needless. "But it's the part more than the book that she'll care about."

"That's right."

"Shall I call Sam in Hollywood and tell him you're flying to Rome with Donna?"

"Good thought. If the office needs me, I'll be at Donna's apartment most of the day tomorrow. Let me give you the phone number."

"Tell her my apartment is at the top of the Spanish Steps. It has the most gorgeous view in Europe," Donna's startlingly familiar voice trilled.

"I'd better cut this short," Craig picked up. "We're stopping by my hotel for my luggage before we head for Orly. We have to be in Rome by nine a.m. Rome time."

"So Donna and Gino can be on the set," Jan figured. *When would she have time to read the book?*

"Right, darling. Grab a pencil and write down the phone number at Donna's apartment."

\*     \*     \*

272

Craig put down the phone and turned to Donna.

"All set?"

"As soon as Gino comes out of the shower." Her face was taut. "Once the film is finished, that character goes out of my life."

"You'll find somebody else," Craig soothed. "You always do. You're Donna Warren. And on the plane," he said with resolve, "you'll read the book."

"No, darling." Donna threw him off base. "I hate reading books. You'll sit with me on the flight. Gino will want to sleep. He's worrying already about how he'll look on camera tomorrow. Today," she giggled as she corrected herself. "And while Gino sleeps, you'll tell me about the book."

"It's not a great book, Donna." Craig was deliberately conscientious. How many great books became films? "It's a page-turner. But the part of Lori can be a great role in your hands. Jan saw you in every scene she wrote. She knew that the women in the audience would suffer with you. You'll show fifty million moviegoers what it's like being divorced and over thirty-five in 1995." He diplomatically lowered the age from forty to thirty-five. "The swinging side and the tormented side. They'll laugh with you and cry with you – and thrill with you when you make a big career-wise move *plus* land your man and hold him. The Nineties woman means to have it all!"

"I know Sam loves the book," Donna said with devious softness. Craig saw the glitter of reality in her eyes. "But I have to be sure about my part. Tell me everything that happens to this girl. Make me see it as a sensational role for me."

\*      \*      \*

Jan saw Lisa and Brian off to school, then concentrated on getting dressed to go in to Craig's office. She would phone Sam around ten o'clock West Coast time. No point in phoning the hospital about Marianne again. She'd called when she woke up

273

at seven. Marianne was on the critical list. But that was to be expected, she consoled herself.

Walking into the reception room of Craig's office Jan felt an immediate awareness of catastrophe. Sally and the editor who had arrived thus far were huddled over a folded back newspaper.

"The bitch!" Sally's voice was unsteady. "The lousy bitch!"

"What's happened?" Alarm zigzagged through Jan.

"The morning newspaper," Sally said furiously. "This column item." She handed over the newspaper and pointed out the item she had red-pencilled.

Jan read and turned to ice:

*'Donna Warren, currently filming in Rome, will be furious when she discovers she is being used to promote a novel by a woman named Janet Ransome. Ransome's writing credits consist of confession stories and porn for the sleaziest of men's magazines. Donna has never seen the so-called manuscript which she is supposedly panting to film.'*

Paula at work! So vindictive that she would try to wreck a property in which she had a financial interest. It couldn't be anybody else.

"A letter from Paula King was delivered by messenger just before you walked in," Sally said. Sally, too – without comprehending – suspected Paula. "Since Craig won't be in today, don't you think you ought to open it?"

"Yes," Jan agreed, her heart pounding. She reached into her purse. "Here's the number where he'll be staying."

Sally took the slip of paper and went into Craig's office for the letter from Paula. Churning at the ugliness of the situation Jan opened the envelope. The letter was brief and to the point. A cheque was enclosed. In view of the disclosure of Jan's background she was withdrawing from the campaign. *That was the joke of the year. Paula was cutting out because her pass had been ignored.*

Paula had deducted what she considered a fair amount for

274

her efforts to date. Satlof was being advised that she was no longer handling promotion for the book. What would Marilyn Kahn – everybody at Satlof Publishing – think when they read that item? That Craig and she were con artists!

"Bad news?" Sally was anxious.

"We'll survive." Jan handed over the letter.

Sally scanned the contents.

"Craig will be livid," Sally predicted. "What can you do?"

"I'm calling Craig to see if Donna's signed." She checked her watch. Calculating the time in Rome. *She* had signed the book contract; it had not yet been signed by Satlof. A verbal agreement wouldn't stand up in court. "We need to issue a rebuttal to that item."

Only now did Jan realize she was trembling. How dare the newspaper make it sound as though she were some sort of charlatan because she had written confessions and stories for the men's magazines! Sure, they had lied about Donna's interest in the book, Jan forced herself to concede. That part had been a gamble that troubled her at the onset. *But Sam wanted Donna for the starring role. And Donna owed Sam a film.*

"Should I try to put the call through to Craig now?" Sally asked. "It's afternoon in Rome."

"Please do."

After she talked to Craig, she'd have to call Marilyn Kahn. Maybe nobody over there had seen the column. But word would reach them fast enough. Someone in Satlof's publicity department must scan the columns daily for items on their writers. Let her be able to tell Marilyn that the item was a lie. That Donna Warren was signed for the film.

In minutes Jan had Craig on the phone.

"Craig, has Donna signed?" Jan asked without preliminaries.

"She'll give me a decision when she finishes shooting today. We're having dinner together. She won't read the book," he admitted with exasperation. "I had to break it down on the flight here. I gave an Academy Award performance." He paused. "You sound uptight. Something go wrong?"

"It's too complicated to go into over the phone. I was just hoping that—"

"Go into it," Craig interrupted.

As succinctly as possible Jan briefed him on her luncheon with Paula and on this morning's repercussions. She listened while he cursed in outrage. She felt sick with apprehension. They had come this far. Would Paula King grind it all down to nothing?

"As soon as I talk with Donna, I'll call you back," Craig promised. "If I was a Catholic, I'd tell you to light a candle. A hundred candles! But thank God for the time difference. If the word is good, you'll be able to tell Marilyn before their office day is over. You'll call Sam out in Hollywood and have him phone that son-of-a-bitch of a columnist and make her eat crow!"

"And if the word is not good?"

"We won't even think about that," Craig said. "Call you later, Jan."

# Chapter Twenty-One

Jan prowled about Craig's office, drank endless cups of coffee. Craig had his business to fall back on if this deal fell through. But her whole future – and the children's – hung on Donna Warren's signing to play Lori in *The Second Time Around*.

Shortly before one, when Sally and the editors had gone out to lunch, Ronnie showed up with take-out food in tow.

"I figured you'd forget to eat," she said when Jan confessed she had not even thought about lunch. "Let's collapse on the sofa in Craig's office and eat. Cornell called just before I left to tell me that the doctors say Marianne is responding well to treatment. They're counting on almost total recovery."

"Thank God for that."

"If Cornell had not acted fast, Marianne would be dead. After this no more aura lady or those other quacks. Marianne will take her medication if Cornell and I have to sit on her. People don't have to die from high blood pressure – they can control it."

While they ate, Jan brought Ronnie up to date. Ronnie had not seen the column, but she comprehended that millions of avid gossip fans had read it.

"I figured Paula would try to kick you in the teeth. Even if it costs her. But Craig's out there fighting. My money is on Craig. When will he call?" Ronnie asked.

"I imagine it'll be around three or four New York time. I won't leave the office until I hear."

"Call me," Ronnie ordered. "If Craig hasn't called by the time my office closes, I'll be over."

The afternoon crept past. Every minute seemed an hour. Jan's anxiety intensified when three o'clock went past without a call. Then four o'clock. At five o'clock Jan called home and told Lisa that she was tied up at Craig's office.

"There's money in the jacket of my corduroy coat," Jan told her. Their hiding place for emergency cash. "Run downstairs and pick up a pizza for Brian and yourself. And fix one of your gorgeous salads," she wheedled.

"Why can't you come home?" Lisa demanded. But Jan knew that Brian and she would be content with pizza and a salad.

"I told you. I have to stay here. I'm waiting for a call from Craig in Rome."

"Is Donna going to be in the movie?"

"That's what I'm waiting to find out." At least, Lisa and Brian hadn't read the item vilifying her, she comforted herself. "Be sure to settle down to homework right after dinner. You have a test tomorrow."

At five thirty the staff prepared to leave.

"I'll lock up," Jan told Sally.

"Would you like me to stay?" Sally was torn between loyalty and social life. Jan knew she was meeting her male room-mate right after work. So far it was platonic. Sally had other ideas.

"No need. There's no telling what time Craig will call. Ronnie will be over in a little while to keep me company."

At twenty-five to six Craig phoned.

"She's signed, Jan!" Craig's voice was vibrant with elation. "In the presence of a Rome lawyer. In triplicate. Call Sam and tell him we have her signature on the contract."

"Craig, that's marvellous!" Her emotions were on a merry-go-round. She couldn't actually absorb – just yet – the fact that they'd won this sweepstake. Donna Warren would play Lori in *The Second Time Around*. There would be a major motion picture produced by Sam Martin. "It's too late to call Marilyn," she realized with regret. "I'm sure the office is closed."

"Try to reach her at home. After you've got through

278

to Sam and asked him to demand a retraction from the columnist."

"Do you have Marilyn's home phone number?" They didn't have to worry about the price of transatlantic calls. Not with Craig's package ready to be sewed up.

"I don't have it. But check all the M Kahns in the Manhattan directory. She'd never list her first name – that's an open invitation to obscene phone callers." Unexpectedly he chuckled. "Paula's done us a favour. This will buy us extra publicity for the book. She's going to hate that," he said with satisfaction.

"If I can't track Marilyn down tonight, I'll catch her as soon as she comes into the office tomorrow," Jan promised.

"I'm taking the two twenty p.m. flight out of Rome tomorrow. I'll arrive at JFK at four thirty p.m. New York time. I should be in my apartment by seven. I'll buzz you the minute I get there."

The ball had been kicked off. *They had a major motion picture.* Next they'd have a major paperback sale. A book club. Foreign sales. With luck Craig would drive the price tag up to a record price for a first novel. It wouldn't matter that a large chunk of that money would be options. The potential was there. They'd make the front page of the *New York Times.* The *Wall Street Journal.*

Feeling herself living in a strange, exciting new world, Jan sat alone in the empty office and tried to assimilate what was happening. It wouldn't be real for her until she sat down with Craig and held that signed contract in her hand. But what could go wrong now? Donna had signed in the presence of an attorney.

What was she doing, just sitting here and talking to herself? Phone Sam. She reached for Craig's Rolodex to check out Sam's phone number, dialled. His secretary reported he was in conference.

"Ask him to call Craig Yarbrough's office in New York, please. As soon as he's free. It's urgent."

"Does he have the number?"

"Yes, but let me give it to you again."

Jan was combing through the M Kahns in the Manhattan

directory when Sam called back. She briefed him on the signing, reassured him with the information that Donna had signed in the presence of a local attorney. When she told him about the column item and their conviction that Paula was responsible, Sam related a malicious Paula King story of his own. He promised that the newspaper would print a retraction.

Jan tried every M Kahn in the phone directory. Two didn't answer. One – obviously not Marilyn – had his answerphone report that he was at his health club and would be home at nine. The others were not Marilyn Kahn. Okay, Jan told herself philosophically. She'd talk to Marilyn first thing in the morning,

Ronnie phoned from her office as Jan was about to leave for home.

"She's signed," Jan reported.

"Baby, you've made it," Ronnie chortled. "If I wasn't stuck here at the office – and I'll be here for hours – we'd go out and celebrate."

"I can't believe it!" One call from Rome and her whole life was changed. Craig had said, '*You start the ball rolling, and it moves ahead on its own momentum.*' "It's like hearing you've won the Irish Sweepstakes."

"You'll get used to it, darling," Ronnie crooned. "Enjoy. Remember, in this world we have to nurture all the great moments that come along. They have to see us through a lot of crud."

Arriving at the apartment, Jan discovered Lisa in the kitchen, busy with salad makings. Brian had agreed reluctantly that it was his responsibility to bring up the pizza.

"Burt called," Lisa remembered. "He's called three times."

"I'll get back to him later." She had not expected Burt to call again. But she'd return this call, she decided. She meant to retrieve the earrings she left at his apartment on Thursday. The earrings Dan had brought her from Sedona. "After I talk to Dan."

"Burt said to call the instant you got in," Lisa rebuked.

"All right," Jan soothed. "I will."

Lisa returned to the kitchen. Jan sat down before the phone.

She had promised herself, after she interrupted Burt in his romantic interlude on Friday evening, that she would never see him again. But the earrings were a strong incentive. Was she being mid-Victorian to be turned off because she knew he played the field? A lot of women – including Ronnie – expected a one-to-one relationship.

Jan forced herself to dial Burt's number, waited for him to pick up.

"Hello." Tonight Burt sounded serene and friendly.

"Lisa said you'd called." She tried not to sound hostile.

"A client gave me two tickets for this evening's performance of *Sunset Boulevard*. He can't make it. Would you like to go?" That aborted telephone conversation might never have happened. "I know it's short notice, but it's a shame to throw away seventh row seats to a great show. I've seen it, but I'd like to see it again."

"I'm free," she said, after an instant of indecision. This was the excuse to pick up her earrings. "Would you like to run over for a quick dinner?" She checked her watch. It would be a mad rush, but the invitation was obligatory.

"It's too late," Burt rejected. "Let's have dinner after the performance."

"Fine." It was difficult to appear casual. Why had she agreed to go to the theatre with him? Why couldn't she have asked him to bring the earrings into his office and leave them with the receptionist? Then she could have picked them up without ever seeing him again. Why were the sensible thoughts always after-thoughts?

"I'll meet you in front of the Minskoff Theatre at a quarter past eight," he said briskly and hung up.

Conscious of time at her back Jan dressed swiftly. It was too late to call Dan. She'd talk to him tomorrow. She chose the grey velvet Ralph Lauren skirt and the full-sleeved grey silk blouse that she had bought to wear with it. It was dressy enough for the theatre and yet casual. Burt tended towards casual wear.

Why did she worry about pleasing Burt? But that was a habit that died hard with women.

She talked briefly with Lisa and Brian. She confided that it seemed definite that Donna Warren would appear in *The Second Time Around*, but she swore them to secrecy for the present. She hurried downstairs and out onto the street to search for a taxi.

She was nervous about snaring a cab this close to theatre time. Her worry was needless. In a moment she spied an unoccupied taxi. Her hand shot upward to signal the driver. She would arrive on schedule.

If nothing went wrong with the book, she could take taxis without this sense of guilt. Jan leaned back and gazed at the passing streets as the taxi shot across to Madison, deserted at this hour, and swung north. Everything that was happening was still veiled in unreality. She wasn't the same Janet Ransome who had awakened this morning. Now she knew her destination. Nothing would go wrong with the book from this point on.

The realization that everything they had fought for was almost within their grasp was simultaneously exciting and frightening. All his life Craig had been convinced this time would arrive. To her it was a new and exotic prospect.

In her mind she tried to consider rationally what lay ahead. With Donna signed, a major paperback sale was guaranteed. All the other goodies would fall into place. The months would speed past, and she'd have to go out and promote the book. Scary but part of the operation. *Would she wake up tomorrow and discover this was all a dream?*

Tomorrow, Jan promised herself, riding on a cloud of exhilaration, she would run out and shop for some special gifts for Lisa and Brian. To make up for the lean birthdays and Christmas this year. They were dear kids, she thought tenderly. Let her be a good mother. Let her raise Lisa and Brian with a skill that would keep them from missing the presence of a father in their lives.

The taxi deposited her in front of the theatre. Already a festive crowd gathered on the sidewalk and in the lobby. A quick survey told her Burt had not arrived. Again she rebuked herself for accepting tonight's invitation. She didn't want to spend an evening in Burt's company.

She stood at the curb and watched for him to arrive. At exactly a quarter past eight he stepped out of a taxi.

"Hi." His eyes were warm and approving as they rested on her. Part of the act? "Have you been waiting long?"

"No, I just arrived."

People were moving into the theatre now. Burt and she joined the procession. They were in choice seats, Jan acknowledged with the first flurry of anticipation. She loved the theatre. This was an unscheduled celebration for what happened in Rome. She wouldn't mention it to Burt. She was disappointed that there had been no time to share the news with Dan. She was eager to see his face light up when she told him Donna had signed. He knew what that meant for the success of the book.

Burt helped her out of her coat. His face wore a reminiscent glow.

"You were wearing that outfit the first time I saw you," he said softly.

"I was." She was surprised that Burt remembered. "At Ronnie's party."

When the lights went down, Burt reached for her hand. He was tense, she thought. He knew she was upset about that phone call. Her voice had told him that, even in that brief exchange. Did he expect to be able to pick up where they had left off? He didn't know her at all, did he?

At intermission they joined the throngs outside the theatre. The air was warm and sweet. Burt talked about the house out at the Hamptons. The house he had meant to show her on that aborted Sunday excursion. He was impatient for the arrival of summer. He relished weekends at the beach.

When the lights flickered, they returned to their seats. Jan found the performance a delight, but Burt seemed restless during

---

the second act. Was it because he had seen the musical before? Not likely. It was great entertainment that could be enjoyed several times. Now Burt was reading the programme. In the middle of a particularly intense scene. Jan suspected he wasn't seeing the words.

She heard a low grunt from him as the curtain descended.

"Are you hungry?" he asked while the audience demanded repeated curtain calls.

"Vaguely." She had settled for a piece of toast and a chunk of cheese as she dressed. Burt had said they'd have dinner after the theatre.

"There's a new pastry shop near my place. Let's grab a cab and go up there."

"Fine." So they wouldn't have dinner, she shrugged this off. Burt seemed upset. Maybe he was working with a problem client. Like the last one who kept demanding changes in construction when Burt thought an apartment was finished.

With all the theatres breaking about this time they walked to Fifth Avenue before they discovered an available taxi. In response to her inquiry about an assignment he had discussed at their last evening together, Burt launched into a lengthy account.

"Look, we're not trying to break speed records," he interrupted himself to castigate the driver. "Slow down!"

Jan was not aware that the driver had been speeding. She sensed an undercurrent of rage in Burt that was unnerving. Unrelated to the speed of the taxi. She had never seen him in a mood like this.

She brought Burt back into the discussion again with the feeling that she was sharing a taxi with a total stranger.

"Stop at this corner," Burt interrupted himself again to instruct the driver, who slowed down and pulled to a stop on the avenue. "Don't you understand English?" Burt snapped. "I said on the corner."

The driver swung about to confront Burt. His face was tinged with a dark red colour.

"I stopped on the corner," he said belligerently. "On the avenue instead of the street because I turned with the light."

"Here." Burt pulled a ten dollar bill from his wallet and handed it to the driver.

"Haven't you got singles?" the driver asked.

Scowling in the light that the driver had switched on in the cab, Burt reached into his pocket.

"I have only three singles."

"All right, let me have that." The driver retreated from belligerency. Intent now on avoiding a fight.

"I have more singles," Jan said hurriedly and dug into her purse. She wouldn't go up to Burt's apartment tonight. Not even for the earrings. In this mood he scared her.

They went into the charming new pastry shop. She had never been to any place twice with Burt. How strange. A waitress led them to a small booth and presented them with menus.

Burt was impatient for the evening to be over, she realized when he looked at his watch. Why had he bothered asking her out? She would have preferred not to have seen him tonight. Or ever again.

Was it because he didn't like winding up a relationship – if what they'd had could be dignified by that name – because he'd been caught in bed with another woman?

Astonishingly they were able to carry on small talk over chocolate mousse cake and espresso.

"You left your earrings up at the apartment," he said when the waitress brought the cheque to their table. "Come up for them?"

Instinctively she knew this wasn't an invitation to bed. He was worried about getting the earrings back to her. To clean off the slate.

"I'll run up with you for the earrings," she agreed, no longer scared. They were playing their final scene.

They walked to Burt's apartment as though this was any other evening when they had been out together. His hand reached for

285

hers as they crossed the street. But she was beginning to accept what she had suspected in uneasy moments. Burt was another man looking for a room-mate. For convenient sex and no expenses because a room-mate would share the rent and the rest of the scene. He had finally got the message that she was a woman with two children and responsibilities she had no intention of shirking. *Not a prospective room-mate.*

Burt never saw past her face and body to the woman inside. Perhaps he wasn't capable of that. He could not see the warmth and love and companionship she might have been able to give him. He was too wrapped up in his own neuroses.

Burt's phone was ringing as they approached the door to his apartment. He rushed to unlock it, then hurried into the bedroom to pick up the phone.

"Hello." He sounded irritated at being disturbed. "I can't talk to you now." The terse voice she remembered. He didn't mean to try to make love to her, did he? They knew it was over. "I can't talk now," he said after a few moments. But he remained on the phone. He was auditioning again for a room-mate, she thought.

Jan glanced about the small living-room. If she could pick up the earrings, she'd just go on alone. Her eyes settled on the stereo. There they were. She crossed to pick up the earrings and walked to the bedroom doorway. Burt looked up with a frown.

"I'll run along," she whispered, and he hung up.

"I'll put you in a taxi," he told Jan.

When he had hailed a cab for her on the southbound avenue, he bent to kiss her goodbye with a warmth she had not expected. But Jan knew it was over for Burt and her – and she was glad.

It had never been truly right for them. She had been vulnerable. She had shut her eyes to the array of small warning signals that were visible from the beginning. Like so many women before her.

She knew now. The only man she wanted in her life was Dan.

# Chapter Twenty-Two

Jan's initial thought when she awoke was that she must call Marilyn Kahn and tell her that Donna had signed for the film The office opened at nine. Marilyn probably arrived between nine thirty and ten. She ought to wait until ten to call.

Her eyes sought the clock. She didn't have to get out of bed for another ten minutes. These final ten minutes were always a cherished luxury. Once she had Lisa and Brian off to school, she would phone Dan and tell him. He'd be happy for her.

It didn't matter now that Paula had been so rotten. And there'd be the added publicity of a retraction. Satlof's promotion department would move ahead with full speed. They didn't need Paula King. No worries now about the Satlof contract coming through. By next March the hardcover would be arriving in the bookstores.

While Lisa and Brian focused on breakfast, she phoned Dan. She was disappointed that he had already left the apartment. But she would talk with him later.

Lisa and Brian left for school. Jan waited impatiently for the moment to arrive when she could try to reach Marilyn. The Satlof office must know about the column item. It was amazing that nobody had phoned about it. But Marilyn knew that Craig was in Paris, she reasoned. She was a sharp lady. She must realize Craig wouldn't be in Paris if he wasn't confident of having the contract signed.

She was just about to dial Satlof Publishing when Peggy phoned.

"Jan, can you come up for coffee?" Her voice was shrill and agitated. "I've got to tell you what Hal just pulled on me!"

"I have to make a call first, Peggy." She hesitated. "I have to stay close to the phone. Why don't you come down here? In about ten minutes."

"In ten minutes," Peggy accepted. She was annoyed at the delay, though. "You won't believe this, Jan!"

Jan managed to free herself of further conversation and hastily dialled Satlof Publishing, asked for Marilyn's extension.

"Hello." Marilyn picked up on the first ring.

Before any discussion of the newspaper item Jan told her that Craig was arriving at JFK tonight. He had Donna's signature on the contract. Marilyn was delighted. Now Jan told her that Sam was demanding a retraction from the newspaper. This, too, pleased Marilyn. Satlof's PR department would take over from Paula.

"We mean to have the book in the stores by mid-November," Marilyn told her. *Not March.* "In time for Christmas business. It's terribly tight, but we can swing it."

Jan was off the phone only a few moments when the door-bell rang.

She opened the door for Peggy and darted into the kitchen to check on the coffee-maker.

"You won't mind that the coffee's been sitting a while, will you?" she asked apologetically. "If it bothers you, I can boil water for instant."

"I won't know what I'm drinking this morning." Peggy's face was etched with agitation. "You know Ralph's been staying with me since he was thrown out of his studio? And it's been so nice. He brings me breakfast in bed every morning, and he cooks exotic ethnic dishes for dinner." She paused. "And when Ralph makes love to me, it's a lot different from Hal's fumbling. He makes me feel important. Special," she summed up defiantly. No matter that he was so much younger than she.

"What happened to upset you?" Jan asked.

"Hal must have had a detective following me." Peggy grimaced. "How else could he know? He called up this morning and threatened to go to court to reopen the alimony agreement. If I'm shacked up with a guy, he said, why should he be paying me alimony? Damn it, I earned that money! I took care of his rotten house for twenty-four years. I raised his two sons!"

"Talk to your attorney about it," Jan advised. "He'll know where you stand."

"I called the lawyer. He's off in California. But I won't let anything happen to my alimony. I told Hal that Ralph is just a friend who's staying a few days while his place is being painted, that he needed to use my studio to finish an assignment. I'll tell Ralph tonight – he'll have to move right out. I can't do anything to jeopardize my alimony."

Jan went into the kitchen to pour coffee for them. Peggy would spend the rest of her life worrying that she might lose her alimony. Why couldn't she let go and begin to live again? For a little while – after Tim left her – she thought her own life was over. That she existed solely for Lisa and Brian. But she was wrong. Dan made her realize that.

"I'm calling Hal back at his office," Peggy decided. "I'll tell him I'm not staying at the apartment. I won't be back until Ralph is gone. Which will be tomorrow," she said insistently. "May I sleep down here tonight? I can bring up some blankets and sleep on the floor." This was the wistful little Louisiana belle Jan had seen on their first encounter. "I'd be so grateful, Jan."

"You'll sleep on the other sofa," Jan said. "The living-room is a little snug with the sofa bed opened up, but you can slide through. It's fairly comfortable."

"I'll tell Ralph he has to go. He can move out any time tomorrow. And if Hal's sneaky detective comes around, he'll find out I'm sleeping here tonight. I'll bring down my own linens and pillows. You won't have to worry about that. Is it all right if I come down around nine? I have a class from six to eight."

289

"Nine o'clock is fine," Jan assured her. "Whenever is comfortable for you." The kids shouldn't be upset; they had their own rooms. And there were two bathrooms to cope with the morning rush. "If I'm not home, Lisa and Brian will be here."

Jan tried several times to reach Dan on the phone, increasingly frustrated that he was not home. She longed to share her news with him. Dan would understand how much it meant to her. After all the years of being a closet writer – because Tim would be embarrassed if her markets became public – it was satisfying to be able to say, 'I'm a writer.' She was a person in her own right. Not just a wife and mother.

Again at six o'clock she tried to reach Dan. Still no answer. At a few minutes past seven, as she was sitting down to dinner with the children, Craig called.

"I was in a taxi at JFK before five thirty," he boasted. "The only delay on the road was once we were in Manhattan. Jan, you want to see the contract?"

"You know I do!" she laughed.

"I figured. I'll bring it over in a little while," he promised. "Now tell me everything Marilyn said when you told her Donna had signed."

Lisa and Brian were excited about Donna Warren appearing in the movie. That was more exciting to them than knowing the book would be published. They were dying to pass on the news to their friends. Very soon they could.

After dinner Lisa and Brian escaped to their rooms. Jan loaded the dishwasher, picked up the assortment of clothes strewn about the living-room and returned them to their respective quarters. When did kids learn that the living-room was not the family dumping ground?

The buzzer from downstairs was a jarring intrusion. But her face lighted. That would be Craig. Peggy would come directly to the apartment.

She pushed the intercom button.

"Yes?"

"Mr Yarbrough is here," the doorman reported.

"Ask him to come up, please."

Jan was waiting at the open door when Craig emerged from the elevator. He sauntered towards her with a wide grin on his handsome, deceptively young face.

"You want to see the contract?" he teased and reached inside his jacket pocket as he walked into the apartment.

"Oh, Craig, you did it!" Jan gazed with awe at the signature on the contract. "You pulled it off."

"Not fully as yet, but I will," he said. "We'll run that prospective money up to one million. For a first novel," he emphasized. "That guarantees us a fortune in free advertising. How does it feel to be almost rich and successful?"

"So wonderful I'm scared," she admitted. It was more than the money. Craig and she had worked to pull off a promotion, and they were succeeding. No literary masterpiece – but great entertainment. The hard work, the gamble was paying off. For all the cynicism that permeated this decade they were living the American dream. Out of nothing they had created something.

"Now I want to hear every little word that passed between Paula and you." Unexpectedly he giggled. "Not to mention the action. And then tell me about Sam and Marilyn. Oh, the original of this is on its way to Sam." He put the contract back into his jacket pocket. "The film won't go into production until well after the book is launched, but it looks damn good in an ad to carry the legend, 'Soon to be a major motion picture starring Donna Warren'."

It was almost ten by the time Craig left. Peggy had not arrived yet. Perhaps her class ran longer than she expected, Jan told herself. On the chance that Peggy might have lost track of time, Jan phoned her. The line was busy. Peggy was in her apartment.

Jan tried Dan again. No answer. It was ridiculous to feel such a compulsion to share her news with Dan, she rebuked herself. So she would tell Dan a day later.

291

Brian emerged from his room to survey the refrigerator. He settled for an apple, announced he was going to bed in a few minutes.

"Peggy didn't come yet?" He was racing through the bedtime routine to free the bathroom for their house guest, Jan understood. In suburbia, she thought with a flicker of amusement, he would never have dared to refer to her friends by their first names.

"I just tried to phone her. The line was busy." Jan suppressed a yawn. She wished Peggy would get down here. She'd hoped to be in bed by eleven. This had been an exhausting day.

When the phone rang again, she was sure it was Peggy. She might have had trouble convincing Ralph that the living arrangement was over.

"Hello."

"I've been tied up all day in some craziness on campus," Dan reported. "I just got home a few minutes ago. Have you heard from Craig?"

"Donna's doing the film!" Jan told him jubilantly, pleased that Dan had called to find out. *He had been thinking about her.* "I didn't completely believe it till he popped over here a little while ago to show me the contract. Satlof is giving the book top priority. They expect to publish in November."

"Jan, that's marvellous! Your worries are over."

"It's a great feeling," she conceded. But she was greedy. She wanted the whole package. Children, career and man. The man being Dan. But how often did life work out that way? She had the kids. And now the book. Be grateful.

"Sleep well," Dan said softly. "I have to settle down now to correct a batch of papers before I call it a night."

"Thanks for calling, Dan. I was trying to reach you all day. I was dying to tell you about the book."

"Shall we have dinner and celebrate?" he asked with an odd self-consciousness.

"I'd love that," Jan accepted. Why did he feel strange about asking her out to dinner?

"Friday night clear?"

"Friday's fine." Any night would be fine.

"I'll talk to you before then. Goodnight, Jan."

Jan put down the phone with a fresh sense of well-being. Dan had thought about her during the day. He had been anxious to know how Craig had made out in Paris. And he was taking her out to dinner on Friday night.

Brian left the bathroom, said goodnight, and closed himself up in his room. A few minutes later Lisa made a final trip to the refrigerator for a glass of apple juice and flipped on the TV while she drank it.

"When's Peggy coming down?" Lisa was curious.

"Any minute," Jan guessed. She debated about preparing for bed. No, she'd wait until Peggy showed up.

"I'm going to sleep." Lisa deposited her glass on the dining table.

"You're going to sleep after you put the glass in the dishwasher," Jan corrected.

"You didn't empty it yet," Lisa pointed out.

"Rinse the glass," Jan redirected. "Then go to bed. The maid's off-duty."

At twenty past eleven she tried again to reach Peggy by phone. The line was still busy. Perhaps Peggy had changed her mind about coming down here to sleep. One way to find out, she reminded herself. She dug her keys out of her purse and headed upstairs to Peggy's apartment.

The stereo in the apartment next to Peggy's was blasting rock. Jan recalled that everybody on the floor had been complaining about the noise. Frowning in rejection of the clamour Jan rang Peggy's doorbell. She heard no sounds from inside the apartment. Peggy must be off the phone. The way this building had been constructed every sound in every apartment was audible out in the corridor.

Peggy did not respond to the bell. Maybe she was in the bathroom. Jan waited a few moments and tried again. She could hear the sound of the ringing inside as her finger remained obstinately on the bell. Would Peggy have gone downstairs for something at this hour?

Jan was suddenly uneasy. Marianne's stroke had made her susceptible to fears. Was Peggy all right? Had she fallen from a step-stool or slipped in the bathroom and hurt herself?

"Peggy?" She rapped sharply on the door. "Peggy?"

Silence greeted her efforts. Slowly she walked down the hall to the elevators. Back in her own apartment she decided to call Dan. He could be more objective than she.

"Dan, I'm sorry to bother you this late," she apologized when he answered the phone.

"No bother," he reassured her, concern in his voice. "You have a problem?"

Jan filled him in on the situation with Peggy.

"Maybe I'm being hysterical to worry about her. But she was supposed to be back at nine. That was more than two hours ago. I know she came back from her class because her phone was busy for ages."

"You have a right to be worried," Dan agreed. "I'll go down to the super's apartment and ask him to go up with his keys. You meet us up there at the door. Okay?"

"I'll go right up," Jan said, her anxiety escalating.

She was waiting at Peggy's door when Dan and the super arrived. It was obvious that the super was irritated at having been disturbed.

"I'll unlock the door," he said, "but you go in alone. Maybe she just fell asleep. You know, some people can sleep through a bombing. I don't want her sore at me for busting in like this."

"I'll go in alone," Jan soothed. Why didn't the idiot in the next apartment turn down the stereo? It was way past eleven.

The super unlocked the door and gestured to Jan to proceed. She turned the knob and walked inside. The living-room was in chaos. Not unusual for Peggy, who loathed picking up. Jan frowned at the phone, dangling on the floor. It had not been in use – merely off the hook.

She turned towards the kitchen alcove. A chill darted through her, immobilizing her for an instant.

"Oh, my God!" The words were wrenched from her as she stared at the crumpled body on the floor. Blood oozed from one breast. The knife that had inflicted the wound lay close to Peggy's body. "Dan!"

Dan charged into the room, the super at his heels.

"Call for an ambulance!" Dan ordered the other man and knelt beside Peggy. "Call the police," he amended his instructions. "She's dead."

For what seemed hours Jan sat on the corner of the sofa with Dan's arm around her while the detectives asked questions about Peggy's murder. She didn't even know Ralph's last name. Only that Peggy had ordered him to move out of the apartment. But there were fingerprints on the knife. The detectives anticipated no problems in identifying and tracking down Peggy's murderer.

Hal was notified by the police. As soon as the body was released by the medical examiner, he would make funeral arrangements. Jan felt as though she were living in a nightmare. Here she sat on Peggy's sofa, that opened up to become Peggy's bed. But Peggy was that plastic bundle that had been carted off to the morgue.

She had worried that Peggy would encounter violence at the hands of a man she might meet through one of her personal ads or somebody she picked up at some singles scene. She met Ralph at that off-off-Broadway group. It wasn't a 'dinner and bed' affair. She'd known him for a while before she let him move in with her. But she had not known him well enough, Jan thought with anguish, reconstructing the murder in her mind. Peggy told him to move out, and he went berserk. The seeds for murder were in Ralph before Peggy ever met him.

At last the detectives dismissed Jan and the two men. Dan walked her back to her apartment.

"I doubt that you'll get much sleep tonight," Dan said wryly. "Try to rest when the children get off to school in the morning."

"You'll have little sleep, too. You have an early class on Wednesdays," Jan remembered with compunction.

"I'll be all right." He took her face between his hands and kissed her gently on the mouth. "Goodnight, Jan."

Inside the apartment Jan stood still for a few moments. She trembled from the touch of Dan's mouth on hers. *That wasn't enough.* Why hadn't he kissed her with the passion he felt? Was he afraid to admit he loved her? What was this wall between them?

# Chapter Twenty-Three

The joy of the progress of the book was dimmed for Jan by Peggy's murder. Within forty-eight hours the police had tracked down Ralph and arrested him. According to the newspapers he would try for an acquittal on the grounds of temporary insanity. Jan prayed he would not be loose on the streets within a year or two.

There was no contact between Peggy's family and her Manhattan friends. It was as though she had never been here, Jan thought uncomfortably. She knew that Peggy had been cremated and her ashes buried in Connecticut only because the super had picked up this information when her ex-husband and one son came to close up her apartment.

Even Lisa and Brian were more subdued than normal. This was their closest brush with big-city violence. Yet it could have happened anywhere, Jan consoled herself. It was circumstances, not place, that brought on Peggy's murder.

Jan was grateful for Dan's frequent presence now. He took her out to dinner once a week. She invited him to the apartment for dinner another evening each week, telling herself that Lisa and Brian enjoyed having him here. She watched wistfully for some sign that the wall he kept between them was about to crumble.

But Dan hid whatever he felt for her behind a screen of solicitude. He knew it would be a long time before she recovered from the shock of Peggy's murder. And a new anxiety brought sleepless nights. Would Dan feel there was no real place in her life for him because of her writing career? Surely Dan was too modern in his thinking to feel that way; she tried to eradicate her fears.

297

Each day Craig reported on fresh activities regarding the book. A substantial book club sale came through. Foreign sales were coming in. Satlof was scheduling an auction for the paperback rights, with a floor of a quarter million dollars.

Early in June – one year from the day when Tim announced he wanted a divorce – the *New York Times* carried a front page story about the 'million dollar first novel'. Ebullient with pleasure and astonishment Karen called to talk about the book. Jan was cornered in the lobby by neighbours. Dan read the story on his way to school, and called to talk about it. They'd expected the story to break – they had not known when it would occur.

"What a birthday present for you," Ronnie said over dinner in Jan's apartment.

"I'd completely forgotten it was my birthday," Jan confessed. "Until I noticed the kids whispering, and then they announced they'd make dinner tonight. And I remembered."

"We called Dan and invited him, too," Lisa reported. "But he has a class tonight."

"Who told him I love red roses?" Jan's eyes were tender as they rested on the exquisite flowers he'd sent.

"Nobody," Lisa said. "I guess Dan likes them, too."

"Shouldn't we bring in the cake now?" Brian asked hopefully.

"Why not? We're all finished," Jan approved.

"Feel any different being thirty-nine?" Ronnie teased.

"Yes." Jan squinted in thought. "It's absurd, I know, but suddenly forty is staring me in the face. Why does forty seem ten years older than thirty-eight?"

"It's a state of mind." Ronnie spoke with a new acceptance since she'd met Todd Stuart. "So what does middle-age mean? The first half of life is over, and the best is coming. What's that poem by Robert Browning? 'Grow old along with me/The best is yet to be—' "

" 'The last of life, for which the first was made,' " Jan picked up. How wonderful it would be to spend the rest of her life with Dan. But could he ever allow himself to love completely after his disastrous first marriage? Such a bad marriage that he never even talked about it.

"Mom, when you started the book, did you think it might earn a million dollars?" Brian was awed by that sum.

"Darling, it won't be a million dollars for me." Jan was serious. Let Brian and Lisa keep their feet on the ground. "I share the money with Craig, first of all. The hardcover house takes fifty per cent of the paperback sale and the—"

"And the IRS takes a big chunk." Brian nodded sagely.

"Will there be enough for a beach house?" Lisa's eyes were eager. "It would be cool to have a beach house."

"Mom, can we buy a beach house?" Brian was impressed by this prospect.

"We'll rent a place out at Montauk for a month this summer," she compromised. Perhaps Dan would come out and visit. It would be beautiful to walk along the beach at night with Dan. "If we can find something available this late."

Ronnie's friend, Todd Stuart, was looking around for a small house for her to rent, though she had not told Lisa and Brian until this moment that this was a possibility. Ronnie and Todd were seeing each other constantly. She was taking bets with herself that within six months they'd be married. Laughter welled in her. After meeting Todd, Ronnie had banished her earlier stipulations about pre-marital arrangements. After a long haul on the singles scene, Ronnie had hit the jackpot.

*     *     *

Tim picked up a copy of the *New York Times*, folded it over, and climbed back behind the wheel of the car. He hated New York, but he liked to know what was happening back there. He'd never leave California. This was his turf. But he'd have to do something fast about landing a job. Anita was throwing too many nasty scenes about their not having enough money.

He detested the shabby mobile home they'd been renting the

past five months. Rents out here were as insane as they were in Manhattan. And Anita kept talking about trying to break into television. She'd be out of her mind to throw over her job. So she had to put up with some roving hands and cheap feels. The tips were sensational in that bar.

He drove home, went inside for a beer, came back out and fell into a chaise. He took a swig of beer, unfolded the *New York Times*. His eyes scanned the front page, settled on the lower left-hand corner. A million bucks for a first novel. Some smart guy who knew all the answers, he thought enviously. Probably packaged out here.

Then he sat upright in shock. *No, it couldn't be Jan.* She wrote shitty confession stories and cheap sex for the men's magazines. This had to be some other Janet Ransome. He skimmed the next few sentences. A divorcée with two children, a girl and a boy. She moved into Manhattan just a year ago, after her divorce. *Christ, it was Jan.*

His first instinct was to phone her. He immediately rejected this. He'd fly back to New York and see her. After all, she had custody of his kids. He'd always known how to handle Jan. He could do it again.

Anita was a sharp chick, but he could handle her, too. She'd understand why he had to fly back. She'd stake him to the plane fare. He grinned as he tried to visualize Jan as a swinging divorcée. She'd faint if a guy made a pass at her.

Tim was whistling when he went to phone about airline schedules from Los Angeles to New York. He meant to be on a plane tomorrow morning.

\*   \*   \*

Jan cleared away the dinner dishes. Striving to brush aside the doubts that had eroded her peace of mind since the night of Peggy's murder. The book was candid in showing the desperation and depression that haunted many of the 'singles' in the city. But

300

it portrayed glamorous and exciting moments, talked about the new openness in approaching men. About the new freedoms.

Would *The Second Time Around* bring unhappy single women – and men – into the city to search for the brass ring they might never find? Would they encounter violence or murder, like Peggy? Ronnie insisted Peggy didn't die because she was part of the singles scene. Peggy was so wrapped up in her own problems, Ronnie kept saying, that she couldn't see that Ralph was psychotic.

Ronnie's words at lunch yesterday echoed in her mind now: *'Jan, women want to meet men, and vice versa. The book shows them the options open to them, but you've made it clear they have to use their heads. If you meet a man at a friend's house for dinner, is that a guarantee he's not psychotic beneath his charming exterior? Most men aren't – but somewhere there'll be a potential killer like Ralph. And men run the same risk. You've said it loud and clear. Women are free today, but let's handle that freedom with care.'*

She had never discussed her feelings about the book with Dan, yet she knew he sensed her doubts. Peggy's murder had brought them closer together than they had ever been. Yet still he held back a part of himself. But enough of this. She had pages of revisions to proofread tonight.

Marilyn was bright. She zeroed in on every scene that had been written too quickly. Jan appreciated her astuteness. They would have a stronger book with the revisions.

From years of habit she shut out the sounds that emerged from the stereos in the two bedrooms and focused on the work before her, starting at the sound of the buzzer. Who could that be? Dan always called before coming up.

She hurried to the intercom and pushed a button.

"Yes?"

"Tim Ransome's coming up," the breezy relief night doorman announced. The only doorman on the job who didn't wait for instructions to send a visitor up to the apartment.

"Thank you." Jan heard herself respond. She was frozen in shock.

301

Tim in New York? They had not heard from him in months, and here he was on their doorstep. *He had heard about the book.* No, she rejected guiltily. Why did she always think the worst about Tim? The story just broke yesterday. How could Tim have heard about it out in California? It was too soon.

She hesitated for a moment, gearing herself for the encounter with Tim, then knocked first on Brian's door and then Lisa's.

"Yeah?" came two voices in concert.

"Out here on the double," she ordered. She recoiled from meeting Tim alone.

"What's the matter, Ma?" Brian seemed concerned.

Lisa poked her head out of her doorway, reluctant to pry herself loose from the stereo.

"Daddy's coming up," Jan told them. He was supposed to be crazy about California. What was he doing in New York? "The doorman just called."

"Daddy's *here*?" Brian's face switched from disbelief to jubilation. "Daddy's coming home?"

"Mom!" Lisa's face was incandescent. She shot to the door and pulled it wide. "Wow!"

Jan's throat constricted. She had told herself she was doing a great job as a single parent. But look at their faces when they knew they'd see Tim in a few minutes. Daddy wasn't coming home, she told herself grimly. Daddy and she were divorced.

Jan flinched as she heard the familiar sound of the elevator coming to a stop at their floor. The door slid open. Tim walked out into the corridor. Bronzed from the California sun. With a slight paunch, she noted subconsciously. Too little exercise and too much beer.

"Daddy! Daddy!" Lisa squealed and rushed into her father's arms. Brian hovered self-consciously at his side, reached for his valise.

"Hey, kids, you both look wonderful. Boy, have I missed you." But not enough to pick up the phone to talk to them, Jan remembered. Tim only phoned when he needed money.

An arm around each child Tim strode towards the door. Jan braced herself to greet him.

"You're looking beautiful," he commented and leaned forward to kiss her on the mouth. Reproachful that she did not respond.

"What brought you to New York?" she asked as the children drew him into the apartment. She managed to keep hostility out of her voice.

"Missed my family," he said softly. His eyes were amorous. He had not looked at her like that in years. It was a game. He had read 'million dollar first novel' and raced here to cut himself into the pie. "Got room for the old man?"

"You can sleep in my bed," Brian said quickly. Jan's mouth dropped in consternation. Her throat was tightening. Tonight Tim could stay. "I'll sleep in my sleeping bag."

"How have things been with you, Jan?" Tim asked, his eyes trailing over her.

"Are you hungry, Daddy?" Lisa inquired before Jan could reply to his question. "We have some roast left from dinner, and I can make you a salad." Lisa had become the salad specialist.

"Sounds great," Tim approved. "Go to it, baby."

He had been away a year. He had written maybe ten postcards in that time. He acted as though he had gone away on a week's business trip. He was still the children's father. He wasn't her husband. *She would not allow him back into her life.*

Brian pulled his father onto the sofa and began a barrage of questions about California. Did he go surfing and scuba diving? Were the freeways really so crazy?

Why was Brian so interested in California? For a fearful moment Jan asked herself if Brian preferred to live with his father. But his father would not want the responsibility of raising him. Nor could she believe that either of the children would choose Tim over her.

Jan sat back in tight silence while Tim ate the cold roast and the salad so proudly prepared for him. Brian brought him instant coffee. The children bubbled over with delight in their father's presence. But even battered children loved the parent who battered them, Jan reminded herself.

She allowed Lisa and Brian to stay up slightly later than usual. But she reminded them that tomorrow was a school day. They wheedled another twenty minutes and then retreated to their respective bedrooms, Brian pulling his father along with him, for which she was grateful.

For what seemed an eternity Jan lay awake on her made-up sofa bed and listened to the low-pitched conversation that emanated from Brian's room. She ought to go in and tell them to go to sleep. Brian had to get up for school in the morning. Yet she could not bring herself to do this.

She must make it clear in the morning that he could not remain in the apartment. Without arousing the children's hostility. Of course he had heard about the book. He didn't fly back to New York one day after the story broke because he 'missed his family'.

Long after Brian and Tim fell asleep, Jan lay staring into the darkness. Angry and frustrated. Tim would use the children to try to push himself back into their lives. It wouldn't work. Let this not create a breach between the children and herself.

Jan awoke the children as usual and got them off to school. Tim slept soundly in Brian's bed. She stared at him dispassionately for a moment before she closed the door to Brian's bedroom when he hurried off to school. She felt nothing for Tim except anger that he dared to invade the apartment this way.

She dressed with compulsive haste and went to the coffee shop on the corner for breakfast, knowing Tim would sleep till noon. After breakfast she phoned Ronnie and told her about Tim's appearance at the apartment.

"Let's meet for lunch," Ronnie said briskly. "A long lunch."

They decided on time and place, and Jan hung up. She knew Ronnie would have to put in a rush morning at the office if she was to take time out for a lengthy luncheon.

Tim wouldn't try to make love to her, would he? Yes, he would. In the early years of their marriage Tim had settled every argument in bed. He was reverting to that approach. He still thought he was the prize stud.

She ought to be back at the apartment when he woke up. She had to let him know he couldn't stay. But she needed time to gear herself for a battle with Tim. She'd have lunch with Ronnie, and then come home about the same time as the children. During the course of the afternoon she'd manage a few minutes alone with Tim. She'd tell him.

Misgivings tugged at her. She'd have to let him remain tonight. But that was all. Tomorrow he could pack his valise and go some place else. He wasn't moving in with them.

Jan looked at her watch. She had an open swathe of time before she was to meet Ronnie. She would walk up to Lord & Taylor on this beautiful June morning and buy something insanely extravagant for herself. Not for the children. That would look like a bribe.

She would have whatever she bought delivered. It would arrive after Tim was gone. Even Tim must understand Brian needed his rest. He wouldn't get it in a sleeping bag on the floor. And Tim was not returning to her bed. Not ever.

Jan went through the morning's shopping and luncheon with Ronnie in a veil of guilt because she was plotting Tim's eviction. Tomorrow morning she had a meeting with Marilyn to go over another segment of the manuscript. By the time she returned, she meant for Tim to be gone.

Jan timed her arrival at the apartment to coincide with that of Lisa and Brian. Tim was awake and watching television. Dirty dishes sat on the dining table. Was he still with that girl? What was her name? Anita. He must not be working if he took off this way for New York. She'd bet that Anita was working.

Tim went into a wrestling act with Lisa. Had Lisa forgotten all the times she'd said to her mother, '*Why don't you divorce him?*'

It startled her to notice an unfamiliarly serious air about Brian this afternoon. The first excitement of seeing his father was wearing off. Brian was wondering how Tim meant to fit into their lives again. He was remembering how Tim walked out of their lives.

"Hey, I'm taking my family out to dinner tonight," Tim announced in high spirits. But *she* wasn't part of his family any more. "Nothing fancy. I'm not exactly flush financially. The deluxe hamburger plate and shakes," he said humorously.

He didn't ask how she was fixed financially. He knew.

All right, she'd tell Tim tomorrow that he had to move on, Jan promised herself. This was not the strategic moment. She'd have to figure a way to remove Tim from their lives without hurting the children. She couldn't bear to appear a monster to Lisa and Brian.

\*     \*     \*

Karen left the office at shortly past three to drive up to the Connecticut house before her dinner appointment. If anyone had told her a week ago that she was considering changing jobs, she would have laughed. But the offer to join McLain & Spier's new resale brokerage arm was too heady to ignore.

She was having dinner with the head of this major developer of New York co-ops at eight. She wished that Jason had not flown out to Chicago on business this morning so that she could have discussed it with him.

But she didn't need to discuss the matter with anybody. She knew when the phone call came this morning that this was a major step upward professionally. No matter what Jason said, she would grab the job. The company had brass to contact her right in her current employer's office. But that showed how eager they were to hire her.

Maybe it was crazy to drive all the way up to Connecticut, but she meant to look absolutely right tonight. The Calvin Klein linen suit that she had bought and sent up to the country house to save on the sales tax was perfect for a business dinner.

She congratulated herself on beating the afternoon rush out of the city. In record time she was pulling up into the circular driveway of the house. No need to put the car into the garage. She'd pick up the suit and drive right back into Manhattan.

She unlocked the door and walked into the foyer. The pair of champagne glasses sitting on the coffee table in the living-room brought her to a halt. She never left glasses sitting around in the living room. *Champagne* glasses?

Now the sounds from the master bedroom assaulted her ears. Jason and some girl. But Jason was in Chicago. No, Jason told her he was flying to Chicago. He was in the bedroom making love to Fran. That super-saleswoman from his office.

She was simultaneously furious, hurt and humiliated. This was the end of the relationship with Jason. She was upset about the coke. But this she would not endure.

She stood still, listening to the sounds from the bedroom. Jason and Fran didn't even know she was here. With cool intent she picked up the two champagne glasses, walked to the fireplace, and smashed the glasses on the hearth. End of relationship.

"Hey!" Jason's alarmed voice emerged from the bedroom. "Who's there?"

By the time Jason appeared in the doorway, she was driving away from the house.

On the trip into New York Karen made her plans. Over the weekend she would go up to the house to remove her clothes. She'd call that twenty-four hour locksmith service in the neighbourhood and have the locks on the door changed tonight. If Jason drove back into town, let him spend the night in Fran's apartment.

She pulled into the garage at a quarter past six. The locksmith would still be open. She'd run right over and arrange for the cylinders to be changed in the locks.

She was aware of a sense of relief that it was over with Jason. She didn't need a man like him in her life. She was

307

*Julie Ellis*

young and attractive and bright. She could survive very well on her own.

Jan was grateful to have the apartment to herself. Tim had gone with Lisa and Brian to Barnes & Noble on Fifth Avenue and Eighteenth Street to look for a paperback on scuba-diving that he insisted they'd love. When Tim was underfoot, the apartment ricocheted with tension. Her whole world seemed in chaos. Alone she had a sense of cherished freedom.

She sat down to phone Dan. He would be home from school by now, she judged. He was scheduled to come to dinner tomorrow night. Afterwards they planned to go to a concert. She would not allow Tim to spoil one moment of the hours she could be with Dan.

Engrossed in the problem of ejecting Tim from the apartment and on the point of dialling Dan's number, she started at the unexpected ring of the phone.

"Hello."

"Jan, it's Karen." Her voice was strained.

"Hi, how are you?"

"I have a great new job coming up," Karen reported. "And I'm breaking up with Jason."

"The drug scene?" She remembered how upset Karen had been about Jason's involvement with coke.

"That and other women. I drove up to the country house to pick up something. Jason was supposed to be in Chicago. He was in the country house. In bed with a girl who works for him. I've made up my mind, Jan. No man will ever come first in my life. I'll find somebody else, sure, but if it doesn't work out, I'll know I have a career that's damned important to me." Karen managed a shaky laugh. "Of course, I'm greedy. I'd like a great career and a great man."

"Talking about a not so great man," Jan said, all at once remembering herself walking into the bedroom where Tim had been making love to Anita. *Men were so stupid in*

308

*their timing.* "Guess who popped into my apartment last night? Tim."

"He'd heard about the book," Karen pinpointed instantly.

"It wasn't his deep love for his family. I'm bracing myself to throw him out."

"Do it fast," Karen said. "But I don't have to tell you that." Like Ronnie, Karen was confident she would banish Tim from her life. Why was she being such a coward about it? "Look, I don't think it'll happen; but if Jason should call you and ask if you know where I am, would you please say you haven't talked to me in days? The phone keeps ringing, but I won't answer. I have a locksmith here now changing the locks on the doors. Jason can make an appointment to pick up his things. But not tonight. I don't feel up to talking to him tonight."

"You'll be okay, Karen," Jan consoled.

Jan sat quietly for a few minutes when she finished talking with Karen. She knew exactly what Tim was after. He meant to inveigle himself into the apartment and then into a remarriage. But this was the end of the line. Like Karen, she knew what she had to do.

She was thirty-nine years old. According to statistics on life expectancy she had half her life ahead of her. She would not spend those years with Tim.

In three years Brian would be in college. Lisa would follow him two years later. They could survive without their father for that period of time. Besides, what did Tim have to offer them? Right now he was playing the loving father role. It wouldn't last.

Jan rose to her feet in sudden decision. She knew exactly what she must do. All her life she had allowed herself to be manipulated. That time was over.

She waited for Tim to return with the children. They came in amid laughter and high spirits. She remembered what marvellous fun Tim could be – when he was so inclined.

"Brian, I want you and Lisa to go over to Baskin and Robbins and pick out a sumptuous icecream cake." With a serene smile she turned to Tim. "We'll celebrate my thirty-ninth birthday belatedly with you." She saw Tim start. He had not remembered her birthday for years. "We won't have dessert when we go out to dinner."

"Why can't Brian pick it out?" Lisa demanded. "Why do I have to go along?"

"So you won't complain later that Brian chose flavours that you hate." Jan made a show of firmness, though her hand was unsteady as she fished a bill from the pocket of her slacks. "Don't rush. Choose something special."

"Next week I may call up the old office," Tim said leisurely when they were alone. He leaned forward to take her hand. She eluded him. "They'll be glad to hear from me. I've seen in the financial section of the *Times* that they've had a lot of turnover in personnel. They know they made a bad mistake in dumping me."

"Tim, I have something here." Jan reached into her purse and pulled out a cheque. "This is made out to you. It's a cheque for ten thousand dollars."

Tim was at first startled, then wary.

"Part of the house money?"

"That saw us through the past year," she brushed this aside. This was *her* money. "Let's stop playing games, Tim. I know why you're here. But there's no place for you in my life. I want you out of this apartment by noon tomorrow morning." Ignoring his flush of anger she extended the cheque. "It's post-dated three days. Call me from California tomorrow night or I'll issue a stop-payment order."

"You stupid bitch!" he lashed at her. But he was holding on to the cheque.

"I used to be stupid," Jan corrected him, giddy with success. "Now I'm smart. You're to tell the children that you had a call from your office. You have to rush back to California tomorrow. That's part of the deal," she emphasized.

"You've changed," he denounced. "You're hard and bitter."

310

"Oh yes, I've changed," Jan conceded. This past year had been a crash course in living. Being with Ronnie and Craig had changed her thinking. Mike and Burt – and especially Dan – had changed her. Sharing with Peggy and Karen, and even Marianne, had changed her. "Now if you'll excuse me, I have an urgent errand. I'll be back soon."

With the apartment keys in one hand Jan waited impatiently at the elevators. Let Dan be home. She couldn't delay another day in talking to him. The 'down' elevator stopped. She hurried inside and pushed '4'. She was in luck. The elevator made no other stops.

Approaching Dan's apartment she realized with soaring relief that he was home. He was listening to the TV news. She rang his bell, churning inside with mixed emotions now, expectancy fighting a battle with sudden misgivings. Had she been misreading Dan's feelings for her? Seeing only what she wished to see?

The door opened.

"Hi." Dan's face brightened. "Come on in."

"I have to talk to you, Dan. I've been so upset these last twenty-four hours." Since Peggy's murder her instinct was to turn to Dan in every major moment. "Tim barged in on us. I'm guessing he read about the book and figured he ought to be sharing. I'm not guessing," she amended. Karen had seen it right away, too. "That's what brought Tim tearing to New York."

"Then you'll be tied up tomorrow night?" Though Dan attempted to be matter of fact, Jan read disappointment in his eyes.

"Absolutely not," she rejected. "I've told Tim he must be out of the apartment by twelve noon tomorrow. I gave him a stake. A post-dated cheque. If he doesn't call me from California tomorrow night, I'm stopping payment. He's furious, but I think he's got the message." She took a deep breath. "I told him there was no room in my life for him. I didn't tell him I was in love with somebody else—"

311

*Julie Ellis*

Dan flinched.

"I figured," he said with resignation. "The night I came back from Sedona – when I took Keith out there at his spring recess—" He saw that Jan looked blank. "My son," he explained awkwardly, remembering now that he had never mentioned a son. "Driving in from JFK that night I saw you walking down Second Avenue in the Sixties. You were holding hands with someone—" His hurt reached out to stab her.

"Dan, that wasn't the man I meant." Her smile was tremulous. Her mind adding up the facts. *The boy in his apartment was his son.* And he'd been distant when he returned from Sedona because he thought she was in love with someone else. "I saw him for a while – when I was trying to run away from myself. When I was afraid there was no room in your life for another woman after a bad marriage. Dan, I love you."

"Jan—" His face was luminous. She had not misread him. He reached to draw her into his arms. "I think I've loved you since that first morning we went in for coffee. But for a while there I had problems with Keith. I had responsibilities to my son – I wasn't free."

"And now?" she questioned while his mouth came down towards hers.

"Keith's fine. I'm free to live my own life. Jan, we've wasted so much damn time—"

She had known Dan would be passionate, she thought with exhilaration, when his mouth released hers. He slid an arm about her waist and prodded her towards the bedroom.

"Dan," she remembered in consternation, "I sent the kids out to buy an icecream cake—"

"So they'll put it into the freezer," he chuckled. "First things first—"

For the first time in thirty-nine years of living, Jan told herself, she felt secure and confident and a whole human being. At last she was a whole woman.